Joseph Knight

James Robertson is the author of the novel *The Fanatic* (also published by Fourth Estate), as well as two collections of short stories, *Close* and *The Ragged Man's Complaint*, several collections of poetry, and a book of Scottish ghost stories. He lives in Fife.

For more information on James Robertson visit *www.4thestate.com/jamesrobertson*

Also by James Robertson

The Fanatic

Joseph Knight

James Robertson

FOURTH ESTATE • *London* and *New York*

This paperback edition first published in 2004
First published in Great Britain in 2003 by
Fourth Estate
A Division of HarperCollins*Publishers*
1 London Bridge Street,
London SE1 9GF
www.4thestate.com

The quotation from *Birds of Heaven* by Ben Okri is reproduced by kind
permission of the publisher, Phoenix

A catalogue record for this book is available from the
British Library

ISBN 978-0-00-715025-0

Typeset by Palimpsest Book Production Limited,
Polmont, Stirlingshire

Printed and bound by CPI Group (UK) Ltd, Croydon, CR0 4YY

MIX
Paper from
responsible sources
FSC™ C007454

For Marianne

For whan fair freedom smiles nae mair,
Care I for life? Shame fa the hair;
A field o'ergrown wi rankest stubble,
The essence of a paltry bubble.

Robert Fergusson, 'Ode to the Gowdspink'

Nations and peoples are largely the stories they feed themselves. If they tell themselves stories that are lies, they will
suffer the future consequences of those lies. If they tell
themselves stories that face their own truths, they will free
their histories for future flowerings.

Ben Okri, *Birds of Heaven*

Acknowledgments

This book is based on true events but it is first and foremost a work of fiction. I have taken many liberties with the historical record and with the characters of historical figures, both famous and less well known, and I have invented entire episodes and characters where the historical record is, to the best of my knowledge, blank.

I could not have written the book at all without the help and advice of many individuals and institutions. The story of Joseph Knight was first suggested to me as a possible subject for a novel by Rob MacKillop. Others who provided information and help of different kinds include Michel Byrne, John Cairns, Angus Calder, Stewart Conn, Douglas Dunn, Amanda Farquhar, Shivaun Hearne, Stuart Kelly, Lindsay Levy, Ellie McDonald, Marianne Mitchelson, David Morrison, Polly Rewt, Ed Scott, Roland Tanner and Iain Whyte.

As ever, the staff of the National Library of Scotland and of Edinburgh City Libraries were extraordinarily helpful. To them, I must add the staff of Dundee City Libraries, and of the National Archives of Scotland. The Keeper of the Library of the Faculty of Advocates granted me permission to consult papers relating to the Knight v. Wedderburn case, for which I am most grateful. I acknowledge the support of the Scottish Arts Council, in the form of a bursary, which allowed me the time to research and write this novel. The Authors' Foundation, administered by the Society of Authors, also gave me financial support without which I would have been unable to travel to Jamaica for further research.

Finally, I am indebted to my agent Sam Boyce and my editors Leo Hollis and Nicholas Pearson for their consistently encouraging guidance and enthusiasm.

James Robertson
August 2002

I

Wedderburn

TO BE SOLD

*A BLACK BOY, about 16 years of age, healthy, strong, and well made, has
had the Measles and small pox, can shave and dress a little, and has been
for these several years accustomed to serve a single Gentleman, both abroad
and at home.*

*For further particulars inquire at Mr Gordon bookseller in the
Parliament-close, Edinburgh, who has full powers to conclude a bargain.*

This advertisement not to be repeated.

EDINBURGH EVENING COURANT, 28 JANUARY 1769

FOR KINGSTON IN JAMAICA

The ship MARY, JOHN MURRAY *Master, now in Leith Harbour, will be
ready to take in goods by the 20th September, and clear to sail by the
fifth October.*

*For freight or passage apply to Alexander Scott Merchant in Edinburgh,
or to the Master at Mrs Ritchie's on the Shore of Leith.*

EDINBURGH EVENING COURANT, 2 SEPTEMBER 1769

Sir John Wedderburn, tall but somewhat stooped with age, stood at the windows of his library, enjoying – as he felt he should every morning he was given grace to do so – the view to the Carse of Gowrie and the Firth of Tay. Ballindean's policies stretched out before him: the lawn in front of the house, the little loch, then the parkland dotted with black cattle, sun-haloed sheep and their impossibly white lambs. Thick ranks of sycamore, birch and pine enclosed the house and its immediate grounds. Beyond the trees, smoke rose from the lums of estate cottages and the village of Inchture and was immediately scattered by a breeze from the east.

Had he ventured outside, Sir John could have looked behind the house, to the north, where the woods thinned out and the land rose to the sheltering Braes of the Carse. But on this morning John Wedderburn was not going anywhere – not while that wind was blowing. The view from the library was, for the time being, all he required. There might have been more majestic landscapes in Scotland, but none that could have pleased him more.

He was seventy-three, thin and angular but with rounded shoulders and a nodding, lantern-jawed face that gave him the appearance of a disgruntled horse leaning over a dyke. Strands of grey hair swept back from his forehead and curled thinly behind his ears. His brow was tanned and his cheeks weathered and taut, as if he had lived most of his life outdoors, but his hands – slender-fingered and soft – belonged more in a room such as the library.

Sunlight shafted in through the window from a watery sky. A huge fire roared and cracked in the grate at one end of the room. There were two armchairs, one on either side of the fire, and a few feet further away – close enough to get the benefit, not so close as to hurt the wood – a heavy writing-table of finest Jamaican mahogany. Near the door a wag-at-the-wa, which had just clanged out ten o'clock, ticked heavily. But it was the rows of books that dominated the room.

Bookshelves ran along two-thirds of the length of the wall behind the table, and reached almost to the ceiling. The volumes were well bound, neatly arranged, and free of dust: biography, history, philosophy, verse, those often rather too delicate creations *novelles* . . . So many books, and so little inclination left to read them. Sir John thought this without turning from the window. He felt them massing behind his back, picked them off in his mind: *The Works of Ossian*, heroic and Highland, whatever Dr Johnson might have said of their authenticity; Edward Long's *History of Jamaica*; Lord Monboddo's six volumes on *The Origin and Progress of Language* (tedious, eccentric – Sir John had given up after half a volume); Smollett's novels – he remembered heavy, sweltering West Indian Sundays much relieved by *Peregrine Pickle* and *Roderick Random*; the poetical works of the ploughman poet Burns and 'the Scotch Milkmaid', Janet Little – little doubt already which of those would last the pace; collections of sermons, treatises on agriculture, political economy, science . . . And two copies of Henry Mackenzie's *Man of Feeling*, because the lassies liked it so much. Sir John had once tried this book and had thrown it down in disgust – grown men bursting into tears over nothing on every third page. 'That is not the *point*, Papa,' his daughter Maria had insisted, 'you are too matter-of-fact!' But that *was* the point. There wasn't a hard bit of fact in the entire book.

The *fact* was, Sir John no longer read much himself, but he subscribed to many publications, and took the lists of the Edinburgh booksellers, mainly for the benefit of his wife Alicia and his daughters. They were all there in the room too, around the fireplace, a series of silhouettes done five or six years before: Alicia, fair and delicate at forty-three; Margaret (child of his first wife – after whom she was named – now nearly thirty and so long neglected by suitors that Sir John had almost given up worrying about it); Maria, Susan, Louisa and Anne (all in their teens). Great readers, every one of them, especially of *novelles* and poetry. Sir John was quietly pleased that his four sons – represented in various individual and group portraits on the opposite wall, and all but the youngest sent out into the world to work – showed little inclination for reading, and none at all for *novelles*.

The library's most recent acquisition, delivered the previous week, was a collection of Border ballads in two volumes, compiled by Walter Scott, Sheriff Depute of Selkirkshire. How appropriate, Sir John had thought as he cut the pages, that so many thieves and ruffians should be rounded up by a sheriff. But there was nothing really wicked in the ballads – nothing that was not safely in the rusted, misty half-dream that was Scotland's past, nothing dangerous to the minds of his daughters. Susan was the one most easily swayed by history, romance and poor taste. But then she was female and seventeen, it was to be expected. She would grow out of it. Books might have some bad in them, but there were, after all, worse things in the world.

The last fifteen years in France had demonstrated that, but Sir John had known it much longer – since, in fact, he was Susan's age. The French had gone quite mad, and now the world was paying for the madness. Two men born of the Revolution strode across the Wedderburn imagination, the one threatening to become a monster, the other already monstrous. Napoleon Bonaparte was the first, a brilliant Corsican soldier, who had temporarily made peace with Britain at Amiens but whose ambitions clearly pointed to further and more devastating campaigns. But worse, far worse, was the second man, the *black* Bonaparte, Toussaint L'Ouverture, the barbarous savage who had turned the French island colony of San Domingo – once the sugar jewel, the sparkling diadem of the West Indies – into a ten-year bloodbath. Toussaint L'Ouverture: the name passed like a cloud over the ruffled, sparkling Tay, and Sir John shuddered.

From the Paris Jacobins this slave had learned the slogans *liberté*, *egalité* and *fraternité*, and had the outrageous idea of applying them to Negroes. He had massacred or expelled the French planters, devastated their plantations, defeated the armies of France, Spain and Britain – forty thousand dead British troops in three years! – and left San Domingo like a weeping scab in the middle of the Caribbean, barely a hundred miles from Jamaica, with Toussaint himself, drunk on power, emperor of the wreckage. Yet in Jamaica, it seemed, his exploits had made him a hero to the blacks. God help them all then, Sir John thought, white and black alike, if they should follow his example.

There was a tap at the door of the library and it opened just wide enough to admit a dark-suited, dark-jowled bullet of a man, whose lined face suggested that he was almost as old as Sir John himself – this despite a thick crop of hair so black that it looked suspiciously like a wig. But these days wigs, even among elderly men, were something of a rarity.

'There's a man Jamieson here frae Dundee, Sir John. He says he has business wi ye.'

Sir John frowned, did not turn. 'What day is it, Aeneas?'

'Thursday.'

'Is it? Well, show him in, then.' He remained at the window.

He had forgotten about Jamieson. These last few weeks his head had been full of other business. First, there had been correspondence with his brother James, whom he had appointed guardian to his children. Although James was only a year and a half younger, he was in better health – fatter, sleeker – and likely to last a few more winters, whereas Sir John had found this last one sorely trying. The cold had scored deep into his flesh, seized up his knee and finger joints, and had him longing for the Caribbean. The thought of more snow and ice was not just depressing, it made him fearful. James might have had his faults in the past, but he surely would not misuse his nephews and nieces.

Then there had been fine-tuning his will. His eldest surviving son, David, who lived in London and managed much of the family's West Indian business from there, would inherit Ballindean, but, steady though David was, Sir John was not willing to let the future hang on the whim of one individual. It had taken too much trouble restoring the family to Perthshire, after the difficulties of more than half a century ago, to permit the work to be undone in a moment. So he had made an entail of all his property, establishing a complex chain of succession tying Ballindean to future generations of the family, and the family to Ballindean. And not just Ballindean, but also Sir John's portions of the estates in Jamaica. David could enjoy his own, and after him so could *his* children, but neither he nor they would be at liberty to sell off the Wedderburn property: it would, barring financial disaster, stay in the family now and for ever. If Sir John wanted to be sure of one thing before he died, it was this: the Wedderburns were back in Scotland for good.

The matter Jamieson had come about had slipped his mind. No – it had been sitting in the dark of his mind, a locked kist in the attic. Perhaps Jamieson had brought the key to it from Dundee?

'Good morning, Sir John.'

Still facing the window, Sir John tried to assess the man from his voice. It was not a deep voice – it almost squeaked. Jamieson had been recommended by the family lawyer – indeed, Mr Duncan had appointed him, and this would be the first time Sir John had clapped eyes on him. What was he? A kind of drudge, a solicitor's devil, a sniffer in middens and other dank places, howking out missing persons and persons one might wish to know about but not be known by. A ferret. Yes, his voice was the squeaking, bitter voice of a ferret.

Sir John turned from the outside light. He was surprised by what he saw. Jamieson was a small, balding man in his forties, wearing ill-fitting black clothes that were so crumpled it was a fair wager he had slept in them. Then again, he had just travelled nine miles on horseback, and although the new turnpike between Dundee and Perth was a vast improvement on what had passed for a road before, this might have been cause enough for his dishevelment. He seemed rather portly and careworn, more like a mole than a ferret. Sir John noted that he was carrying nothing – no leather case, no sheaf of papers, no casket of evidence. This was not encouraging. But then, what had he expected him to bring?

'Good morning, sir. Is it cold out?'

'A wee thing chilly, Sir John. That east wind is aye blawin.'

'Very well. There is the fire if you wish to warm yourself.'

Jamieson hotched awkwardly near the door. Sir John kept up his sour face, but inwardly he smiled. Perhaps the man thought it would be impertinent to come between a laird and his hearth just to warm one's backside. Perhaps he suspected that the laird was toying with him. Well, he was entitled to his suspicions. It was his job.

7

When it became clear that Wedderburn was not going to speak, Jamieson coughed and filled the silence himself.

'Aboot the, eh, maitter I was instructed tae inquire intae, Sir John. I received the commission at the end o January and I hae been workin awa diligently ever since. I hae sent oot numerous letters, checked parish records, questioned shipping agents, mill overseers, members o the criminal classes . . . I regret tae say that I am unable tae gie ye ony satisfactory report.'

'Is that so? Why then are you here?'

'It was intimated tae me that the maitter was of some . . . was tae be conducted wi the ootmaist discretion. I felt it only richt I should bring ye this disappointin news mysel.'

Wedderburn sucked in his cheeks till it seemed his whole face was about to collapse. 'It *is* disappointing, sir. Can you report nothing at all?'

'Extensive inquiry has been made, and no jist in Dundee. I had hoped for information frae the agent in Perth that first worked on the person's behalf, a Mr Davidson . . .'

Wedderburn glowered. 'Ah, yes, I mind that name.'

'. . . but he has been very ill and unable tae see me. I hae been in Edinburgh, Kinross, Fife, Angus – but withoot ony success. In short, nae trace o the person has been uncovered.'

'Let us not be shy, sir. His name is Knight. Joseph Knight.'

'Aye, sir.'

'He cannot simply have disappeared.'

'Wi respect, Sir John, there's ony number o things micht hae happened. He micht be deid.'

'What makes you think that?' Wedderburn said sharply.

'I'm no sayin I dae. But it micht be possible. For aw that, he micht be in London. Or America. Africa even.'

'I hardly think so.' Now Wedderburn was beginning to suspect Jamieson of toying with *him*. 'Mr Jamieson, I do not doubt that you cannot find the man, but no *trace* of him? Not a word? Nobody with a memory? A man like that surely does not just disappear.'

'That's whit he seems tae hae done, sir. Disappeared.' Jamieson coughed. 'And his wife wi him.'

'You mean his wife *as well*?'

'Aye, sir, of course. As we've no found either o them, we dinna ken if she's yet *wi* him.'

Sir John thought of the wife. The Thomson woman. She would long since have lost any charms she once had. He had a sudden, startling image of her, a twisted, witch-like hag, clinging to the back of Joseph Knight like a curse. He gave his head a shake, moved towards the fire.' 'It's odd. It is not as if he is inconspicuous.'

'Which is why I say,' Jamieson said, following. 'were he yet in Dundee, I would hae discovered it. A black man in Dundee is a kenspeckle body. But as soon as ye reach tae Edinburgh, or the west, it's a different proposition.'

'He's still a black man. He must stand out.'

'There's mair o them in Scotland than ye micht imagine. Maistly in Glasgow and roond aboot. Wi the trade tae the Indies, ye ken. It's no like Bristol or Liverpool, sir, whaur I'm tellt they are very numerous, but there's mair here than ye'd think.'

'Is that so?' Sir John was irritated by the suggestion that this man knew more about Negroes than he.

'In the west, aye. There's a line or twa I pit oot in that airt that I've no reeled in yet. No that I'm ower hopeful, but . . .'

Wedderburn tilted a furrowed brow at him: *explain further what you mean.*

Jamieson coughed again. 'Ye'll be aware o the present revolutionary spirit that's rife amang certain trades, sir? Weavers and spinners and the like. There's a secret society brewin up discontent, ye'll maybe hae heard o it? The United Scotsmen, as they cry themsels.'

Wedderburn found himself getting annoyed. Jamieson seemed incapable of coming at a point directly. He always wheedled and sneaked his way up to it. 'Why should they interest me? I am not a political man.'

'Nor I, sir.'

'But they interest you?'

'It's my work.'

'You are a spy.'

Jamieson blinked, mole-like. 'Weel . . .'

'You are a spy. You turn men's coats. You buy men and their secrets. Am I right?'

'It's why ye employed me,' Jamieson said flatly.

'Mr Duncan employed you. Never mind. Go on with your United Scotsmen.'

Jamieson paused, as if recollecting something he had memorised earlier. 'In pursuin a certain line o inquiry intae the activities o this combination,' he said, 'on behalf o some gentlemen wi considerable interests in the linen manufactories in Dundee and Fife, I had occasion tae make contact wi some o the weavers o Paisley. There is a black man in that toun – no *oor* black man – a respectable and loyal subject – and as it appears there is a web o contacts no jist amang the weavers but amang the Negroes o the west, I thocht something micht come back by way o him. But there's been naething thus far.'

'This *loyal Negro*,' Wedderburn said, stretching out the phrase as if to test if it would snap, 'what is his name?'

'Peter Burnet. A weaver.'

'You met him?'

'No. I wrote tae him.'

'And you expect a reply?'

'I dinna ken.'

Sir John snorted. 'Well, well, if that is all, that is all. Knight may be furth of Scotland altogether, as you say.'

'I could appoint agents in London, sir. Time would be a factor, but if ye were willin . . .'

Something in Wedderburn's eyes brought Jamieson to a halt. There was a deep thought turning in there, an assessment. Then Wedderburn shook his head, as if ridding himself of the thought. Later, Jamieson would curse himself for not paying more attention, for not seeing it as a warning signal. He had seen the same head-shaking gesture earlier, when Knight's wife had been mentioned. As if there were something in Wedderburn's mind that he couldn't get out.

Wedderburn said, 'No. It's not important.'

If it was not important, Jamieson thought, why had he been traipsing around the countryside for two months? Not that he was going to complain, since the fee was substantial, but in his experience even wealthy gentlemen – especially them – did not hire him for trivialities.

He ventured an opinion. 'Tae reach further afield, sir, we

could try a discreet advertisement in ane o the newspapers. "Information regarding the whereaboots of the following individual . . . a small reward offered" – that kind o thing. If he disna read the papers, somebody that kens him micht.'

'Oh, he reads the papers, Mr Jamieson, be assured of that. He is a very thorough reader.'

'Weel, then . . .' Again, Jamieson saw that struggle in Wedderburn's eyes. Hot, then cold. Anger? Guilt? Something old but still raw. And behind Wedderburn, above the fire, he saw something else: flanked by several smaller silhouettes, a large painting in which three men posed on a kind of wooden porch. Their clothes were old-fashioned – from forty or fifty years back, perhaps – and the painting was no masterpiece, but they were unmistakably Wedderburns. All three had Sir John's high brow and long jaw. The porch was attached to a house, and was partly in shadow. Bright green, foreign-looking shrubs and an absurdly blue sky provided a crude contrast to the shade and to the unsmiling faces of the men. The scene must be Jamaica. One of the men – probably the one in the middle, Jamieson thought – had to be Sir John.

'No, I do not wish it,' Wedderburn said. Jamieson dragged his attention back to the old laird. 'I believe you are right when you say he is no longer here. And in any case, the nature of these Negroes . . . Put such a notice in the press, there would be dozens of them thigging and sorning at my gates. No, we'll not pursue that line.'

'I only thocht, if it's a maitter o compensation . . .'

Sir John drew himself up, squaring his shoulders against their stoop. 'Compensation? What do you mean by that, sir?'

Jamieson thought of a dog with its birse up, but the image did not quite fit. It was more as if the raw thing in Wedderburn had suddenly manifested itself on his skin, like a disease. Jamieson took a couple of steps back towards the door. 'Jist that . . . weel . . . for Joseph Knight. The case is auld enough noo . . . Time saftens sair herts. I presumed . . .'

'Well, *don't*!' The word shot from Wedderburn's mouth like a dog after a cat. Jamieson retreated further. 'Your presumption is not what I hired you for – nor your couthy proverbs. Your task was to find Joseph Knight, nothing more. And you have failed.

11

You presumed that I seek him out to pay him some money? To make amends of some kind? *I* pay *him* compensation? Oh, you have read me very wrong, sir!'

'I see that, I see that,' Jamieson said, though what he was most clearly seeing was his fee floating down the Tay. 'No whit I meant at all, Sir John. I beg your pardon – oomph!'

A further detonation from Wedderburn was forestalled by this minor one from Jamieson, triggered by the opening of the library door, the handle of which had dunted him sharply in the small of the back. A tall, dark-haired girl in a white muslin dress entered.

'Oh, I am sorry.' It was not clear if she was addressing Jamieson, now rubbing his kidneys and screwing up his face, or her father.

'What is it, Susan?' Sir John said. 'It is not yet noon.'

'I forgot, Papa. I came for a book.' She had her father's serious, thin face, and an adolescent awkwardness of posture.

'You will have to come back for it, then.' Wedderburn turned to Jamieson. He made a sudden stab at joviality. 'My daughter, sir, reads books as a sheep eats grass, incessantly, and as you have discovered she lets nobody stand in her way. I make it a rule that this room is mine, and mine alone, every morning, or I'd have no peace. But I don't have it anyway. My dear, you must find something else to occupy you for an hour and a half. Should you not be at your task?'

'I've finished my task, and now I've to read a book while Maister MacRoy helps Anne with hers. Could I not . . . ?'

Sir John held up a finger. 'We are discussing business matters. Your book will have to wait. Do some sums. Now – away with you!' He half shouted this, half laughed it. Jamieson could see the intention: Wedderburn assumed that the lassie had overheard him roaring at Jamieson, and wanted her to think that that had been all light-hearted too. Sounding ever more conciliatory for her benefit, he moved over to the writing-table, saying, 'I thank you for your efforts, Mr Jamieson. I imagine it's tedious work. Off you go, miss.'

'I thole it, sir, I thole it,' Jamieson said, as the door closed behind Susan. He was content to play along with her father's pretence. He had had no idea, when approached by the lawyer to carry out a search, that Wedderburn would still be so sore. Twenty-four years had passed since the case was decided: Jamieson had had two wives and eight children in that time, and his eldest three were all grown and flown from the nest. Although most folk had forgotten the case – Joseph Knight, a Negro of Africa *v.* John Wedderburn of Ballindean – obviously Wedderburn . . . But obviously what? Jamieson's curiosity, which had been professional until this moment, suddenly became more personal.

Not that it was his concern if the old laird still nursed a grievance – if he did not, there would not, presumably, have been any work for Archibald Jamieson – but seeing it exposed in that way, then hastily concealed from the daughter . . . Jamieson was impressed, intrigued even. He looked again at the Jamaican painting. The men in it were young, in their twenties or thirties. If it was John Wedderburn in the middle, the other two must be his brothers. Jamieson wondered if Knight had already become a possession when the painting was done.

Wedderburn was now seated, setting out paper, ink and pen. 'I think our business is concluded,' he said, glancing up. 'You'll send your bill to Mr Duncan? He'll expect a full account of your activities.'

This was it? The matter sealed? What was Wedderburn trying to do?

'Aye, certainly, Sir John,' Jamieson heard himself say. 'Thank ye. It's an honour tae hae been o service, sir. Tae a gentleman such as yoursel.' He took a chance. 'That, eh, painting. If I micht . . .' He advanced towards it. 'Is that yoursel in the middle, Sir John?'

Wedderburn glowered at him. 'It is.'

'It's very fine,' Jamieson said, peering closer. 'A very fine likeness.'

Wedderburn half rose from his chair. 'No it is not. It's poorly executed. The artist . . . well, one had to settle for what one could get out there. Now –' He gestured at the door, sat down again, began to write.

'Of course.' Jamieson, still contemplating the painting, stepped away from it. But he could not resist touching Wedderburn's wound one more time.

'Ye'll be, I dout ... ye'll be ane o the *great* Wedderburns? Like Lord Loughborough, the Chancellor o England? Ye'll be o *his* faimly, sir?'

Sir John Wedderburn stopped writing, looked at Jamieson as if at a worm. 'No, sir. Lord Loughborough is of mine. Good day.'

Jamieson turned and hurried from the library.

In the hallway he paused to catch his breath, half disgusted at his own sycophancy, half pleased at its effect. Almost at once he became aware of a shadow hovering on the stairs above him. It was Aeneas MacRoy, the sneering creature who had inspected him like a school laddie before announcing his arrival to Wedderburn. MacRoy descended without a word. His deep-set dark brown eyes flickered to a silver salver that sat on a nearby half-moon table, as if he expected Jamieson to try to steal it. He led him out the way he had come in, past the kitchen and the wash-house, down a freezing stone passage and across to the stables where his horse was tethered. Only then did MacRoy speak.

'That didna tak lang, did it?'

'No.'

'And it's a fair ride back tae Dundee.' The implication was that Jamieson had wasted everybody's time, including his own. Jamieson was half inclined to agree, but did not want to admit it.

'Aye.'

'Wi this wind ye'll likely hae a face as hard as a kirk door by the time ye win hame.' Without waiting for a further response, MacRoy hurried back into the house.

Jamieson, pondering the probable accuracy of the prediction and the grim satisfaction with which MacRoy had uttered it, warmed himself for a minute at the horse's flank. It was a long trip for a twenty-minute interview. He could, of course, have made his report to Mr Duncan, Wedderburn's lawyer, but he had wanted to see Ballindean and its laird for himself. Jamieson had spied on unfaithful wives and husbands, eavesdropped on radicals, hunted down cheats, thieves, eloping daughters and dissolute sons, but he had never had to search for a black man before. He had been curious to see the master who was still

14

chasing a runaway slave after twenty-four years. And now, having seen him, he was even more puzzled. Wedderburn's sudden burst of bad temper had been counter-balanced by apparent indifference as to Knight's fate. What was Wedderburn's motivation? Jamieson could not figure it out. He wondered if he was losing his touch.

Yet why should he think that? He'd not performed badly over the United Scotsmen, an affair that had involved much discreet inquiry and cultivation of dubious acquaintances, and a little danger. He had attended, in disguise, a meeting of radicals at Cupar, narrowly avoided a severe beating in the back streets of Dundee, and helped the authorities chase a notable agitator out of the country. This kind of work was paid for by the proprietors of the new manufactories that were going up everywhere, changing the face of the country. Jamieson did it because it was there, and because it paid better than his other work, copying documents. He liked the owners neither more nor less than he liked the weavers. As he had told Wedderburn, he did not consider himself political.

He was about to mount up when he realised he was not the only human being in the stable. The lassie, Susan, emerged from one of the stalls, herself and the white dress now protected from dirt and cold by a black cloak clutched close about her.

'I know the matter you were here to see my father about,' she said.

'Oh aye?'

'Oh aye,' she echoed. 'I heard at the door.'

Jamieson considered the combination of her directness of speech and her hunched, uneasy stance. He said cautiously, 'I dout your faither wouldna be best pleased aboot that. Or aboot ye waitin oot here on such a mornin.'

'Ma faither disna ken aboot either,' she retorted, a perfect mimic. 'And I wasna waitin on *you*. Since I hadna a book tae read, and nae task either, I cam oot tae see the horses.'

He could not help smiling. 'But ye kent I would be here sooner or later.'

'And I ken aboot Joseph Knight,' she said. Then, reverting to English: 'Don't you think it's an interesting name?'

15

'Is it?'

'Biblical,' she said, 'but chivalric too, and mysterious. The Black Knight. I think of him as a chevalier of darkness.'

'Aye, weel,' Jamieson said, 'your faither disna share that view.'

'Papa never mentions him. But we all know about him, it's hardly a secret. My sisters and I. And Mama too, although she wasn't married to Papa when it happened. My other brothers and sisters – the old, half ones – even they were too young to remember much about it now, but we all know.'

'How's that?'

'The servants, of course – the older ones. And Aeneas MacRoy with a drink in him.'

'Him that convoyed me in and oot? Aye, whit sort o a man is that? Some kind o major-domo?'

'He thinks he is, though it's Mama that runs the household. Aeneas is our schoolmaster.'

'The times are tolerant, when lassies cry their dominie by his Christian name.'

She laughed. 'Only behind his back. In the schoolroom he's strictly Maister MacRoy.'

'It's a queer dominie that gangs aboot like a servant, showin folk in tae his maister. He must leave aff teachin ye as aften as he taks it up.'

'Aeneas has been here so long nobody is concerned about what it's fitting for him to do or not do. He and Papa are old comrades – from the Forty-five. I don't think Papa notices any more whether Aeneas is tutoring us or skulking in a corner or chewing his dinner thirty-two times to aid the digestion – he does that, you know.'

'Frae the thrawn look on him, it disna work.' Jamieson was gratified to see a smile break over Susan's face. 'Onywey, whit does he ken aboot Joseph Knight?'

'Oh, this and that. He doesn't say much about him, and then only when he's drunk, but you can tell it's deep in him yet. And my uncle James, he doesn't mind speaking about it – the case I mean.'

'Is he in the picture wi your faither?'

'The one above the fire? Yes, on the left. The roguish-looking one. He *was* a rogue then, apparently.'

16

'Faith, whit way is that tae speak aboot your uncle?'

'It's only what my father says. He doesn't mean it harshly. But you can see him curl up inside if the plantations are mentioned when my uncle visits. Papa always stamps out the first few words that might blow in Joseph Knight's direction. I know, I've watched for it. Did Papa tell you who painted that picture?'

'He didna, na.'

'My uncle Alexander. He died not long after he painted it. Do you know who else is in it?'

'Anither uncle o yours.'

'That's right. Uncle Peter. He died in Jamaica too. But not just him.'

Jamieson frowned. The lassie was haivering. 'There's jist the three o them,' he said.

'You didn't look closely enough. It's very dark on that porch. Yet it's the middle of the day.'

'Whit are ye sayin, miss?'

She took a step back, and he realised his question had come out quite fiercely.

'Joseph Knight is there too. Or he was once. Papa had him painted out after the court case.'

'How dae ye ken that?'

'Because I do. I must have looked at that painting a thousand times. There's somebody there under that heavy shadow. You can just make him out. And I'm sure he's black. Who else could it be?'

Jamieson shrugged. Now he wanted to go back into the library. The lassie seemed to have a lively imagination, but why would she come up with such a story? Then again, why would Wedderburn go to that trouble? Why not just take the painting down, destroy it?

'If your faither had that done, it was lang afore ye were born. Did he tell ye that was whit happened?'

'No, but it's obvious, isn't it? I think Papa was ashamed. He thinks the court case was a great stain on the family, and of course it was, but not for the reasons he thinks.'

'Whit dae *you* think?'

'That Joseph Knight must have been very brave. And right.'

17

And clad in shining armour, Jamieson added into himself. He said: 'Ye dinna approve o slavery?'

'Do you?'

'I dinna think muckle aboot it.' It existed. It was a fact of life. That was what he thought.

'Well, you should.'

'*You* dinna like it, then?'

'How could I? How can anybody? It makes me ill to think of it. There are associations formed to abolish it. I'm going to join one and fight it.'

'There's associations formed tae fecht aw kinds o things. That disna mak them richt. It's slavery that biggit this fine hoose, and bocht aw thae books ye read.'

'That's not my fault. Nobody should be a slave. That's what it was all about, wasn't it, the court case? Whether you *could* be, in Scotland. What I don't understand is why Papa wants to find him now, after all this time?'

'I dinna ken.'

'Not because *he's* had a change of heart, anyway. You thought that, and he nearly took your head off.'

'Ye've sherp lugs, miss. Whit was the book ye wanted?'

'Oh, I hadn't one in mind. I'll devour anything. Like a sheep.' She bleated and he laughed. 'It's strange work you have,' she said.

'I work tae eat, like maist folk. I dae whit I dae.'

'Look for people?'

'That. And this, and thon.'

'What's your horse's name?'

'I dinna ken. I hired it. I dinna keep a horse.'

She clapped the horse's neck. 'Imagine not knowing her name. What if she wouldn't do as she was bid, or something feared her?'

Jamieson smiled. 'Miss, this is the maist biddable horse I was ever on. It jist gangs whaur ye nidge it wi your knees. If I spoke tae it I would probably fleg the puir beast.'

'Do you think he's still alive? Knight, I mean.'

'I dinna ken.'

'Ye dinna ken much. I think he's dead. We'd have heard otherwise. There's not much news goes by Ballindean, one

18

way or the other. Either from visitors, or newspapers, or the servants.'

'The world's a bigger place than Ballindean,' Jamieson said. 'He could be onywhaur in it.' He made to leave.

'Old Aeneas hated him,' she said, as if desperate to keep him a minute longer.

'Whit gars ye say that?'

'Aeneas hates everything. No, that's not fair. He likes my sister Annie. But he hated Knight. It was an *affaire de coeur*,' she added pointedly.

Jamieson was interested, but pretended he was not; adjusted a saddle-strap. He was torn between believing her and dismissing her. He said, 'Ye're gey young tae ken aboot such things, are ye no?'

'No,' she said. 'Books are full of them. But this was a real one. Joseph Knight won the heart of the woman Aeneas wanted. That's why he hated him. More for that than because he was a Negro. How could you hate someone just for their colour?'

Jamieson had had enough. He swung himself up into the saddle. 'It's easy, miss. Folk dinna need muckle o an excuse, believe me, for love or hate. Ye'll find that oot for yoursel.'

'Leave love alone,' Susan said, with a bluntness Jamieson was certain she would not use to a man of her own class, though she might to one of her sisters. 'Love's not at fault. You old men are all the same. You're like my father. You don't believe in love, or goodness of any kind.'

Jamieson was rather shocked. He *felt* old when she said it. He was only forty-six; Sir John Wedderburn could easily be *his* father.

'Na,' he said, 'I dinna. And I dout Joseph Knight didna either. And nor would you if you were him. Ye'd best get inside, miss, afore ye catch cauld and I catch the blame.'

She looked disappointed, either in him or the fact that he was leaving. 'Well, *au revoir*, Monsieur Jamieson,' she said, following him out and slapping the horse's rump. 'And if ever you find him, be sure and let us know, father and me.'

*　　*　　*

19

Conversations tended to continue in Susan Wedderburn's imagination long after they had ended in reality. Especially conversations that, like books, took her outwith the policies of Ballindean. But such conversations were rare. Her full sisters, though she was fond of them, were too childish, too light-headed or infatuated with marriage to give her what she needed. Her half-sister Margaret, twelve years older, was too dull. Her mother was too protective, saw serious or heated discussion as a threat either to her own domestic tranquillity or to her daughters' prospects of safe, suitable unions. Maister MacRoy's mind seldom strayed beyond the set lessons of the schoolroom. Susan felt starved of adventures but had no idea what form those adventures might take.

Her father had had adventures at her age. She knew his stories of the Forty-five inside out. They had once thrilled her, but lately she could not separate them from the brooding presence of the dominie, who had been at Culloden too, but who was about as romantic as a goat. All that Jacobite passion belonged in another age, it had nothing to do with her. The Forty-five might have been tragic and stirring but it was also hopeless and useless and ancient. What she wanted was an adventure that was happening now, that touched *her*, one that was not yet over.

Round, balding but mysterious Mr Jamieson from Dundee had therefore been immediately interesting to her. When, outside the library door, she had heard the forbidden name Joseph Knight mentioned, Jamieson had become almost exotic, an emissary from a distant kingdom. In the stable, she had told Jamieson that he *should* think about slavery, but he had shrugged her off. Now she heard that conversation go off in a different direction, Jamieson challenging her challenge: *why* should he think about slavery? *He* was not the one living off the proceeds of Jamaican plantations. *He* was not the child of a planter. What was slavery to him but a distant, vague fact of life? Whereas to her . . .

What was it to her? She talked of anti-slavery societies but she knew nothing about them, and no one who belonged to one. She read occasionally of such people in the weekly papers. They seemed mostly to be evangelicals and seceders –

non-conformists at the opposite end of the religious spectrum from the Episcopalian Wedderburns – or, worse, radicals and revolutionaries. Almost all of her knowledge of slavery had come from her father, and from the books in his library.

Her head was full of other conversations: the ones she had teased out of her father over the years. Nowadays he refused to be drawn, but there had been times when he had seemed to enjoy her questions – but only if they were safe questions.

'Is it like this in Jamaica, Papa?'

'Is it like what, Susan?' They were walking in the woods above the house. She must have been eleven or twelve. It was late spring, the ground was thick with bluebells, the trees were putting on their new leaves.

'Like *this*. Are the trees and flowers like this?'

'No,' he said. 'Bigger, and greener and brighter by far. You never saw trees the like of them. So tall you often cannot see the tops. But when you can, there are great red flowers growing out of them. And further down, other plants grow up the trunks – creepers and climbing things bursting with flowers, and with leaves the size of dinner plates; in fact sometimes they are used for dinner plates. And everything lush and green – greens of every shade you can imagine. And that is in the winter, though the seasons hardly exist. Winter there is like our summer only hotter. You think you will be shrivelled away by the heat and then the rain comes and everything becomes still more green – darker and yet brilliant too. And always hot, hot, hot. I cannot describe it.'

But he could, and she knew he was describing a picture in his head that he was happy should be in hers too. He would tell her of huge butterflies, flying beetles the size of small birds; birds that could hover in one place by beating their wings so fast they were a blur and made a droning sound like bees while their long thin beaks drank from flowers; rag-winged crows as big as buzzards, wheeling over the fields in sixes, eights, dozens; multi-coloured parrots, big-chinned pelicans, prim white egrets that rode on the backs of the cattle; insects that drove you mad at night with their incessant chirping, whistling frogs, spiders that could build webs big enough to catch small birds; crocodiles that lived in the swamps, mosquitoes that fed on you year in, year out, and that you never got used to. Coconut trees, banana trees, trees laden with strange fruits never seen in Scotland. It was, her father said, like a huge, hot, overgrown garden.

'Like the Garden of Eden?' she asked.

He laughed. 'In a way, yes.'

'Is there a serpent, then?'

'Only you would ask that, my dear. Yes, there are snakes, but not dangerous ones.'

Then came the questions that were closer to home. What was the house like, she wanted to know. Was it smaller or bigger than Ballindean? How many rooms were there? Was there a view? Was there a town nearby? And what about the people?

'Well, there was me, and your uncle James, and your other uncles that you never knew. We had many Scotsmen for our neighbours. There are many there still.'

'But the people who grew the sugar?'

'We grew the sugar . . .'

'No, who grew it, cut it . . .'

'You mean the Negroes?'

She felt her pulse quicken. Yes, yes, yes, the Negroes. She thought of them flitting through the shady jungle, mysterious, dangerous, beautiful as the blood-red flowers on the trees. One minute you would see them, the next they'd be gone. They were beyond her. But her father had known them.

At first she had thought he was reluctant to talk of them. Later she felt that he just had very little to say about them, as if somehow he had noticed them less than he had the land and its creatures. Some Negroes were black and some were brown, he said, some were not far from white. They were lazy or hard-working, they were weak or strong, they were mostly foolish and childlike. She grew to believe that he did not find them very interesting.

So she read what she could in Mr Long's book on Jamaica, and in other books she found on the higher shelves in the library. And though all that she read in these books confirmed what her father told her, they said more too: about the brutishness, the immorality, the craftiness of Negroes. Because of their nature, she read, it was necessary to control them, to punish the lazy and the wicked, to crush them lest they try to rebel. All this seemed sensible, though sordid. But the more she read, the more she began to glimpse an argument that the books always sought, with wonderful plausibility, to dismiss. The argument was never properly articulated. It was mentioned only to be ridiculed as ignorant, ill-informed, malicious, naïve. Thumbing through these volumes, she lost sight of the flitting figures in the red-flowered jungle; felt instead a growing sense of unease, a sense that things were being kept from her.

'Why do they have to bring so many in the slave ships?'

He said calmly, 'Because there are more needed than could possibly be raised on the island.'

'But why are they treated so cruelly?' She felt anxious and unhappy asking the question: she knew her father would hate it.

'It is not cruel, Susan,' he said. 'How else could they be brought?'

'But it *is* cruel. It is horrible to think of children being torn from their mothers and fathers, husbands from wives, sisters from brothers, and carried off to a land so far from their home, and made to work so hard. It *must* be cruel.'

'Susan, I do not know where you find such ideas but you should believe them no more than you believe fairy tales. Some people are cruel. That is true the world over. Some people are cruel here in Scotland. In Africa people are horribly cruel. But we were not cruel to the slaves. They were treated kindly when they behaved, and chastised only when it was necessary. That is how it is there still. That is how your Papa is with you, child. Sometimes I have to be angry with you. That does not mean I do not love you.'

'Did you love the slaves?'

She saw the shock in his eyes.

'Of course not. They were not my children. But it was our Christian duty to look after them.'

'Is it Christian to keep them as slaves?'

'I do not wish to discuss this further,' her father said. 'But I will say this, since you speak of what is or is not Christian. The Negroes are not Christians. They are different from us in many ways, not just in their colour. They are not quite human in the way that we are. It has been tried and found impossible to teach

23

them to be refined and civil like us. They can do so much, and no more. That is their nature.'

'But *we* are Christians. And don't some of them come to be baptised and make very good Christians?'

'Most make very bad ones. Susan, we will not talk any more about this. You are a child. You have no idea what it is like in the Indies, let alone in Africa. Believe me, I am your father. There never was a race of people constitutionally better suited – better *created* – to be the property of others.'

But she did not – quite – believe him. She read the books again. She overheard disturbing snatches of conversation when her uncle James came to visit. And she heard stories from the older servants about Joseph Knight, the slave her father had brought back with him to Ballindean.

Then, in the library one day, when she was about fourteen, the sunlight caught the painting above the fireplace in such a way that she suddenly glimpsed a new figure in the gloom. Uncle Sandy's picture. She had looked at it so often that the shock of what she saw now made her gasp, as if she had seen a ghost. There was no one else in the room. She stood as close as she could, peered at the painting straight on, from the left, from the right. The oil gleamed back at her. Behind the oil was a leg, a shoulder, a face. A man.

From then on she learned to use the library at times when her father was out or away from home. She started to use the books as none of her sisters did, *to find things out*. And when she was alone she would stand for long minutes in front of the painting, gazing at the porch where Joseph Knight had been – where the outline of him still was if you were wise to it. She would close her eyes and see him running through the trees. He was naked. He was young. He was extremely handsome.

Right from the start she had known she must not mention him to her father. The servants did not even have to warn her, she knew it from their hushed tones. She understood it from the bitterness that sometimes seeped out of Maister MacRoy. She wanted to ask somebody about the figure in the painting, but she did not dare. It was a secret. If her father found out that she knew it, he would be angry. He might take the painting away. She must do nothing to provoke that.

So Joseph Knight remained at Ballindean yet was always missing, visible yet invisible, present yet absent in all the real and imagined conversations she had ever had. That was part of the thrill of hearing him named by Mr Jamieson. It made him seem alive, even though as she had told Jamieson she thought he must be dead. For years she had sensed Knight's ghost in the library: in the books themselves, in old letters folded and forgotten inside the books, in every nook and on every shelf. He was there but not there. Jamieson had been so close and yet had not spotted Knight in the painting, because he had not known to look. But she had known. And now she knew she would have to look again; that there must be more of Joseph Knight somewhere in that room.

Alone again, Sir John Wedderburn briefly regretted being so sharp with Jamieson. But then, the man had been presumptuous – and a sycophant when his presumption met resistance. Sir John stood and went to inspect the picture of himself, James and Peter. Not a good painting. Its amateurishness had always annoyed him. He should take it down, put it somewhere else or get rid of it all together. But he knew he would not. He had been having this argument with himself for thirty years. The painting mattered. It was one of only two things that survived of his brother Sandy. He went back to the table.

Jamieson's suggestion that he was some mere branch of the Wedderburn tree had irritated him. Just because cousin Loughborough had been in the public eye! Even against somebody as insignificant as Jamieson it was necessary to defend the family name against incursions, especially when they involved a plotter and trimmer like Loughborough, whose whole history had been one of eliminating any Scottish traits – accent, acquaintances, principles – that might have hindered his political progress in England. Sir John, though he spoke good English, still sounded Scotch enough, and that was with twenty years in the West Indies, where the whites generally turned to speaking like their slaves. Lord Loughborough, on the other hand, had taken lessons in his youth from some Irish speech pedlar, had planed out his vowels and Scotticisms till nobody would laugh at him in London. Ah well, Loughborough was at an end now.

They all were, their generation – redding up their affairs as best they could.

Aeneas's quiet knock came again and he slid in, closing the door behind him. 'He's awa,' he said.

'Good.'

'Is there onything ye want done?'

'No.' The question seemed innocent enough, but the implication was, did anything need to be done about *him*? Jamieson. Aeneas watched out for his master like an old dog. With his grizzled, unsmiling loyalty he might have been better suited for a soldier than a schoolmaster. *Might have been*. Wedderburn smiled – there was a whole other life in that phrase.

'You know what day it is tomorrow, Aeneas?'

'Aye. The sixteenth.'

'Fifty-six years,' Sir John said.

'Aye, Sir John.'

April the sixteenth. The date never escaped them. There were anniversaries scattered through the calendar that Sir John always observed with a sombre heart: so far this year there had been the martyrdom of Charles I, at the end of January, and the death of his first, dear wife Margaret in March; and late in November he would mourn, yet again, his father. But tomorrow it was Culloden.

'You'll come and drink a toast with me?'

'Jist oorsels?' MacRoy asked.

'Of course.' It was never anyone but themselves. Everybody else was too young, or dead.

'Nearly sixty years, damn it,' Sir John said. 'A lifetime away, a world away. Dear God, somebody will be writing a *novelle* about it next!'

'It'll no tell the truth, a *novelle*,' Aeneas said.

'No, it won't. The women will love it. But we're still here. We know the truth.'

'Aye.'

'What a life, Aeneas, eh?' Sir John said. 'What a life! Out in '45 – there's not many left that can say that! And you, too. We were out together.'

Out. What a tiny, enormous word. At sixteen Sir John had

26

marched to Derby. At seventeen – Susan's age – he had been at Culloden. At eighteen he had been an exile in Jamaica.

Life, the poets said, was a splashing mountain burn becoming a deep, smooth river flowing to the sea. Sir John did not see it like that. For him life was a broken expanse of land without design or cultivation, patchworked with bog and rocky outcrops. A trackless moor covered by low cloud – or by smoke. What connected one memory to another, this moment to that moment? You turned around and lost sight of someone, your bearings went astray, you could only dimly see what you had thought was a certain landmark.

What had a frightened boy on a battlefield to do with an aged laird in Perthshire, putting his affairs in order, folding away his years? What had a boy on the run called John Thomson to do with an old man called John Wedderburn? What had a black boy with some impossible name, chasing birds in an unknown village in Africa, to do with a man called Joseph Knight, sitting in a courtroom in Edinburgh? What had these lives to do with each other? They seemed quite distinct. Separate people. There was no continuous stream, only a torn, faded, incomplete map of wilderness.

He shook his head. He must have dozed. Some time had passed – the clock said half-past eleven – and Aeneas had gone away again; if he had actually been there and not part of a dream. Sir John was disturbed by this idea. Recently he had been having sensations of doubt like that all the time: was he awake or dreaming? It was very unmanly. And he didn't really believe that idle nonsense anyway, about the trackless moor. It made everything so pointless. Better to think of God, and, God willing, a place in heaven. *There* was the stream of life, *there* was the eternal sea into which all must flow. He had been hirpling about just now like some kind of atheist! Like the infidel Hume on his deathbed teasing Boswell about oblivion – knowing full well that Bozzy would just *have* to tell everybody about it. Hume who had been so terribly intelligent that he could imagine himself unable to imagine! Think himself insentient! Deny the very stirrings of his soul! Idiot Hume, too clever for his own salvation, telling Boswell, 'If there *were* a future state, I think I could give as good an account of my life as most people.' A risky hypothesis to put before God, but then again, Sir John had lately been thinking the same.

He, of course, was no atheist. When the day came, he would be able to give a fair account of himself. He had always tried to do things right. He had not wilfully done evil. Honour, courage, Christian decency – he believed in these things, had lived his life according to such standards. You were put here in this life and all you could do was get through it as well as you were able, and that was what he had done.

Reminded of Boswell, Sir John stood up and wandered his shelves, identifying the spines of the *Life* of Dr Johnson. He had never been able to fight his way through the whole of that work, but there were passages that he knew almost by heart. 'I cannot too highly praise the speech which Mr Henry Dundas generously contributed to the cause of the sooty stranger.' That was one. He had read that a dozen times, never got beyond it to the next page. It just made him angry.

Changed times. Dundas had spent the 1790s stalling the parliamentary efforts of Mr William Wilberforce to abolish the slave trade, conscious then of the detrimental effect abolition would have on the West Indian plantations, Sir John's among them. Yet he had shown only disdain for the Wedderburn interests when he had spoken for the 'sooty stranger' in that courtroom in 1778.

It was all politics of course: Dundas had told Parliament that he wanted to end slavery when the economic conditions were right. He had meant the political conditions. But now he was out of office, resigned as His Majesty's Secretary for War along with the rest of Pitt's Government. Even Harry Dundas had to come to an end eventually.

'Changed times.' Sir John said the words out loud, as if to remind himself of the present, and his presence in it. It didn't do to dwell too much on the past. But increasingly, that was what he did – dwelt on the past, or in it, or tried to shore it up against the tide. For the last twelve months Sir John had been firing off letters to various persons in the Government, imploring them not to listen to Wilberforce and his abolitionist cronies who seized on every reported brutality, exaggerated it tenfold and then claimed it as the norm in the plantations. As if one bad master made an argument against the entire system. Was a fornicating minister an argument against religion, a drunken laird a reason to abolish property? Few of these meddlers had even been in the West Indies. None of them had ever tried to rid Negroes of indolence, deceit and stupidity, to instil decency and honesty in them and raise them above the animals. Everybody could see what happened when Negroes got loose. A Toussaint L'Ouverture appeared, wielding a machete.

This, Sir John told himself, was one reason he had wanted Joseph Knight found. Nothing to do with money, or setting up a meeting. He had wanted to know if Knight still existed. He had wanted an example.

Joseph Knight – a Negro who had had the best advantages and opportunities, the best master, who had been instructed and baptised in the Christian religion, and who, even in these circumstances, had turned out a knave, an impostor, a traitor. If he still lived, by now he would undoubtedly have sunk into obscurity, destitution, superstition and depravity. He had been heading down that road even before the court case was over. If he could have been found, if he could have been held up as evidence . . .

But there had been another reason to find him. Again, to see if he still existed, although this time it was not about the public interest. It was about locating a missing, personal landmark. Joseph Knight was *missing* from his life, had been these last two dozen years. Once he had always been there, quiet, reliable (so it seemed), an unmistakable, visible sign of Wedderburn's success, of his return from exile, of his triumph over adversity. Even now, in spite of everything, Sir John would have enjoyed being able to say, 'That one was *mine*.'

With an effort Sir John turned in his chair to the wall behind the table, where there was a small etching of his father, the 5th Baronet of Blackness. His neck and shoulders protested, and he shuffled the chair round. When he looked at the etching, he sometimes thought the likeness very good, sometimes poor (unlike the Jamaica painting, which always looked poor). This was because for so long now the portrait of his father had been more real than the man: these days it was a question of asking how good a likeness his father would have been of it. It was a thin, horsy, straight face, with large worried eyes and a broad forehead capped with a neat curled wig. The etching had been done from memory by a female cousin, after the execution. His father had been forty-two when he died. Sometimes when Sir John stared at the etching he imagined his father alive again, and ageing, becoming more like *him*. What a strange thing – that he should have become his father's father.

The pinprick of a tear started in one eye, and he stabbed it dry with his forefinger.

He could not be bothered now with the letter he had started. He had been going to write to James down at Inveresk – something about the guardianship – but it could wait. Invariably, thinking of Joseph and Jamaica made him think of James too, his only surviving sibling. Their eldest brother had died at the age of five, leaving John heir to their father's baronetcy. Three other brothers were long dead, two of them in Jamaica, and dead also were their four sisters. John and James were all that survived of the seed of their father. With James he had shared more of the adventures of his life than with any of the others, yet in character they remained utterly different. They seldom saw each other now. To or from Inveresk, which lay across two firths and down the coast beyond Edinburgh, was a long journey for old men.

He got up and went over to the window again. The east wind was still biting at the leafless branches of the trees beyond the small oval loch. Better to be inside looking out, on a day like this, than outside looking in. Ballindean, for all its fine south-facing location, was not the bonniest of houses anyway. Sir John had made many improvements since buying it in 1769, but more than once he had wondered how much one could really do with an old house. If he were forty again, perhaps he would knock it all down and start anew.

Being stuck inside made him restless. He went towards the writing-table, paused. Somewhere in there, deep in one of the drawers, beneath a jumble of old letters and papers, lay a small calf-bound book, a journal, now beginning to crumble at the edges. For years he had meant to destroy it – James and he, after long discussion, had determined that this was the proper thing to do – but the journal was, apart from the painting, the only surviving memento of his young brother Alexander, who had kept it, sporadically, for four years in Jamaica. Apart from James and himself, the three brothers who had survived to adulthood had all died within a few years of one another, back in the 1760s; Peter and Alexander in the Indies; David, whom he had never really known, in London. But it was Sandy he regretted most.

Dead at what? – twenty-four, twenty-five? Peter had lasted well into his thirties, had at least settled in the Indies, was making a success of things there when the yellow fever carried him off. But poor Sandy had never settled. And the way he had died – Sir John could not bear to think about it. If Sandy could have held on just a few years more, he might have come home safe like James and himself. Or if he had come back with him in '63, John's first return – that would have saved him. Now all that was left of him was the journal and the painting. Typical Sandy, to do one thing inadequately, and another thing worse. The picture was poor, but the journal was awful.

The painting was saved by its sentimental value. It was crude and clumsy – the sky was too thick, the faces too flat – but it captured something of the house in Jamaica, and its naïve execution was Sandy through and through. It was also the only image he had of Peter. And it was part of the family's story.

The journal's contents were a quite different matter. They were certainly not for the gentle eyes of his wife and daughters. What Sandy had written was weak, febrile, disgusting. It left a vile taste in the mouth. But it, too, was Sandy. John Wedderburn kept it for that reason, but it stayed buried in the drawer.

It was the record of a life cut short, wasted. Sir John did not like waste of any kind. He looked at the inviting armchairs by the hearth, and decided against getting out the journal. One day soon, perhaps, a last glance – then into the fire with it. Right now, he wanted to sleep.

II

Darkness

Drummossie Moor, 16 April 1746

Sir John Wedderburn, 5th Baronet of Blackness, forty-two years of age and feeling sixty, spoke to his son side-mouthed and out of the hearing of the troops drawn up a few paces in front. 'The men are dead on their feet. I fear this may be the end, John.'

His caution was hardly necessary: most of them, though not yet dead, were half asleep, heads bowed, bonnets scrugged down against the wind and wet. The army stretched in thin grey lines across the sodden moor. Opposite them the Government forces waited in solid red blocks.

'We are cold and hungry and exhausted,' the father said. 'Cumberland's men are fat and rested and twice our number. It is not a happy meeting.'

'We have won against the odds before,' the son said. 'And they are not desperate like us.' Making a virtue out of desperation had turned his lips blue. He was shivering uncontrollably, and as he spoke another squall of sleet, colder and more vicious than snow, battered over the moor and hit him full on the face, forcing him to turn away from his father.

Two months before, he had celebrated, if that was the word, his seventeenth birthday by toasting the Jacobite army's capture of Inverness. But even then it had been obvious that Prince Charles Edward Stewart and his Council were divided and running out of options. Even then, all young John Wedderburn had wanted was to go home. And now this. A shattered, sullen remnant of at most five thousand men, aching from a stumbling, useless march through the night – a failed attempt to surprise Cumberland's camp with a dawn attack – and a misty afternoon laced with sleet and bitter wind. It was April, but felt more like midwinter.

Sir John put his arm around his son's shoulders, pulling him close. An observer might have thought he was simply trying to rub warmth into him. He spoke urgently into his ear. 'John, when this starts the outcome will be clear in a matter of minutes.

If we take the fight to them perhaps we have a chance. But the MacDonalds have no belly for it on the left. They are nursing their injured pride, and without them this army has no backbone.'

'*We* are its backbone,' the boy said, sweeping his arm at the two battalions of Lord Ogilvy's regiment formed up in front of them: Angus men, drawn from the glens of Isla, Clova and Prosen; from the Sidlaws, Forfar and Dundee. Hard, silent cottars from lands straddling the Highland–Lowland divide, they had marched without complaint the hundreds of miles to Derby, then back to Scotland and all the way to this bleak northern moor. Some had been killed, others had slipped away to Inverness in search of food, a few had deserted and headed back south to their homes, but nearly five hundred remained, relatively well armed with musket and sword, still maintaining the discipline which had begun to break down among the northern clansmen.

Because of his social position, young John Wedderburn was a captain in the Glen Prosen company raised by his uncle Robert. To him was given the honour of carrying the colours, which were snapping and billowing angrily a few yards away, kept upright for the time being, and with great difficulty, by a tiny drummer boy jacked between the staff and the wet ground; and though Wedderburn was too young to lead troops into battle, and acted more as an aide de camp to Lord Ogilvy, he felt it his duty to hold out some hope of success. 'We are the army's backbone,' he said again, trying to convince himself.

His father shook his head. Hopelessness was all over his face.

Poverty was what had led Sir John to throw in his lot with the Prince. Although he had inherited the title Baronet of Blackness on the death of his father, it had come without land, since one of the 4th Baronet's last acts had been to sell the estate, on the edge of Dundee, in a desperate attempt to make ends meet. Since then, the family had been living on a run-down farm at Newtyle, a few miles to the north-west of the town. Lured by the prospect of reward into what had not then seemed a mad and impossible enterprise, the new Baronet had allowed himself to be persuaded to accept an appointment as collector of excise for the Prince, and now he feared all those receipts held by the merchants and magistrates of Perth and Dundee – receipts which bore his signature. They had been signs of his diligence. Now they were paper witnesses to his complicity.

'Listen to me,' he urged. 'If it goes badly, do not wait for the end. Ride away before it is too late.'

'Leave my men, sir? Desert the colours? How can I do that?'

'We are being held in reserve here. *Your* men may not even be called upon to engage. If it comes to a retreat, you'll only be a step ahead of them. In a way you'll be leading them.'

The boy blinked at the ground, as if dazed by the lameness of this reasoning. 'And you?' he mumbled. 'What about you?'

'I'll not be far behind you. I'll stay with my Lord Ogilvy as long as I can, but I'll not wait to be killed if that's all there is to be had from the affair. Nor, I doubt, will he. Don't look affronted, lad. There's no shame in this, no disgrace. Better to live for another day, if there's to be one, than be butchered in a bog.' He looked around quickly, as if expecting the Prince to walk by and accuse him of treachery. 'John, I am your father. Do you love me?'

'Yes, Papa, of course.'

'Then honour and obey me.'

A thin series of cheers went up in front as Lord Ogilvy and the Duke of Perth rode along the line, waving their hats. Ogilvy's regiment was in the second line of the army. To the right, seventy yards ahead, and only three hundred from the red coats of the Government forces, were the men of Atholl, who had been given the place usually taken by the MacDonalds, who felt insulted as a result. In return for this privilege, the Atholl men were up to their shins in bog, and crowded together by a dyke running along their right between them and the river Nairn. Across the moor Cumberland's drums were rattling away like hailstones. Shouts from the Highland officers drifted up into the heavy air. Men began to stamp their feet, check their powder and muskets. It was just after one o'clock.

'I must get back to Lord Ogilvy,' said Sir John, 'and you must take your position.' Their horses were being held by a servant twenty yards away, and they started towards them. As they went, there was a roar from the left: the Jacobites' paltry collection of artillery had begun firing at the enemy.

A minute later the response came from Cumberland's three-pounders and mortars. Roundshot whistled overhead, thudding into the ground just behind the waiting Jacobite troops. Mud and heather showered up and splattered down again. Somebody screamed in agony. The enemy artillery had found the range at the first attempt.

'God help us!' said Sir John. He seized his son's arm again. 'I beg you, do not ride for Inverness. If the battle's lost Inverness will be lost too, and they will show no mercy to those they find there.' A mortar shell screamed overhead and exploded thirty yards away. 'Turn south as soon as you can, and get back to the lands you know. Get into Badenoch, past Ruthven, and keep riding. Lose yourself in the mountains. Take the Lairig Ghru or one of the other passes, and keep moving till you come in above the Dee. You'll know where you are from there?'

'Of course. There's no need for all this, Papa.'

They were shouting at each other now as the roundshot crashed around them. Smoke was blowing thickly across the field, but already their own guns were firing only sporadically, while the Government bombardment intensified.

'There's every need. I wish it were not so. A hard time is coming on us all.' Another volley flew so low overhead that they fell to the ground, flattened by the turbulence, and when they rose they were both streaked from chest to knee in black mud and scraps of heather. Their horses were panicking, the servant struggling to control them. As they mounted, Sir John bellowed his last instructions. 'Get across the Dee and over the hills again, by the Monega Road, till you come into Glen Isla. Seek out Mr Arthur, the minister. He got the living from your uncle Robert, who vouches for him. He will give you shelter till I can come up with you.'

'If you're only just behind me, we'll meet long before Glen Isla.'

'Aye, that's right, John. But you're not to wait on me, do you understand?'

A band of smoke mixed with driving rain half obscured father from son. When it cleared a little, young John turned his horse to join his troops, lifting the colours as he went from the numb hands of the drummer boy, who promptly collapsed, covered his head with his arms and started to scream.

The men of Angus were standing firm against the bombardment;

so far the shot had either gone over their heads or fallen short. In front of them, though, it was a different story. As the enemy guns shortened their range, the iron balls drove great lanes through the ranks of shivering Highlanders. They tore off limbs like rags, punched holes that removed entire guts from men who were still standing, and left others dead or beyond repair on the freezing wet ground among their comrades. MacLeans, Maclachlans, Frasers, Camerons, the roundshot slaughtered them with perfect indifference. But even through the steady crack and thud of cannon fire young John Wedderburn could hear the frantic cries of the Highland officers: 'Dùinibh a-steach! Dùinibh a-steach!' Close up! Close up!

Runners were scurrying back and forth between the front line and the commanders at the rear, yet nobody seemed to be in control. Wedderburn watched with rising horror. 'Dùinibh a-steach!' he heard again. But tightening the ranks only made them more vulnerable. Why were the men not ordered to advance? Were they all to die without striking a blow?

The Jacobite artillery had now ceased firing entirely. Briefly the enemy's guns also fell silent. But then they began again, this time loaded with grapeshot, withering sprays of lead pellets that ripped through the clans like scythes through a field of oats. To stand and take this, after everything else, was intolerable. First the MacLeans, then all the Highlanders still surviving in the centre and right, threw off their plaids, gripped their claymores and staggered forward through the bog, screaming into the grapeshot gale as they went. They left behind them a carpet of bodies and body parts. When they were halfway across the moor the Government infantry's muskets opened up on them.

The Angus men waited in reserve, helplessly watching the carnage. Young John Wedderburn's terrified mare was stamping and snorting, and in bringing her under control he let her run a few paces. He glanced back through the drifting lines of smoke to see if he could spot his father. A hundred yards away a group of horsemen seemed to be moving away from the battle. John Wedderburn screwed his eyes against the smoke. He could see, he thought, the Prince among them, but not his father. He could not see him anywhere at all.

*　　*　　*

There followed a dream of flight, stretching over days. The retreat his father had hinted at did not exist, only a stream of men and horses fleeing south in total disorder. John Wedderburn was carried along by this current. Shame barely crossed his mind: his only thought was to get away. He saw many of his own Glen Prosen company running in the same direction, showing not the least concern for his ignoble behaviour. This did not relieve the sickness in his stomach. Somewhere in the last minutes of the battle he had let go the colours and had not seen them since, but the sickness was not guilt, it was fear. By the time he reached Moy the men were straggled for miles along the road, some barely able to keep moving, others asleep where they had sat down for a minute's respite. The ground was littered with discarded weapons and uniforms, forgotten bonnets, broken shoes. John paused to rest his horse, which was lathered and unsteady from being ridden too hard. He knew he should let her walk unburdened for a while, but when more riders came up and reported that the redcoats were slaughtering any male they caught – fit, wounded, young, old, armed or weaponless – he remounted and whipped the beast south again.

Twenty miles on, as night fell, he found himself alone. Fording the pounding, numbing Spey, the mare collapsed in midstream and John had to abandon her, then fight his way across on legs like blocks of stone, bawling out animal noises of rage and exhaustion. He had not eaten since dawn, was completely drenched, frozen, shattered, frightened, friendless, and now without a horse.

He stumbled on through the gloom towards the great hulks of the Cairngorms; knew he must stop and find shelter. Not far from the river he came across a huddle of houses crouched low as dogs and every one in darkness. He knocked at the first. He was sure there were people inside but there was no answer. He pushed; the door was barred. He tried the next one: the same. At the last house, despairing, he did not knock but leant against the door, and it opened under his weight. He stepped inside, closed the door behind him.

A woman's voice said, 'Cò tha siud?' – Who's there? – and something else fast and challenging, he could not make out what: 'Ma 's ann a thoirt an èiginn orm a thàinig thu, tha mi

40

cho cruaidh ri cloich; ma 's ann dha mo spùinneadh, chan eil càil agam ach seann phoit.' 'Tha mi le Teàrlach,' he said, not caring any more. I am for Charles. The voice muttered something else; it was coming from a recess at one end of the room and sounded like an acceptance, if not exactly an invitation. The room was warm, the air thick with the smell of peat, and as his eyes adjusted he saw a bank of glowing red a few feet away. He went towards it, dripping at every step, and lay down in front of the fire. In a minute, he thought, I will take off my wet things, but just for now . . . Seconds later he was asleep.

He woke, his joints seized, still stretched on the dirt floor of the house. The fire was blazing now; steam poured from his clothes like hill mist. Stiff and shivery, he slowly pulled himself upright, began to feel the blood in him again. There was a bed set into one wall, and in it, watching him intently, was a very old woman.

John Wedderburn's Gaelic was sparse – learned on the march to Derby from soldiers who had laughed good-naturedly at his efforts while appreciating the fact that he made them – and the woman had a rapid and almost impenetrable intonation. By slowing her down, he gathered that he had slept the better part of a day, that she was too old now to get out of bed except to feed the fire, which she had done before he woke up, and that so long as he fetched more peats from behind the house he was welcome to eat what little food she had, as she would die before him. He went out for the peats – there was not a flicker of life in the other houses – brought in several loads and stacked them in a corner, as if by prolonging the fire he could prolong the woman's life and thus maybe his own, but there appeared to be nothing to eat in any case. He took off his boots and stuck them almost in the fire to dry them out, hung his tunic over the back of the one wooden chair in the place. When he tentatively asked about food, the woman signalled him nearer, and pulled from beneath the bedding a small poke, at the bottom of which were a few handfuls of oatmeal. He shook his head – not if that was all she had – but she insisted, again saying that she would die before him. Then she laughed, a toothless rasp, and added something that he had to get her to repeat three times. By the time he understood, there was no joke left in it: she would *probably* die before him, unless the redcoats arrived before he left.

He mixed some of the meal with water in her one blackened pot and put it on the fire. She would not take any of the porridge when it was ready, so he ate it all: a dozen mouthfuls. Nor was she interested in the money he offered her – one or two of the few coins he had in a purse slung round his neck beneath his shirt – but she did gesture to him to pass his tunic over to her. He laid it across her lap as she sat up in bed, and she felt the brass buttons with crooked fingers. Then she indicated to him to look under the bed.

There was an old wooden kist there. Opening it, the first item he came upon was a grey shepherd's plaid, filthy and matted as a sheep's winter coat. She nodded eagerly, apparently having given up trying to speak to him: he was to take it. She proceeded to pull the buttons of his tunic with surprising strength, and they disappeared under the blankets to join the meal poke. She signed that he must throw the tunic on the fire. He did so, watched it smoulder, then catch and blaze. With a stick he stabbed at it, a cuff, a sleeve, the collar, till the evidence of his visit was all gone. He put on more peats. Knowing it was time to move on, not wishing to go, wishing somehow he could stay in the cottage for years, he sat staring into the flames for a while, then stood and turned to the old woman still sitting in the bed. 'Tapadh leibh,' he said. She nodded. 'Tapadh leibhse.' Thank *you*. He put on his boots, hot and white-stained, wrapped the plaid around himself, and stepped back out into the world.

Nothing after that but walking and sleeping. That first night he managed perhaps six miles before stopping, not wanting to get deep into the mountains without seeing roughly where he was. He slept in the plaid among the roots of a huge pine tree, and the night, though cold, was at least dry. Early next morning, hungry again, he followed a track that headed south-east, rising steeply alongside a burn in spate. By instinct rather than knowledge he believed this to be the northern end of the pass known as the Lairig Ghru. He had stood at the other end, more than twenty miles away, while his father pointed out the route, but he had never walked it. Part of him feared travelling in daylight, but the ache in his belly told him he must risk it: it would take a day, and beyond it he still had another full day at least, probably two, to get into Glen Isla. If he travelled only at night, hunger would beat him. Also, the morning was sunny and dry, but the weather might change at any moment. He fixed his mind on the Reverend Arthur, and pressed on.

Huge, bleak, snow-covered hills rose on either side of him. The path faded and often disappeared altogether. The sun vanished behind clouds. Sleet, heavy rain and brief patches of sunlight succeeded one another. As he climbed higher, he entered the cloud itself, and the moisture enveloped him, lying greasily on the plaid. If he heard a sound that might be another traveller, he left the path and hunkered behind a rock. But nobody came. There were others in these hills, he could sense them, but they were all moving as discreetly as he, and all in much the same direction. He wondered if his father was one of them.

On Deeside there were more people in evidence, country folk going about their daily business, also many ragged men, of varying ages but all in some kind of distress, on their way to somewhere. The atmosphere was oppressive. It was as if a veil of some indefinable material had been dropped over the Highlands, clinging invisibly to everything: everybody knew what had happened; everybody knew that, whether they had been involved or not, they would suffer for it.

The cottars were wary but not unkind. John got half a thick oatcake from one wife, an egg from another. Information about the battle was cautiously sought in return: nothing so direct as 'Were you there?' – although it was obvious that he and the other men had sprung from *some*where – but what news he might have heard about this or that person who seemed against their will to have got caught up in that affair in the north. He could not help them, thanked them for the food, wandered on. Soon his boots cracked and split: they had been wet too often, and dried too fast. The sole of each foot was a mass of blisters. He crossed the Clunie Water, limped into Glen Shee, met a shepherd who pointed out to him the drovers' track known as the Monega Road over the next set of hills, and started to climb. The weather turned foul again. He slipped on mud and rock, dragged himself through wet, treacherous snow, nearly fell off a cliff, screamed his despair to the relentless sky. He found the path, lost it again, walked through the night because it was too cold to stop, and in the morning came like a ghost to the head of lovely Glen Isla. There he sat down and he wept. There were still several miles to go before he reached the manse, but at last he was in a place he recognised.

Edinburgh, May 1746

To say that the Reverend William Arthur was nervous would be something of an understatement. He was terrified. A respectable, law-abiding man of the cloth – admittedly from an Angus parish full of Episcopalians, a fact which placed him in a proximity to the rebels that many of his kirk brethren found disagreeable if not downright suspect – here he was in Edinburgh, at the General Assembly of the Church of Scotland as by law Established, not a month after the crushing of those same rebels, in the company of a young man who had been, who still was, *out*! He was, in short, harbouring a criminal, a boy who had been present at Culloden and the earlier engagements, and whose unhappy father was languishing in custody at Inverness, or perhaps by this time even in London, awaiting trial. Should it be revealed that John Thomson, the minister's footman, was not John Thomson at all – and was that not too *obvious*, too *ordinary*, a name for a footman? – Glen Isla would be deprived of its pastor and the pastor of his living, if not his life.

The Reverend Arthur did not take pleasure from rubbing shoulders with trouble. He had obligations to the family, of course; he sympathised, even, but he had been thinking uncharitable thoughts about the Wedderburns all week. Between times he had been praying hard: for forgiveness if he had done wrong; for strength if he was doing right; but most of all, he was praying that John Thomson would quickly leave his service, go to London, and never come chapping at the door of his manse again.

The spectral figure, in an astonishingly filthy shepherd's plaid, had barely been able to speak when it appeared just before dinner on that chilly April day. Young John had managed only a few words about the battle, his uncle Robert Wedderburn, and his hope of sanctuary. By the time Mrs Arthur and a maid had bundled the lad indoors, stripped him, bathed him and put him to bed in the attic, away from prying eyes, dinner had been quite spoiled. An urgent discussion had ensued about what to do with him, always supposing he did not die of his ordeal.

It had been Mrs Arthur, more moved than her husband, more seduced by emotion, who had thought of the General Assembly, which would be taking place in little over a fortnight. The Reverend would be setting out early, as he had other business in the capital. He would not normally go to Edinburgh without a servant, but old Tam Tosh, who might have accompanied him, was so arthritic these days that he dropped anything heavier than a comb: now here was a young fellow ready made, and quite plain-looking too. Busy Edinburgh would be safer for the boy than these glens into which inquisitive soldiers would soon be marching. Reluctantly, Mr Arthur had agreed. On the road between Angus and the capital, John Wedderburn had been lost and John Thomson born.

They were lodged in the Canongate, and when the minister went out he preferred it if John Thomson went too. This was because the lad would not stay in their room alone, but wandered the streets speaking to God knew who. Worse, he wrote letters to his mother in a clumsy code that a spy would crack on the first page, asking for news of his father, and rounding off with requests that she, Lady Wedderburn, send him, John Thomson, more clothes, and that she remember him to his aunt! Mr Arthur felt it necessary to regulate his servant's supply of paper and ink, and to keep him by his side as much as possible.

The only consolation was that Edinburgh, which barely half a year earlier had been swooning at the feet of the Chevalier, was now so fervently back in the Hanoverian fold that nobody thought any *rebels* in the town – for of course everybody understood that plenty were there – posed any great threat to national security. How conveniently, for example, certain non-combative poets and booksellers, famed for their Jacobite sympathies, had absented themselves from the capital during the occupation, and how easily they had returned to resume a peaceful life and, tentatively at first, to write songs of heroism and betrayal.

In spite of this, Mr Arthur was less inclined to break out in a cold sweat if he could keep John Thomson under his close personal observation. He had him attend him to St Giles' for the General Assembly, which venerable body humbly composed a thank-you letter to His Royal Highness, the Duke of Cumberland. The letter praised the Duke's generous resolution in delivering the Scottish Church and Nation from the Jacobite army; acknowledged the many fatigues he had endured and the alarming dangers he had run in pursuing that ungrateful and rebellious crew; expressed the Church's great joy in the complete victory he had now obtained by the bravery of his Royal Father's troops, led on by his own wise conduct and animated by his heroic example; and, finally, prayed that the Lord of Hosts, Who had hitherto covered his head in the day of battle, might yet guard his precious life, and crown him with the same glorious success, and that his illustrious name might be transmitted with still greater glory to latest posterity. This was approved, applauded and dispatched by His Royal Highness's most obliged, most obedient and most humble servants, the ministers and elders of the Kirk: a letter so nauseatingly obsequious that it made Mr Arthur feel quite ill as he voted for it.

Fortunately for the minister, his purgatory did not extend beyond the duration of the General Assembly. John Thomson, a half-hysterical, frozen, wasted child a fortnight past, had come back to life in the miraculous way of youth, and intended to set off at once for London. There, according to information contained in a note from his brother James to their mother, and communicated by her to the minister (a paper trail that made Mr Arthur shudder), a ship had docked bearing such prize captives as the Earl of Kilmarnock, the Lords Balmerino and Cromartie, Sir James Kinloch and Sir John Wedderburn. The prisoners had been distributed to jails as yet unknown, to await the gathering of evidence against them. Clearly, the eldest unincarcerated male Wedderburn's place was at his father's side, or as close to it as he could get without being detected and put there literally. Greatly relieved, the Reverend Arthur returned alone to Glen Isla. John Thomson boarded a vessel at Leith, and worked his passage south to the English capital.

London, June–November 1746

In London young John, now neither Thomson nor Wedderburn, was given safe lodging and subsistence by a relative, a Mr Paterson, through whom he was also reunited with his brother. James, just fifteen years old, as one who had not been out, was at liberty to travel where he wanted throughout the kingdom. As soon as he had heard of his father's capture he had mounted his favourite pony and headed south, putting up in byres and stables on the way. Anger and the snorting of cattle had kept him awake most nights: anger at not having been at Culloden, anger at his father's capture, at his father for having *been* captured, at John for *not* having been; this burning rage had driven him all the way to London. There he had found that his father was in the new jail at Southwark along with a number of other Jacobite gentlemen. They were being treated, all things considered, with the courtesy their social status demanded. In the Highlands, meanwhile, poor men were being shot on sight, their wives and daugters raped, their cottages burnt and their cattle slaughtered. Large numbers of destitute peasants, brought out on pain of death by their chiefs, were being condemned to transportation. Now, with John's arrival, James's anger began to settle like the bed of a fire, his character to harden into something new and purposeful.

James looked like a Wedderburn but he was darker-haired, softer-skinned, more lightly built than his brother. He had been making women fall for him since before he was conscious of his own charms. As a bairn he had had a smile and an eye that could melt most female hearts, and in London it was no different, except that now he was aware of his power. John used to watch him, and was envious of the ease with which he attracted women, the way he toyed with them, the disdain with which he dismissed them.

James seemed also to take a certain satisfaction from being the only connection between his older brother and their father. He was allowed regular access to the prison, bringing Sir John fresh linen, soap, books, tobacco and a few other luxuries. James and young John spent much time together, and too much money, in coffee houses and taverns. This earned a rebuke or two from the father, which James took almost as a mark of appreciation. In August he turned sixteen. He bought himself an interesting present: a whore in Covent Garden.

In Southwark jail Sir John Wedderburn kept good heart: he was glad to have one son near him; glad, too, to hear that John was, for the moment, out of harm's way. He wrote to his wife, and heard back from her how, with his other children, she now lived in straitened circumstances in Dundee, having been ejected from the farm at Newtyle. This was a sore blow, but they had never had much money anyway. He would find a way to make amends.

He was confident that the longer he was held at Southwark, the more the Government's attitude to minor players like himself would soften. After all, he had not actually killed anybody. He would be tried, no doubt; found guilty, certainly; but the bloodletting that had lasted all summer would surely satisfy even the Duke of Cumberland's desire for vengeance. Banishment, for a spell, that surely was the most likely outcome. They would go to France. Life would begin again.

He was, however, anxious about John, whose name was on the lists of wanted rebels, with the designation 'Where Now. *Not Known*' next to it. The lad could not stay in London indefinitely. The Wedderburns were a far-flung family, with enterprising cousins scattered across the globe. Mr Paterson, for example, had considerable interests in the West Indies. Arrangements were made to spirit John out of the country. John was reluctant to fall in with them but his father, via James, insisted. By the end of September, he was gone.

When the trial came on in November, the Crown presented its evidence with ferocity. Receipts from Dundee and Perth, bearing the Baronet's signature, showing how those towns had been forcibly relieved of duties and other monies for the Prince's service, were thrust under the jurors' noses. Witnesses swore to his presence in arms at Culloden, Prestonpans and Derby (a place he had never been, never having left Scotland). None of this was unexpected, but the prosecutors' outraged zeal was, and the jurors were infected by it.

They did not even leave the courtroom to find him guilty of high treason, whereupon the court, having asked Sir John if he had anything to say for himself, and receiving no reply, proceeded to pronounce judgment and award execution against him: 'that the said Sir John do return to the Jail from whence he came and from thence be drawn to the place of Execution and when he cometh there that he be hanged by the Neck but *not* till he be dead and that he be therefore cut down alive and that his Bowels be then taken out and burnt before his Face and that his Head be then severed from his Body and that his Body be divided into four Quarters and that those be at the Disposal of our said present Sovereign Lord the King'.

This was on 15 November. The sentence was shared by several other gentlemen who now, perhaps, wished that they had been peasants after all. Various appeals and entreaties were made, but to no avail. Cumberland himself insisted on the sentences being carried out in full: 'Good God,' he spluttered, juice cascading over his chins as he worked his way through a bucket of oysters, 'did we gather all these miscreants up in order to let them go again? No, no. Examples must be made.'

But of all this the 5th Baronet of Blackness's eldest son and heir was quite ignorant. Before the end of summer John had left London, and had crossed the ocean: another stage on the dream-like flight that had begun on Drummossie Moor, and from which he did not know when he would come to rest.

Kingston, January–March 1747

John Wedderburn slowly came awake again, and found himself, as his eighteenth birthday approached, no longer a boy. He had been in Jamaica for half a year, acclimatising, or being 'seasoned', as the term was. Europeans, it was said, needed this period of adjustment, preferably twice as long, even more than Africans, though it was the latter who would eventually be toiling all day under the Caribbean sun. But while the Africans were not allowed to be idle in their first months in the island, but were given light tasks such as weeding or cattle-minding, or indoor work, John Wedderburn was expected to do almost nothing. He was kept at his relative Mr Paterson's expense, and grew increasingly bored.

Company was not hard to find, but, to begin with, he avoided it. He felt like an exile, not yet a West Indian but a Scot, on the run from England. He kept himself to himself. Riding from one part of the island to another on a borrowed horse, he inspected some plantations, their great white houses and simple slave villages, watched the slaves at work in the cane fields, saw the sugar being processed in the mills, learned the difference between creoles and Africa-born blacks and the obsessive gradations of blood-mix that lay between black and white: sambo, mulatto, quadroon, octaroon, musteefino. These designations also taught him an important lesson: there were no gradations of whiteness. In the purity of your race, if you were white, lay your salvation.

As his own skin became burnt by the sun, he thought of this, and determined to keep himself pure. He wanted to save himself. He thought of home and its whiteness, something to which he had never before given any consideration. Now, surrounded by black people, he saw in his mind the overwhelming whiteness of Scotland.

In Kingston, he spent these lone months wandering the grim,

gaudy streets, taking in their odd mixture of dust and humidity, of squalor and sweat, of crudeness and finery. He got caught time and again in astonishing downpours. A baking hot sky would be transformed in mid-afternoon, in a matter of minutes, into something dark and menacing. Then the rain would come, vertical sheets of warm, sweet-smelling water, quite unlike the insidious, creeping drizzle of Scotland. Half an hour later the sky would be clear again and the ground bone-dry.

Compared with London, Kingston was a village but it lacked the quaintness of a village. The streets were lined with wooden shacks and larger wood- and brick-built houses, the latter often with shaded porches along their entire front where white men and women sat and observed the world. The few really substantial buildings were used by the island's administration or by the wealthiest merchants and planters. King Street, the wide main thoroughfare, was always busy with carts and carriages. There were stores with the latest fashions, furnishings and domestic supplies imported from Europe. Inns and boarding houses, rough-looking drinking shops and slightly more genteel coffee rooms filled the gaps. It was a male town faced in some quarters with a chipped female veneer.

At first sight, it was a place where blacks and whites seemed to mingle on equal terms. But this was a false picture. Most of the apparently free blacks were slaves employed in various trades – coopers, carriers, carpenters, blacksmiths, seamstresses, laundresses. If they were not working for their own master they were working for someone else's, charging a fee, some of which they were permitted to keep. These men and women existed in a halfway state between slavery and freedom, and their whole manner, their better clothes, their sprightliness and the speed at which they worked, all seemed to suggest to John Wedderburn that they had somehow been 'improved' beyond the condition of those labouring on the plantations. This he found interesting.

Ships arrived daily from Britain, Guinea and the American colonies. Down at the waterfront John watched vast quantities of goods being offloaded and tried to calculate what they must be worth. A miserable, foul-smelling guardhouse was there too, and a gibbet, on which were suspended cages containing the remnants of slaves who had committed some crime or other.

A man passing by, seeing him standing there, asked him what he was staring at. Embarrassed, John Wedderburn waved an arm widely. 'Everything,' he said. 'It's all so busy.'

'No,' the man said, 'you were looking at *something*, not everything. You were looking at *that*.' He was smoking a pipe, and pointed at the gibbet with it.

John began to speak, but the man interrupted him.

'And you're as well to look at it, lad. Because without that, *everything* is nothing.' He spat on the ground. 'We're at war.'

John looked again at the carcasses in the cages. 'The French?' he asked. 'Were they in league with the French?'

'Bugger the French. We're at war with *them*.' He sucked on his pipe again. 'You'll see if I'm not right,' he said.

Months after his arrival, a letter reached John via Mr Paterson's business. The letter had been weeks on board a ship crossing the Atlantic. It was written in his father's hand. He opened it eagerly, forgetting how much time must have passed since its composition. It was very brief, a few lines only:

27 November 1746

Dear John,
    Today I got notice that I am to be executed tomorrow.

The paper swam before his vision, his heart doubled its pace. With an effort he focused on the writing again.

I was proved reviewed by the Prince at Edinburgh with a small sword and pair of pistols when you know I was not in arms there, the injustice and untruth of which with a great many other things I designed to have expatiated more fully upon if I had time. I hear that while you stayed here you parted too easily from your money which will not do, I need not tell you to take care and please Mr Paterson.

Damn Mr Paterson! Mr Paterson was in London! He, John Wedderburn, was stuck in the Indies, and all his father could do – had been able to do – was complain about untruths and tell him to curb his spending. *Take care*. Take care of what, his

53

empty purse? His browning skin? O God, Papa was dead! What had they done to him? They had wiped him clean away. As if to emphasise that awful fact, the letter was not even signed.

He tried to persuade himself that there might have been a reprieve, but he knew it could not be. A week, a month passed: no joyous, God-praising letter in the same hand arrived. Instead, in January, came his brother James to confirm the news.

The boys spent a week getting drunk together, which would not have pleased Mr Paterson if he had got to hear, but he did not, since Mr Paterson's representatives were often to be found joining in the sessions. When they were on their own, the brothers tried to make sense of what had happened, where and who they now were.

'Are you the sixth Baronet of Blackness, then?' James wanted to know. 'Now that Papa is dead.'

'I don't see how I can be. We lost Blackness years ago. We've even lost the farm at Newtyle.'

'But Papa kept the title, did he not?'

'I think it will be taken anyway, James, on account of our being out. At the moment I don't care, I don't feel like a baronet.'

James looked angry. 'Well, if you don't want the title I'll have it. You dishonour Papa talking like that. He was strong right to the end.'

Then James told John of their father's last night alive. To pre-empt last-minute applications for mercy it had been intended to keep the date of execution a secret from those about to die. On the evening of 27 November, James had been allowed in to see him. Sir John had been in the middle of a game of backgammon, and James had sat down beside him to watch. A few minutes later, a jailer had approached and whispered something in the father's ear. Sir John had paused, his finger resting on one of the stones, as if contemplating what move to make. 'Friend,' he had said to the jailer, 'would you kindly stand out of the light till I finish this game?' Then, having played it out, he had put his arm around James and called for wine. When the men around him all had glasses, he told them the news: 'I regret to tell you that I am to be executed tomorrow. There is no time for an appeal. I therefore ask you to join me in a farewell toast and then to indulge me with some solitude. My son is here, and I have letters to write.'

After the wine was drunk, he and James were given space alone. Sir John wrote half a dozen brief letters: one to his wife; one to John in Jamaica; three to relatives in Scotland entreating them to look after his family; and one to His Royal Highness, Prince Charles Edward Stewart.

'He showed me that one,' James said. 'He wanted me to see that he remained loyal even after what had happened. He said we were all poor and he hoped the Prince would protect us. He sealed it up and gave it to me with the others, to give to Mr Paterson.'

'*Will* the Prince protect us?' John asked.

'Of course he won't. How can he? He's away to France and he'll not be back. I doubt Papa expected much from that quarter. The point is, though, *he* never wavered. And we must never waver. If we do, we will vanish.'

As Papa had vanished, John thought, but he said nothing. Perhaps James also felt the irony of his own remark. In the prison, even at that late stage, he had tried to persuade their father to do something to save himself. Ever since the sentence there had been a steady flow of visitors at night, including assorted vendors of ale and port, barbers, tailors and whores, all of whom anticipated doing some kind of business. Men condemned to death, after all, might as well spend what money they had left, either to look their best before the gallows crowd, catch the pox or drink themselves into oblivion. James had proposed that they pay one of the whores to lose some of her clothes – on a permanent basis – and get his father out in them. Sir John had dismissed this scheme: 'Do you know how many hairy big-boned women are stopped leaving prisons on occasions like this, James? I do not wish to be discovered in such circumstances and ill-used on my last night on earth. I'm as well dying now as twenty years hence.' Then he had blessed the boy, embraced him and sent him away. 'Do not come here tomorrow. There will be nothing more to say. You will only make it harder for me to die.'

'And did you obey him?' John asked.

'Aye. I did not see him at the prison again.' James closed his eyes. He was shaking. John put his hand on his brother's arm. James opened his eyes again. 'I saw him later,' he said. 'At Kennington.'

But it would be a long time before he would say what he had seen there.

John had finally adjusted to the climate. James appeared to need no seasoning. His energy and curiosity were astonishing. Kingston veterans marvelled at him. He had a hundred schemes to make the best of their situation: to make money, lots of it; to work hard and live hard; and one day, to go back to Scotland.

John concurred with all of these propositions, especially the last one. He was more cautious, less certain that they would succeed, but he would put his back to the wheel and make it turn. His father's reproach about the money rankled: it would rankle for twenty years. The last thing he had thought to say to him: *you parted too easily from your money which will not do*. Very well then: he would amass wealth. He would not squander it. He would not be the prodigal son. He would be the 6th Baronet. He would go home to enjoy his own again.

He was not the only one thinking along these lines. The island was something of a Jacobite refuge. Every boat, from America or Europe, disgorged another young or middle-aged man who found it expedient to sojourn in the sun for a few years. Some only lasted a few weeks: the sun was no friendlier than Butcher Cumberland. Those who ignored the dire warnings of old hands about the wrong food and drink, yellow fever and mosquitoes, the importance of clean water and the dangers of dirty cuts and grazes, dropped by the dozen. But the Wedderburns survived, working for one or other of Mr Paterson's enterprises – he had stores in Kingston, and his agents acted on behalf of a number of plantations across the island. Another Jacobite exile and one of their old Perthshire friends, George Kinloch, had been made overseer of a small plantation in the west, near the port of Savanna-la-Mar. They were pleased for George, and when they went to visit him they liked what they saw of that end of the island. 'There are opportunities here,' James said. 'There are great opportunities.'

One afternoon, John found his brother downing rum in a

Kingston grog shop with two men of very different physical appearance. One was yet another Scot, not much older, black-haired, clean-shaven, neatly dressed. In his white linen shirt and light, black short coat he seemed to be coping well with the heat. His whole air was one of self-assurance. This was David Fyfe, a medical graduate of Edinburgh who had been in Jamaica eight months. The other man was huge, sixtyish, bulb-nosed and florid. A once white, now tobacco-yellow peruke, in a style that might have been fashionable under Queen Anne, was crammed on his wrinkled forehead, and this, together with the combined weight of a thick brown coat and ornately brocaded waistcoat, was causing him to sweat like a fountain.

James shouted John over and called for another chair, another glass and another bottle of rum. It was both hard and easy to believe he was still only sixteen.

'Davie, James,' John greeted them, taking the seat.

'This,' said James to the fat man, 'is my esteemed elder brother John Wedderburn, late of Scotland, now a colonist like the rest of us. John, it is my pleasure and so forth to introduce Mr Thomas Underwood of – where did you say again?'

'Amity Plantation, sir, in the parish of Westmoreland, county of Cornwall. *My* pleasure, sir, and an honour. Always an honour to meet another Scotchman. Not that it's difficult here. You're almost as numerous as the negers. No offence, naturally.'

He spoke with a mild Yorkshire accent, the words interspersed with heavy rasping breaths and much wiping of the brow. His unsuitable dress, clearly the chief source of his discomfort, seemed to indicate a newcomer. In fact Mr Underwood had been on the island nearly thirty years, but would never get used to the heat. He had small eyes made smaller by the encroaching folds of his cheeks. He tipped his fleshy head at John.

'Now, sir, it's all one to me, I assure you, but were you *out*?'

John had an idea that Mr Underwood, through James, already knew the answer. He drew himself up proudly: 'That, sir, is not a question one gentleman expects to be asked by another.'

Underwood shrugged. 'I'll take that as an aye. No, no, don't be offended, Mr Wedderburn, I don't care a bit, and you'll find very few folk as do. We're an island of tolerance – we're only here to get rich after all, and you can't hold *that* against nobody. I only ask on account of you Scotchmen are such a curious breed. You'll murder each other over crowns and creeds at home, but here the loyalest of you falls on his rebel compatriot like a brother. The sun does something to you it don't do to Englishmen: it seems to dry up all your grudges.'

'Mr Underwood's plantation,' James said, 'is not far from where George Kinloch is. Mr Underwood knows George quite well.'

'Indeed I do,' Underwood said. 'Not a grudge on that gentleman's person.'

'And what brings you to Kingston, sir?' John asked.

'A scramble, sir,' Underwood said. 'Tomorrow morning. I'm hoping to pick up some cheap slaves to replace half a dozen I lost at Christmas to the flux.'

'But there's a regular market at Savanna-la-Mar,' John said. 'Surely it's a long and hazardous trip to come all this way for slaves?'

'Oh, dreadful hazardous,' Underwood agreed with enthusiasm. 'A hundred miles and more on roads that would shake the teeth out of many men – not that you can call them roads, in some parts. But I've been visiting friends here, you see, and they've given me some fine heavy bits of furniture which I intend to ship home along with the new slaves, if I can get some. Are you in the market for slaves yourself, Mr Wedderburn?' he asked John.

'Not yet,' said John.

'But we will be,' said James.

'You should come along with me in the morning. I can show you what to look out for when you're buying them up cheap. In a scramble, I mean.'

'What,' says James, 'is a scramble?'

'Just what it sounds like. The shipmasters have sorted their negers out by the time they get here, they've decided which ones they can sell at premium, which ones are ailing, which ones are feeble-minded, that kind of thing. They sell the best to folk as know what they want and have money to pay for it, they auction the weakest for whatever they can get, which is precious little, and them that's left, the middling sort you might say, are put to a scramble. A set price is fixed beforehand, same for each slave, so if you've a good eye you can pick up an excellent bargain. Oh, but you have to be quick on your feet to beat t'others. Come along with me in the morning and I'll show you how it's done.'

'We'll be there,' James said at once. 'How about yourself, Davie?'

'No, I'll be seeing enough Negroes as it is. I've a long day tomorrow. Three plantations and a hundred and fifty slaves to inspect.'

'Ill?' Underwood said. 'Not a contagion, I hope?'

'No, a routine visit. A stitch in time, you'll understand, or more likely a poultice or an incision, may save nine. Nine slaves, that is,' he explained to the Wedderburns, 'for which a master may have paid a great deal of money.'

'How's *your* master, Davie?' John asked. 'Still alive?'

'Very sickly,' said Davie Fyfe with a wide grin.

'Excellent,' said James. 'You'll be a rich man soon.'

'What d'you mean?' Underwood asked.

'The surgeon Davie works for,' James said, 'has been ill for months. If he doesn't want to expire here he'll have to go back to England.'

'In which case he'll be dead before the Azores,' Fyfe said.

'So whatever happens,' James said, 'Davie will inherit the business, and probably at a knockdown price, won't you, Davie?'

'I'm hoping so. If you can stay fit yourself, there's a fortune to be made here from doctoring.'

'Oh, you needn't tell me that, sir,' said Underwood. 'The bills I pay for doctoring! They would keep a lord and his castle back in England! I'm not complaining, mind you – if you get a surgeon in quick, he can save you far more in slaves than what he'll charge you for his time. He can spot a fever before it turns into a forest fire, the flux before it becomes a flood, if you understand me. Negers go down in parties, Mr Wedderburn. One gets a fever, they all get it. But a good surgeon – and I'll say this, a good surgeon's nearly always a Scotch surgeon, begging your master's pardon, Mr Fyfe – a good surgeon will nip that fever in the bud, and kill it. He might in the process kill the slave as has it, which is a loss to be borne of course, but I warrant you, it makes t'others get better quick. Am I right, sir?'

Davie Fyfe acknowledged that he was quite right. 'Except,'

he added, 'that a good surgeon never *kills* his patient, though the patient might unavoidably die of the attempt to make him well.'

'A slip of the tongue, sir,' said Underwood, slipping his own round another shot of rum. 'And of course it depends on the illness. And the slave. There's some negers can withstand any amount of fever, but will go down in a day with the yaws. There's other negers live with the yaws like it's their mother, but give them a touch of fever, they're dead before morning. Am I right, Mr Fyfe?'

'Quite right.'

'I have seen the yaws,' said James. 'What causes it?'

'Seen it?' Underwood exploded. 'I should think you have! You can't be very long here without seeing the yaws! Oh, but you don't want to know about it, young man. Do he, Mr Fyfe? Very nasty, very nasty. But you have to know about it, to know Negroes. Mr Fyfe will tell you about the yaws. Makes me shudder just to think on it.'

Davie Fyfe opened his mouth to explain the yaws, but Underwood had hit on a favourite theme, and rolled on unstoppably.

'I take a great pride,' he said, 'in knowing my Negroes. I'm a fair man, and I don't believe in mistreating them. Punishment, yes, but that's not mistreating them if they deserve it, that's treating them same as you'd treat anything in your charge, black, white or beast of the field. There's men I know,' he went on, shaking his head and in the process showering the table with sweat, 'as have no respect for your African at all. They forget that he's a human being. A bad planter don't break them in as he should, he don't season them over a twelvemonth, he puts them out in the field far too early, and then he wonders why they die on him and he's wasted his money. That's almost like murder, in my book. You can pay a terrible price for a fine Coromantee, a terrible price, but if you don't look after him, well, you may as well have put your money on a horse with three legs. No, a good planter, such as I believe I am, knows his Negroes, and if you, Mr Wedderburn, and your young brother here, are to flourish in Jamaica, I'd advise you to know your Negroes too. Come along to the scramble with me tomorrow, and you can make a start. Truth of the matter is, you can't prosper here without keeping slaves, and if you want to keep them you have to understand them, the different types of them. Do you follow me?'

'You must tell us more, sir,' James said, signalling for more rum and winking at John. 'How many *types* of them are there?'

'Oh, limitless, limitless,' said Underwood. 'Guinea, you see, where they come from, is bigger than, oh, England and Scotland and France put together. Far bigger. And what is Guinea? Is it a great kingdom, like France, like England? A fine country like your Scotland, sirs? No, it's a jumble of little kingdoms and tribes and desert and swamp and forest, all mixed up together. That's where your neger comes from, and there's many of them very glad to get out of it, though they don't think so at the time they're taken, which is understandable. But if they stayed, chances are they'd be eaten by savage lions, or by other negers, or they'd be killed by them, or they'd starve, or die of thirst – there's a hundred ways of dying in Guinea, Mr Wedderburn, and none of them's nice. Or they'd be made slaves of by the Moors, which you may be sure is a sight worse than being a slave here in the Indies. A great deal worse. Am I right, Mr Fyfe?'

Mr Fyfe opined that he might well be, but as he had never been to Guinea he could not tell.

'Nor I,' said Underwood, 'but there's plenty as has. All the captains of the slave ships, they have, and I talk to them as part of my policy of knowing my Negroes. Anyway, as to *types*, Mr Wedderburn, there's your creoles of course, to begin with – that's them that's born here in the Indies and has forgotten whatever African tribe they once was. Then, of the Africans, the full-blooded freshly imported slaves, well, I'd say there's four types, speaking in a general kind of way. First, there's your Eboes. They come mostly from Benin, that's the underbelly part of Guinea. They're the least useful, in my opinion, though they fetch them over in droves. A very timid type, and rather prone to killing themselves of despair, I'm sorry to say. You'll see a lot of them in the scramble tomorrow, I don't doubt. Then there's your Pawpaws and your Nagoes, from a bit further north. Now these are very excellent Negroes if they'll live, very docile and well-disposed creatures, and never the least trouble, but they die off easy from a lack of character – am I going too fast, sir?' He asked this of James, who had produced a pocket book and stub of blacklead pencil and was taking rapid notes. James waved him on. 'The third type is your Mandingo. He's a clever fellow, too clever in fact, he can learn to read and write and do his sums very quick, but he's lazy, and much given to theft. And then,' said the fat planter grandly, as if announcing a prize bull, 'there's your Coromantee, from the Gold Coast. He's the cream of Africans, stands head and shoulders above the rest. Firm of body, firm of mind, brave, strong, extraordinary powerful worker in the field – but proud too, stubborn, and ferocious when roused. You have to watch Coromantees like a hawk, gentlemen, but you'll get more work out of one of them in a week than you'll get out of six Eboes. Am I not correct, Mr Fyfe?' he finished, by way of variation.

'Indeed you are, sir,' said Davie Fyfe, 'and to what you've said I'll add that, being of a strong constitution, they don't get so sick as the others.'

'We should have some Coromantees then,' said James to his brother, 'when we are planters. They sound like the negers for us.'

'And how,' said John, 'do you intend that we pay for them?'

James did not answer that question then. Nor did he address it the following day, when they went to the scramble with Underwood and saw him in action picking up bargains. A large wooden pen had been filled with a couple of hundred Africans. Once a set price had been agreed, a drum sounded, the gates were opened and in rushed the planters or their overseers, each carrying a coil of rope identified by a couple of handkerchiefs tied to it.

Underwood, sweat lashing off him and his wig toppling on his head like a skein of yellow knitting, moved with amazing speed, grabbing at the arms of terrified Africans, quickly inserting a thumb into some of their mouths to check the state of their teeth, slipping his hand between their buttocks (it was known for ships' surgeons to stop slaves' anuses with oakum, to disguise the fact that they had the flux), pummelling and punching at their legs to test them for strength, and all the while playing out the rope, the loose end of which James had offered to hold.

'Bring it round, sir, enclose them, that one, that one there, sir, the big bullish one,' Underwood roared, making himself heard above a similar racket issuing from the mouth of every other white man in the scrum. James darted after Underwood like an elf behind an ogre. Every few seconds he turned back to John, who was following at a distance and doing his best to avoid bodily contact with anyone. There was an appalled look in James's eyes, but he was also laughing uproariously. He began to wave the rope-end in black faces, and when they cowered or shied away his laugh got louder. It was as if, having decided to do something distasteful, he discovered that he quite enjoyed it.

In less than a quarter of an hour, Underwood had got himself seven new slaves, corralled by the rope like unwilling participants in some grotesque parlour game, and was settling up with the slave-ship captains.

That evening, long after Underwood had loaded his new purchases on board ship for Westmoreland, the brothers discussed the scramble over supper in their lodgings.

'It was disgusting,' John said.

'You mean it offended you?' James asked. 'Your moral sensibilities?'

'No, I mean it disgusted me. The noise and sweat and brutishness of it.'

'It was impressive, too, though,' James said. 'Not Underwood – he's a buffoon. But the fact that a man like that has such power over others.'

'He certainly had no compunction about checking his wares.' John had an image of the fat planter's fingers running over black skin.

'You'll have to do the same,' James said, 'so you'd better get used to it. And you will. It doesn't have to be so uncivilised.' A sly look came over his face and he leaned forward. 'Listen, John, here's what I propose. We'll be planters, and we'll be better than the likes of Underwood, far better. But first we'll be surgeons. I've been thinking about it all day. Davie'll teach us, he'll take us on as apprentices when he gets the business, he'll not have to pay us much, not till we learn a little anyway. Well, you needn't look so gloomy, you must have seen a fair

63

display of wounds, quite a pack of sick men, in the last year or two.'

'It's true. But all those black bodies crushed together. It unnerved me.'

'Well, treating them's only common sense, surely, and luck, and having a strong belly. After what you've been through it'll be bairn's play; and if you can manage it, I can. And we'll use our fees to *buy* slaves. We'll do it right, though, not like that madness this forenoon. We'll go direct to the slave ships, and buy us some Coromantees.'

'But we've no qualifications,' John protested. 'The island is awash with surgeons, real surgeons.'

'Ah, but we're Scotch, which Mr Underwood seems to consider as fine a qualification as any. And how many of these *real* surgeons you speak of have ever been challenged to produce their degrees? We studied in Glasgow, or Aberdeen, or Edinburgh, it doesn't matter which, none of the medical men here are young enough to say it's odd how they never met us in the dissecting room – except Davie, and he'll not betray us. And if we're lacking our papers it's because of our political *indiscretions*, which obliged us to leave a wee bit hurriedly. Nobody will care, if only we're competent. There's to be an amnesty soon anyway, they're saying, for folk like you that were out. So we must practise, and get competence, and Davie's the man that will help us to get it. And in any event it'll only be practising on slaves, so we can afford a few minor mistakes. A few major ones, even.'

'We'd need land, too,' said John. 'No point in having slaves if we've nowhere to work them.'

'There's land a-plenty here. But we'll keep an eye out for what's already been reclaimed and planted. Buy a share in a small plantation, buy the whole of it, and build it up.'

'Maybe to leeward,' John said, 'in the west, where Underwood and George Kinloch are. Westmoreland's the youngest parish, it's not so congested as this end.'

'Aye,' James said, 'we'll get over to leeward in a while. But first we'll be doctors. What do you say?'

John Wedderburn thought of touching black flesh, cutting into it, gangrenous rot, infestations, flux, fever. He remembered the limb-scattered field of Culloden. Surely he could steel himself. Surely he could.

He smiled at his brother. 'You're a scoundrel, James. I say we shall be doctors.'

Glen Isla, 1760

A dozen miles north and west of Savanna-la-Mar, the main town and port of Westmoreland, the westernmost parish of Jamaica, the soil-rich plain of the Cabarita river gave way to the lower slopes of the mountains. Here, a rough road curled up into the hills, and the landscape took on a wilder aspect than that of the sugar-growing flat land that stretched down to the sea. Wilder, and yet somehow comfortingly familiar. Up in the hills the heat was less intense, less humid. If you discounted the size and abundance of the vegetation, you could almost believe yourself to be in a Scottish glen.

This was what John Wedderburn had thought when he had first inspected the area with a view to buying property, two or three years after his arrival in Jamaica. A further ten years had passed, and the place was now his home. The refuge-like feel of it had led him to name it Glen Isla.

It had been a time of constant, grinding, back-breaking labour. The Wedderburns had become rich. These two facts were connected, indirectly. The labour had been overseen by them, but actually carried out by slaves. Not that they had been idle: they had worked, first as doctors, then as planters, as hard as any other white gentlemen in Jamaica, but they had also had a large helping of luck – of the kind that really involves no luck at all, but only patience till somebody dies. In 1751, John had come into a substantial inheritance left by a great-uncle in Perthshire, and this they had used to purchase two parcels of land. The first, Bluecastle, was down near the coast, a few miles west of Savanna, an old-established cane plantation in need of new management. James had taken that on. The second was Glen Isla.

The house at Glen Isla was situated in an elevated position just over the crest of the escarpment that rose from the sugar plain. An area two hundred yards in width had been cleared of trees all around the house, so that it had unobstructed views of all the approaches – highly necessary in times of slave unrest. Where the rough parkland created by the tree-felling ended, the track to the house joined the public south–north road that twisted across the mountains into Hanover parish, eventually reaching Montego Bay twenty arduous miles away on the north coast.

A quarter mile in the other direction, there was a viewpoint on the escarpment from which one could look out over the plain as far as the sea, and take in the entire estate – the hardwood forest still thick on the hills, the cane fields, the Chocho river snaking through them to join the Cabarita, the mill and storehouses, and the slave huts laid out in rows close to the produce-growing fields.

It was Good Friday, early in April. James had come over the previous night, and after breakfast the two brothers rode out to the viewpoint to watch the last of the cane being cut and brought in for crushing. It had been an excellent crop, both at Glen Isla and at Bluecastle, where the work was all but done. Already the sun was blazing. The Wedderburns dismounted and let the horses loose to stand in the shade. Down below, the plantation looked like a toy, a model of a plantation. They could see one group of slaves harvesting the cane, another line coming behind them piling it on to ox-drawn carts. Further back, women were carrying loads of cane on their heads into the mill, from which came the faint, repetitive clank of machinery. Elsewhere a handful of children were herding cattle by the river, and a couple of men were stripping the branches off a fallen tree, preparing to clear it from the water. Since the sugar crop was almost in, other slaves had been diverted to the fields kept for growing provisions, and were making the ground ready for yams and cabbages. It was as picturesque and peaceful a scene as any planter could hope to look upon. There was something almost unreal about its perfection. Everywhere was a sense of industry, fertility, domesticity, prosperity. By the end of the week the sugar would be drying, the hogsheads waiting to be filled. Another season over.

These were the thoughts going through John Wedderburn's mind when his brother said, 'We have come a long way since London, have we not?'

'I was just thinking that. Aye, we have. It's not the road we expected to take, but . . .'

'. . . but it's been paved with gold, eh?'

'Now, perhaps,' John said. 'Not at first. As you said, we have come a long way.'

'Do you remember what it was like breaking in some of this land? And how little we got out of it in the first year?'

'I do,' John said. 'You were angry with me. You said we'd moved too soon, should have stuck with ginger and indigo for another season or two.'

'Aye, well, you were right. The sugar price shot up. You're a better farmer than me, I don't deny it. But I was always the better doctor.'

They spoke like middle-aged men, contentedly competitive with each other, looking back on decades, but John was not long turned thirty-one, James still only twenty-nine, and both still had plenty of ambitions left. Chief among these was to make enough money to go home; to see their mother and sisters again; to convert some of their wealth into Scottish land, while still leaving enough in Jamaica to go on multiplying. Their two younger brothers, Peter and Alexander, had joined them some years before, and might in due course be left to manage things on the plantations. Back in Scotland, their politics were fast becoming not only forgiven but positively romantic. Another few years would wash the slate quite clean, turn their Jacobite past into an asset. And they would still be young enough to wed, to seed their own Scots sons and daughters.

The desire to get home was what kept them going, squeezing as much out of the plantations and the slaves as possible without jeopardising the whole enterprise. It was this that differentiated them from planters like Underwood, whom they still saw from time to time, although they had long overtaken him in wealth and social prestige. All Underwood's loud talk about knowing his Negroes and getting rich quick was a front for bumbling inefficiency and absence of resolve. He still sweated like a pig. He had never got used to Jamaica because he had never made up his mind to escape.

Some of his information, though, had been useful. He had been right, for example, about the Coromantees: they were the best slaves you could get, and the Wedderburns had made a point of buying only them. They had developed good connections with certain shipping companies and their captains, and had looked for preferential treatment at the markets, since they were prepared to pay the best prices.

What exactly a Coromantee was, however, was less certain. It had become clear to the Wedderburns very quickly that they were not dealing with a distinct tribe or race when they demanded Coromantees: they would buy a dozen and find four different languages spoken among them. John tried to discover more about the designation. The traders at Savanna were not sure, but thought it derived from an old settlement on the Gold Coast, Kromantine, the site of the first English slave station a century before. It was, in other words, little more than an export stamp.

'What does it matter?' James had said, when John told him what he had learned. 'I don't give a damn what they're called, so long as nobody sells us a bad one.'

As for Underwood's faith in the abilities of Scotch doctors, it was shared by many planters, which was both gratifying and useful, but largely misconceived. The brothers knew this because, with minimal training, they had both practised as Scotch doctors these last thirteen years, though only James still did much in that line. His claim that he was a better doctor was based on a bolder and more cold-blooded approach than John would ever be capable of. Davie Fyfe had given them a basic knowledge. The rest, as James had divined at sixteen, was a crude mix of guesswork, trial and error, and common sense.

Bleeding, blistering and purging: these were the basic cures most doctors relied on. Release the blood, scorch the skin, sluice out the bowels, and you might, just might, remove whatever the sickness was. The Wedderburns had learned the application of leeches and of the scalpel, the preparation of emetics, the uses of fire, steam, nitre, tartar, mercury; any number of potions, powders and pills patented in Europe or America by medical men whose names were attached to them but who could never be held accountable for their inefficacy. Mercury for the pox; opium to quell pain; 'tapping' to relieve dropsy; for dysentery – the bloody flux – bleeding, purging, puking, sweating, anything to cleanse the body of a condition which carried off more slaves than any other. Doctoring was a chancy business, a gamble. There was, of course, an inexhaustible supply of patients on whom to try out new methods, but this was itself part of the problem. Whenever they thought they were on top of some outbreak of illness, thousands more Africans arrived in the island after months at sea in filthy, disease-ridden holds, bringing new strains of tropical ailments with them.

The Wedderburns had often discussed slave health with other doctors and planters. There were soft fools like Underwood who thought they knew their slaves but paid more attention to the quacks who spouted medical jargon and charged exorbitant fees for the privilege of hearing it. There were hard fools who treated every African wound as self-inflicted, every sign of lethargy as malingering, every desperate fever as one more indicator of the degraded racial origins of their slaves. And then there were the calculating, thoughtful, observant ones – like the Wedderburns – who saw each dead or debilitated slave as a loss of fifty or sixty pounds sterling, each sound and working one as the same sum spread over ten, twenty or thirty years. One school of thought argued that it was good economy to extract the maximum labour for the least expense from your slaves, use them up and start again. Another school, to which the Wedderburns subscribed, believed the opposite: that it paid to keep your Negroes in reasonable health. Nobody, however, could be accused of getting things out of proportion. Whatever your thinking, it was not in the end about slave welfare. It was about money.

Now John and James Wedderburn were looking down from Glen Isla on the source of that money. 'Half a life,' said James. 'Or not much less, anyway. That's how long we've been here.' Then he began to laugh.

'What?' John asked. 'What's so amusing?'

'Just that I was thinking, our father was the fifth Baronet of Black*ness*, whereas you have become the first Baronet of *Black*ness.'

'Very good, James.'

'But think of it, John. In '45, Papa took only you as his retinue. Were the opportunity to arise again, you could bring four dozen Coromantees to the Prince's standard. That's a whole Highland glen.'

'And you could bring a company of your own black bairns.' In the last year, James had delivered two of the girls that kept house at Bluecastle of babies which he freely admitted were his own. Boys, both thriving. 'We may soon be able to count them in dozens also.'

'Well, and what of it?' James was still grinning at his brother, who was staring steadfastly ahead.

'You know how little Papa would have approved of that . . . miscegenation of which you are so fond.'

'I'm not sure I do. I never spoke to him about matters of the flesh, even though we had that time together in the prison.' This was a dig at John, a reminder of his exclusion from those visits. 'But in any event you are not him, and Abba and Jenny are not yours. Well, I suppose you have a part share in them. Not that you make any claim on it – not that I'd object if you did. For all practical purposes they're mine to do with what I like.'

'That's evident. I hope you'll not live to regret it.'

'I'll not. And nor will the lassies, if the bairns live.' A challenge had entered James's voice. 'I've told you before, I'm going to set them free, mothers and bairns, if they reach ten years. I've told them too.'

'It'll be throwing money away.'

'Perhaps. But I'll not have my own blood chained for life.'

'That's very noble of you.'

'Ach, John, you should learn to relax. You're so cold. Are you never tempted yourself?'

'I intend to marry a Scotswoman whenever I return home.'

'As do I. A good, clean, virginal, white Scotswoman. Or maybe a rich widow. Marriage is a different matter altogether. But I could not tolerate this heat and this life without the black lassies to relieve my passion. It keeps the fever out of me.'

'You really do think that, don't you?'

'Well, look at me. Fit and healthy. Mind you, so are you.'

'We are different.'

'Aye, hot and cold. I'm rum and you're ice. Perhaps that's just our different ways of surviving here. But I can't be like you.'

'Nor I like you. We've always been different. But we complement one another.'

'We do here. We've had to. It was not always like that. I'd have been too hot for Scotland in '45. If I'd been allowed to come with you, I'd probably have concluded my life at Culloden, or with Papa in London.'

'Well, you should thank God you did not. Think what you'd have missed. And thank Him that those days are by with, James. I may never warm to a German king but I'll live under one readily enough when I go home.'

'You'd not come out for Charles, if he came again?'

'No, and nor would you and well you know it. I'd not offer my sword to a Stewart now, even if there were one worthy of it. There's too much to lose.' They looked again at the wealth creation going on below. 'Half a lifetime, James, as you say. We were boys then, both of us. Just the eighteen months between us, but I, you'll mind, was sixteen and thus old enough to die for a cause. Not now. Now I am old enough *not* to die for a cause. There is only one cause – one's own self and one's family –'

'Which you don't yet have –'

'You forget Mama and our sisters. One's self, one's family, and the prosperity of these. Nothing else matters.'

'And the relief of passion,' said James. 'That matters to me a great deal.'

They remounted and rode downhill, threading in and out of the shade until the road levelled out, then struck off towards the mill. Wilson, the bookkeeper, was managing operations. There were other white overseers in the fields, but the three of them were the only white men in the mill – the distiller, boilerman, packers, coopers and other skilled workers were all black. The place was a clammy hive of activity. The noise and heat and sweet stench of the crushed cane were oppressive and heady. After a few minutes the Wedderburns left Wilson and his men to it, and rode back to the coolness of the house.

Within a fortnight, the rest of the cane was in, cut and crushed. From the mill's boilers vast quantities of liquid had been run off to make low wines for the slaves and rum for the mother country; the remaining juice had been cooled, allowed to granulate, and packed into hogsheads. The fields lay slashed and brown, ready to be planted for the next season. The field gangs were exhausted, the mill slaves hardly less so. Crop Over: a holiday for all of them. From their hut village down on the plain, the noise of their singing and drumming drifted up.

The Wedderburns were tolerant of it: the sounds, hesitating almost deferentially at the open windows, enhanced their own sense of superiority, of being *proprietors*. John imagined a big house in Scotland where the lowing of cattle beside a bright splashing burn might have the same effect. Such a house would be far more substantial and imposing than the wood, clay and brick edifice he had here, grand though this was in comparison with the accommodations of his white overseers, let alone the slaves' huts. There would be a tree-lined avenue, perhaps, leading up to the porticoed entrance; stone columns and balconies instead of the wooden porch; enormous, roaring fireplaces in carpeted drawing room and oak-panelled dining room. Not these sweating uneven walls that were home to a multitude of scurrying beetles, cockroaches and green lizards. On evenings when he was by himself, John Wedderburn walked the rooms of that imagined house: sometimes he walked them alone; sometimes with a graceful, lily-white lady on his arm.

For Crop Over he had granted the slaves a few goats to slaughter, and made presents of some bolts of Lancashire coloured cotton for the women to turn into gaudy holiday clothes – a gesture, he was pleased to think, that far exceeded the annual suit of working clothes island law obliged him to provide each slave. Not that anyone ever checked – which made his provision still nobler. Who was going to check? His neighbours? The magistrates from Savanna? And who, more to the point, was going to complain?

He had worked out a few years ago that if he could keep one in every three acres of the estate under cane, and from them produce around a ton of sugar for each slave, at current prices he would achieve a very acceptable profit. Another third of the land he devoted to animal grazing and provision-growing for the house and workforce, and the final portion – mostly on the hills – was woodland, from which he was gradually extracting some excellent timber. This year, by a combination of working the blacks hard and storm-free weather, the sugar crop had been excellent. Although his calculations were not complete, he estimated it at nearly one and a half tons per slave. Furthermore, Britain and France were at war, struggling for territorial control of North America and economic mastery of India, and occasionally attacking some of each other's smaller Caribbean islands. The war had driven the London sugar price up to thirty-five shillings a hundredweight. He had every reason to feel thankful to Providence, and therefore generous to his workforce.

James was over from Bluecastle for an extended dinner. Their younger brothers Peter and Alexander were also there. Peter was twenty-four, Sandy a year younger. They divided their time between the two estates, depending on where they were most needed. Neither of them had responded well to the climate when they first arrived, but Peter had gradually acquired some strength, and his natural enthusiasm had helped him overcome bouts of illness. He was not particularly clever or imaginative, but went along with whatever plans John and James proposed. John thought that in many ways these were the best characteristics for surviving in the West Indies.

Sandy was a different case. He had been sick as a dog on the passage out, and swore he would never get in a boat again. Six years on, he was still weak and liable to come down with fever at any time. John had considered sending him back home but the thought of the journey appalled Sandy so much that he was stirred to try to keep up with Peter. The strain and anxiety never really left his face, however, and it did not take much to throw him into a depression. James, though he indulged Sandy when he was trying to be manful, was also less patient than John when he was not, and as a result Sandy spent as much time as he could at Glen Isla, where fewer demands were made of him.

George Kinloch, now a successful planter in his own right, was expected for dinner. Davie Fyfe, the thriving doctor, also now in the west, had come in the company of Charles Hodge, a Savanna merchant who had supplied most of the furnishings for the house. In the absence of a wife John Wedderburn had depended on Mr Hodge to fit him out from the shipments that came in from London and Boston. Hodge, he understood, depended in turn on Mrs Hodge's taste, and judging by the sumptuous decor of their own town house on Great George Street she knew what she liked. But she was also sensible:

she realised that an unmarried planter was looking for comfort, not necessarily extravagance; for practicality, but then again not austerity; that such a man was not over concerned with fashion, but equally did not wish his friends to think him a primitive. So she had taught her husband how to navigate these tricky waters, cultivate the confidence of the planters, encourage them to spend wisely yet often, and thus bring the Hodges' own money-making vessel safely into port.

The only slaves at Glen Isla not yet celebrating Crop Over were the domestics: the cooks, maids, butler and footman required to prepare, serve and remove the long parade of dishes their master and his guests would work their way through over the duration of a three-hour dinner. But as their daily tasks were much lighter than those of the field and mill workers, they could hardly expect to be released so readily. There were, in any case, not that many of them. Three maids, Mary, Peach and Bess, doubled up as kitchen hands helping Naomi the cook. Two men, Jacob and Julius, acted as butler and footman, but of this pair it was not quite certain where the duties of one ended and of the other began.

Unlike some of the really fabulously wealthy planters, for whom such details were a reflection of their prestige, John Wedderburn did not care much about this casual attitude to job demarcation. It did not seem important in a place that, even though he had spent his entire adult life there, he still regarded as only a temporary home. When he went back to Scotland it would be different. He would want to do things right there: in Scotland, doing things right would matter. And with this in mind he intended, some day soon, to begin to train up a slave to take home with him as his personal servant. Not Jacob or Julius: they were too set in their ways. Someone younger, more pliant, who could look after his clothes and toilet, be a faithful companion, a memento of his Jamaican days to be admired by neighbours, friends and guests.

By and large, the domestic work at Glen Isla did get done, for all six domestics were aware that they could be relegated to field labour in an instant. They were also kept on their toes by the tongue-lashings and occasional blows of John Wedderburn's housekeeper, Phoebe.

He could hardly think of Phoebe without prefixing her name, as James jokingly once had, with the word 'formidable'. She was a creole who had come with the estate at Bluecastle, but James had quickly taken a dislike to her exacting sense of what was proper, and packed her off to work for his brother. Tall and thin, her face pitted with the marks of childhood smallpox, she was no beauty; but she had a head for economy and a nose for discovering theft or laziness, and though Jacob and Julius drove her to distraction at times, she managed them and the others well.

Between her and John Wedderburn there was little affection, certainly no intimacy, only a mutual respect for each other's cool style. The other slaves feared her, and she despised them: she had cut herself off from them, and did not join in their social life. She had learnt to read, and pored endlessly over an old Bible her master had given her, fancying herself a Christian, although she had never asked for instruction in the faith. She had a room to herself in the house, and probably expected to be given her freedom one day. John expected that one day he would probably give it to her. But if or when that day came, he knew she would not leap for joy, pack her bag and turn her back on the plantation. Where could she go? She would go on running the house, as though she had been free to leave all along but had chosen not to.

The white men lounged in the porch for an hour, drinking Madeira to work up an appetite. Hodge, the only one of them tolerating a wig in the afternoon heat, had brought some books for John Wedderburn: two for him to borrow – *Observations in Husbandry* by Edward Lisle, and *The Gardener's Dictionary* edited by Philip Miller – and one that he had ordered to buy, the shorter, octavo edition of Samuel Johnson's *Dictionary*, which, though not five years old, was already famous. The work was passed around, definitions read out and admired or disputed. Mr Hodge observed that it was a book all the more remarkable because its author, so he had it on good authority, was a slovenly brute who went for weeks without changing his shirt and was given to physical violence against any who offended him.

George Kinloch arrived with some even more interesting

literature: two rampant Parisian *novelles* – seized from a French ship captured sailing from San Domingo to Florida – which, from their ragged state, seemed already to have been read by a good proportion of both the French and British plantocracy. An etching on the title page of one, of a semi-naked courtesan spread over some cushions, looking invitingly over her shoulder and pointing her voluptuous *derrière* in the reader's direction, showed what to expect; the other's title page had been torn out. Peter gleefully seized the one with the picture; Sandy, although his French was rudimentary, made a show of licking his lips over the text of the other.

James smiled at them smugly: 'Those that can, do. Those that canna, read.'

'Or they read and *then* do, wi a swollen imagination,' Kinloch said.

They sat down to eat at two. The marathon began with stewed snook and ketchup sauce. There was a dish of boiled crabs, a tureen full of mangrove oysters, the juices to be soaked up with cassava bread, and all to be chased with great pitchers of porter. Then came boiled salt beef with rice, spinach-like callaloo, green peas and yams; four varieties of bird – snipe, coot, teal and squab – shot by the Wedderburns and roasted en masse; a plum pudding; three kinds of cheese; plantains, pawpaws, oranges, pineapple, watermelon in honey, chocolate sauce. There was some excellent claret, also taken from the French vessel, which Mr Hodge had bought at the knockdown price of five pounds the hogshead and which he was bottling and selling to the Savanna taverns at five pounds a dozen; but he had generously supplied the present party with three dozen at cost. And John produced a very acceptable punch made up of rum, Madeira, claret and wild cinnamon.

The courses merged into one another and by four o'clock the table was piled with half-empty plates and the debris of demolished wildfowl, fruit skins, stones and unfinished pudding. The maids removed what they thought was done with, and were bellowed at if they lifted a glass or a dish too soon. Eventually, having first ensured that there was plenty of drink still available, John dismissed them.

'There's one bonnie and two passable there, John,' Peter said.

'Peach *is* a peach. I suppose you'll have sent her to wait for you in your bed.'

'You know I have not,' John said. 'I told them they could go down to the dancing, and redd up in the morning.'

'I can't believe you keep her only for decoration.'

'I don't. I keep her to work, nothing more.' There was irritation in John's voice. He knew that Peter was needling him, and that James was enjoying seeing him look uncomfortable.

'If we were at Bluecastle,' Peter insisted, 'James would have packed them off to bed the minute they'd finished waiting table.'

'You had better take your dinner there, then, if I'm failing you as a host.'

'If we were at Bluecastle,' James said, 'we might have fucked them *on* the table. But we must respect our elder brother's sense of decorum, Peter.'

George Kinloch roared with laughter. 'I'm wi James on this matter, John, but of course I bow to your wishes. It's not as if we canna restrain oorsels once in a while.'

Mr Hodge coughed and squirmed in his seat. He was looking pale and sweaty. 'I keep only the ugliest female negers about the house,' he said. 'I'm not like you fellows, I can't afford to yield to temptation. Mrs Hodge wouldn't stand for it.'

'Well, sir,' said Kinloch, 'you are in the happy state of not requiring to be tempted. For a fellow without matrimonial ties in this climate, it's a necessity. It's simply unreasonable to expect him to behave himsel when he's surrounded by half-clothed sable bitches like thae.'

'Brother John behaves,' Alexander said quietly, as if he were not quite sure whether he wanted to be part of the discussion. John looked at him sharply. Sandy was performing in his usual manner, trailing along in the wake of others.

'Oh, why's that?' Kinloch demanded.

'B-because he has the dignity of the family name to uphold.'

'Do you not indulge yourself *at all*, sir?' Hodge asked. 'I'm certain, if it were I –'

'No, I do not,' John interrupted him, giving Sandy a thin smile. He was well used to this from his brothers, but he had no wish to explain himself to Hodge. James and Peter in particular, and Sandy increasingly, could not understand his abstinence. All the planters did it – took the best-looking slave women for themselves: there was no shame and little discretion about it, as the clusters of mulatto bairns running around every plantation proved. You took them willing or not, gently or by force, and that was all there was to it. But John had no interest in coupling with slaves he might be whipping the next day. In fact, the thought revolted him. How, though, did you explain this to your three brothers, who were sometimes to be heard comparing notes on the performance of a girl they had each had at different times?

It was Davie Fyfe, the doctor, who came to his rescue: 'Frankly, I am sick of treating half the population in this island for the clap. There's nothing like drawing a discharge of pus from another man's member to encourage you to keep to the straight and narrow.' He looked round the table, but was careful that his gaze did not linger on any one face. A few seconds' silence proved too much for Sandy, though.

'Who else here has been syringed by Davie?' he said. It came out almost as a shout. John shook his head in exasperation.

'Oh, Sandy!' James said. 'That's the last time I congress with any of *your* past bedfellows.'

'It's no secret, is it?' Sandy said. 'We all get the clap sooner or later.'

'Not I,' John said.

'The later ye are, the mair chance,' Kinloch said.

'It depends on who's been there before you,' James said. 'Eh, Sandy?'

'That's why I always like to get in first,' Sandy said.

Again, John winced at his youngest brother's forced bravado. He worried for him – that in his efforts to keep up with the pace set by James and Peter, he would burn himself out.

'I hear Mr Collins flogged a girl almost to death for clapping him,' said Peter. 'But who's to say she did not catch it from him, if Davie's not pulling our legs. That would seem a trifle unfair.'

'I never fash mysel wi the fairness or otherwise of another man's use o the whip,' Kinloch said. 'Ye never ken all the circumstances. Ye see some neger greeting in the bilboes, or knocked senseless by her master, and ye feel it's cruel. Then ye discover she was stealing, or feigning illness, or she wouldna do as she was tellt, in bed or oot o it. Mr Collins doubtless had another grievance forby the clap.'

'There's some men I would not have at my table, though,' said John, 'on account of the manner they treat their slaves.'

'Such as?' Kinloch sounded touchy.

'Well, Tom Irvine.'

'Auld Tom?' said Kinloch. 'What's Tom done to upset ye, man?'

'He's a rough and ready kind of man,' said Hodge, 'fierce at times I'm sure, but he doesn't strike me as anything out of the ordinary.' The merchant suddenly pulled off his wig and swiped at a mosquito, then laid the wig in his lap. His bald head gleamed with rivulets of sweat.

'He degrades himself,' said John. 'He does not care if the blacks see him as a brute. In fact he revels in it.'

'Then Mr Hodge's observation is correct,' said Davie Fyfe. 'There's plenty like him.'

'Sometimes it's necessary,' said Kinloch.

'No,' said John, 'it is necessary to be strict, to punish where punishment is due. Of course we can all agree on that. But Irvine – no, I'd not have him at my table.' He made a rasping sound in his throat.

'What on earth is it he's done?' Hodge asked.

'We were down there three weeks ago,' James explained. 'His crop was all in – you know he hasn't as much land, and what he has is poor, badly drained – and we thought we might hire some of his slaves to help finish ours. But they were in such a miserable, wasted condition we'd never have got the work out of them to make it worthwhile. We went to see him and he was wandering about in just his shirt. Said he'd lost his breeks and couldn't be bothered to look for them. The place was stinking. One of his lassies had asked if she could go to tend her garden as there was nothing to be done in the house, so he shat in the hall and told her to clean that up.'

'Maybe he is demented,' said Kinloch. 'The heat, Mr Hodge.' But Mr Hodge had gone rather quiet, and did not seem to hear.

'Is Mr Collins demented?' asked Fyfe.

'Collins? Of course not. Why?'

'I heard if he catches a slave eating cane, he flogs him and has another slave shit in his mouth. Then he gags him for a few hours. Or he has one slave piss on the face of another. Is that the behaviour of a sane man?'

'It may not be pleasant,' said Kinloch, 'but it's no mad. If it was him doing the shitting and pissing, I grant that might suggest an unbalanced mind. But he instructs another neger to do it. He maintains his ain dignity.'

'For God's sake,' John Wedderburn said. There was a round of more or less revolted laughter from the others, which he at last joined in. The story was neither new nor particularly shocking. They might not have stooped quite to good old Tom Irvine's level, or Collins's, or at least if they had they were not saying, but they had done other things – dripped hot wax into wounds opened by whipping, rubbed salt or hot peppers in them. Or, more to the point, *they* had not actually done these things: they had had others do them – white employees, other slaves – and watched. Or not watched. Like Collins, they had kept their distance, and thus their dignity.

'In any case,' Kinloch added, 'eating shit is just a step frae eating dirt. I suppose some of them don't mind it much.'

There was silence around the table as they all considered this. Dirt-eating was one of the great mysteries of the plantations. Some slaves had a craving for the ground, clay in particular. Nothing was more likely to send a white man into a fit of revulsion than the sight of an African grovelling in the field, stuffing his face with soil. Nothing brought down the lash so fiercely. It was like watching some wild beast sniffing and scraping at a midden. It seemed to mark the distinction between the races more clearly than anything.

'We have a case of that just now,' said John, passing round a new bottle of claret. 'A boy called Plato. We've had to strap him to a board to keep him from it. Did you see him today, James?'

'On my way up. I've put him in a hut away from the others. He has a sore breaking out on his face that I fear may be the start of the yaws. I've told that old witch Peggy to look after him – nothing kills her, and her herbs and potions will not hurt him – may even be of help. I looked in his mouth. He has worms there.'

'From the dirt, nae doubt,' said Kinloch.

'I'm not so sure,' James said. 'Davie and I have been giving this some thought. I begin to wonder if it's not the other way round – if the dirt does not come from the worms.'

Kinloch snorted. 'That's ridiculous!'

'Well,' said Fyfe, 'why should the soil which gives us our good crops cause so many ailments among the slaves? A dirt-eater comes down with everything: the flux, dropsy, fatigue, stupidity –'

'And there ye pit your finger on the nub,' said Kinloch. 'Idleness and idiocy. The only thing that will cure thae ills is a thrashing. A good sound Negro never came doun wi dirt-eating.'

'But George,' said James, 'suppose for a moment that a good sound Negro did. What would be the cause of it? Suppose, for example, that he got the ground itch – you'll agree any Negro can get that between his toes?'

'We'd get it if we didna wear shoes. Ye're no wanting to gie them all shoes, are ye?'

'The ground itch is caused by hook worms,' said James, ignoring the question. 'You clean out the scabs, bathe the feet, and with time the itch is gone. But suppose the worms – some of them – get under the skin, and into the blood. Where do they go? They go through the blood to the lungs. Your good Negro coughs to clear his lungs. This brings the worms to his mouth. He takes a drink. The worms are carried into his gut. They feed there. The slave, consequently, is constantly hungry. He has a craving for whatever will fill his belly. The cane, or the ground it grows on. The worms grow inside him. They lay their eggs. The good Negro shits in the cane field. His shit is full of eggs. Need I go on?'

'I see,' said Kinloch. 'Ye mean getting one slave to shit in another's mouth may spread the worms?'

'For God's sake, man,' said Fyfe, 'forget about that. The ground is covered in hook worms. All we're saying is, if Plato is infested with worms, maybe that's the cause of his dirt-eating. Not the other way round.'

'It's the same with the yaws,' James went on. 'It never seems

82

to come on its own. And you'll grant that not even the most devious malingerer can feign it.'

'He'd be a magician if he could,' said John. 'And mad.' The raspberry-like sores and eruptions on face and body, the weeping tubercules and ulcers, the swellings and blisters on soles of feet and palms of hand, the obvious and intense pain caused by all this – nobody could, or would want to, fake the yaws.

'It's their foul habits,' Kinloch said decisively, reaching for a third slice of cold plum pudding. 'If they didna live such filthy lives we wouldna lose so many o them. Ye never see a white person wi the yaws.'

'Perhaps that's because our houses are bigger, airier,' said Fyfe. 'We die of all the other things they have, though. Yellow fever, the flux, dropsy. And then we have our own diseases: I never saw a Negro with the gout, or the dry belly-ache.'

'Ye're contradicting yoursels,' said Kinloch. 'First ye say that we're like them, then that we're no. I ken where I stand. I'm as like a neger as a – as a thoroughbred horse is like an Arab's camel.'

'I only wonder,' said Fyfe, 'if we exchanged places with them, if we'd exchange diseases too. As you said yourself, if we took off our shoes . . .'

Charles Hodge, who had been sitting, eyes closed, trying to contain a growing disagreement between his stomach and either the oysters or the topic under discussion, suddenly startled everyone with a drawling laugh. 'Haw! Exchange places, sir? Haw! Take off our shoes! That's the kind of metaphysical . . . perprosal you'd expect from a Scotchman. It's a impossibility. Mr Kinloch is right. We are horses, not camels!'

He stood up, knocking his chair over, and swayed out of the room to be sick. The others watched him go, only vaguely interested in seeing if he made it outdoors. If he did not, it would just be one more mess for the maids to clear up in the morning.

'All Davie is saying,' said John, 'is we should take more care of them. That's Christian if nothing else.'

'Oh man, dinna let them near Christ!' Kinloch exploded. 'Christ and kindness are troublemakers on a plantation. If ye gie them a sniff at Christ, they'll say they're saved and that makes them as good as ony white man. Treat them wi kindness and they'll repay ye wi idleness, complaints, grievances. It's but a step frae there to resentment and plotting.'

'Kindness doesn't enter into it,' said James Wedderburn. 'And I'm not interested in saving their souls either. I want as much work out of my slaves as you. I want as much money out of the crop. The best way to get that is healthy slaves. How much does a slave cost? A good one, a young, fit, Africa-born Coromantee?'

'Fifty pound,' said Kinloch.

'Sixty,' said James.

'Ye're being robbed.'

'Well, give or leave the ten pounds, it's a high price. I want that slave to last ten years at least. Perhaps twenty.'

'Away!'

'I have to season him for a year –'

'Six months.'

'– feed him and clothe him while he lives. I want him free of worms, yellow fever, the flux, poxes, consumption, the yaws – anything that stops him working. If I whip him every time he is ill, that is more time lost while he mends. Whip a slave for theft, or insolence, or running away, or refusing to work – of course. But let's be sure we whip them for the right things. Oh, and I want him to make me a lot more slave bairns too. I don't practise kindness, George. I practise economy.'

Except when it comes to your own slave bairns, John thought, but he said nothing.

'I prefer common sense. If ye treat a black soft, ye soften yoursel. Then ye think ye'll ease their labour a bit, gie them better hooses. The next thing ye're beginning to doubt the haill institution.'

'You're over-harsh, George,' said John. 'We are not tyrants.'

'Aye we are,' said Kinloch. 'We maist certainly are. We hae to be. It's the only honest way. If ye look at the thing true, ye'll agree.'

Later, long after Hodge had been put to bed with a bucket beside his head, and Kinloch and Fyfe, blazing drunk and barely able to stand, had somehow mounted their horses and trotted off homeward, the four Wedderburns played a few rather listless hands of rummy. They were all staying the night at Glen Isla. In the darkness the singing and drumming from the slave huts rose and faded on a light breeze.

James kept lifting his head, as if trying to catch something of the songs, almost as if he were envious of a better party. Peter pulled out his dirty book and, between turns, studied the pages for salacious passages, silently mouthing the French as he read. Alexander yawned constantly. Only John was concentrating much on the cards.

At last James flung down his hand. 'Damn it, John, Peter was right. I could devour that Peach just now. Or any of them. Let's go down for them.'

John shook his head. 'That, I think, even George Kinloch would think unwise at this time of night.'

'Well, can we not send for them?'

'No one to send. Unless you want to ask the formidable Phoebe. No? You'll just have to suffer alone then. Drink some more wine.'

Sandy stood up. 'I'm for my bed,' he said. He sidled out, clutching the other French book.

'Don't be up all night now,' Peter called after him, but this drew no response.

'He's writing a *novelle* himself, I think,' Peter told the others.

'What?' James frowned at him.

'He's writing something anyway. He's been scribbling away in a book since Christmas. But he keeps it hidden and he denies it if you ask.'

'Between that and his sketches, he's becoming quite an artist,' James said derisively.

'Leave him alone,' said John. 'We've all little enough privacy here as it is. Let him be.'

James yawned. 'I'm for my bed, too. By the way, Geordie Kinloch was right about one thing.'

'What?' John asked.

'About us being tyrants. Benevolent we may be, but tyrants is what we are.'

'James, you're not surely feeling guilty?'

'Not a bit of it. And it's not madness either. It's a natural state of affairs. It has to be. God's providence. What other reason for

85

such a distinction between the races? So we may as well make the best of it.'

'But,' John said, 'it behooves us to behave like civilised men. A lass like Peach – whip her if she's troublesome, but why mistreat her if she is a good girl? That is my view, and will continue to be.'

'No shitting in the hall for you, then,' James said. It was hard to tell if he was mocking John again. There was a trace of laughter in his voice, in the brightness of his eyes, but his mouth was unsmiling. He stood up, drank off the last of his wine.

'By God, though, a night like this, does it not make you yearn for a wife?'

'There's Mrs Hodge in Savanna unoccupied,' said Peter, glancing up. 'You should have ridden off with the others.'

This did finally produce a laugh from James. 'You are trespassing on the bounds of propriety, Peter. Be sensible. Why would I want all the trouble of seducing a white woman? In a country like this? And as for a wife, well, I was jesting. I don't have the patience for *that*. Not yet, at least.'

86

Dundee, May 1802

The weather had finally turned, it was warm and sunny, and the four younger Wedderburn girls were in town. They were in high spirits at the prospect of a day in Dundee. Their half-sister Margaret had avoided having to chaperone them by pointing out that there was not room inside the carriage for them all, and that she had no desire to go. So Aeneas MacRoy was accompanying them, sitting up with the stableman, William Wicks, who was at the reins. At the old West Port the girls decanted, and MacRoy, after telling Wicks to drive to the shore where the horses could feed and rest before the return journey, got down stiff-legged from his seat and followed them at a discreet distance. He had been instructed by Lady Wedderburn, who was in bed with a cold, to keep an eye on her girls: Dundee could be rough, even in daylight, and MacRoy's task was to make sure the lassies did not wander away from the main streets and into trouble.

MacRoy reckoned they were safe enough, with or without his assistance. Generally speaking, the poor and desperate robbed and bludgeoned one another, not their social betters. There was less risk involved. The fact that it was he – a man of sixty-eight, and hirpling somewhat these days – who had been entrusted with the girls' protection, suggested that not even their mother anticipated any difficulty. What could she be expecting? A band of brigands to carry them off to Araby? And what, in such an eventuality, could an aged dominie do to stop them? Then again, it would be a bold brigand who would cross Aeneas MacRoy. Small and ancient he might be, but he was still a force to be reckoned with when roused. Tough as knotted wood and fierce as a wildcat, especially if the Wedderburn honour was at stake. Lady Alicia had known him twenty years. She did not really understand him, but because her husband trusted him, so did she.

The sisters intended to visit Madame Bouchonne's in the

Overgait, as she had recently advertised a large consignment of materials and designs newly arrived from London and the Continent. They wanted – or at least three of them wanted – to promenade up and down the Nethergait and High Street, to see what else might be new, and of course to be seen: the Wedderburn name was embedded in Dundee history – merchants, ministers, landowners, lawyers, burgesses, soldiers – and everybody knew who they were. Perhaps they would run into other ladies in from the country. They would almost certainly meet a cousin or two. They would take tea at the New Inn, where who knew what interesting persons might also be passing the afternoon? A gallant young captain from the Forfar Militia perhaps, or better still a major in the Perthshire Regiment. And after all else, there would be the elephant. Fourteen-year-old Annie very badly wanted to see the elephant.

Aeneas MacRoy planned to watch them for a few minutes, then slip off to one of a number of dram shops he knew, and while away an hour before meeting them at the inn.

Susan, lingering in the wake of her sisters, had come to town in a mood of ambivalence. It was not that she did not want to be here – there was, after all, so much to see compared with the fine but too peaceful surroundings of Ballindean. Dundee was thriving, noisy, its narrow central area a constant mêlée of vehicles and hurrying people. It had a population approaching twenty-five thousand, which made it bigger than Perth and almost as big as Paisley. Dundee's spinners and weavers had something of a reputation for radicalism, which appealed to Susan as much as it appalled her mother. There were, apparently, some truly dreadful backstreets and wynds, inhabited by characters who would, according to Aeneas MacRoy, stab you with a look. The thought of these dangerous places and people sent a thrill through her.

The huge new steam-driven flax mills built on the burns running down from Lochee might seem monstrous, but she could not help but be impressed by their power. Likewise the bustling harbour – with its intoxicating mix of foreign-looking sailors and merchants, and its hubbub of strange tongues; its ships carrying grain and linen to England and Holland; barrels of salted herring to the Indies (herring, she'd read, was a staple of the slaves' diet), to Danzig and Riga, and bringing in iron, copper, tar and pine boards from Sweden and Norway – the harbour both intimidated and exhilarated her. And Dundee's main streets and fine location below the Law, overlooking the gleaming firth, were gracious and charming. All this Susan saw and understood – much more so, she felt certain, than her sisters; and that was the source of her ambivalence. She would rather be here on her own, in disguise perhaps, able to walk the streets unnoticed and in her own time, not as part of a Wedderburn parade.

She was looking forward to fussy Madame Bouchonne only for the opportunity to laugh secretly at her and her claims of aristocratic blood and narrow escape from Madame Guillotine. Her outrageous accent could not possibly be Parisian, as she maintained, but was surely grafted on to something closer to home – Ayrshire, perhaps, or Dumfries – and her name bore an uncanny resemblance to Buchan or Buchanan. Madame Bouchonne might be a rare and exotic flower which her sisters would be loath to see wither, but Susan would rather have browsed for hours in the booksellers' at the Cross, without Annie tugging at her sleeve. She wanted to go *into* the mills, see the men and women working there in their strange new crowded way, like a nest of ants. She wanted to talk to the weavers at their looms. She wanted to wander without sisters or chaperone, to sit by the harbour and drink in its sights and smells. But she could not do these things: she was hemmed in by her skirts and stays and family name. She wanted to be – for a day, or a week, or a year – a *boy* of seventeen.

She was beginning to feel that she had put enough yards between herself and her sisters almost to be not counted as one of them, when a man suddenly stepped from a close in front of her. She put out her hand in fright, but disappointingly he did not try to stab her with a look or any other implement. He stopped abruptly to avoid bumping into her, and made a short bow of apology.

'Mr Jamieson!' she said.

The plumpish man in his crumpled black clothes looked startled, then broke into a smile, friendly yet slightly awkward, even humble. It was enough to renew in Susan the confidence that came with being a Wedderburn. What she most disliked about herself was also one of her strongest attributes.

'Miss Wedderburn. Ye've come tae shed licht on oor dark toun.'

She looked up at the blue sky, then at the busy street. 'That's hardly necessary.' Then, peering into the close from which he had emerged: 'Although down there, perhaps . . . Is that where you stay?'

'Na, na,' he said. 'I was, em, looking for someone.'

'Not Joseph Knight still?' she asked. She wasn't sure if she wanted to laugh. Glancing ahead she saw her sisters slowing, becoming aware of her absence. She stepped quickly into the close mouth, cleeking Jamieson by the elbow and taking him with her.

'Miss, I dinna think . . .'

'I'm no awa tae kiss ye!' she said, turning the accent on, and loud enough to make him start and even put a finger towards her lips.

'Guidsakes, ye'll hae me apprehended!'

'Apprehended? That's a word much used in your trade, I suppose. And did you find this someone you were looking for?'

'No, I – he's oot. I'll get him again.'

'What a strange life you lead. Always hunting folk. You never explained –'

Maria, Louisa and Anne passed on the street, Anne calling her name.

'Ye'd better go, miss.'

'But what about Mr Knight? Have you found him yet?'

'I've no been looking. No since your faither –' He broke off: this was ridiculous, being interrogated by a child. Why did he find himself so tongue-tied? 'No, I've no found him.'

'Oh,' she said, turning to go. 'That's a shame, because I have. Goodbye, Mr Jamieson.'

Now it was he who pulled her in from the street. 'What d'ye mean? Where?'

'Unhand me, sir!' she said, straight out of a *novelle*, and laughed because Jamieson seemed so astounded at the violence of his own reaction. But then, realising there was not much time left, she hurried on. 'Perhaps you need my help.'

'Your faither disna want me tae . . . Whit is it ye ken?'

'It's information . . . from my uncle. I'm not sure whether I should give it to you.' She saw how eager he looked. 'Where may I reach you?'

'Here,' he said. There was a tremor of excitement in his voice. 'I mean, no *here*. In the toun. An address tae Archibald Jamieson at St Clement's Lane will find me.'

'St Clement's Lane,' she said. 'Well, I *may* write.' She started to go.

'Miss Wedderburn – I dinna ken – I wouldna want ye tae cross your faither. Ye've a clever heid on ye, but ye're jist a lassie.'

'Leave my *faither* to me,' she said. 'You're not him. *Au revoir*.'

She darted off again, back into the light. Jamieson followed her to the close entry, stopped on seeing her sisters flocking round her, heard a snatch of her excuse: '– thought it might be picturesque. It is not.' Momentarily Anne peered in, and shrunk away at sight of him scowling in the shadows. Then they were gone, along the Nethergait in a flurry of skirts and chatter, leaving Jamieson not quite sure what had happened, what kind of conversation he had had. All he knew was that he felt the same tingle of excitement he had when tracking down radicals, or being within reach of a vital piece of information.

He was made very certain of what happened next, though. As he made to leave the close for the third time, he was met with a rock-hard fist that grabbed a handful of his shirt front and a good clump of chest hairs beneath it. It bore him back into the mirk and slammed him against the stonework. Jamieson grunted, tried to work himself free, but the other man's grip was unshakeable. The arm that pinioned him was quivering with the exertion but solid as an iron bar. Without relaxing his hold, Aeneas MacRoy made a suggestion: 'I think you and me should hae a wee conversation.'

Jamieson nodded, tried to speak, found when he did that all the breath had been punched from his lungs. He nodded more vigorously. Slowly, MacRoy eased off, let go of him, stepped away. 'For God's sake,' Jamieson said, massaging his chest. 'Ye're a schoolmaister. And this is a guid shirt.'

'Be glad I dinna mak ye eat it,' MacRoy growled. It was an

absurd threat but his voice and rage-darkened face gave it an unnerving force. Jamieson, who mixed with villains of various hues in the course of business, wondered if he was losing his touch. First he had got out of his depth in his interview with the laird, then the laird's lassie had unsettled him, and now the laird's dominie had caught him off-guard. MacRoy said, 'I ken a place where we'll no be disturbed.'

They continued on down the close, away from the Nethergait, towards the shore. Jamieson knew where he was being taken. Just before they reached the end of the close, MacRoy stooped at a low entrance to one side, and pushed open a door. It led into a dingy drinking shop, damp-smelling even on such a warm, breezy spring day. Two sailors were slumped insensible across a table, one on either side, heads touching as they snored. A few other battered, scraped and uneven tables and benches were the only items of furniture, and MacRoy and Jamieson the only conscious customers. A couple of guttering candles fixed on makeshift shelves by their own wax gave off a greasy half-glow that only made the room gloomier. From behind a high counter in an even darker recess of the room, a thin, slurring voice piped out: 'Aye, sirs. Whit'll it be?'

'D'ye ken this place?' MacRoy asked.

'I've been here,' said Jamieson. 'Aye, Nannie,' he said to the counter. Then, to MacRoy, 'But I dinna frequent it unless I hae tae.'

MacRoy spat on the floor. 'I dae,' he said. 'I *frequent* it.' He made it sound like a word only an Edinburgh fop would use. 'No because I hae tae. I *like* it.'

Jamieson looked at him. Outside, the older man's head had barely reached his shoulder. In this putrid hole there seemed to be more of MacRoy, as if occupying preferred territory hardened and thickened his bones; made him, not fleshier, but somehow more *cadaverous*. Regaining his composure as they approached the counter, Jamieson decided that MacRoy did not so much frighten as repulse him.

The landlady revealed herself: a spindle of a woman, skinny as her voice, wearing a filthy apron over a coarse dress of indeterminate colour and material. An equally colourless lace cap sat on a nest of hair so tangled and matted that it seemed a comb, if applied to it, would either snap or vanish for ever. The woman leant heavily on her hands, swaying slightly. 'Whit'll it be?' she said again. She was clearly very drunk.

'Whisky,' said MacRoy.

'Cask or bottle? Cask's cheaper, bottle's better.'

'Nannie, ye're a cheatin hure,' Jamieson said, feeling the need to reassert himself in front of MacRoy. 'It's the exact same stuff, whichever vessel ye tak it frae.'

Nannie stared at him. 'Oh, it's yoursel. I didna ken ye at first.' Names seemed beyond her. 'And wha's this wi ye? Weel, sir, I've no seen you for a while either. I didna ken ye kent each ither.'

'We dinna,' said MacRoy. 'We'll sit ower there.'

They went to a table by the single, dirt-encrusted window, through which was cast a scabby, useless portion of the daylight. Nannie tottered across with a jug of whisky and a couple of tumblers no cleaner than the window. Jamieson produced a handkerchief and dichted one of them out. MacRoy poured into both glasses and set the jug down on the table with a crack, watching the other man coldly without releasing the handle. The landlady was still hotching unsteadily beside them.

'Noo, Nannie,' MacRoy said, without taking his eye off Jamieson, 'get back tae your fuckin midden and lea us alane.' She scuttled off. Into himself, Jamieson admitted to being impressed by the schoolmaster's language. The enforced bottling up of curse words, which life at Ballindean must require, doubtless improved their flavour when finally uncorked.

MacRoy pulled a clay pipe and a tobacco pouch from his jacket, studiously packed the pipe, got up to catch a light from one of the candles, cowped his first dram, nodded at Jamieson to do the same, refilled both glasses, sat back and puffed at the pipe. 'So whit's your business wi Miss Wedderburn?' he said.

'Nane o your concern.'

MacRoy laughed, leant forward. 'Listen tae me, man. I didna like ye when I saw ye at the hoose, an I dinna like ye noo. I like ye even less when I see ye whisperin secrets doun a close tae a lassie that I'm lookin efter. No my concern? That's a Wedderburn lassie. She sits in my schoolroom. Ye're no fit tae be in the same hoose.'

'Maybe that's why we bade in the close ootby.' Jamieson was feeling better with every minute that passed. He took off the second dram. He was getting the measure of auld Aeneas now, beginning to understand what drove him.

'I could hae broke your neck back there,' MacRoy said.

'How did ye no?'

'I want tae ken whit your business is wi her.'

'And I've tellt ye, nae business o yours.'

'I'll find oot. She'll tell me.'

'Whit'll ye dae, threaten her? Thrapple her in the stables like ye did me? I dinna think so, Maister MacRoy.'

'If Sir John hears o this, he'll hae ye locked up. Or beaten up, ane or tither.'

'Noo ye're cleekin at straes, Aeneas. This is a free country, awmaist. Ye michtna like folk haein a conversation but ye canna prevent it. And I dinna think ye'll be tellin Sir John either. He'd be wantin tae ken hoo ye let the thing happen at aw. And onywey, whit *has* happened? A few words exchanged in passing? Nae crime there.'

MacRoy took another drink. His brow furrowed deeper still. He stared at Jamieson with pure hatred. Or was it something else? Jealousy? And suddenly Jamieson knew who MacRoy was really staring at.

'This is aboot the neger. I ken it is.'

Jamieson smiled. Ye could hae taen the words oot ma mooth, he thought. He said, 'Whit neger? I dinna see a neger. Does Miss Wedderburn ken ony negers? We can ask Nannie if she's had ony coming in aff the ships lately.' He half rose to call her over. MacRoy's hand shot across the table and gripped his wrist. Jamieson sat down. The hand released him, slid back again.

'Joseph Knight,' said MacRoy. 'It's aboot him.'

'Are ye tellin me or speirin?'

'Fine I ken that's whit ye cam tae see Sir John aboot. Tae seek him oot. Weel, ye'll no succeed. He's deid. Deid and gane tae hell.'

'Ye're sure o that?'

'That's whaur he should be. And it's whaur ye'll be if ye dinna keep awa frae Miss Susan.'

'Man, man, calm yoursel. Tell me aboot this. Ye're jealous. Noo, ye canna be jealous o *me*. Naething to be jealous aboot – look at me. It was a pure accident meetin Miss Wedderburn. Ye

94

ken that. But Joseph Knight, that's a different story. Wha was it ye wantit *him* tae keep awa frae?'

MacRoy took more whisky. His gaze shifted, first to the window, then to the sleeping sailors, finally back to Jamieson. 'I mind aince,' he said, 'gaun intae Dundee wi him on the cairt. Wull Wicks – no the laddie, his faither, that's deid noo – Wull and I were awa tae fetch some plenishin for the hoose, and we were tae tak the slave in tae a barber at the Cross, that was tae gie him trainin in dressin hair or some such. And there wasna muckle talk on the road, but Wull says tae him, "Look at ye in your finery. Look at your hauns. The loofs o them are saft as a lady's. They cry ye a slave but it's clear enough tae me wha the slaves is aboot here. No you wi your work-shy hauns an hoose-bred ways, Joseph Knight. I would be a slave in a minute if I could get leevin like you, man." I mind that, aye, every word o it. And the neger never said a word back, jist sat there wi a sneer on his mooth. He was a slave but he thocht he was better nor the rest o us, that's certain.'

It was as if a tightly wound spring was being gradually released inside MacRoy. 'He had nae richt. Whit was he? A neger. Sir John's neger brocht back frae the plantations. He was lucky tae be here. Sir John treated him mair like a son than a slave. Better than a servant. He should hae been grateful for that, brocht oot o savagery and made a Christian in a daicent Christian country. But that wasna enough for him, na. He had tae hae mair. And mair and mair. He had tae hae awthing. He had tae hae *her*. But she was mine. She should hae been mine.'

'Wha's that?'

'Annie. Ann Thomson. The neger turned her heid, and broke Sir John's hert. That's whit he did.'

'Sir John's hert? *His* hert's no broken. That's jist an auld man wantin tae redd up his affairs. And Joseph Knight's ane o them. Whit happened tae him and Ann Thomson?'

'Happen tae them?' MacRoy said. 'Ye ken whit happened.'

'Na,' Jamieson said. 'I dinna.'

'Fuck you, then.'

'Why dae ye say Knight broke Wedderburn's hert? Whit was there atween them?'

But Aeneas MacRoy had had enough. He drained the whisky

in his glass, stood up, put his face down two inches from Jamieson's. His eyes were furious and watery. 'He broke his hert,' he repeated. 'He and Ann Thomson betrayed him. They're deid and rotting in hell. Or they should be. Stay awa frae her,' he said, stepping back, his voice rising. 'I'll kill ye if ye dinna stay awa frae her.' Then he was stumbling across the dark room, back through the miserable door out into the close, gone.

Jamieson swirled the last of his whisky, contemplating the snoring sailors. They looked so peaceful, so untrauchled by life. A shame they should be in such a hole. But it was, he suspected, heaven compared with their ship.

He pondered MacRoy's confused messages, decided there was more sound than substance in the threat. Who had he meant by 'her' anyway? Susan Wedderburn? Ann Thomson? Maybe MacRoy did not really know himself. Just as he seemed confused about whose heart had been broken by Joseph and Annie. The poor auld miserable bastard.

Jamieson stared at the table. 'Damn him!' he said out loud. MacRoy had not left a penny for the whisky.

After a while he got up and went over to the counter. 'How much, ye auld thief?' But Nannie, like the sailors, was fast asleep. Jamieson put a few coins on the counter and stepped, a little unsteadily, outside.

Aeneas MacRoy felt the spirit racing through his blood. He did not feel disabled by it – on the contrary, he felt liberated. He walked briskly back up to the Nethergait, stormed eastward along it and only came to a halt at the Cross, when his bad leg almost gave way beneath him and he realised he had been putting far too much weight on it. The New Inn was in front of him. He would have to go in and find the lassies. He took a moment to compose himself, straighten his clothes, wipe the sweat from his face.

Sometimes he almost brought himself to thank God that he was now, probably, too old actually to kill anyone. The violence had always been in him, but he had always contained, controlled it. When it boiled in him, it came up against the iron-hard shell he showed to the world, and had to subside. Or it came out in

96

the whisky, a flame like a fire-eater's breath. Or it was diffused in memories.

He minded the stir caused in the town by John Wedderburn's coming home in '68, to stay with his mother and sisters in their house in the Nethergait. How he had styled himself Sir John from the first, although the title had been forfeited by his father, and how folk either did not care or dared not challenge him. Dundee had buzzed with tales of the immense riches he had amassed in the Indies; and there was the young black man, too – handsome, got up in a fine blue suit with gold braid and a profusion of lace at neck and cuffs – who followed his master everywhere. Genteel citizens made sure their calling cards reached Sir John in the Nethergait. Many in the town were still romantically, if not politically, Jacobite, and those who were not saw no harm in welcoming one who had been 'out' but was now back and had the potential to spend so much money. And this sentiment grew stronger, as it became known that Sir John was looking about for two things to make his homecoming complete: a large property, and a young wife.

Aeneas MacRoy bided his time. After more than twenty years, to wait another few months was no trial. He kept a school for the sons of small merchants and farmers and took an unsteady income from it, constantly in thrall to the vicissitudes of harvests and markets. At that time the roll had fallen to a mere half dozen. Sir John's return was timeous. It was not that MacRoy had nursed a plan over the years; it was simply that he had always believed that the Wedderburns would come back, and that when they did he might be able, in some small way, to profit by it.

In the summer of 1769 it became known that Sir John had an eye on the Ballindean property, and was negotiating its purchase with the owner, Carnegy of Craigie. He had his other eye on Margaret Ogilvy, twenty-year-old daughter of his former commander Lord David Ogilvy. His lordship was still exiled in France, but she, having been born and spent her earliest years there, was now living at Cortachy Castle, the family's ancestral home. Before the year was out, a marriage had taken place, the couple had moved into the ancient, somewhat decrepit house at Ballindean, and were accumulating servants. Naturally, the slave went with them.

Early on the first morning of the new year, Aeneas MacRoy happed himself against the cold and made the long walk out to Ballindean. He might have sent a letter in advance, to introduce himself, but he knew that the Wedderburns were at home, and he had the means to get an audience. Day had come by the time he turned in at Ballindean's gates. There was a light frost on the ground, and the loch was dark against the sparkling grass. Aeneas strode up to the front door. The place was silent. He battered at the door. Eventually a maid came to open it.

'Is the laird aboot?' said Aeneas MacRoy.

She looked him up and down suspiciously. A bonnie, black-haired thing with a proud look about her. She said, 'Wha is it wants him?'

'Tell him Aeneas MacRoy.'

'Whit?'

'Aeneas MacRoy.'

'He'll no see ye.'

'Aye he will.'

'Lord, man,' said the maid, 'it's Ne'erday. What ails ye? Ye're ower late for a hogmanay.'

'I'd hae come yestreen if it was for that. Here, tak this yoursel, and gie him this. He'll see me.'

He handed her a penny and a folded piece of cloth tied up with string. She slipped the coin away but stood looking doubtfully at the cloth.

'On ye go, lass,' he said. 'Ye're lettin aw the heat oot the hoose.'

'Ye'll need tae wait ootby,' she said.

'Fine. I'll be in soon enough.'

She shut the door on him and disappeared. She was gone fully ten minutes. Aeneas waited, stamping his feet on the stone step.

The door opened again. 'Ye're tae come in,' she said, wide-eyed.

'Didna I say I would?'

The library was in a state of chaos. Chests full of books were piled against one wall, paintings in heavy frames against another. Chairs and other bits of furniture were stacked in the middle of the room. It was chilly, but a fire was catching in the grate. John Wedderburn, wearing slippers and breeches and a loose shirt, and a smoking jacket over all, was clearly not long out of his bed. He was standing to one side of the fire, running a faded but still colourful cloth between his hands. 'Who are you?' he said.

'Sir, my name is Aeneas MacRoy.'

Wedderburn stared hard at him. The name meant something, but he could not place it. MacRoy could see him struggling, trying to remember.

'Where did you get this?'

'Ye ken whaur, sir.'

'Is that some kind of a threat?'

'Oh no, sir.'

'I'll not be trifled with,' said Wedderburn. 'As you can see, I am just arrived in this house. State your business so I can decide if I need to waste my time on it.'

'Ye'll maybe no mind, sir, efter Culloden, hoo the reidcoats gaithered up aw the colours they had captured. They took them tae Edinburgh, and there the public hangman burnt them at the Cross. But they didna burn this ane. The Glen Prosen company's. Oors.'

John Wedderburn was looking down a tunnel of years. His clenched hands gripped the colours as if to tear the cloth apart. 'Who are you?' he said again.

'Sir, I am the drummer laddie that fell a-greetin when the cannon shot cam ower us. But later I stopped greetin. I saved the colours when aw else was lost.'

'Good God.'

'And I thocht I would tak this opportunity tae return them tae ye, seein as hoo ye hae returned hame yoursel, and I'm richt glad tae see ye, sir.'

'Good God,' Wedderburn repeated. 'The wee drummer. I mind you now. Aeneas. The wanderer. The Highland men called you Angus in their own tongue.'

'Aye, sir.'

'Now I see you as if it were yesterday.'

'It is twenty-four years in April, sir.'

'How old were you then, Aeneas?'

'Jist chappin twal, sir.'

Wedderburn put the colours down on a table, stepped forward and shook Aeneas MacRoy by the hand. 'Well, this is a fine meeting. And you have kept this all that time? That was a dangerous thing to do in the first years.'

'Ah, weel, there's nae bulk tae it.'

'You shame me, that it ever left my hand.'

'I think there was little tae be shamed aboot that day, wi us being sae young, sir. The shame was in the men that chose tae fecht on that ground.'

'Ah, now, Aeneas, we'll not rake over all that – not now, at any rate. But you, well, you saved yourself?'

'Aye. When I had left aff greetin I ran aw the way tae Inverness and a woman hid me in her roof for a month, and I was that wee they never kent I was there. And efter the month I walked back tae Dundee, whaur my mither bade.'

'You had a father?'

'He was deid lang afore. That's why I ran aff tae join the Prince's army, though my mither didna want me tae. When I got hame she begged a future for me frae the minister. I'd haen some schooling, sir, I could read and write, and the minister thocht I would prosper if I got mair. He pit me in for a mortification at the grammar school, and they gied me it. They taught me Latin, and mathematics, and logic, and a wheen ither things. I was there fower year, and when I cam oot, I wasna the drummer laddie that gaed in.'

'You had more book-learning than I ever had,' said Wedderburn. He found glasses and a bottle of whisky, and poured them drams. 'Here's to the auld cause, then,' he said, and they both drank, but there was a little awkwardness in it. 'It is finished now, of course,' Wedderburn added, 'but there's no disgrace in toasting what's past.'

'And whit's tae come,' said Aeneas MacRoy, raising his glass, and they drank again. Sir John asked how he now lived, and Aeneas told him about his tiny school in Dundee. As he talked, Wedderburn's glance kept sliding to the colours lying on the table.

'Ye'll have acquired a good deal more knowledge, then, over the years?'

'Oh, aye. I hae the French, leastwise I can read and write

it though I dinna speak it aften or weel, and the Scriptures of course, and the algebra and geometry and suchlike. I can gie the lads as guid a grounding as they'll get withoot gaun tae the college, *if* their faithers let them stay.'

'They don't always appreciate your efforts?'

'If ye're a fermer ye set mair store by your son's muckle hauns than by his Latin. If ye're a merchant ye carena hoo he spells, sae being's he can coont. I canna blame them but it means the attendance is gey irregular.'

'And the fees too?'

'Aye.'

Wedderburn was silent for a moment, contemplating. 'I have a fellow here that's anxious to get an education,' he said at last, 'and I am happy that he should get one. Nothing fancy, but to read and write and so forth. Would you come out to teach him?'

'I would. But it's a lang road for jist the ae student.'

'I'd make it worth your while. And it wouldn't need to be often – he only wants to read and write a little. I don't want him getting ideas above his station. And in a few years there will be more students for you, God willing. Wedderburns. I would want them to get a good Scotch education – straight, honest, useful. You might be the man to provide that. Not that they may not need some other expertise. A music teacher if there's lassies; a fencing master for the boys. But what was it you said, a good grounding . . . ?'

'I can dae that and mair.'

'You're direct. That's a good Scotch trait. I may not speak much Scotch these days but I have not forgotten where I'm from.'

'That's why ye cam back. Ye dinna speak Scotch but ye soond it. And I ken there's a fashion amang the gentles for riddin themsels o Scotch words – weel, I hae the English, and can teach it.' He paused. 'I have trained myself to stop and start my Scotch like a spigot.' This last sentence was delivered with a deliberate, slow emphasis, its broad vowels and burred consonants much reduced.

'I think I like your Scotch better. We'll see. If I took you on, it would be better if you bade here. There's room.'

'I would hae tae close the school then.'

'Well, one thing at a time. You'll need to meet my lady's approval, of course. But there are other things than teaching bairns you could help me with. And before all that, there's this.' He picked up the colours. 'I'm grateful for what you did, Aeneas, and I'm glad you have come and sought me out. Do you make a gift of this to me?'

'Aye. It was never mine.'

'It is the past. We drank to the past, and you mentioned the future. This is the future.' He made as if to throw the colours into the fire, watching for Aeneas's reaction. There was none. 'You do not flinch.'

'It has served its purpose.'

'You kept it all this time.'

MacRoy shrugged.

Wedderburn nodded. 'I suppose it is still, in theory, dangerous.' He paused. 'You know what happened to my father?'

'Aye, sir. Awbody kent.'

The colours were hanging from Wedderburn's hand. 'If I told you that I would not follow this now, what would you think?'

'I'd think ye'd be mad tae say ony different. Things are no the same noo.'

Sir John nodded approvingly. 'Well, then.' He began to fold up the colours. 'But I would never destroy it. Men died for that cause. My father died for it.'

'I ken.'

'My wife's father may die an exile for it. I will make a gift of it to her, as you did to me. Things like this should not be cast away.' He laid the cloth down on a table. 'Now,' he said, 'you'd better take a look at your student. He's keen, but he starts from a base of near total ignorance.'

'Ah. He's a servant?'

'His name is Joseph Knight.'

'The neger ye brocht hame.'

'The very same. Let's see where he has got to. I think you'll find him interesting, Maister MacRoy.'

'Maister MacRoy.'

'Aye?'

102

'Maister MacRoy!'

He came awake, found himself half standing, half leaning against a wall.

'Are you all right?' Annie and Louisa Wedderburn were staring anxiously at him. Behind them he could see the older girls, Maria and Susan, looking far less concerned, smiling, smirking a little even. He recovered himself as best he could.

'There ye are. I was coming tae look for ye. But the heat . . . I jist needed tae rest for a minute. Did ye meet onybody?'

'Nobody we could marry,' Louisa said.

'Now may we see the elephant?' Annie asked.

'I think we may,' said MacRoy. 'It's no aften an elephant comes tae Dundee.'

A show of wild animals had been travelling from Edinburgh via Stirling and Perth, and, according to a notice in the *Dundee Magazine*, it was set up in the Meadows behind the Murraygait. The grass had been thinned by the passage of many feet. MacRoy handed over the entrance fee for them all – he would reclaim it from Lady Alicia – and they wandered along the cages.

MacRoy paid as much heed to the possible attentions of pursepicks as he did to the exhibits. The beasts were a sorry-looking lot in any case – a bedraggled family of lions, a skeerie pair of zebras, a threadbare tiger, a bear that paced back and forth like a madman in a cell. The cages were cramped and filthy, the smell overpowering. Even the keepers – dark, bearded men in baggy red pantaloons and big-sleeved silk shirts that had seen better days – seemed infected with sadness, as if they had journeyed one or two towns too far from home, and were not sure how to get back.

In the last enclosure was the elephant. This was not the huge, trumpeting African creature Annie had hoped for from pictures, but a tuskless, timid-looking Indian one. Here, for an extra penny, they could buy a bag of cakes and feed it. It ate with a kind of baleful indifference, its wet, snottery trunk curling out mechanically to take the food through the bars. Annie looked very disappointed.

'They're supposed to be exceedingly wise,' Louisa said, trying to cheer Annie up.

'It just looks exceedingly bored,' Maria said.

Annie disposed of the cakes very quickly. 'Can we go now?' she asked. Tears were welling up in her eyes.

It was Susan's belief that if Aeneas MacRoy had a soft spot for anybody, it was for Annie. Sometimes she would catch him looking in her own direction before making some small gesture of affection towards her youngest sister. It was as if he was seeking Susan's approval to be kind. This was what happened now. He glanced at Susan, then lightly touched Annie's cheek with one gnarled finger.

'Dinna fash, child,' he said. 'It is a beast oot o its place and climate. If ye saw it in India it would appear a mighty creature.'

'Poor thing. I'll never see India, and neither will it again.'

They began to walk away. Susan saw Aeneas's brow furrow as he thought of something.

'Years ago,' he said to Annie, 'lang or even I was born, or your faither, they say anither elephant came tae Dundee. It was an ill-willed, cheatin kind o man that brocht it, and the beast was sick, and fell doun and died in the street. And the man, wha'd hoped tae mak a power o siller frae showin it, abandoned it where it fell and disappeared.'

'Did they catch him?'

'They didna ken whaur he was. And here was this muckle heap o stinkin flesh declinin on the street. The guid folk o Dundee held their nebs and strippit it doun tae the banes, because they'd heard an elephant was made aw o ivory, and they thocht tae reap something frae it, but then they found it was jist the twa muckle teeth that were ivory. But the provost had the surgeons o Dundee pit aw the pieces back thegither, and they made a skeleton o it again, and exhibited it. And it was a great wonder and folk cam frae far and wide tae see it.

'Weel, the owner got tae hear o this braw skeleton and he cam back tae claim it for his ain. He said he had sellt it tae the surgeons o Edinburgh, and they cam tae tak it awa tae *their* toun. But the Dundee folk prevented it. They said the owner hadna the richt, for he hadna treatit the beast weel, but had taen it oot o its torrid hame country, and brocht it tae these cauld northern airts, and stervit it and beaten it and taen it in wee ferry boats and ower craigy mountain roads whaur it had nae wish tae gang. And so it stayed whaur it had died, here in Dundee.'

'Is it here still?' Annie asked.

'I dinna ken, child. But if it is, I think it's lang laid tae rest.'

'I don't know, Maister MacRoy,' Susan said, 'that that's any better an end for an elephant than to be stuck in that cage.'

'I don't know either, miss,' Aeneas MacRoy said. 'But it maks a better story.'

It seemed to cheer Annie up slightly, at least. Then, making their way back, they passed stalls where the show people were dispensing potions and cures and had set out on red cloths displays of little wooden toys and boxes, thimbles, mirrors and cheap jewellery. Set slightly apart from these stands was a brightly coloured booth which announced itself as the residence of a gypsy spaewife. Maria and Louisa suggested they all have their fortunes told.

MacRoy looked sceptical. The lightness that had entered his voice in the telling of the elephant story disappeared. 'That is aw superstition and trickery,' he growled. 'Your faither wouldna be pleased tae think I let ye spend guid siller on such trash.'

'Then don't tell him,' said Susan, who suddenly thought it a good plan. 'And we'll not.'

'Well, if we do it,' Maria said, 'we must tell nobody, not even each other. We must go in one by one, and then write down what she tells us in a letter and seal it for a time – a month, say – and see what comes. And after a month we'll open the letters and read what was said.'

'But nothing may happen in a month,' Louisa said.

'Well, two or three months then. And even then nothing may happen at all, in which case Maister MacRoy will be proved right, that it is trash, but harmless. And if the spaewife tells something that comes true, well, it will only be a mystery how she knew, nothing more.'

MacRoy saw that they were determined, and he saw also that they had a hold on him because of his earlier lapse. 'I canna prevent whit I dinna see,' he said. 'I am awa for a dander roond the Meadows tae cool my heid. I'll see ye back at the entrance in a half-oor.'

He trudged off. His leg was hurting a good deal now. He had

walked too far on it. After a few minutes he stopped and sat down under a tree. A light breeze got up. He did not sleep again. The whisky and the violence had left him, and it was pleasant to sit in the shade and take the pressure off his leg.

He thought again of his first visit to Ballindean. How, on being shown out by the same bonnie maid, he had teased her for having kept him in the cold so long. 'Ye'll ken tae let me in when I come again,' he had said. She'd looked at him as if she did not care. 'A penny like the day will aye get ye in,' she said. 'Oh, there's a toll tae pay each time, is there?' he asked. 'And dae I get onything for my penny?' 'Ye micht,' she said, with the briefest of smiles, and closed the door on him. He felt like skipping all the nine miles back to Dundee.

He wondered now, if he had been to a spaewife before then, what she would have said; if she would have been able to see him there, happy as a gowk from his successful interview with Sir John and his first sighting of Annie Thomson. Would she have warned him against her? And what if he had been to a spaewife even earlier, at ten or eleven, before he knew any better, just a year or so before Culloden? Could she have seen him screaming and shaking on the moor, drowned out by the guns; getting to his feet, stumbling away, tripping over the staff of the abandoned colours; tearing the flag off and stuffing it in his shirt, and running, running, running to Inverness? He wondered if she could have told him that all his life thereafter would be a hardening against the memory of that terrible place.

He wondered. And he saw that, whatever she might have said, it would not have changed a thing; that in any case he would never have believed her.

Ballindean, May 1802 / Jamaica, 1760

Sir John Wedderburn and Aeneas MacRoy had been for a walk around the loch. Sir John was surprised at how tired it had made him – it was barely a half-mile circuit, yet his legs felt shaky and his head light. Now they were back in the library. He was seated at his writing-table and MacRoy was updating him on the girls' progress at their lessons, but Sir John had other things on his mind and interrupted him.

'What do you think of that painting?'

MacRoy followed his glance. 'The big ane? You and your brithers in Jamaica?'

'Yes. What do you make of it?'

MacRoy shrugged. 'It's a fine big painting.'

'I was thinking of taking it down.'

'Aye, weel . . .'

'It irritates me.'

'It's been there a lang time.'

'Yes, that's why it irritates me. I feel like a change.'

'We could hae it doun in a minute. But whit would ye pit in its place?'

'I don't know. There are plenty of other paintings in the house. A landscape, perhaps. Something more Scottish.' He paused. 'But I would feel disloyal to my dead brothers if I removed it. I've told you one of them painted it?'

'Aye, Sir John.' MacRoy looked bored. They had discussed the painting in this manner often in the past.

'Loyalty, Aeneas. That's an item in short supply these days.'

MacRoy's eyes narrowed. 'Hae I displeased ye in onything?'

'You? No, not at all. I was speaking in a general way. I was thinking about the younger people today. Do you think they would come out for a cause as we did?'

'No. But the world is changed. We baith ken that.'

'Yes, I suppose so.' He sighed. 'Well, anyway, I have some

letters to write. I'm sure you're doing a fine job with my daughters' education. If there's nothing giving you cause for concern . . .'

'Everything is under control.'

'Good. That'll be all then, Aeneas, for now.'

'Very weel, Sir John.'

MacRoy slid out. Sir John felt only slightly guilty about his lack of interest in the girls' French verbs. Likewise, his letters: though he did have some to write, they were not urgent. Nothing much seemed urgent any more. He simply liked to be alone. Of late even MacRoy's formerly tolerable presence was becoming oppressive. The outside world made Sir John feel not only exhausted but nervous, as if it conspired against him. In here, among his books and papers, he felt its threat less acutely.

Funny how MacRoy had taken his remark about loyalty personally. Loyalty was a tricky concept, complex and yet fundamentally simple. Sir John had been loyal to the Stewart cause as a youth. Now, because his allegiance was to the Crown, it was also to the house of Hanover, and yet he did not feel like a traitor. Something had shifted but he did not feel compromised. Did Aeneas feel the same? Did he care? In a way, they were like the 'loyalists' back in the American Revolution. Many who had previously been Jacobites had steadfastly refused to become rebels against the mother country. But then, loyalty was not about revolution or rebellion. It was about honour.

This was why even now, so many years after it, he was always punctilious in describing the Forty-five as a *rising*. To call it a rebellion was to debase the cause and its motives, to make it sound like something quite different. He had never been a rebel; nor had his father. When he thought of rebels, he thought of slaves. He thought of Joseph Knight. He thought of Tacky.

In Jamaica, around Easter of 1760, he had begun to feel uneasy even as he surveyed yet another successful season for his plantations. He would wake in the night and listen for something beyond the chirking of the cicadas and the whine of mosquitoes. He could not identify the source of his disquiet. The fear of rebellion had always been there, like the night sounds. The words of the man on the Kingston waterfront would come back to him from time to time: 'We're at war with *them*.' But in

1760 the unease had been something more than habit. It had worried away at him like a touch of fever.

And yes, looking back from safe, cool Perthshire, he did associate rebellion with heat, as if it came *from* the heat, from tropical storms. Was that how it had been – an indefinable substance boiling up in clouds, seeping through the air as the rains approached? Or had he heard it in the conch-shell call that roused the slaves to work before dawn but that might also be a call to revolt? Had he smelt it in the sweat glistening on black backs; seen it flashing in the eyes of young men who would hesitate a second before carrying out some task; felt it in the sullenness of the young women? Had that been its sound rattling through the ripening cane fields, grumbling among the slave huts, whispering over the house roof at night?

There had been more visible signs. One morning, on the road to Savanna-la-Mar, he saw two slaves belonging to a neighbour, men known to him by sight, who had shaved their heads clean. Over the next few days, he saw others who had done the same. Women, too. This was something definite, something one could get hold of and worry about. There was some debate among the planters as to what it meant; talk of a cult or a conspiracy, of witchcraft, of obeah men concocting magic to ward off bullets, of strange rituals performed at night while the masters slept. Concerns were expressed about the preponderance of Coromantees in the district: they were powerful workers, but that made them dangerous too. Someone, possibly Underwood, made a remark that circulated with the unease: trouble among the slaves, wherever and whenever it broke out, started not in Jamaica, but in Africa.

There had been a kind of general delusion among the planters, Sir John thought. It was easy to see it from Ballindean, forty years on, especially after the business with Knight. Underwood had thought he knew his slaves. In a quite different way, John Wedderburn had thought he knew his. They had all thought it. But the truth was, slaves were unknowable. The so-called Coromantees were named after a place neither they nor their masters had ever been to. The Africa-born slaves had names and languages that ran like subterranean rivers beneath the surface names and the new language they acquired. They wore their faces like masks. How could they have been anything *but* unknowable?

Sir John remembered James making a joke in very bad taste one day, at a gathering of planters in Savanna – a meal at an inn to mark some occasion or other. What would that have been? The king's birthday perhaps? Yes, that was it, and James stood up and toasted 'The king over the water', and when some bullish English idiot challenged him – to be a Jacobite was still thought to incline a man to France – James very coolly said, 'But he is over the water, is he not? Surely we'd have heard if he was coming to Sav?' Everybody else laughed and eventually, after some muttering, the English bull did too. But that wasn't the real faux pas. It was later that James overreached himself.

The talk had turned to slave names. Somebody facetiously claimed to have the holiest plantation, because so many of his slaves – Abraham, Job, Ruth, Hannah, Moses – had Biblical names. And somebody else said he then must have the noblest, for all his slaves had Roman names. And a third man said that it didn't matter what polish you put on them, all the slaves had African names underneath, which meant, though the planters might think they were in the British West Indies, they must in fact all be planters in Dahomey. And James said, filling his glass: 'All those classical names we give them – Achilles, Hector, Nero, Plato –'

'Cato, Cassius,' a voice chipped in helpfully.

'Brutus.'

'Hannibal.'

'Dido.'

'Silvia.'

'Sibyl.'

'Quite.' James nodded his thanks for the contributions. 'Strange that the one name you never hear is the one that might fit best.'

'What's that? Stupidus?'

'Spartacus,' said James.

There was a gaping silence. Somebody knocked over a glass. James tapped cigar ash on to a plate, looked around with an innocent smile. He caught John shaking his head at him. Others were doing the same.

'I apologise, gentlemen,' he said at last, but still smiling serenely. 'It was just a thought.'

That was James through and through: always testing, pushing, upsetting people. The Jacobite toast might have led to a fight, but the Spartacus quip, invoking the name of the rebel slave who had almost destroyed ancient Rome, was far too serious for white men to scuffle over. A stranger hearing James on that occasion might have taken him for some kind of abolitionist, or a planter with a bad conscience at least. But no, James was beyond all such considerations. That was why he could come out with such a remark – the implications did not bother him at all. It was the others, some of them anyway, who had bad consciences.

Communication from one end of the island to the other was slow in 1760. It might take four days over land to Kingston, more in the wet season. Strange, then, to think that the Wedderburns' slaves knew something was afoot before their masters did. Or maybe not so strange. After all, they had a network between plantations and towns – between lovers, relatives, journeying craftsmen, runners of errands, children – that the whites had no access to.

Things were pretty slack in the days before the explosion. Slaves came and went with remarkable liberty. Some were like dogs, absenting themselves for a few days, knowing they would get a thrashing for it when they returned, but considering it worth it. Like dogs they almost scorned their punishments, severe though they were. How different, thinking back, every-thing was from how the planters thought it: yes, they held the slaves in bondage, yes, they controlled their lives – but under the surface, even in the unshaded light of day, it was the black population that ran the place. A hundred and sixty thousand slaves on the island, and barely sixteen thousand whites: how could it be otherwise? Nothing could function without them.

This had been the source of John Wedderburn's fear, that year when Tacky's war broke out: the knowledge that at all times, every hour of every season, day and night, only a hair's breadth separated the planters' immense prosperity from its utter destruction.

There were three big young men in the great gang at Glen Isla –

Mungo, Cuffy and Charlie. John Wedderburn had bought them two years before and seasoned them with care, put them to work only when they were ready. They were a team, fine glistening men with an easy strength that seemed to eat up whatever task they were given. John admired them and liked to think that they admired him. Usually they were open-faced and cheerful, often singing at their work, but two weeks after Easter they appeared one morning with heads clean-shaven and mouths set tight, silent, refusing to look the Wedderburns in the eye. Sandy was at Glen Isla at the time, recuperating from one of his many bouts of sickness. John tried to coax the slaves out of their mood.

'What's the matter, Charlie? Why you shave your head?'

'Me not know, massa.'

This seemed such a foolish answer that it made John and Sandy laugh.

'You not know? You did it and you don't know why?'

'Me not do it, massa.'

'Who, then?'

'Me do it.' This was Mungo. 'Then Charlie do Cuffy, Cuffy do me.'

'But why?'

'It mek mi hat fit,' said Charlie unconvincingly, and put his wide-brimmed hat on to prove the point.

'Then why no smile? What's the matter?'

Charlie looked at the ground. Sandy turned to the others. 'Why is he not smiling?'

Mungo looked at Cuffy. Cuffy half shrugged. Neither spoke.

John said, 'If I give him a whipping, then I'll find out why. You want a whipping, Charlie?'

'No, massa.'

'Then why you not smile?'

'Not feel well.'

'You not feel well either, Mungo? Cuffy? You all sick?'

Cuffy nodded his head very slowly. 'Yes, massa, we all sick,' he said. 'We all sick and we all tired.'

Sandy exchanged a glance with John and laughed. 'Is that all?'

Silence.

112

'They're just idle,' Sandy said. There was no response.

'Well, Crop Over soon come,' John said, not wishing to prolong matters. 'Then you all get rest. Now go to work.'

The three men ambled off to join the rest of the gang.

Sandy grinned at John. 'Imbeciles.'

'Aye,' said John. 'Let's hope so anyway.' He felt almost sorry for Charlie. The others seemed to be leading him on. Charlie reminded him of somebody. He couldn't think who for a minute, until he realised that it was Sandy, always waiting for a cue, always looking for approval. John was shocked – that his own brother should have any resemblance to a black man.

That was the day the first news filtered in from St Mary's parish, eighty miles to the north-east. Mr Hodge rode up from Savanna in a lather, having spent the morning listening to a man who had come from the capital, Spanish Town, with the most incredible story. Hodge told it to John and Sandy on the porch of the house at Glen Isla. A few days after Easter a hundred Coromantees on two estates in St Mary had risen up, headed for Port Maria and broken into the arsenal there, killing the sentinel. Armed with guns and ammunition, they had moved from one plantation to another, firing the cane and buildings, and killing anyone, white or black, who tried to stop them. Other slaves, in groups of a dozen, twenty, thirty, had joined them. Their leader was a Gold Coast man called Tacky.

Hodge was short on hard facts but replete with horror stories. Overseers and owners were being slaughtered by the score, their hearts cut out and eaten, their blood drunk. Loyal slaves were being horribly beaten, mutilated and dismembered, white women were being raped fifty times before having their throats slit. The merchant's eyes popped at the thought. John Wedderburn filled him with rum.

'And this Spanish Town man, he witnessed all this?'

'No, no,' said Hodge. 'But he had it from the survivors. The whole parish is ablaze.'

Sandy Wedderburn had turned pale. 'And the militia?' he asked. 'The regular troops? Where are they? Are they not engaging them?'

John made a calming motion with his hand.

'Yes, indeed,' said Hodge breathlessly. 'They are out after them now. As soon as word got to Spanish Town, the Council met in emergency session. An infantry detachment set off for St Mary's by way of Archer's Ridge, another was sent from Port Royal, and a third from Kingston. Martial law is declared – the militia is out too, yes, indeed. And they've sent for the Maroons of that district. They're a cowardly lot but they know better than to side with the slaves.'

'The Maroons are not cowards,' Sandy said, with sudden vehemence. 'Are they, John?'

'No,' said John, 'they are not. You should know better, Mr Hodge.'

The Maroons represented something difficult and contra-dictory in Jamaican life: blacks who were free – symbolic to the slaves, defiant of whites, but distinct from both and careful to maintain the distinction. They had fought the British to a standstill in the thirties and established their independence and freedom in the mountain areas by formal treaty. In return they had agreed not to accept runaway slaves into their towns, and to support the British in defending the island against invasion or slave rebellion.

Hodge turned pink and swallowed more rum. 'The fact is,' he said sulkily, 'that the island is turned upside down because of this Tacky and his rabble.'

'I suspect there's little to fash about,' John said. 'Eh, Sandy? It has taken ten days for this news to reach us. In all probability the worst of it is already over, and the ringleaders are dead or in irons.'

Hodge was disappointed by this cool reaction. 'But Savanna is in an uproar,' he insisted. 'The militia is to be called out at once, all absent slaves notified to the authorities, all landowners to report –'

'Wait, wait, wait,' John said. 'Where is the policy in uproar? If we panic, we'll encourage any hotheads who might be thinking of trouble. If life goes on as normal, they will hear rumours but before they know whether to act on them they will hear a certainty – that the revolt is crushed.'

'I do think these are more than rumours, sir,' Hodge said. 'I have heard them myself. And in any event, surely a show of strength –'

'Go back to Mrs Hodge,' said John. 'She is doubtless much exercised by what she has heard. Give *her* your show of strength. And our regards, sir. You should be at her side.'

'Yes, yes, well, perhaps you're right.' Hodge brightened again at the prospect of a frantic dash home to his wife. There was something heroic in galloping to and fro. And what news he would bring of the state of unpreparedness he had found up country! The Wedderburns virtually asking to be butchered in their beds! He knocked back the last of his rum. 'I shall set off at once. There's an hour yet before dark.'

Once he was gone, John turned to his brother. 'Now, Sandy, this doesn't alter what I've just said to Mr Hodge, but I want you to ride down to Bluecastle and tell James what we have heard. Leave out the hysterics, but have him see if any of his slaves are missing. I'll do the same here. Tell him to make certain of all his guns. We're as well to be safe as not.'

But both plantations were quiet. For the next few weeks the rebellion touched them only in the form of more tales of thousands of slaves rampaging through the windward parishes, of Maroon hunting parties retreating under heavy fire, of British troops ambushed and cut to ribbons. The name Tacky grew like a thundercloud over these stories.

The Westmoreland planters gathered in the last of their sugar crop against the impending rainy season. The first of the downpours turned the naked cane fields into mud. John Wedderburn was still confident, with each passing day, that the revolt would not spread to leeward. Then, in the week of Whitsun, Hodge's lurid nightmares came true.

Sandy was still at Glen Isla. He was making sketches of different aspects of the plantation – the house, the factory, the slave village, the gangs at work in the fields. His draughtsmanship was competent but lifeless, but John was happy to leave him to it. It would be a record of a kind, and at least gave Sandy a role that nobody else claimed. The trouble was, he believed himself much better than he was. He wanted John to sit for his portrait.

The two Wedderburns were got out of their beds one night by a partly furious, partly frightened Phoebe. She had heard gunfire in the distance. The three of them stepped out on to the porch.

Over westward, rising from the plains, a red glow fringed the edge of the hills. John sniffed. 'What is that?'

They all stood sniffing. Faint at first, but growing stronger every minute, a thick, rich, sweet smell. It became pungent and overwhelming. It was the smell of burning sugar.

They sat up till morning, waiting for something to happen.

At dawn a party of soldiers rode up to the house. Phoebe supplied them with breakfast washed down with rum and water grog. They had been out all night. Some miles away, a Captain Forrest's slaves had risen: they had killed Forrest's attorney and overseer while they were at their supper. Whole barns packed with barrels of sugar had been torched. Slaves from three more plantations had also taken off, looting, setting buildings alight and arming themselves with guns and machetes. A different detachment of troops had been attacked. One man had been badly chopped, two others had had narrow escapes. The soldiers drank all the grog, then their officer announced that they had to get back to Savanna, to prepare for another night on patrol.

There was something almost comic about the way the whites took to careering around the countryside. Half of them were full of bravado, half of them of fear, and nearly all of them were drunk. Some days, Peter joined in, taking Sandy with him. Peter was in his element: he was a good horseman, and a fair marksman. Sandy was far from happy, but, urged on by Peter, he went anyway. The older brothers thought that it might do him good. He was so nervy, so frail, so easily brought down by the heat, so seldom confident in his dealings with the blacks. Perhaps dashing about with Peter would toughen him up.

John and James remained on the plantations. Over the next day or two, it became clear that the situation was serious. Smoke drifted across their land. A dozen white people had been killed in the vicinity, and several hundred slaves were reported out. Some planters were forced to abandon their property and take refuge with neighbours. Tom Irvine's entire workforce ransacked his house and destroyed it. He escaped into the woods and was found by militiamen next day, minus his trousers, his feet cut to ribbons. The men who brought him in thought he had gone insane. But he had not. He was simply in pain, and incandescent with rage that his slaves had ruined his life.

116

At Glen Isla at this time, apart from whichever Wedderburns were present, there were only two white men left – the others had been called up by the militia. The two were Wilson, the bookkeeper, and Brownlee, who oversaw the gangs and supervised the black slave-drivers. Phoebe could also be trusted, but Jacob and Julius would be no match for the field slaves, and the house lassies could not be depended upon – they were always in an intrigue with some man or other. It seemed a very thin line of defence.

'And yet we have gone for years turning our backs on men armed with knives and axes,' John said to James, who had come up from Bluecastle to discuss the situation. 'I've taken a couple of them shooting, shown them how to prime and fire a gun. We let them come and go freely enough. We are fair masters. We only punish them when they are bad. Why should they turn on us now?'

'Old Underwood would say – no, not him, he's too soft – Geordie Kinloch would say, that you have just volunteered yourself to be slaughtered. Why should they turn on us now? For the very reason that you have asked the question – your guard is down. You don't believe them capable of rising against you? That is treating them as men like yourself. A fatal error, brother. So George Kinloch would tell you.'

'What do you think?'

'You know me. I have no sentiment when it comes to negers. It is a matter of economy. I'm inclined to agree with George, but I will say this: you know your own negers better than he does.'

'That's what I was thinking. I'm going to put it to the test. I intend to arm the best men I have here, and have them protect us and themselves from destruction.'

James nodded. 'Well, you'll not be the only one. Which slaves do you have in mind?'

'Mungo, Cuffy, Charlie. Some others.'

'Fine boys, fine boys. But they're still negers after all. Keep a spare loaded musket in your closet, John.'

James headed back to Bluecastle. In the evening John summoned Brownlee, opened a bottle of rum for him, and told him his plans. Brownlee was a decent man, strict but not malicious to the slaves. He was not keen at first – thought it very risky in the current atmosphere. The entire plantation was talking about the revolt. John pressed his case. It was precisely for this reason that they had to seize the initiative. What were their options? Four white men, however well organised, could not stay awake for ever, could not fend off forty or fifty Coromantees if it came to that. Arm eight of the best slaves, divide the watch among John, Sandy, Brownlee and Wilson with two negers apiece, offer them rewards for their loyalty and remind them of the terrible punishments that would, sooner or later, be the lot of the rebels. It was the surest way to keep the place calm and undamaged and themselves alive. John Wedderburn had no intention of seeing all his industry go, like Tom Irvine's, up in smoke. Brownlee at last agreed that he might be right.

'We'll start in the morning,' John said. 'My brother is due back from patrol this evening. He and I will get the guns ready. Tomorrow, have the gangs go out as usual, but we'll bring the men we want up here to the house. I want Mungo, Cuffy and Charlie – we'll turn their coats before they think of it themselves. I'll write down some other names. You'll have some ideas yourself, I expect.'

In the end, the experiment was never tried, for two reasons. When Sandy rode in an hour later, the first story he told was of a planter over by Broughton, who had had the same idea two days before. He had paraded twenty of his best slaves in front of his house, given them a speech along the lines outlined by John to Brownlee, and armed them with muskets, whereupon they had had a brief discussion among themselves, assured him they meant him no harm, thanked him for the weaponry, saluted him with a wave of their hats and marched off to join their rebel brothers. At Savanna a decree had been issued, with immediate effect, that no slaves were to be given guns, and that none was to be permitted off a plantation without a valid ticket from his master explaining the reason for his journey. Any slave found without a ticket would be taken into custody and the owner fined.

The second reason was that, in the morning, John's three Coromantees, and another dozen slaves, all men, were discovered to have left Glen Isla during the night.

Brownlee and Wilson now went about their duties permanently armed. Sandy rode up the road into the hills and reported it busy with parties of mounted militia and foot soldiers, cautiously probing north towards Montego Bay. Others were escorting miserable-looking batches of captured rebels south to Savanna. Jolting laboriously in the same direction were wagons loaded with the prize possessions (and the wives and children if they had them) of shocked planters, bound for the relative safety of the town. Sandy went with the northbound troops for a few miles, saw several burnt-out planters' houses, counted fourteen black corpses hanging from trees at the roadside. These ones had been summarily executed and strung up as a warning. Those taken prisoner could expect less merciful treatment.

At the end of May a man-of-war was in the roadstead at Savanna, and offloaded a hundred and twenty men of His Majesty's 49th Regiment. They joined a company of the 74th, a fairly full complement of the Westmoreland Militia, and two detachments of Maroons. Troops had also arrived to bolster the militia on the north coast, at Lucea and Montego Bay. These forces now began to move inland, sweeping the country before them, driving the rebels back into the central highlands and forests. All four Wedderburns now took turns out with the militia. It was, John thought, their duty to do so.

The rebels were hard to dislodge from their bolt-holes in the woods and hills. They were well organised and well armed. This was 'look behind' country, where a man could easily give pursuers the slip among trees and through gullies. When the fight was taken to the rebels, they either melted away or put up such resistance that the troops withdrew. Colonel Cudjoe, the Maroon leader, made the best progress, a fact which was galling to the white officers. This went on throughout June and July. But gradually the number of slaves still out was being whittled down. It was increasingly hard for them to get provisions, and they were using up their ammunition hunting for food. Each day now, parties of them were found hanging in the woods, having taken their own lives rather than surrender. Sometimes bloody heaps of women and children were found on the ground in the same places, slaughtered by their men. The white soldiers considered this a mark of African bestiality.

Very few slaves gave themselves up voluntarily. One by one, the missing Glen Isla men were accounted for. Mungo was found hanged. Soon only Charlie and Cuffy were still out there, either free or dead.

In the east of the island, normality had all but been restored. The mighty Tacky had been run down and shot by a Maroon. His head was displayed on a pole on the highway to Spanish Town. In the west, another rebel leader – called Wager by his white master, Apongo by his black comrades – was wounded in a skirmish on the Cabarita river, and taken to Savanna for trial.

There, retribution was already underway. Slow-burning and hanging in chains were among the recommended methods of punishment. Both were ordered for Apongo, reputedly once a prince in his homeland, now a parcel of meat for the executioner: three days of hanging, then burning from the feet up. He was, in a sense, lucky: he died of his wounds on the second day, before they could take him down.

Every day during most of July, Savanna was the scene of such spectacles. A few townsfolk complained – about the smell. The outlying white population made visits to the square where the executions took place: it was not enough that justice was done, it had to be seen to be done. Some brought slaves to watch, knowing that they would tell their friends what they had witnessed.

In August, the Wedderburns got word that their Cuffy was taken, along with another three men. John and James travelled down to Savanna. There was no question of trying to save him, even had they wished to. No question either that he would be found guilty and condemned to death. But it was customary for a master to exchange farewells with one of his slaves before execution. It was a necessary end to a relationship that had gone wrong. Closure. And the slave might have a last request, or wish to apologise, or simply be glad to see a familiar face. Never let it be said that the system was without a measure of humanity.

Likewise it was customary to provide the condemned man with a good meal. This was to give him sustenance for his long days on the gibbet. Cuffy and two of his comrades were not known to have killed anyone, nor were they leaders, so they

120

were spared the fire. The fourth man, found guilty of inciting others to rebel and of killing a soldier, was to be burnt.

The gibbet was shaped like a huge H on a platform. From the crossbeam were suspended three contraptions like seven-foot-high birdcages. Cuffy and the other two were given some bread and cheese and a mug of grog each, then they were strung up in chains within these cages and hoisted above the crowd. There they were to hang, without further food or water, naked except for loincloths, through the blazing days and the humid, mosquito-thick nights, until they died.

On the second day the Wedderburns stood beneath the gibbet and called up.

'Cuffy!'

'Why did you do it, Cuffy?'

Cuffy craned his head down towards their voices. His eyes were puffed and weeping, barely open at all. His tongue was swollen, which made it hard for them to understand him.

'That you, massa?'

'It's me, Cuffy. Why did you do it?'

'I tole you, massa . . . I tole you back then. Me sick, me tired.'

John shouted back. 'No, not your head, you fool. Why did you go out?'

'The same. Me sick, me tired. Go out, get better.'

On the third day they brought out the man who was to be burnt. He was stapled to the ground by a series of hoops hammered in over his arms and legs, till he was quite unable to move anything but his head. A couple of silent, hooded men built a fire near the man's feet. Then they applied brands to his left foot. It twitched, began to blister and to give off a greasy smoke. The man's head twisted back and forth, but he did not utter a sound. Cuffy and one of the other men on the gibbet called encouragingly to him in words the white people did not understand. The third one hung motionless, head on chest, oblivious to the proceedings, to anything but his own suffering.

John was keen to get back to Glen Isla. It was James who had insisted that they wait another day, to see if Cuffy survived till morning, to see the start of the burning. They had spent the night in a Savanna tavern. John's head was sore. The sun was making

121

him dizzy. The executioners, unable to bear the heat, had long since removed their hoods. They were brutal-looking men, white ex-convicts who had traded their own deaths to become butchers of slaves.

'What you saying now, Cuffy?' James asked.

'Me tell mi brudder, this day he be in Africa. That's where I be gwan, that's where we all be gwan.'

John turned away. 'I've had enough,' he said to James. 'Are you coming with me?'

'You go on,' said James quietly. 'I'll come later. I'll stay with Cuffy a while.'

But he was not looking at Cuffy. He was staring at the staked-out man, who still had neither spoken nor cried out, whose left foot was now a charred stump. James hunkered down, watching intently. His face displayed no emotion. John walked away.

The plantation was like a grave that evening. Brownlee and Wilson were sitting on the porch of the great house, muskets primed and within easy reach, drinking porter and swatting at mosquitoes. John was exhausted. He exchanged a few words with them, said they were welcome to sleep at the house till things were back to normal. Then he went inside to bed.

James did not return the next day, nor the next. It was only at the end of the fifth day since Cuffy had been put up on the gibbet that he appeared, grimy with dust and looking as though he had not slept all week. This was not far from the truth.

'He's gone,' he said. He and John were sitting out where Brownlee and Wilson had been two nights before, drinking again. Sometimes it seemed drink was the only thing that was a constant in their lives; that without it they would cease to exist. 'He died this afternoon. One of the others is still alive, just. Their courage is almost equal to their stupidity.'

'I could not thole it,' said John. 'I am sick of this slaughter.'

'They brought it on themselves. I have no sympathy for them. They know that too. We have had no trouble at Bluecastle.' He gave John a glance, briefly critical. 'But I do admire their courage. The one they burnt never uttered a word.'

John shook his head. He did not want to hear about it, but in the gloom James did not see the gesture, or chose not to.

'I watched them burn their way up both his legs and one half of one arm, over the course of an hour or two. He never groaned or spoke at all, yet they kept him conscious all the while, with water and spirits. I would not have believed it had I not seen it. Then one of them got too close. Somehow he got his remaining hand free, snatched at the brand the fellow was holding and threw it at his face.' He gave a short, dry laugh of amazement. 'We all applauded him, those of us still there, and they strangled him. It was almost as if he had won.'

'I cannot think how you could bear to watch it.'

'I have seen worse,' said James.

Silence, except for the ceaseless cicadas. John thought about what he had just heard. He knew they were both thinking of the same thing, their father's death.

'Was it really worse than that?' he asked.

James said, 'This was only a neger.' Then, his voice suddenly weak with fatigue, he went on, 'If it's all the same to you, I'll not go back to Bluecastle tonight. It's been quite an ordeal. I'll stop here if I may.'

'You are welcome. You know you are always welcome.'

In the morning, over a late breakfast, James was much recovered. He had borrowed a razor and shaved, washed most of the dirt off his face. He was, John knew, easily the more handsome of the pair of them.

'Now,' James said. 'Business again. There is ground to be made up. You must restock.'

'What?'

'You must restock with the greatest speed and the least cost. How many have you lost?'

'Slaves, you mean?'

'Of course.'

'Twelve.'

'You'll be due compensation, for those that did not kill themselves that is. You must get your claim in early, ahead of the rush. The St Mary's people will already be lodging their petitions. There's a loss, of course, bound to be – I doubt the Assembly will pay more than forty pound a head for an executed slave – but it's better than nothing, and will help when you buy fresh. I never thought of it, but a crushed

123

rebellion must be good for the slave ships, must quicken the market.'

'James, you never fail to astonish me. I have not thought so far ahead.'

'It is not far at all. If you buy now, you'll not be able to use the new negers fully till they're seasoned. That's next year. You're short of twelve Coromantees. That's a serious deficiency.'

'Eleven, till Charlie's found.'

'Ah, Charlie, yes. Do you know, are there any of the slaves executed so far whose owners are not known?'

'Not that I am aware.'

'You could put in a claim if we were certain of them. Well, perhaps not. You had better not risk it. But Charlie is another matter.'

'He's dead, I should think. Rotting on a tree somewhere.'

'Well, if that's the case, let's be clear it was not his own doing, but that he was hanged on the spot. Sandy can vouch for it – saw the militia or the Maroons do it. Then, if Charlie *should* come back, and assuming you've not declared him as absent – you've not, have you? –'

'I never thought Charlie would rebel. It was against his character. The others urged him to it, I'm sure . . .' Again he caught that sharp look that James had given him the night before. 'No, I've not declared him.'

'Then the price of Charlie staying alive, which he is sure to accept, is that he ceases to be Charlie. Give him a new name when they call for a full registration. That's coming too, John, when this is over – the island has had a grievous shock. That way you may get forty pound for the old Charlie, and a life of labour from the new one.'

'It's somewhat irregular . . .'

James burst out laughing. 'This rebellion is irregular! For God's sake, John, Jamaica is irregular, this whole life is irregular! Do you think you'll be the only one making false returns? Were you not already considering it, by not listing Charlie as an absentee? Or were you going soft on him?'

'Not soft, no. But I believe he went against his will.'

'Take that to its logical conclusion, John, and there's an end to slavery tomorrow. We must let them all go home to Africa,

124

because they went from there against their will. Suppress your qualms, brother. You've done your duty in this affair, you've been out with the militia, we all have. You're a respected man, nobody will dare question your returns. For one slave? You could put in for a further dozen and nobody would challenge you.'

'Well, we shall see.'

James stood up to go. 'Do it, John,' he said. 'Do not waver. I can read you like a book. If you waver, you will lose everything.'

Late in August Charlie did come back, as John Wedderburn had guessed he would, as he had even hoped. He slunk in one night and in the morning tried to join the great gang as if nothing had happened, as if he had been there throughout those three months. Brownlee immediately threw him in fetters and sent word to the house.

Sir John, in his library at Ballindean, safe from the outside world, could remember seeing Charlie prostrate in the mud, the irons on his strong ankles and wrists, fear on his face. 'Are you sorry?' he had asked him. And a string of other questions: 'What am I going to do with you? Where have you been? What have you done? Have you hurt anyone? Killed anyone? Stolen anything? Do you know what will happen to you if I hand you in? Do you know what *should* happen to you?' And on and on. To each question, Charlie made apologetic, humble replies. He had to. He understood, they both understood, that he had no choice. The mere fact that his master was bothering to ask the questions . . .

Brownlee was against it. The other slaves knew who he was, knew he had been out. It would set a bad example. It would show too much leniency for the worst of crimes.

But there was leniency and leniency. 'I do not intend to make this easy for him,' John Wedderburn told Brownlee. He felt that he should not have to justify himself to the overseer.

His brother's words were still in his ears. James's motivation for saving Charlie was purely financial – it was, literally, about saving money. But for John there was more. Charlie did not remind him only of Sandy: he reminded him of himself. A man went out for a while, and came back to find that the world had changed for ever.

'Your name is Newman,' John told Charlie. 'You hear me? Your name is Newman. I never want to hear of Charlie again. I hear of Charlie, I find Charlie. I turn him in. You understand? You are Newman now. Understand?'

Newman understood.

Then John said to Brownlee, 'This Newman is a bad fellow. I want the badness flogged out of him. Fifty stripes, salt in the wounds. Today. The same next week. Every week till he has had five hundred stripes. He'll not be a bad example. He'll be a good one.'

Sir John remembered seeing the neger quail. His lips moved, as if he wanted to say something. John Wedderburn cut him off: 'You are lucky to be allowed to live.'

Sometimes the library was not so safe. It contained shadows. The books seemed to move on the shelves. Outside was warm and bright, with a fine southerly breeze blowing. It would be better to be outside, walking without a purpose. But his legs wouldn't take it. He couldn't get round the loch without several rests. Come the winter, he would be stuck where he was, in a room full of ghosts and pictures.

And there was worse. Lately, Sir John had been finding himself forgetting the things he intended to do. It was deeply disturbing, like coming into a room and finding yourself already there. Or expecting to see someone who had been long dead, then remembering their death, then seeing them anyway. And there was *something*, what was it, something he had been mean-ing to do for weeks. Something connected with Jamaica, with Charlie . . .

Sandy. Poor Sandy had been appalled by what he had learned from John and James of the executions in Savanna. He had hated the details, but had wanted them over and over. And James had given them to him, fed Sandy's fascination. A bad sign. Sir John wished he had spotted it. But he had not read Sandy's journal till it was far, far too late.

He opened the third drawer down on the left of the writing-table, rummaged among the papers there, his fingers seeking for the familiar shape, the soft calf cover of his dead brother's journal. After a minute, exasperated at his own slowness, he pulled the entire drawer out and emptied the contents on to the table. His hands pushed aside accounts, letters, a magnifying glass, a memorandum book, visiting cards – clearing a path through the accretions of his life to Sandy's journal.

It was not there.

Dundee, May 1802

Archibald Jamieson ate breakfast at eight o'clock, alone as always. Sliced ham, bread and honey, coffee, a wee spark of whisky to set the day going. The boys were away out, and Mrs Jamieson seldom rose before midday. She was not a strong woman, not a well woman. Jamieson told himself this often, to remind himself why he must not lose patience with her. But he had been patient for so long – almost since the day they were married, it seemed. Which was now – he pondered for a second, knife poised above the honeycomb, as if he did not know precisely already, as if there was someone else in the room who had asked him – fifteen years past. His first wife Mary had given him five children in seven years, expiring with the stillborn sixth. Janet – he had married her six months later – had managed only two in twice as long, and both of them dead within a year. Nor could he expect any more now, as their sporadic marital conjugations had come to a complete end some while ago. To compensate, he made weekly, paying visits to a woman in Pirie's Land from whom he was assured there would be no embarrassing disclosures and (he had mixed feelings about this) no bairns. The day he met Susan Wedderburn, it had been this woman, not some mysterious man, he had been to see.

His eldest son was a midshipman in the navy; his daughters were married and mothers themselves; his younger sons were scholars at the grammar school. Mary's bairns. He was so proud of them all. Yet the new Mrs Jamieson – he thought of her as that still, even after fifteen years – was wearied by his family. She insisted that the boys quell their noise in the house and complained about the cost and bother of clothing and feeding them, although she had precious little to do with either activity.

The maid, Betty Fraser, took care of all that. Ugly as a soo's snoot, Betty, but Jamieson sometimes cast a covetous eye over her extensive rump. She could give him more bairns, no question, and mother them well too. Not that he needed more. Why this obsession with increasing his offspring? He had fine sons, daughters, grandchildren – and never enough siller to pay for them all. But he couldn't help it: he loved bairns, loved the noise and mess and heat of them. Sometimes he wished they were all Egyptians, brown as nuts, tumbling around the country in a cart, camping out on the shores of lochs, catching a fish or a rabbit or two, and scraping a living out of tin and woodwork. The tinklarian life, as he had heard someone describe it the other day. He'd like that, and the lads would too. It would be romantic. But the new Mrs Jamieson – she'd die of fright at the mere suggestion.

It was romance that had attracted him to Janet fifteen years before. She had been such a contrast to Mary, who had been all rosy-cheeked practicality, soap and bustle, never happier than when she had a bairn wriggling in her arms and two more crawling under her feet. He had adored Mary, especially because of the gift of their children, but there had been nothing intriguing or alluring, and certainly nothing difficult about her. Mary had been exactly the way she appeared. Janet Hunter had been quite another proposition: willowy, pale, quiet-spoken, conscious of her looks and of the effect they had on him, yet not vain. She was the third daughter of a lawyer who occasionally gave Jamieson work, and who to his immense surprise had not objected when he began to pay Janet visits. In fact the father had been a good deal more encouraging than she, who had given no sign that she might be responsible for the healing of the wounded heart of Archibald Jamieson, and certainly had seemed astonished when he proposed to her after only a few weeks. Was it not too soon after his wife's death, she had asked. Was he certain of his feelings? What made him hopeful of hers? It was as if she were conducting an interview on behalf of a third person, the true object of his intentions. He fumbled through his answers, and his awkwardness seemed to make her warm to him. She asked for a week to consider, during which time there should be no contact at all.

She was testing the depth of his desire. He did not realise how much he had fallen for her. By the sixth day he was practically drowning in love, half demented with fear that she would turn him down. Her father, meeting him in the street that day, apologised for his daughter and for Archibald having to tolerate such obduracy. This, he lamented, was the way of the modern world, where young women thought it amusing or their right not to be at once grateful for any offer of marriage they were made. But on the seventh day, Janet smiled peacefully and accepted him.

Leaving his children in the care of Betty Fraser, they had a two-day honeymoon in Montrose, the most dreamlike two days Archie Jamieson had ever experienced. And that was – had been – the thing about Janet: she was a lily, a singing bird, a shepherdess from some pastoral poem. But like most pale, poetic shepherdesses she was fond neither of animals nor the countryside. It also became very clear that she looked her best, and was best company, when unencumbered with bairns, bills, domestic crises or even domestic normality. Within two years, and despite Archie's endless efforts to ease her sense of oppression, the life went out of their marriage as it went out of her two babies, and Mr and Mrs Jamieson settled into a kind of routine of evasion.

And so it had been ever since. They never fought, they never made love (not, at least, with each other), they talked only of things that it was necessary to talk of in order for the routine to continue. He spent long days away at work, she spent long mornings in bed, and at night occupied herself with sewing or reading a book. Archie wondered how it could have come to this: he could still feel the kick of his heart from the week she kept him waiting. But there never seemed to be time now to make things better between them, perhaps because things never seemed to be quite bad enough. It was his hope that when, in a year or so, his youngest boy left school, he and the new Mrs Jamieson would be able to make a fresh start. What he did not know was whether she had the same hope. Nor did he know whether he would be able to bring himself to end his excursions to Pirie's Land before the fresh start was tried.

Meanwhile, the work went on. He had begun as a clerk for the town council thirty years before, a bright lad quick at copying and sums, then had moved into legal work, impressing his employers with his dogged ability to persevere at the worm-like syntax and intricate minutiae of memorials, assignations, petitions, protestations, representations, missives, mandates and obligatours. But clerkship also involved running errands and seeking out information, and Archie had found this far more stimulating. Over the years he had developed the excavation of facts as an independent sideline, and while he still turned in a fair number of pages every week for this lawyer or that, he preferred the less regular, more risky – financially and physically – side of his work. He was a kind of primitive detective. It might never make him rich, but it kept him agile.

He was not always proud of what he did, but, as he used to tell himself, pride came before a fall so he was as well not to be. The sneaking, snooving side of his work was hardly manly, and it had brought a couple of beatings down on his head. The alarm over the United Scotsmen, his having to delve deep into the plots of disaffected weavers – that had involved him in deceit and trickery and he was glad that, for the time being at least, the political situation had quietened.

He was no radical. He was a king's man, a Scotsman and a Briton. He could see the other point of view, and he wished no ill on any man for speaking his mind, but he believed in a settled constitution and, by and large, that the propertied classes knew what they were about. That was how they had become propertied. Although there were exceptions. There were exceptions to any rule.

Betty came in with a fresh pot of coffee and laid a package down on the table at his elbow. 'A laddie jist cam by wi that,' she said.

He picked it up, inspected the seal.

'The penny post laddie?'

'Is there a penny stamped on it?' She looked at him as if at an idiot, a look he found strangely comforting. 'Na, jist a street laddie.'

'Still there?'

'He was halfway doun the street afore I had the door open. So it'll be some o your mischievous business that's in it.' She gave the package a stare not dissimilar to the one she had given him, and went out again.

There was something special about a delivery one was not expecting. Jamieson delayed the moment of opening, lengthening the pleasure of anticipation. It was a neat, small package but it also somehow had *bulk*. The address was written in a feminine hand. The dripped wax of the seal did not bear a sender's mark. He broke it open. Inside was a brief note:

I told you I had found Mr K. He was hiding in my father's writing-desk. My uncle – Alexander, the one that did the painting, not James – has told me all about him. We always understood it was yellow fever killed uncle A. but it was not that alone – what do you think?

When I saw you in Dundee I had not read this fully but only glanced at it. The wickedness and cruelty of life in the plantations I always suspected but now I know. The horrors of how they lived are beyond what I can express.

I don't think Mr K. will be missed. My father is very wandered of late. Start at March of 1762.

You must try to find him.

S.W.

He unwrapped, from a piece of (he sniffed) slightly scented linen, what appeared to be a private journal. Old, yellowing pages, the ink faded badly in places. Did it count as stolen property? Borrowed, perhaps. One thing was sure: he could not return it to its rightful owner, who, it would appear, did not know it was gone. Jamieson sipped his coffee, glanced at the opening pages:

1760
Tuesday, 1st January. Blewcastle. This day I ressolve to make note of events both interesting & dull, so as not to forget them. I am here 6 years now and can not mind one yr from an other so this will be my task to do so. Also it may impruve my riting which is none too strong.

Drank in the Yr with James & Peter. Head now like a drum. No more to rite here.

Wednesday, 2nd January. Peter's birth day. He is 24. We

drunk his health – John, James, I, Dav. Fyfe. James made
him gift of the house maid Nesta for the night. I had her
at Christmas but did not say.

Saturday, 12th January. Wt James & Peter shooting duck
at the river. We got 10 brase of coot but the moskitos
plaged us terible.

Saturday, 19th January. To Savanna with John &
Peter where we train with the milisher. We rode down
ystrdy & stayd at Mr Hodge. Wt his lady there we was
best behaved. In the morning exercises & drill outside
the town. John as an offiser and one of the few thats
been in a war is disapointd with state of the foot which
is composd mostly of town folk & book kepers. You
never saw a stranger mix of jackits & britches posing
as uniforms. If not for the carabines muskats & sords a
plenty among us we wd put little fear in the Negroes and
none in the French.
   Herd that Tom Irvine very sick wt the gowt & dropsy.
It is not lookd for him to live long with the rainy season
aproaching. England wd treat him more kindly but Peter
says he can never go back to England as the ladies ther
wd object to him shitting in the parler.

Jamieson found all this only mildly interesting. The debase-
ments of the plantocracy, he suspected, had probably changed
little in forty years. But no wonder Susan was shocked – the word
'shitting' written in her uncle's hand; the nocturnal services of
Nesta. How these old words would jump from the page in the
douce surroundings of Ballindean!
   Reading the journal would presumably have washed some of
the gloss off her view of the world. It would certainly confirm her
distaste for slavery. Perhaps she had copied out passages ready
to quote at anti-slavery meetings. Then again, such meetings
would have to exist. Public demonstrations against slavery were
not exactly common in Dundee. Jamieson had heard of Quakers
and Methodists ranting and frothing in Bristol and Liverpool, but
there had never been anything like that here. Ladies wrote to

their friends asking them to abstain from buying cloth dyed with indigo, or drinking coffee, or eating sugar – that was about the extent of the agitation.

As Jamieson had admitted to Miss Wedderburn, he had never thought much about slavery, and he reckoned he was typical. An abolitionist tract had come into his hand recently, in a coffee shop of all places. It had been headlined SLAVERY POISONS EVERY LIFE IT TOUCHES. He had skimmed through it, found it rational, and put it aside. If that is true, he had thought at the time, we are all poisoned, each and every one of us. And Miss Susan Wedderburn, he thought now, and all her brothers and sisters, had been poisoned since birth.

He tried to analyse her motivation in sending him the journal. Why would she expect him to be interested? Why would she want a stranger to know the secrets of her family? Was this her way of easing the guilt? But why choose him, Archibald Jamieson?

The answer came back at once: *because* he was an outsider, nothing to do with Ballindean or the Jamaica plantations. She needed him like a doctor. She wanted him to extract the poison.

Well, he would not do it. The Wedderburns, father and daughter, could do their own dirty work.

Archibald Jamieson sat tapping the journal with his fingers for fully two minutes. He looked at her note again. Joseph Knight was in the journal, she said. Yet she insisted that he try to find him. Why? It was absolutely nothing to do with him. His search had revealed nothing, and the case was closed. He had been paid by Wedderburn's lawyer, Mr Duncan. Nevertheless, there was something about Joseph Knight that still intrigued him. What it was, he could not say. Perhaps it was simply his own curiosity, his pleasure in digging out hidden information . . .

He reached for the coffee, refilled his cup, turned forward to the date she had mentioned, and began to read again.

Jamaica, 1762

Saturday 6th March, 1762. Glen Isla. This last week spent preparing the mill & such for the cane. Peter has a way with the machinary and with Wilsons help he keeps the negers in line, they will slack so soon as yr back is turnd. Wilson sees to clening out the old hogs heads and repare of looss staves &c. We are back & for between Blewcastle and heer all week as James away doctoring. John says from the look of it we'll have our best crop yet.

This evening after dinner Peter took the sulky wt a new young horse in the traces, and showd us his skill. The sulky being light & frale you think it will coup at any moment but P. is so fine a driver he held it on the balance. The horse ran as if the weels was chasing it. We stood on the porch and cheerd wheniver he came round the house, Jacob & Julius whoping and leeping with delight below us till Phebe chase them inside. Later Jacob tell me, Massa Peter go like the wind, him fly-y-y!

Rosanna James' maid or house keeper as she stiles herself comes fleeing to Glen Isla this night. She says he bate her most crool and shes taken the chance of his absince to beg our protection. We do not dowt she is a lying hoor.

Sunday 7th March. We have word that the *Katharine* is a day off Savanna. It is a year and four months since she was last here and John did trade with her master Capt. Knight, not long after Tacky. Then he boght 6 Koromanties off him, to make up half of them we lost in the revolt. John boght a further 10 about a year past from an other ship, I forget the master, but we lost 4 of these to yellow fever and the rest are not sesond where as Knights all florish. John & James say they never boght a falty slave of him yet, only wicked ones that went out in the rebellion. That will not happen again, says Jo., we'll keep them on a titer rope from now, God protect us.

Rosanna does show sines of rough treetment tho she may deserve it. She has stripes across her back very angry looking, also she is wt child, we can not but think this is an other of James's conquests. If so or indeed even if the bairn is not his he probly shld not have struck her. John at first says she must go back to Blewcastle and she grew histerical falling at his feet &c. At last John says she can stay and be put to work by Pheobe till he has spoken wt James. She's to sleep with Peach, an envy to us all. She is not ill looking her self and Peter says he may intrude him self atween them if the bed be wide enogh. But knowing John's views he will not try it.

Wednesday 10th March. Savanna. John & I to Sav to meet with Knight & dine with him. Jo. says its time I was aboord a slave ship & saw how the negroes come to us. The ship has come thro feerce wether and lost a score of blacks to the bloody flux but Knight is well plesed with what he has left and says theres many good ones to be had. To-morrow we bord to make our choise ahead of the crowd.

Knight is a big feerce looking man but wt a tender side to him. He has thick long red hair and a grate shaggy rusty baird, parts of it bleeched out by the salt and sun. With its many various shades he resembils a Scotch bull. You allmost look for his hornes but he has none in fact is amable tho runs his ship from what he tells us with strict disipline. Tis the only way to do it he says. No man can long stay master of such a tribe of villanes as make up a ships crew if he be weak, and he wd be both weak and a fool if he relaxd his vigill on three hunderd Africans made despirate by their dismall situation. He spoke long of his wife in Liverpool, he has not seen her a year, and three children a boy and 2 girls. He says one more passage to Ginea will suffise him, he will remove to the cuntry and grow fat on eggs and beef. He seems

136

fat enough already tho tis hard to tell under all the hair.
We sat till late and he staid with us at the inn trusting
to his crew the villanes to have all in preperation for us
to-morrow.

Thursday 11th March. By long boat to the *Katharine*.
Have not been a board a sea going vesell since I got heer
8 years ago. I was so greevous sick coming over I am
made unesy at the meer thought of it. The prospect of
seeing Scotland again so plesing in it self is diminishd by
fear of the pasage.

The ships side reard up above us like the wall of a grate
tower. The day fine and the water flat cawm so it was
less of an anxety to me than mite have been. We climbed
abord and an astonishing site met our eyes.

There displayd along chanes across the middel part
of the deck, was the cargoe or part of it for Capt.
Knight assurd us he only broght up the best he had,
the others older weak or sicklie being yet confind to
the belly of the beest. In any case it was not posibill
to have all the Africans above decks at once, from a
shortage of space and of fettirs and chanes forby the fear
of them louping into the sea. I past an unfastend hach
that must go to the slave deck the stench eminating
from it was such as I never hope to smell agane. I
reeld from it. John saw me and says in a low voyce,
they will have cleend it out, think what it was like a
week past.

The slaves look very fine many of them. There is a
grater proportian of wimen & yung girls than ever before.
At his last visit Cap. Knight was impressd by the tales he
hard of Tacky & Apongo, and there was many planters
toled him they wd not buy Koromanties agane they were
too dangerus. The generall notion has been to breed more
creeols, if they are borne into slavery they will not object
to it so much but see it as their natural state. All ways til
now there has been more males than females and some
of the wimen not fertil, or their young do not survive.
Its even said some smuther them rather than let them

137

growe up in bondage, it is hard to beleeve this cruwelty of females.

In spite of this fear of the Koromanties Knights best slaves are the same, Gold Cost ones and he knows John & James will still pay top prise for them, as will others for they are the best workers in spite of the risk.

Knight did not stray far from our side but he did let us inspect them pritty close, making them stand turn around bend jump open their mouths &c. This as ever is somwhat repugnent to me. John also says he does not like to tuch them too close but will do so to ashure himself of ther quality. They were all well rubbd with pawm oil to make them glissen, had been given pipes & tobacko to put them in better humor and their wool was all shaven so one cd not so easy tell an older man from a young one but there were no tricks with calk or die as some practis. Knight knows we Wedderburns are good customers and tis not in his interest to cheet us.

After an hour or more we had made our choyse. John wanted six men and six wimen and found them, but Knights prices were steep. He wanted £60 a man and 40 each for the females. Six hunderd the lot, and John says five hunderd, Knight comes down to five 50 but will not buge from there. We go to his cwarters to drink a glass & come to a bargin, and that is when we saw the boy.

He was a fine looking fellow, no more than 10 or 11 years, quite tall & well built tho slender and even in the few steps we saw him take he had a grase of movment that was charming to behold, & tho he did not smile or speek he seemd blest with a contenance that in other circumstanses might be sunny and most pleesing to the eye. He broght in a bottle of madeera and glasses on a wooden tray and set it on a table. Then it was as if he did not now what to do – indeed he did not, he stode staring not sullen or stupid but as if lost til Knight usherd him away back on deck, kindly & not roghly. I saw Johns eyes narro as the lad went up.

How do you come by that boy, he asks Knight.

Just the way I come by them all, Mr Wedderburn, says Kt. He was sold to me on a beech for a prise.

John asks who it was sold him, and the captane pulls at the bottom of his baird while soking up madeera through the top of it. Now thats a hard question sir, he says, I'll have it somewhar recorded in the ledger. But then he said he delt with many traders white & black, mostly black, in many places, and cdnt ritely remember. But it was on a beech he did mind, for he said from the boys look it appeerd he had never seen a beech before or the sea or a ship. Knight says, he stared and stared even as you seen him do just now gentilmen. You cd almost sware you saw the cogs a turning in his head, taking it all in. O he's a brite one Mr Wedderburn and no mistake. The world comes to him, he dont go to it.

John observd that the boy was let go pritty free about the ship serving the Capt. & so forth and was he not feerd he would escape or try to free his cuntrymen? But as Capt. Kt pointed out where was he to escape save into the jaws of a shark between Guina & Anteega their first port of call, and even now he would drown if he tried swiming to shore. As for aiding the other slaves, an eye was kept out for that but he was a favorit among the crew and lived more wt them than wt the slaves. Then was the Capt. planing on keping him? I cd see that this was what he had in mind, but J's questions made him considir the matter a fresh. Was you intrested in him yore self Mr Wedderburn? I mite be says J., he's fine looking, as you say, I have a mind to trane a lad up for a purpos. Oh he's very fine, says K., he would be an exselent adition to a gentelmans househald. Well, says John, you shall have yr 5 & 50 if you let me have the boy too. K. splutterd a bit as he cd have sold the boy for 30 seperate but John begun to look impashent & as if about to leeve & perhaps Knight saw the hole bargin slipping from his grasp for sudenly he reeches out his muckil paw and sezes J's hand. Let us seel it with a toast says he, poring from the bottle agane. To the Wedderburns their futur prosperity and the excillent sarvisses of Joseph Knight.

I'm obligd to you sir, says John, wt a look at me, which led me to understand he ws thinking as I was, that the Capt. recomended him self some what too strong. By the way, John says, does the boy have a name? K.: *That* is his name, sir, Joseph Knight, and may he sarve you well. I named him after me, thats *my* name – Joseph. Which was the first we new of it.

He called for the boy agan & in he come, he new not the words perhaps but he new the sound of the Cap's voice & stood wating instrucsions. Aynt you a good boy, Joseph? says Knight and the lad says back *goo boy* like a parret, not a smile or a flicker on his face. Yore to go with your new master now, says Knight. This is Mr Wedderburn. You be good he'll be a good master to you. Black Joseph says agane *goo boy* not having I am certane the slitest comprihension that he had just changd hands, and John smiles and claps him on the head. White Joseph roard with laghter.

I dont no why but tho this concluded our bisiness and all seemd well for us & the boy I felt a strong urge to get out of that cabbin and back on dry land. Acordingly I was much releved soon after when having finishd the bottil & John paying part sum to Knight we left taking the boy Joseph with us and the 12 Kromanties were removd from the lines & made redy to be loded ashore & broght to Glen Isla, & Knight to be payed the remander by our agent in Sav.

Befor we went to bed I asked John what purpos he had in mind for the boy, who meantime had been put to sleep wt Jacob & Julius. John said, we will see how he does, but I mean to take him home. When we say home of course we mean only one plase and that is deer old Scotland.

Friday 9th April. Blewcastle. Good Friday. On this day was Christ naled to the Cross for our sins. This the day of his execushon. The jews wanted it. The Romans carried it out. Now we the Christians remember it.

Sunday 11th April. Glen Isla. Easter, or pickny Chrismas as the negers call it. Christ risen. A holyday for them & for us too. We do not go to church, it is too far, but have a short servise here with the house servents, led by John with Bible reading & a psalm. John had Joseph stand befor him holding the Bible open from which he red.

Peter & James here for dinnar but James away erly as meeting wt a cluch of docters in Sav including Davie Fife & an other Scot Crookshank that Ive met but once befor and did not like, he is a sly slidy kind of felow.

Before he left James sees/speeks with Rosana now with a mity belly on her, then with John & agrees to sell her back to her 1st mistress. A complicatd bisness. From Peter I got the full story while they ware out the room.

Rosanna was first a slave on the Duglas estates and maid to Lady Duglas. James as phisician attended Lady D. these 3 or 4 yrs and also some of the slaves. He saw Rosanna there and desird her. This does not surprise me for James desires many that are not half so cumly but it wd have been as Peter says too grate an improprity to buy her for the sole purpose of lying with her, Lady Ds sense of virtue wd not thole it. So James engagd this Crookshank to aproach Lady Duglas and offer for Rosanna, a very good prise, then deliver her over to James. Well I do not now the truth of it wether J. was at falt tho he is hardly a villane, and Peter says some mite charge James with wickednes but the fact is the pius Lady D was willing to sell her maid to Crookshank, a man far less respectd than James. Thus did Rosana come to Blewcastle and Peter reminded me tho in truth I'd forgot it if I ever knew that at least one of the black bairnes running lose there already is James's by Rosanna. Now she is dew to deliver up an other to him but she protests aganst his ill treetment hence her arrival heer. In short she wishes to return to the Duglasses & they seem prepard to have her. But James has made it an absolut clawse of the contract that the child is free from birth even tho the mother is not. I no not whethir James insists this from pride of blood or because he can not bare

141

to see 2 slaves sold for the price of 1. Peter thinks the former. I say the thing is not proven. The out come is Rosanna is to go from here befor her time is due. This is a blow to yung Joseph K. who has taken to her like his own mother.

Tuesday 27th April. Blewcastle. Feeverish. Hard put to it to see to rite. My pen wanders like spider. Horid visions on walls. Blood. Too weak.

Monday 17th May. Glen Isla. I have been visited by the fever dog agane this past month. Have been very sick & not fit for a thing, as above. Bad dreams of fire, hanging, buchery. They moved me back heer as tis cooler, James comes as often as he can to atend me. Am a little beter to day. Cd scarce keep down any food & have lost much weght thro sweats & purges. James has done his best for me but admits it must run its corse. He says he has grater faith in some of the slave remedies for fever than in his own medecine.

The girl Rosana left here last week, her mother is an o-beeah woman of note in Kingston & James intends to consult wt her – not for this bowt of the fever but for future ones – when next he has ocasion to go there or if she come to see her new grand child, that must come soon from the size of Rosanna when she departd. The witches name is Talkee Amy she runs a shop for her master a marchant Mr Payne. I was there 3 yr ago so James tells me but I do not recall it. She sells cheese chints milk etc. on Paynes behaf & all kind of smuggld & secret goods on her own, as root potiones & such like that the blacks & many whites especialy wimen hold in great esteme.

Yung Joseph has been around my bed side much. He speeks little but you no he is lerning all the time. He helps me walk around the room & will sit for hours wt me. Tho we can not converse much both from the lack of comon langage & my illnes yet I feel he is a comforting presens. He smiles as if to say he nows I will be well agane & some how I beleve it. These visions & dreams tho signify different.

It ocurrs to me if he is 12 or there abouts as wd seem then he was born about the year 1750 when I my self was 12 this makes a kind of bond betwene us. More over I was just 16 when I came here & have felt as adrift perhaps as he, as torn from mother & home as he.

Some wd say we are different as I did not have to come but no, I had to it was desird of me by the others, I could scarse resist. Also being better bred a Scot a white man I have a greater sensibillity of my ordeel, so – poor Joseph but poorer Sandy. He had a great affecton for Rosanna & she for him she wd cuddel & hug him & he liked that as if he had found his mother agane so it was sad for them to be parted tho the Duglasses are not far & it may be they can visit each other. I am struck by Capt. Knights words who gave him his name. *The world comes to him.* I often ponder what he ment. I think he ment he is wise. His look is wise. James says show me a wise neger & I'll show you a crafty one.

This riting tires me. I pray for this ilness to pass.

Friday 21st May. Much beter today. For the first time step out side in the evening & walk about the house park. Joseph wt me. We speak with Mary & Peach they seem pleasd to see me up. Mary specialy is warm and tuches my cheek most tender, they are more tuching than us. Some I cant bear ther tuch but Mary is lite of tuch and color, I cd grow to like her. She & Peach fuss Joseph to make up for his loss. He does not trust them, shies away from them as he never did from Rosana & who can say he is not right since thair afection may be taken from him at any time.

Monday 14th June. Blewcastle. James at Lady Duglass today. She tells him Rosanna is deliverd of a male child 2 weeks past, both are well so there was no nesecity for him to see her. As a doctor that is. Of corse there is some delecasy regarding the child's provinance at lest as far as

143

Lady D. is concernd tho every body betwixt here & Sav must suspeck James of being the father & in deed Lady D. must know also or the mater of the child being free wd not have arisen. Rosanna has called him Robert. James semes torn between pride & rage, but all redy casts his eye else where I'm sure. Tis ever thus wt my brother. We all John exceptid enjoy the lassies flesh but James takes a pride in the frutes of his labors where as the thoght of siring a black bairn is disgusting to me. I can lie wt the lassies but I do not want them bringing forth proginy. Some times I think of being befor God the judge, if you had black bairns they wd be the mark of yore sin. Then you wd be cast into the darknes for etternity. I fear Hell wich I think never crosses Ja's mind.

Thursday 24th June. We have letters today from Mama & our sisters at Dundee. How fine it is to see ther hand. They tell us Margaret (who does not rite) is well & settld at Blair, she is wt child. Kate, Susanna & Agatha each apend a page or 2 to Mamas news. All well, as is she. Agatha is now turnd twenty, I wd not now her she says. The house in the Nether gait is dispond to Mama & them which is a relef to John – shd the girls not marry they will be sicur of home & incom. Mama wishes they were not in the town all yr but there is little else for it til we come home & take them to the contry agane. They may go to Blair but only for a spell. At once I sat to rite them but there is so littel news to tell or that I *can* tell. The letter must bild over days. John speks of going to Scotland next yr to redd up our afairs & prepar the way for our return. I wish I may be well enogh to go wt him. Jamaica is killing me.

Lacking news I thought of a better plan. I will paint John James and Peter, perhaps my self also, for Mama. If I go home next yr I will take the portrats wt me, if John goes by him self he may take them.

Saturday 17th July. Glen Isla. More days abed. I am all bone my flesh is an old mans. I can not move or if I do I faint pewk ake til my head bursts & my back semes about to break. This dog is a obstinat beest. James comes, he is never sick, it is not fare. He says he will bring the witch, she is here from Kingstown. I do not want her.

Joseph is not to go to the feelds. John has decided it. He is given over to Pheebe & the house hold to lern to be a foot man or Johns vally or some such I do not care. He is given a blue jackit wt brass butons knee britches bukled shoes & stokings which he seldom wares. They make him a play thing a monkey. He comes less to me now just in the evenings from time to time. He still says little enogh. I used to think his smile was frendly but now I think it cuning. Did he smile to see me getting well or because he saw me sick? His friend is Newman. This is C— as was, his name is Forbidden. Strange that at first I thoght of him as NewMAN, but now he has become NEWman and thus his old self is slowly forgot. But he nows who he is & we now. His back bares the reminder, stripes like weel ruts across the sholders. O God who will pay for such in the final reckening? I fear, we Ws.

This book is a weekness or wd be thoght so by the others if they read it.

Wednesday 21st July: She has been! A feerce old 'good-dame' as they wd say at home. Wrinkeld as a stick. She spoke with such a mix of African & Kingstown I could catch barely 3 in every 10 words she said. She ran her fingers over me with not the leest concern whare they went. James was most impacent with her but she wd not be hurried. At last she went away to make up some hellish brew a kind of leaf tea. I have drunk this three times sinse. The first time I was sick the second I fell asleep before I cd finish it & it spilld on the bed. The third time was just now. It tastes like thin mud but my head does not ache so.

Thursday 22nd July. She came again expressd her self well pleesed with me. Joseph was there at her side she spoke much & quick to him & continewed outside on the porch, I know not what of. Do they try to poyson me? Later when I asked him what she told him he said only a Nancy story. It must have been a long one. Nancy is the spider in ther stories, he is a sleekat body & makes his way in life by navery. The negers admire him because he outwits the grater beasts.

Saturday 24th July. On my feet once more. The tea is drunk & I am better for it. Talkee Amy is away to Kingston. How she gets thare I do not no perhaps she flies.

Monday 9th August. I got Mary to come to me last night. She did redily enogh. She has been playing with me this past month so I thogt I would play her back. But strange to say when she crept in to my bed the desire ebbd away & we lay like bairns together. The sleep was good untrubled. She went this morning erly saying she liked it, tho I suspect her lagh. I liked it too. Peter must not see this nor James they alredy think I am a poor enugh apoligy for a man.

Saturday 14th August. I have had so little to do with the plantations of late I loss all sense of the laburs. The new cane is planting, other crops also, thare is more land being cleerd & broken for next season but I have no interest in any of it. John goes about things with out involving me. James at Blewcastle more and more, doctering less and less as Peter is divertd by his own work as a wheelrite and carrage bilder at wich he hopes to prosper. I would help more if I did not get so ill. This contry is not for me. I long for home cold Scotland.

Saturday 21st August. I have begun to plan out the painting. Have decided to do all together, John James & Peter, here at Glen Isla. I have skeches of them all and can work with out making them sit or stand for hours which James for one says he will not abide. I will have them standing on the porch and sitting beside them will

146

be A.W., the Artist, an enigmattic figure wt a knowing look as if to say here are these fine fellowes lords of their domayns in Jamaica, and I am the man that shows them to you.

Monday 20th September. Mary who has been coming to me some nites for a month & more tells me she may not doe so any more. She says this as we lie together. I ask why. She says she has an other man now. I laghd at this saying, Mary, you may have an other man but you have one master & I am he. She shook her head, no my master is not you but yr brother, pleese do not make me stay. What I *pleese* is what you must do I said. I askd what man. She said, It is Newman. I was angry I said you dont throw me over for a neger & I made to enter her but the anger was spent & I cd not. Then she held me. I suckeld on her she let me. In the morning she was gone.

Sunday 3rd October. They all conspire. I went to John and askd him if he fuckd with Mary. He was cold. I fuck with none of them, he said. I do not beleeve him. I said, she is betraying you, she is wt Newman. John said, that is her consern, leave her alone.

Later I saw Joseph with Newman they were wispering. Mary will not look at me. It is cleer they all combine agaynst me. I have seen Peter & James also, they lagh at me. Well, I too can play that game.

I askd Phebe about Mary, how is her work. P says she is slip shod. I will have her out of here.

Tuesday 5th October. John away to Sav today & tomorrow. I had a long talk wt Phebe. She is a sowr bitch but this serves my purpose. I said to her if Mary is slip shod you need not put up with it. Was there not an other young girl that cd be trayned from afresh to do what she was told and do it better? P. said there was plenty that wd like the chance to work in the house. Very well I said, you fetch one that you like and send Mary to me. Wd the master not object, Phebe says. I too am yr master I said,

147

why do you people not see that, we are all your masters and you must do as we bid. P. nodded her head at me, there was a gleme in her eye as if she knew what I was about, which I did not like. She went out and preccently Mary comes in.

You are dismissd from here, I said, you are to go to the second gang. Why, she had the nerve to ask. You know why, I said, you are lazy and impewdent and Phebe says you are beyond listning to her. That is not trew, she says. I said, do you call me a lier. I had a whip in my lap and now I struck it wt force against the chair. No, she says, but why must I go? I told you, you are a disapointment to me, I said, and to Phebe. She says, I will tell Mr John when he returns from Sav. I said, it will be a negers word agaynst his brothers. I will not go, she says. I stood up and struck her in the face with the whip handel saying aye you will or you will get the other end of this bewty across yr back. So she went to the feelds a weeping.

Thursday 7th October. John home late last nite. Erly this morning he must have been aprised by Phebe of what has passd. He came to me and askd why I wishd Mary punishd by being put from the house. I told him he shd ask his housekeper. He said but I know this is yr doing. I said, has Phebe said that? He said yes but it is no mistery, I know what is between you & Mary. There is nothing, I said. If Mary comes greeting to you will you beleve her over me? He said I know what I will beleve but I will not humilate you by bringing her back. He turned his back on me to go. I said, she is lucky the 2d gangs labors are as nothing to the firsts. He did not look at me. I will not humilate you more than you have your self, he said, and went out.

Sunday 10th October. I am wicked I am wicked. God forgive me for she will not. Saw Newman today. He lookd on me with hate. Joseph is serly & avoyds me. I wd have him whippd but he is Johns I dare not.

Tuesday 12th October. Today as I went to the fields I was struck by a blinding pain & fell to the ground. I thoght perhaps I was attacked by Newman. They came to help me & put me to bed. It was the sun or God. All my strenth has fled again.

John came by this evening. I asked him to restore her to the house. He said that was not posible they wd see it as weaknes. Then he said, *I* see it as weaknes, Sandy, you are sick but you have yr self to blame. I beleve he wd like me to die. I will not give him that satisfaction. To tired to rite more.

Saturday 27th November. Papa died this day. John shut away by him self. The day is hot & sunny but the mood of the place is gloomy. So it is this & each November. Worked on the painting. It is all but done. I have left my self out after all since I feel I am hardly here in the flesh any more. Instead I have put in Joseph, The Faithfull Servant.

Saturday 25th December. Glen Isla. Christmas. I have not ritten heer neer a month. Mary is with Newman he can keep her. She is aling John tells me too soft for the field work. She will go to the 3rd gang to repare. I do not care.

I determin to make a fresh start. I am better. We are all asembled for prayers and then a great dinner. James Peter John & I. Joseph serves the wine. Before the meal I presented the painting to them. Only John knew I had been working on it, and even he I had not let see it. They all aplauded and admired it, nor do I think they were humoring me. Peter says you have captured us very well, and James says espeshally since we never sat for you. John says to Joseph do you see your self, you will look out from that picter for a hunderd yrs and never age a day. None of us will, said Peter. Then James said, but why did you not paint yr self with us. I said, because the painting is for Mama and she will have no need to see me in it. Peter says why not. I said because I will give it to her in person. I am going home.

I thought this might cause a row but far from it, they beemed even more. John says, let us drink to that. Then, looking at me, here is to Scotland we will be there next Christmas. We drank and wished each other happy Christmas. I said they make little of Christmas at home. John said the calvenists may do what they want with their black beeked soles, we will mark it there as here. He smiled at me. I thoght of snow. Strangely I felt warm thinking of it. I long for it. I will make my self better so I can see snow again.

Dundee, May 1802 / Jamaica, 1763

Archibald Jamieson, after a day copying screeds of legal argument about a boundary dispute between two Angus farmers,
was taking advantage of the late evening light to finish reading
the Wedderburn journal. He was not quite certain why he was
bothering. Sandy Wedderburn's jottings were such a mix of
feebleness, spite and delusion, quite apart from being badly
written and poorly spelt – an offence to his clerical sensibilities
– that Jamieson found it hard to persuade himself there was
anything useful to be got out of them. Still, he read on.

He kept wondering about Susan, whether she had read these
pages through tears of rage or between fits of vomiting. The fact
that she had sent the journal to him suggested that she had
not – could not – confront her father with it. This still left an
unanswered question: what did she expect Archie Jamieson to
do with it?

She seemed to have been right about one thing: Sandy had
painted Joseph Knight into that picture above the fireplace. So
who had painted him out? Would Sir John really have done that,
or had it done, and still left the thing hanging so prominently? He
hadn't even appeared to like it, had been dismissive of 'the artist'
– 'one had to settle for what one could get out there'. Hardly the
affectionate tone a man might be expected to use of his dead
brother's memory.

Perhaps, though, Sandy's journal had supplied Sir John's
motivation for keeping it on display: *you will look out from that
picture for a hundred years and never age a day.* For a wealthy,
settled, successful family, the Wedderburns seemed beset with
insecurities.

Saturday 1st January 1763. Glen Isla. This New Yr's
night is moderate compard wt last. The brothers kept
well up wt drink & cards & a cluster of companyons but

151

I slipt away shortly after midnight. I have found a new companyon of my own. It is – a poem!

I found it among Johns books. It is The Grave. A somber piece by a Edinburgh minister Robert Blair whos task is to 'paint the gloomy horrors of the Tomb'. If his soul was black beekd, as John put it, I no not but his poem is dark. He died the yr our father died it says. It is befor me now. Copying from it is an efort and it makes me see how adrift is my spelling. But that is its mildest lesson. In every line of it are hints of Papa & us & them (the negers) & what must come to us all:

> What is this world?
> What but a spacious burial-field unwall'd,
> Strew'd with death's spoils, the spoils of animals,
> Savage and tame, and full of dead men's bones?

There is truth in it & in this:

> 'Tis here all meet!
> The shivering Icelander, and sun-burnt Moor;
> Men of all climes, that never met before . . .
> Here the o'erloaded slave flings down his burden
> From his gall'd shoulders, and when the cruel tyrant,
> With all his guards and tools of power about him,
> Is meditating new unheard-of hardships,
> Mocks his short arm, and quick as thought escapes
> Where tyrants vex not, and the weary rest.

That is fearsome in its nearness. You wd think the man had bene here. It is a strange comfort tho, a cold littel passion, this book. The others wd hate it. Has J. ever read it? I can not think he has. The pages seem unturnd, tho the damp has made them moldy.

Tuesday 11th January. Mary colapsd in the fields. The party she was wt was bairns & old haggs. By chance I was observing them from curiossity not because they need supervising they were only gathring grass for the cattel.

She saw me at a distance & straitened her self looking
at me. Then she gave a cry & fell to the ground. 2 of the
old use-less wimen went to aid her. I wd have driven
them off as I beleved it too much coinsidence she shd
fall in front of me, & that she was faining, til she went
into great twistings & I cd not dout her pain. Then from
between her legs suddenly thare bloomd a great stane of
blood on the ground & she was deliverd of an abortion.
Newman who is in the first gang did not now of it at first.
Joseph was with the 3d gang as he often is when bored
wt the house, he strips off his finery & defies Johns plans
for him. He ran to fech Newman. Nothing but chanes
wd have kept that neger at his labour he hurried to her
& gathering her up he caried her to ther hut. His passion
was such that none of us dared prevent him nor did we
make him returne to his work this day. She lies very sick.
John wd have sent for James but Newman swoar he wd
not let him touch her & got the old wimen to tend her.
J. says he will let it pass but if she shold die he will have
Newman punished for his obstinasy.

Wednesday 12th January. I can not but help think some
how it is my falt. This is foolish I know & certanly the
fetus was not mine but had I not put her to the feelds it
might not have happened.

Friday 14th January. She is dead. God forgive me.

Saturday 15th January. Newman gone. I would go too if
I could.

Sunday 16th January.

       Here too the petty tyrant . . .
  Who fix'd his iron talons on the poor,
    And gripp'd them like some lordly beast of prey,
    Deaf to the forceful cries of gnawing hunger,
    And piteous plaintive voice of misery
    (as if a slave was not a shred of nature,

Of the same common nature with his lord),
Now tame and humble, like a child that's whipp'd,
Shakes hands with dust, and calls the worms his
    kinsman . . .

Tuesday 18th January. John says if he is not back to morrow he must send to the maroons to track him which they will do for a sum. He says he must be sene to hunt him or they will all run off.

Friday 21st January. The maroons think he has gone to the mountains whare he will perrish if they do not find him first or if he does not come to ther town. Which ever of these they say they will return him here.

Sunday 30th January. John plans to leave for Scotland no later than the start of May. With good wether we may make Liverpool or Greenock in 7 wks. He will have power of atturny for Peter & James (& me tho I will be there also God willing) to settle what family business he can. That is 5 months & we shall see home mother sisters, all.

Tuesday 1st February. Newman is found. The maroons broght him in this morning on the back of a pony. Where ever he went when he left Glen Isla, he came back & hangd him self in the woods a mile fr the house. I went with one of them he showd me the spot, a dark shady place wt very tall trees. He had climbd one attachd the rope to a branch & dropt from it. It was hard to reach him & cut him down the neger told me. Stood a while till the moskitoes drove us away.

It is strange to think that he died twice, once as Charlie once as Newman. In deed he may have died once at leest even before then in Africa. Perhaps that is all slave lives are, a number of deaths. Perhaps all life is only a number of deaths.

Self-murder is a grevous sin yet I can not sensure him for it. Blair says to take your own life is like rushing into the presence of the Judge daring him to do his worst

– 'Unheard-of tortures must be reservd for such'. Yet Newman had sufferd much already you think he cd thole what ever the Supreme Being in his infinit wisdom dispensd. Is this blasphemmy? I care not. I do not even no if negers are broght befor God to be judgd, or if that is a fate reservd only for us ther masters. But then what weght of sin will be on our backs.

Thursday 17th February. This day I askd John if he means to purchase land & house when we are at home. He says he intends to look. Blackness is gone from us & tho we have the properties in Dundee he wants to be a laird with cattel game &c. some where not far from where we grew up. There is no question of him not coming back here. He knows *my* feelings on this subject but says *he* must be in Jamaica 5 or 10 yrs more. If 10 he wd still be only in his middle forties. Plenty of time he asures me to marry rase children *become a Scotsman again*. Are you not a Scotsman here? I askd. Are you? he replied. Is James? We are none of us. We are but sojorners here. If you go to seek gold you take it away and bild a palace you do not bide in the hole where you find it. He is right of coarse. But for me if once I reach Scotland I will not take my foot from it again.

Friday 18th February. Joseph like a specter these days – silent here a moment gone the next. He performes his duties around the house and garden well but with out the least sign of interest. He is bereft of Rosana of Mary of Newman maybe this is the cause. What does he mind of Africa his own people his mother? Does he have emotion or passion? He does not show it.

Tuesday 8th March. I do not sleep much these nts. The dreams are back. Hanging men burning men. Yet phisickly I am as well as I have been in a twelfmonth.

Tuesday 12th April. A ship the *Mary* is at Savanna loading with sugar & other goods and sails for Cork Dublin &

Greenock by the month end. John has ritten to sicure
us places abord her. The name does not escape me nor
Peter who remarkd that I wd once more have a berth in
Mary which I was obligd to take in good spirits tho I did
not feel it. So they know too! Of course they hv alwayes
known. There are no secrets here. You can not shit in
the privvy but some neger goes past & wishes you good
morning.

John now twice as active as ever compleeting busines,
seeing frends & redding the estate agaynst all dificulties
over the next yr but he insists I rest easy so as to be well
for the jurney, the others say the same. But I am well!
They wish to be rid of me. I will thole that as I wish to be
rid of Jamaica.

Thursday 19th May. God mocks me for mocking Him.
This entry is a desparate sadnes. After all my hopes of
last month – of the last year! – John is gone wtout me.
He cd not delay, the *Mary* wd not since the winds were
faverable. The curst dog came back & worrid me sore not
a day after I last wrote & has left me like a rag. I cd not
move from my bed til this week. They talkd of getting me
aboard but the pasage to Scotland wd surely have killd
me even if the jurney to Sav had not. I tried to make my
self believe I cd manage it. I stood from the bed one time
to pruve it & fell on my face after 2 steps.

James came & ministerd as before. He wd not permitt
me to be moved. I beggd him to get the Kingstown
witch but she did not or wd not come. I felt something
in James that he did not want her here tho he did not
say so. Why did she not come? Ja. says I am too much
weakened to go alone on an other ship. I cd take Joseph
to look after me but my dear brother will not allow it I
suppose he fears what wd become of him shd I die. But
does he fear for me? I only want to go home & now Ja.
puts the boys interests befor mine. He who beats fucks
buys & sells them will not give one to save his own
brother. Or does he serve the interest of an other brother
since Joseph is Johns? Well these are curst transactions.

156

I shall surely die if I stay in this rottin island. We shall all die.

Friday 20th May. Woke sudenly from a bad dream to find Joseph stood at my bed side, I was shockd thinking at first he was part of the dream, he was so close to me and on his face was that evill smile. I seezed his rist befor he cd step away, he is become stronger than me but I put all my strenth in to gripping him. I said still half asleep, what are you doing, have you come to kill me? He said no, the fever will do that. He tried to step away but I held him tite, pulld my self up in the bed. If I'd had a whip or stick I wd have bate him sore for that remark, as it was I struck him wt the flat of my hand across his face. You are a wicked boy. J: No massa. I struck him again. You are a wicked boy. J: Yes massa. Why do you say the fever will kill me? J: Talkee Amy say so. Why does she not come to help me? J: She say she help you before. Why do you not help me? J: I dont want to. I struck his face. You do as I tell you. J: No. I struck him again. I am yr master. J: No, that is Massa John. I only do what *he* say. Do you do everything he say? J: Yes. Have you been in his bed? J: No. I struck him. Have you been in his bed? J: No. If he commanded it, you wd. J: No. I struck him. Yes, he is yr master. J: But he does not own me. I struck him. He owns you. J: Not here (hitting his hand on his chest). I struck his face again. We all own you. J: No, none of you. You will never own me. I made to strike him another time but he escaped my hand and ran out. I lay back exawsted. The depth of his insolense astounds me. I hate him as he hates me. As they all hate me.

Friday 27th May. James comes to see me. We playd a game of back gamon but my mind did not stick to it & he did not have the patiens to play badly & show me mercy. After he gamond me 3 times I pushd the bord away & we sat in silence a while.

I said Papa was playing this when they told him he was to die.

James said So I have told you often enogh. What of it?

Tell me agane I said. Doutless I sounded like a child but he told me. The night before in the prison. Papas request of him not to come the next morning. And James did not go to the prison but he went to Kenington common waring an old coat & a hat pulld down low so shd Papa look at him he wd not see him but only a stranger in the crowd. And what a crowd it was a mad cheering shouting mob that spat & whisseld as they drew them on sleds thro the streets. James pushd his way to the scaffold & watchd. How cd he watch? But he has told me so well that I see it my self now – Papa walking unaided up the steps in his shirt brave & unbent & given a space to pray & then the rope put about his neck. The drop James watching in silence the people all chering about him Papa choking his face turning blew. They were expert in their craft the men who killd him. They let him die till the last minute then they stopt him. They revivd him wt brandy & showd him the buckit where they wd burn his bowells then they laid him out & opend his white shirt & cut him open & pulld them out & held him sitting while they showd him them & plungd them in the fire. And his eyes were fixt straght ahead as if he lookd not at what they were doing but thro to another place. And so the life went from him. Our father.

Then James said a thing he never told me befor in all the times he has spoke of this. He had by dint of much elboing & burroing got him self almost to the foot of the platform. When they held Papa there by the sholders in his death throws he was but a few yds away. He said, I always thoght he must be seeing the angels coming for him or Jesus at the rt hand of God. It was a mercy to me to think that. But now I dont believe it.

I trembld to hear this. You do not believe in God I askd. No he said thats not what I ment. I mean that Papa was not seeing God or angels. He was staring at me. A stranger. It did not matter who I was he fixd his eyes on me. I am sure he did not recognise me. It was life he saw that he stared at so hard. He did not wish to go even then after what they had done to him. He did not wish to be taken from this world.

You can not know that I said. How can you know that?

He said, because I have seen it since.

Archibald Jamieson was surprised at the abruptness with which the journal ended. He came out of it as if rudely awakened. Those last lines ran down to the bottom of a right-hand page, and half the book still remained. He turned the leaf expecting more of Sandy's increasingly morbid ramblings – there was nothing! Nothing but blank, mottled space. Jamieson felt cheated by it, abandoned by Alexander Wedderburn, and he felt a further great emptiness – the absence of Joseph Knight. The boy abused by the invalid man – defying him, but then vanishing, as Sandy Wedderburn himself vanished with the last of the entries. It was as if the ending of the journal deprived them both of life.

Susan's note had led him to believe that the journal contained a clue as to Knight's whereabouts, but he saw now that that was impossible. How could something written by a dead man years before Knight even arrived in Scotland reveal him in the present? Nevertheless . . . Jamieson turned the pages quickly, just in case. Nothing, nothing, nothing – until the final page, where in the same laboured hand he saw the following:

> Sure, 'tis a serious thing to die! my soul!
> What a strange moment must it be, when near
> Thy journey's end thou hast the gulf in view.

More of the death poem. God, somebody should have rescued him from that! Jamieson looked again at Susan's note: *We always understood it was yellow fever killed uncle A. but it was not that alone – what do you think?* Suicide? Perhaps the journal ended so suddenly because Sandy killed himself. But Jamieson didn't think so. Suicide required a special kind of courage – the courage of slaves, perhaps, the courage of despair – and Sandy had not been endowed with courage of any sort. A sneevilling kind of creature altogether. No, he would have let the fever eat him away sooner than injure himself. He would probably have decided to kill himself only when he was too feeble to accomplish it. Then he would have had something else to complain about.

Jamieson was surprised at his own cynicism. He realised that he had become very angry, reading this inadequate document composed by an inadequate man when he himself was a mere bairn. Had it made Susan angry? Or had she just wanted the thing out of the house?

It took Archibald Jamieson the rest of the day to pinpoint the cause of his anger. When his boys kissed him goodnight on their way to bed, he understood. It was not the insipid, petty nastiness of Sandy Wedderburn that enraged him. It was the negligence, the poverty of emotion of all the Wedderburns. He was silently furious on behalf of the boy Joseph who, if he still lived, would now be a man five or six years older than himself. What kind of man would such neglect have made? But Archibald Jamieson did not really see the man. He kept seeing the boy. He loved children. He detested the thought of a child being treated with such – indifference.

Ballindean, June 1802

Inveresk Lodge
Midlothian
Sunday, 20th June

Dear Brother

Thank you for yours of the 15th. You do not mention your health, but from Isabella who has had a letter from Alicia I gather that it remains middling at best, which grieves me. I hoped this warmer weather had eased your bones and calmed your mind. I fear my news may do little to alleviate what suffering you may have.

Do not distress yourself concerning the future of the plantations. Though the abolitionists now make a mighty noise and I do not doubt in time will succeed in their aims, that time is some long way off, certainly beyond the span that remains to you and me. The plantations were established by practice and commerce not on a moral whim, and it is commerce not whining morality that will bring about future changes, including perhaps a general but *gradual* manumission. Do not write too intemperately to London, you will only aggravate the spirits of those in high places who sympathise with the meddlers. Our best argument is the current disaster in San Domingo – dreadful stories emanating now of the savage cruelties inflicted on white and black alike. How strange that one's hopes in that quarter should rest with Bonaparte! The one thing that may be said in his favour is that his own despotic designs will surely not tolerate those of Toussaint L'Ouverture, and that he will attempt to restore order to that sorry colony.

Should our own colonies be inflamed in like manner, not only would their prosperity and stability and the mother country's trade with them be destroyed, but so too would the lives of thousands of Negroes, who would be slaughtered or die of starvation. Tell *that* to the zealots who call for black 'freedom'! Let Wilberforce and his friends spout, there are men of better sense who know what would be the inevitable outcome of their schemes. But I know I need not preach this at you, John. In any case, this peace with France cannot last long, and when the war recommences the claims of patriotism will subdue the fervour for making all men equal regardless of property, creed or colour.

You write to ask if by chance I took away Alexander's pocket book or journal of his last years on this earth. I think you must be confused, John. That object I'm sure was destroyed many years since. We both felt it was a dishonour to his memory and ours, the wanderings of a diseased brain. I am almost certain we together consigned it to the flames one day at Ballindean, or at least we agreed that you would burn it. I trust you did. Remember we said, a little sadly, that the painting was a better memorial to him since he was not in it. Do not upset yourself on this matter. The journal is gone, and you are only deceived by the passage of time.

But I must also tell you that I too am visited by a ghost from our West Indian days. You will remember at the time of your trouble in the courts how we got word of the arrival of Robert Wedderburn (so styled) in this country, and how, some short time after, he reached Edinburgh and came chapping at my door. I sent him off smartly enough on that occasion, but he has surfaced again, making importunate applications on account of our relationship, and, what enrages me more, making them not to me but to my son Andrew in London, who has been plagued by his effrontery. I know I need expect no sympathy from you on this matter, John, since you always disapproved. The villain, not content with being a freeman, as he was made at birth, continues to crave assistance on the strength of his name though he is a fit and bold fellow well able to turn a day's work, but you know how they never like to do that if it can be avoided. *Of course I will deny all his claims.* I write you this only as a warning that he may approach Ballindean, by letter I mean, as he seems from Andrew's account to have a special regard for you as one who may be sympathetic, based on spurious legends passed to him by his people about your taking in his mother &c. He is devious and may not deal directly with you but with your family. Be on your guard against him!

I hope and trust that it will come to nothing, and that once rebuffed firmly on all fronts he will go back to being a tailor or to preaching, in which I understand he engages in a ranting style having turned Methodist. Is not all this miserably predictable? But I felt it only right to forewarn you, far though you are from the metropolitan clamour.

We are all well here. I may come north before the summer is over, and hope you are in better health when you receive a visit from

Your affectionate brother,

James

Sir John Wedderburn observed the shake of his hand as he let the paper fall into his lap. He was sitting at the fireplace, and while he did not feel cold, he was not hot either. The weather had gone off since James had written his letter. Today was damp and cloudy; they had lit a fire for him. Crouched over a fire at midsummer – what was he coming to? He grued at that: knew precisely what he was coming to. The End – like one of the lassies' damned *novelles*. He lifted the letter again, scanned it. Too many words. His brother's writing was getting hard to read. So James did not have the journal. It had been a long shot. Maybe James was right. Maybe they *had* burnt it. He hoped so. When was the last time he had actually looked at it, rather than just thought of looking at it? But it had been in that drawer, surely it had. Nobody else could have taken it. Nobody else would have known it was there, or cared what it was. Only he cared any more about Sandy.

Terrible it had been, leaving Sandy bedridden when he had sailed on the *Mary* in '63. If Sandy could have been got home then, things might have been different. The physical wasting of him had been bad enough, but the sapping of his spirit had been still more distressing. James had done his best but then grown impatient. John himself had been unable to trust Sandy with any responsibility. It had been easier just to leave him be, leave him to his jottings and sketchings and complaints. James, Peter and he had come to the same conclusion as Sandy himself: Scotland was the only place for him. But getting him there had proved impossible. In the flurry of last-minute arrangements, they had even forgotten about packing up the painting.

Arriving home, John had of course had to calm Mama's worries about Sandy – yes, he had been ill, and this had prevented his return, but he was also working hard, was needed on the plantations. That was untrue, but then John discovered quickly that there were many aspects of life in Jamaica that, back in Scotland, were better disguised, glossed over or suppressed. The plantations became like places in a dream almost before he stepped ashore. When asked, he found it hard to recall even quite simple facts about them.

Apart from the failure to take Sandy and his picture with him, the trip to Scotland had been a success. One of his main tasks was to make sure that his mother and sisters were properly established in Dundee. He also had a number of legal documents drawn up on behalf of himself and the brothers, and travelled a good deal – to Edinburgh, to Aberdeen, and extensively throughout Forfarshire and Perthshire. He had not intended to buy on this occasion, nor did he, but he surveyed the land knowing that somewhere between Dundee and Perth, among his old childhood haunts, he would find a suitable place to settle.

In Edinburgh he found a few old comrades whose Jacobitism was forgiven though not forgotten, but apart from memories he had little in common with them. He trod warily between the firmly Hanoverian establishment and the relics of the cause, and found that a great many other folk did the same, and were none the worse for it. He avoided any meeting that had even a whiff of conspiracy about it. Not that there was much of that. Most of the gatherings he attended were social ones – balls, soirées, oyster suppers. Edinburgh was loud not with the march of a Highland army and the din of bagpipes, but with *ideas*.

The *Caledonian Mercury* was full of announcements of new treatises by historians, agriculturists, philosophers: Kames's *Elements of Criticism* was an astonishing best-seller; Hume's *History of England* was just out, as was *A Critical Dissertation on the Works of Ossian* by Hugh Blair, the minister of the High Kirk at St Giles and Professor of Rhetoric at the University. Arguments over the authenticity of those heroic Gaelic poems were raging in the taverns and coffee shops – if duels were not actually being fought in defence of their honour, challenges were certainly being thumped on table-tops. The magistrates had ordered the draining of the Nor' Loch, and a new bridge was to be built over it, leading to an as yet imaginary new town on the north side. The world John Wedderburn had fled from in '46 was changing. Plainly, by the time he came back in a few more years, it would have all but gone.

Returning to Jamaica, he had the sense of re-entering a place much less likely to alter in the coming years. Year in, year out, the cane fields produced their riches, the gangs swung their way through them, slaves were bought, seasoned, used up, replaced. Planters would go on making improvements to their great houses, to methods of production, and yes, to the conditions in which their slaves lived and worked, because it was in their interests to do so. But fundamentally the structure of life and of society did not change – whereas in Scotland everything was being upturned, and much of it for the good. It was almost as if, in leaving Scotland and going back, then leaving again, John Wedderburn was stepping through a magic glass into an unreal world. It was not always clear which world was which. The glass inverted the old and the new. If he went back through it one more time, he would find himself in a place that was strangely familiar, that was different and yet was home.

A number of things pushed him towards that final sea voyage. There was the letter from his sister Katherine, gently and without alarm reminding him that their mother was now entering on her sixties, and becoming a little frail. There were the immense profits of the years of war against the French which meant a rapid reduction in what he owed to his creditors and consequently less need for him to stay managing the plantations. And there was Sandy's death.

Sandy never acclimatised, never became immune to the various sicknesses and fevers that from time to time swept through the island. In May of 1764, not more than three months after John's return, he was brought down with yellow fever. First he burned up with it, then he became almost comatose, his pulse barely detectable. His eyes enlarged and the whites turned a grimy parchment colour, his skin jaundiced. He awoke, vomited and voided till there was nothing left to come out. Then he lay still, and cooler, and it seemed as though he might make a recovery. But it was only a brief remission. They made him drink as much water as he could but it came through him thick and viscose as if he were a sugar factory, and his stools were like tar. He puked up blood. He became delirious, shouting one minute about hellfire, the next about being caught in a snowstorm. He went into a fit of hiccups that were devastating to watch, that convulsed his chest and twisted his mouth into a horrible grimace. When things reached this stage, John left James to do what he could. Davie Fyfe came, but it was hopeless.

'Even if we were better doctors than we are, we could not save him,' said James. 'Davie cannot save him. Nobody can save him . . .' It was as if he had not finished the sentence, as if he meant to add 'from himself'.

'It is my fault,' John said. 'I should have tried harder to get him home.'

'You would only have killed him sooner,' James said. 'It is nobody's fault.'

They found the journal, and first John, then James, read it through. They never showed it to Peter. It made an extra bond between the two elder brothers. They debated burning it even then, but decided against it. 'We'll keep it as a kind of warning,' John said. They understood each other: the journal was a symbol of weakness, of the destructive power of weakness. Sandy was what they must never become.

Once he was dead and buried, the settled, rhythmic Jamaican world re-established itself, continued to turn as if nothing had happened, just as it continued whether you lost two or twenty slaves in a year. What was death to this place, one white death, a hundred black deaths? They were nothing. John's desire to get back to Scotland increased.

Then in October 1766 there was a small but deadly slave rising on a neighbouring estate which spread to some of his own Coromantees: a bookkeeper and three or four other whites, and a number of slaves who refused to join the rebels, were killed. The revolt was quickly put down, and those involved either shot in the fighting or executed later. For a brief moment, there was a danger that the great house at Glen Isla would be attacked, that John Wedderburn's own life was at risk. It seemed like a throwback to another age, a re-enactment of events that should have been consigned to history. He was thirty-seven years old. He felt he should no longer have to face such unpleasantness. He did not want to die a violent death. Nor did he want to die like Sandy. He wanted to die old and grey, surrounded by his children. It was time, finally and permanently, to go home.

But like the hero in a fairy tale, he could not pass from the unreal to the real (if that was where he was going) without taking with him a token. It would serve as a reminder of where he had been, and what had happened there. It would mark the source of the riches that would continue to flow across the Atlantic and feed his third life.

The token, Joseph Knight, had turned in a few years from boy to man, had become a tall, handsome, affable youth of eighteen or so. Sir John remembered Joseph's complete lack of enthusiasm for the journey. 'But I will show you things that will astonish and amaze you,' he had told him. 'I will show you a country that you cannot even dream of. Joseph, we are going home.' And then Joseph had smiled slightly, as if he were already making an effort to imagine the place.

Sir John Wedderburn looked at his brother James's letter lying in his lap. He glanced over it again. There was nothing in it he liked – plantation worries, bothersome Negroes, Sandy's sad ravings. He felt an urge to get rid of it.

With sudden determination, thinking of the lost journal, he leant forward and thrust the letter into the fire.

III

Enlightenment

MUIRTON IN PERTHSHIRE JUNE 3RD 1768

RUN AWAY from Captain Oliphant Kinloch, a NEGRO SLAVE, a stout lad, well made, 17 years of age, five feet seven inches high, had on a dark coloured thickset coat and vest, buckskin breeches, a blue surtout coat, with a crimson velvet collar, and done round the edges with crimson velvet, a black velvet cap, and answers to the name of LONDON. Any person apprehending the said NEGRO SLAVE, and lodging him in any of his Majesty's gaols, by applying to Mr James Smyth, writer to the Signet, Edinburgh, or the proprietor at Muirton, shall receive twenty shillings sterl. besides their expences. He, among other things, carried off a silver Watch, which he offers to sale, it is hoped will be stopt for the proprietor, a fellow servant's behoof.

N.B. As every person knows the penalty of harbouring a slave, any person that does will be prosecute in terms of the act of parliament.

EDINBURGH EVENING COURANT, 8 JUNE 1768

FOR MONTEGO BAY, LUCEA, AND SAVANNA-LA-MAR, JAMAICA

The ship CHRISTIANA, ROBERT BAIN Master, now lying at Greenock, will be ready to take on board goods by the 20th curt., and clear to sail by the 20th January.

For freight or passage, apply to Sommervel, Gordon and Co., merchants in Glasgow, or the Master in Greenock.

The C— is a fine large vessel, armed with ten carriage guns, and has excellent accommodation for passengers.

CALEDONIAN MERCURY, 17 JANUARY 1788

III

Enlightenment

Edinburgh, 17 August 1773

Mr John Maclaurin strode towards the top of the Grassmarket, on his way to what promised to be an interesting dinner at James's Court. He was a tall man, a little above six feet, who seemed even taller because of his gaunt thinness, gangly limbs and ungraceful stride. A long, disapproving nose was further exaggerated by a receding chin, and yet his gloomy features were misleading, for he was quick-witted, and generally excellent company. A languid way of speaking disguised a powerful intellect. He was capable of fierce opinions, especially where either Scotland or natural justice were under fire, but they were often immediately succeeded by gales of laughter, as if his anger were only a front put up to see which of his friends he could make jump the highest.

Ten minutes earlier he had climbed out of his carriage at the West Port and sent it back home, to Dreghorn Castle. There, in the lee of the Pentland Hills to the south-west of the city, he had left his wife Esther for the afternoon – somewhat against both their wills, as she was within days of producing their eighth child in ten years, and they were both nervous. So far they had been moderately unlucky: three of the children had not survived, two of those that had were sickly. Mr Maclaurin felt perhaps he should be at home. Mrs Maclaurin did too, but had pushed him out, since an opportunity like this would probably never come again. In any case his anxiety would make hers worse. By the time, in the early evening, he walked down the High Street to the Tron, where he could hire a hackney-coach to take him home, Esther would have gone to bed.

It was approaching three o'clock, a fashionable whole hour later than the usual time for dinner, but then his hosts prided themselves on keeping abreast of fashion. He was to dine at the home of James and Margaret Boswell, and meet, for the first time, the great Dr Samuel Johnson. Maclaurin was of two minds about this encounter. On the one hand, he was intrigued by the Englishman's literary brilliance and his reputation for erudite conversation. On the other, he was scunnered at hearing endlessly of these virtues from Bozzy, who, though a close friend – they were both advocates, and often jousted before the Bench – did not know when to shut up about his fat favourite. Boswell squirmed with evident delight every time he recounted another of Johnson's barbs against the Scotch. Maclaurin was not sure how he himself would react if he were baited, but he hoped it would be with dignity and spirit.

Boswell, of course, having persuaded Johnson to come not only as far north as Edinburgh but to go with him even unto the wildest retreats of the Western Isles, was in his element: showing off the doctor to as many of his acquaintances as he could fit into half a week of hastily arranged dinners; and in return attempting to impress Johnson with the length and breadth of Scottish genius. At thirty-eight, Maclaurin was six years older than Bozzy, and sometimes found his friend's irrepressibility wearing. Today, he supposed, he had been invited as an example of a kind of middling, middle-aged Scotch lawyerish intelligence. Well, Johnson would see what he would see . . .

The afternoon was windless and warm, but against it, owing to a habitual fear of catching cold, Maclaurin was defended by an unseasonably heavy coat. Possibly this obsession with draughts, sneezes and dry stockings was related to the loss of three children: it might also have derived from the history of his father, Colin Maclaurin. A gifted mathematician, he had become professor of that subject at Aberdeen at the age of nineteen, moving to the chair at Edinburgh eight years later. He had exhausted himself organising the city defences against the Jacobite army in 1745, escaped to York when his efforts came to nothing, returned in poor health the following year, caught a chill and expired. John Maclaurin was ten years away from the age his father had been when he died, and was determined, for the sake of whichever of his own children grew to adulthood, to get well beyond it.

The High Street was reached from the Grassmarket via the West Bow, a narrow twisted ascent less like a thoroughfare than a mountain pass. It rose so steeply that even fit walkers found it taxing on the legs. Half medieval and half derelict, every cranny and corner occupied as a place of residence or business or both simultaneously, dotted with mysterious doors and curious airy passageways leading apparently to nowhere, disfigured by unnatural protuberances and impossibly angled outshots, liberally decorated with sign boards, shop names and drying-poles festooned with all manner of clothing and bedding, the West Bow was as densely crowded at its upper storeys as it was at ground level. Maclaurin was always thrilled by its packed riot of colour and noise, and by the fact that this confusion of a street was a kind of trial, a pilgrim's progress, out of which one emerged on to the wider, airier and brighter Lawnmarket and the great cascade of the High Street pouring down from Castlehill to Holyrood. Going up the West Bow, he felt as though he were in a fable.

It had at one time been home to one of Maclaurin's friends, Andrew Crosbie, one of the most successful advocates in Edinburgh. Until a few years before, Crosbie had inhabited a dingy flat among the silversmiths and coppersmiths of the Bow, from which it was a mere step to the howffs of the Grassmarket, where he had habitually drunk himself into oblivion. But – sign of the times – the inelegant advocate had flitted and built himself an elegant house in the new Edinburgh, at St Andrew Square, a minute's walk from the residence of Mr David Hume, and now Crosbie drank at home more than abroad. Would drink himself to an early grave, Maclaurin believed, which would be a pity, for despite his lack of social graces Crosbie had a brilliant and humane mind which he used to great effect in the courts. The two men got on very well. Although Crosbie thought Maclaurin would have been a long-faced Presbyterian girner in an earlier age, and Maclaurin had no doubt that Crosbie would have been a gouty old Restoration soak, they shared a passion for fair play which overcame such prejudices.

The same friendly sparring marked Maclaurin's relationship with Bozzy. Boswell had once told him why he was so drawn to the rituals of high Anglicanism, and so repelled by Presbyterianism: the English service filled him with joy and made him think of heaven, while sitting in a kirk filled him with gloom and made him think of hell. 'And so it should,' Maclaurin had told him unhelpfully, even though he himself had outgrown all but the semblance of religious adherence.

On the High Street the bustle was scarcely diminished, and yet the town was quieter than usual. The Court of Session had just risen for the summer recess, and lawyers and clients alike were fleeing hot, smelly Edinburgh for more salubrious rural retreats. The Maclaurins had a town house in Brown Square, near Greyfriars, but it had been Esther's wish to have her confinement amid the peace, trees and fresh breezes of Dreghorn, and Maclaurin, though he loved Auld Reikie, equally loved to get away from it.

James's Court was across the Lawnmarket on the north side, a towering tenement of eight storeys, with sweeping views towards Fife. The Boswells had one of the finest sets of apartments within this building, which at fifty years old was a mere juvenile in the medieval part of town. Their house was entered at ground level from the street and – almost unheard of – had its own second floor connected by an internal staircase.

A servant opened the door to Maclaurin, but Boswell himself charged out to greet him like a toy on a spring.

'The Sage is here, he is *here*!' He clasped his friend by the hand, and seemed almost, Maclaurin feared, about to kiss him. 'How very *good* to see you, John.'

'Ye saw me only on Friday,' said Maclaurin dryly. 'I had nae idea ye missed me sae muckle.' He was gratified to see Boswell wince at his Scotticisms – precisely the effect he had anticipated – and wondered about dropping a few more into the course of the afternoon.

Boswell read his mind. 'Now, now, don't embarrass me, John,' he said, which only made Maclaurin determined to try.

He was handed on to Mrs Boswell, who was not much calmer than her husband. 'Mr Johnson is not altogether the easiest guest,' she confided. 'I gave him my own bedroom, to make him feel more comfortable, but he will not stay in it, but roams around the house at all hours, and frightens the maid. I procure him the best food I can, and he eats it all but without seeming to taste it. And what a man for tea! We must make several gallons a day. Not that I should object, and I do wish James, since he is so influenced by him, might follow his example and drink more of it and less wine. But then, he will turn the candles upside down when they don't burn bright, and the wax drips all over the carpet . . . Still, I must not complain. He is a very great man, which excuses everything, does it not? How is Mrs Maclaurin?' Looking pale and tired (she had a five-month-old child and they were trying for another – Maclaurin, being aware of Boswell's sexual appetite, imagined this involved some fairly strenuous conjugating), she brought him into the drawing room.

It was quite spacious, almost palatial by old Edinburgh standards, though nothing to the grand new accommodations going up across the Nor' Loch. Maclaurin knew the four men already present: old Sir Alexander Dick of Prestonfield, scientist, physician and expert on the healthful properties of that strange Russian beast the rhubarb; James Gregory, a brilliant young doctor who might have had Sir Alexander as his patron had his own father not been Professor of Medicine at the University; Dr John Boswell, James's amiable but rather odd uncle; and Sir David Dalrymple, Lord Hailes, author and arbiter of polite taste, and a judge before whom the two advocates pled on a regular basis.

Hailes was only forty-seven but had the bearing of a man ten years older, possibly because he had been a judge nearly that long. Almost uniquely among the Scottish gentry at this period, he had been educated at Eton, a fact which partly accounted for the thin, reedy timbre of his voice, as though all his vowels had been strained through a sieve. Other judges, including Boswell's father Lord Auchinleck, prided themselves on the retention of both Scots pronunciation and vocabulary, but Scotticisms were entirely absent from Hailes's speech. Boswell envied and admired his sense of good taste, his anglicised bearing, his huge library, and the fact that he was one of the few 'North British' intellectuals whose work Johnson admired.

These four gentlemen were seated or standing in a semi-circle, their backs obscuring from Maclaurin's view the object of their attention, who at that moment emitted a long, low growl in response to something one of them had said. Maclaurin turned to Boswell, who had bounced in behind him. 'Is he out of humour?'

'No, no, he is in excellent form,' said Boswell. 'That is his laugh. I'll introduce you.'

Samuel Johnson was sixty-four, and wore his years as if he

had had all of them since birth. Crumpled, ungainly-looking, in dowdy, brown and far from spotless clothes, he was a kind of wide, heavy version of Maclaurin himself. He glowered with inquisitive but short-sighted eyes from under a large brow, on top of which was settled a bushy, greyish wig, half rose to take Maclaurin's hand, then subsided again with a series of grunts. But there was a smile playing on his lips, betraying his delight at being the principal, the only *real* attraction in the room – Margaret Boswell may have been young and pretty, but she was not *significant*. Only the Boswells' black cat, asleep on a window-seat, seemed unimpressed by him.

'We have heard much of your proposed expedition, sir,' Maclaurin said, deciding for the moment to speak English, as a courtesy to Johnson. 'It is quite an undertaking.'

'What do you say?' Johnson barked. 'You will have to speak up. I am hard of hearing.'

'Your expedition tae the Highlands,' Maclaurin barked back, changing his mind. 'Div ye no fear ye may be pittin ower muckle on yoursel?'

Johnson waggled a finger in his right ear and made a face, but he had understood perfectly well. 'Not at all,' he said. 'I have absolute confidence in Mr Boswell. My load shall be as nothing to his, since he will also have me to bear.'

'I hope he hasna misled ye that the roads are straight and the inns luxurious.'

'It would be a very green man who swallowed such a tale,' said Johnson, 'if Edinburgh is typical. When I got off the coach here on Saturday, I was thirsty and had some lemonade at the inn while word was sent to Mr Boswell that I had arrived. I asked for the lemonade to be sweetened, whereupon the waiter picked up a lump of sugar with his greasy fingers and dropped it in the glass. *Not* a good introduction. I threw the contents out of the window.'

'You learn Edinburgh habits quickly enough, then,' said Maclaurin. 'That is what we do with the disagreeable contents of any container.'

'So I have smelt,' said Johnson gruffly. 'And the waiter was lucky not to follow, since he was certainly disagreeable.'

'You see, John,' said Boswell nervously, 'if you disparage your own country, it is only an encouragement to him.'

'Frae whit ye hae tellt me, James, praising it has the same effect.'

Johnson growled for several seconds, apparently very happy with Maclaurin's sparring.

'When do you set out?' Maclaurin asked.

'Tomorrow morning,' Boswell said. 'We are bound first for St Andrews, then up the coast to Aberdeen, across to Inverness, and thence to Skye and the other islands.'

'I envy you, sir,' said Maclaurin to Johnson. 'There are few enough Scots that have seen a tenth of what you are about to see. It will be a great adventure.'

They were summoned for dinner shortly after this, and moved through to the dining room. Lord Hailes was put opposite Johnson, and the pair of them dominated the conversation as Boswell had hoped they would. Literature, language, art, manners – these were the subjects served up along with ashets loaded with grouse, mutton and beef; there were mountains of vegetables and several bottles of claret, although in deference to Johnson's abstinence the others restrained themselves more than they would usually have done. Boswell was in ecstasies and could barely stay seated during the meal. At the other end of the table, Sir Alexander and Gregory devoted themselves to Mrs Boswell, while James's uncle played with his food and dumbly inclined his head in whichever direction the conversation sounded more entertaining.

Afterwards, Johnson and Maclaurin discussed poetry. Maclaurin was an occasional poet, and had brought two of his own productions for comment, epitaphs on his father the mathematician. Johnson was appreciative of one, which was in English, but more critical of the other, which was in Latin. He then reeled off a huge list of all the men Boswell had introduced to him since his arrival – 'some,' he muttered conspiratorially, 'a good deal more interesting than others'. From breakfast to dinner a steady stream of blind poets, professors of this and that, doctors, lawyers and philosophers had come and gone. William Robertson, the Principal of the University, had not left his side all the previous day. Supper last night had been shared with two advocates, Mr Andrew Crosbie and Mr Robert Cullen.

'And what did you make of Mr Crosbie?' Maclaurin asked.

'I liked him,' said Johnson. 'With his heaviness and ugliness and absence of tact, and his dislike of cant – well, there is something endearing in a man of that sort, do you not think?' He looked at Maclaurin slyly.

'And young Mr Cullen? I ken them so well, you see, it is interesting to hear the impression they make on one who meets them for the first time.'

'Cullen?' Johnson considered for a moment. 'Very charming. A very polished and witty fellow.'

'We call him "courteous Cullen",' said Maclaurin, 'because he is all that you say he is. But at times he rides his wit very close to falling off it.'

'I should not like to see that – he did not seem vain. Give me an example.'

'Well, he is an excellent mimic, but mimicry is a dangerous sport. I was at a dinner not so long ago, where he entertained the company with a round of imitations of some of his advocate colleagues – myself included, by the way, done very sharp. The Lord President was there – Lord Arniston – and he was much amused, and invited Cullen to include some of the Bench in his performance. Well, Cullen couldna resist the temptation and did a splendid Monboddo discoursing on the speech patterns of the orang-outang, a Kames *bitching* this and *bitching* that, and a Gardenstone sharing snuff with his pet pig, causing us all to erupt. Says the President, "Why have ye left me oot? I canna allow it. Ye must dae me also." Cullen caught himself at the edge of the precipice and stepped back, said he thought he should not do it, but his lordship insisted – virtually commanded it. So Cullen took him off, the spitting image, and of course we were all in fits again. All, that is, save one.'

Hailes, who had been half listening, chuckled into himself. 'I really should not be hearing this,' he said.

''Tis nae secret, my lord,' said Maclaurin. 'I'm surprised ye've no heard it afore.'

'Oh, doubtless I was buried in my books,' said Hailes. 'I lead a retiring life out at Inveresk, sir,' he said to Johnson.

'What was the outcome?' Johnson asked.

'The President bore it with as good a grace as he could muster,' said Maclaurin, 'which wasna much. It must have been like looking in a very unflattering glass. When we had control of ourselves again he looked Cullen full in the face and said, "Very amusing, Mr Robert, very amusing, truly. Ye're a clever lad, very clever. But just let me tell ye – that's no way to rise at the Bar!"'

Johnson did not actually growl at this, but rocked back and forth, his shoulders shaking. 'If I'd known, I would have asked for Mr Cullen's Monboddo last night,' he said eventually. 'There was never so much nonsense spoken so learnedly as by Monboddo.'

'You know him, then?'

Johnson grimaced. 'Is it possible *not* to know him? His views precede him like trumpets. I have met him, yes, but only once. When he comes to London he gets into company for which I have no liking, so our paths do not cross. Does he still make that journey on horseback?'

'Oh, aye. All the way, and all the way back. He disdains a coach – a coach is a modern effeminacy to him.'

'That is a mad prejudice against convenience, surely. To travel on horseback in the Highlands, where no coach *could* go, is a necessity, but to London . . . Well, anyway, we were talking of him yesterday at dinner, and of that belief of his you mentioned a minute ago, that if one invited an orang-outang to dinner *it* might be taught to converse also. This is a ridiculous notion in itself. I find it doubly worrying in one whose trade it is to rectify error.'

'Lord Monboddo,' answered Maclaurin, 'if I understand him right, believes everything may be *possible*. That is, if we can *imagine* something, then it is not beyond comprehension, therefore it is possible for it to be.'

'You defend him as Mr Crosbie defended him,' said Johnson. 'And I say to you what I said to Mr Crosbie – it is as possible that the orang-outang does *not* speak, as that he speaks. However, you have a point. I should have thought it not possible to find a Monboddo; yet *he* exists.'

Johnson went on to describe the tour Boswell and Principal Robertson had taken him on, around the Royal Infirmary, the abbey and palace of Holyrood, and the kirk of St Giles, which was divided within into four separate churches, each congregation having its own minister and a different degree of Presbyterian rigour according to its taste. Dr Robertson, Johnson said, had explained to him some of the enthusiasms still at large in the Church of Scotland, which he and the Moderate party sought to keep at bay; especially in the matter of patronage. Johnson, as a high Anglican, thoroughly approved of the right of land-owners to appoint ministers to livings that they endowed, and to overrule the preference of congregations. This, however, was an unlucky topic: Maclaurin had cut his teeth as an advocate in the ecclesiastical courts of the General Assembly, held annually at St Giles', and had always pleaded on behalf of the opposition. When Johnson made a remark about superstitious peasants voting to be harangued every Sabbath by bigoted maniacs, Maclaurin flushed with anger. 'Just because the members o a congregation uphaud the richt to choose their ain minister disna mak them aw fanatics,' he said loudly, and with deliberate Scots emphasis.

Across the room, Boswell, who had been cornered by his uncle, caught the rumble and hurried over anxiously to defuse the situation. But Johnson was equanimity itself.

'Bozzy, Bozzy, this is your friend. I will not fight with a friend of yours, in spite of his warlike tones. A blockhead or a rogue is my enemy, but not a man of principle such as Mr Maclaurin.'

'I am happy to hear you say it,' said Boswell, shooting Maclaurin a warning glance.

'Not tonight anyway,' Johnson added. 'I do not say I would not take up arms against him in other circumstances. It is not a good idea always to treat your opponent with respect. Others may think that a sign of weakness, that your deference implies an admission of the justness of his cause. Would you not agree, Mr Maclaurin?'

'In some circumstances, aye,' Maclaurin said, calming down. 'Of course, as an advocate, one seldom pleads the causes closest to one's heart.'

'Very well said, sir. A lawyer has no business to have a heart. I go further: he has no business with the justice or injustice of the cause which he undertakes – he should be concerned only with the evidence, and its presentation, and leave the matter of justice to the judge and jury. However –' he paused, as if mustering his thoughts on some previously postponed subject '– I did not mean principally the law. I was thinking of your good Dr Beattie, who has attacked Mr Hume for *his* attack on religion.' He paused again: *pay attention, gentlemen, I am going to pronounce.* Boswell hushed the room. 'Now some people have thought Dr Beattie rude to ridicule Hume, but I applaud him. When a man sets himself up as being so much cleverer than the rest of us, and than all ages before us, can he be surprised if another man comes and laughs at him?'

Maclaurin was looking bemused at this sudden change of subject. 'We touched on this yesterday,' Boswell explained.

'There's no much ye didna touch on, it seems,' said Maclaurin.

'But as I said to you then, sir,' Boswell said to Johnson, 'it is impossible not to *like* Hume, in spite of what he has written. He is much better than his books.'

'You see?' Johnson said to Maclaurin. 'My point exactly. Bozzy, by his weakness for Mr Hume's company, and for fear of causing him offence, half surrenders to him. Whereas, if Mr Hume is the great man he thinks himself, we may deride his opinions all day and it will be like throwing peas against a rock. So there is not the slightest need to be polite with him. I wonder,' he said, 'whether it is Hume's being a blockhead that makes him a rogue, or his being a rogue that makes him a blockhead.'

'Oh, I must protest,' said Boswell. 'He is neither. I know him well.'

'We all do,' said Lord Hailes, but Johnson surged on as if he had not heard.

'Another fact endears Dr Beattie to me, and diminishes Mr Hume. It is a remark Hume makes in one of his essays about Negroes being naturally inferior to white men. They have never, he declares – not *ever* in the course of time – produced a single man of ingenuity or invention! And not just Negroes, but yellow and brown men, men of all other shades. You wonder if Mr Hume has ever heard of China. He says he *has* heard of a black man whose learning is highly spoken of, but thinks it likely this poor fellow has acquired a few simple accomplishments and can repeat them like a parrot. He means, I believe, a Mr Francis Williams, a Latin scholar and poet of note, who was educated at Cambridge. Does this mean that all men educated at Cambridge are mimicking parakeets? No, apparently only the coloured ones. And this, gentlemen, is your worthy and intelligent David Hume. Dr Beattie quite rightly deplores his offensive and ill-founded opinions.'

'Even supposing it to be an error of judgment,' said Hailes, 'that opinion, that footnote as I recall it, is, I think, twenty years old or more.'

'That is no excuse, sir, since Mr Hume declared his genius long before that, and *inserted* the footnote in later editions. He draws his conclusions from hearsay and an abhorrence of blackness, which in any man of sense is an ignorant way of going about things – in a philosopher it is inexcusable. Boswell will support me against such ignorance, won't you, James? He knows my man Francis Barber – my freely engaged and paid *servant*, I should say – who is as black as that cat in the window, and than whom a nobler and more civilised white man does not exist. Oh, but I forgot. Boswell is an enthusiast for slavery.'

Boswell tried to protest. 'This is unfair, sir. You know my regard for Mr Barber.'

'But not for his fellows,' Johnson said with glee. 'You see, gentlemen, while I celebrated Lord Mansfield's recent decision in favour of Somerset the slave, I believe my friend here was disturbed by it. It seemed to him to presage disaster for our empire. How does Scotland read it, gentlemen?'

There was an awkward silence. The previous year, England's Lord Chief Justice had ruled that a Virginia planter who had brought a slave into the country did not have the right to take him away again against his will. Johnson frowned at the lack of response.

'You have considered it, surely? Lord Mansfield is one of you, or once was. We got him young, I admit, and made something of him, but he is still a Scotchman. His judgment must interest you for that reason, if no other.'

Maclaurin, who was looking particularly uncomfortable, coughed. 'A similar case arose here a few years ago,' he said. 'It was due to come before the Court of Session but it did not, because the slave's master died, and so the issue was not resolved.'

Hailes said, 'There was an even earlier case, in the fifties. But on that occasion, the slave died during the process.'

'I see,' Johnson said. 'So you ought to have made your own judgment by now, but death has cheated you twice? How disappointing.'

'There will be a third time, I hae nae doubt,' said Maclaurin. 'And when it comes, I hope we will be as bold for liberty as the court in England.'

Hailes agreed. 'It is only a matter of time.'

'I am very glad to hear it,' Johnson said, smiling. 'And, Mr Maclaurin – I share your hope. But if you read Mansfield's judgment carefully, you will find it is not so much for liberty, as for the man Somerset. It does not say slavery is illegal, only that Somerset, now he is in England, cannot be compelled by his master to go back to Virginia. The effect is that Somerset, by being on English soil, has become free, but Lord Mansfield has not freed all slaves in England, let alone in the colonies. He is very specific on this point.'

'It's true enough,' Hailes said. 'He found it a very tricky issue. Somebody told me he rather hoped the case would go away, as ours did, because so much is at stake.'

'So much *money* is at stake, you mean,' Johnson said.

'I suppose that's what he had in mind,' Hailes said.

Boswell's uncle, looking permanently startled at the mighty intellects he found himself among, had been fluttering at the edges of this discussion for a minute or two. Now, unexpectedly, he spoke. 'Lord Mansfield, of course, has a slave of his own.'

Everybody stared at him. Dr Boswell seemed more surprised that he had been in possession of this information than the others were that he had released it. James came to his uncle's rescue. 'That is true, very true, I'd forgotten it. A domestic servant, I believe. But was she not the natural child of a relative of his lordship's? Something makes me think she was.'

'I could not say,' Dr Boswell said softly.

'Yes, a captain in the navy or something. And Mansfield took her into his own household when she was very young. Quite admirable, really.'

'But still, she is a slave, is she?' Maclaurin asked.

'I doubt she is kept in chains,' James Boswell said tersely.

'But perhaps if she is not free,' said his uncle, 'her being in the house might affect Lord Mansfield's, ah, judgment. That is all I meant.' As if this contribution had been altogether too much for him, Dr Boswell slid away again towards the door.

'This person I was talking to,' Lord Hailes said, 'did say that Mansfield was quite upset at having to reach a decision at all! Apparently he remarked that – now, let me get this right – that he would have all masters think their Negroes free, and all Negroes think themselves not, and then both would behave a great deal better.'

'Did Mansfield really say that?' Boswell asked.

'That's what I understand. It is a touch disingenuous, but . . .'

'But masterful,' Boswell said. 'Poor law but very practical.'

Maclaurin sniffed. 'I see now how his lordship rose to such eminence in England. He abandoned all principle and became a sophist.'

'Now, John, are we so much more principled here? We like sugar quite as much as the English.'

Johnson was looking very pleased with himself – like a man who had put a cat in a doocot. 'Well, well, we shall see, won't we? When this matter next comes before the Scottish courts, your liking for principle, Mr Maclaurin, for getting to the root of the matter, may serve you well.'

Maclaurin was about to rise to this jibe, but Johnson reached out and touched his arm lightly. 'I am serious, sir. I do not make fun of you. Let not *your* justice be dashed on the rock of expediency.'

Later, riding home to Dreghorn through the warm evening with the carriage window closed tight and his collar turned up, Maclaurin thought back over the last few hours. He'd be able to amuse Esther in the morning with details of Dr Johnson's bear-like qualities, his coarseness, his taste, his intelligence, his stupidity. The dislike of Hume, for instance, on account of his lack of religion, seemed to Maclaurin to display a narrowness of mind, an intolerance, which Johnson would have been the first to condemn in a Scotsman. How did Johnson reconcile the fact that men of faith whom he admired, such as Principal William Robertson, were also great friends of the infidel Hume? Or that Boswell, of whom he was so fond, was fond of Hume? All who actually knew Hume – as a man rather than as a demon – were fond of him: a more affable, charming, easy and entertaining companion it was impossible to imagine. He was now living off St Andrew Square in comfortable but somewhat slipshod circumstances, looked after by a housekeeper whom some said was his bide-in lover and others – on no better evidence than her rather masculine features – a man in disguise. As conversant with his cat as with old friends, and indulging his latest passion for the art of cookery, Hume was growing ever fatter and ever more relaxed about the prospect of not going to heaven when he died. Not going anywhere, in fact.

Johnson, it seemed, had latched on to a few of Hume's less intelligent remarks and made mountains out of them. The footnote about Negroes was silly and inexcusable, Maclaurin conceded. But elsewhere in his writings – he could not think where – he felt sure that Hume took as firm a stand against slavery as Johnson, or as his friend Adam Smith. 'Cruel and oppressive', surely he used some such phrase? And James Beattie up in Aberdeen might be a more staunch, more vociferous opponent of slavery, but, compared with Hume, he was not very bright.

Then again, Maclaurin thought, intelligence and political rectitude were not the same thing. Indeed, sometimes the former kicked hardest against the latter if it was imposed by stupid though well-intentioned people.

The hackney rattled on along the Colinton road. Maclaurin confessed to himself, as the lights of the city fell away, that these thoughts were not prompted by Johnson's conversation alone. He shuddered, feeling again the chill of embarrassment that had risen in him when he had mentioned the Scottish case, 'similar' to Somerset's, that had come to nothing. He had been involved in that case, and had felt bad about it ever since, because he had been on the wrong side.

Of course, an advocate could not be 'on the wrong side'. *A lawyer has no business to have a heart*, as Johnson had said. There was the difficulty. Maclaurin had taken the case – it was unprofessional, unheard of, for an advocate to decline business when approached by a solicitor, unless he had a personal interest in it – and then had discovered, too late, that he did indeed have a heart. He had been retained by the master, a doctor in Fife, to plead against his slave's bid for freedom. This slave, Davie Spens – he had taken the surname of the minister of Wemyss who had baptised him – had deserted the doctor after acquiring Christianity, and settled on a farm where he had got work and lodging. The doctor had wanted to send him back to the Indies and sell him to some planter.

The case was to have been heard in the Court of Session. It had seemed a straightforward case of rights in property. But the more Maclaurin had gathered information for the memorial he was to submit to the court, the less he had liked what he was doing. The arguments and authorities were strong and plentiful enough, but morally how could he prepare such material knowing that, if he won the case, he would be condemning a man who had tasted liberty to lifelong bondage? Maclaurin had had a few sleepless nights, torn between his duty as a lawyer and his feelings as a human being. It had been an immense relief to him when the doctor suddenly died and the case against Spens was dropped.

That had been only three and a half years ago. At least Maclaurin knew now where he would stand when the issue next came before the law. He remembered the shame he had felt on learning that a fund for Spens's defence had been set up among the colliers and salters of Wemyss parish, and that his lawyers had waived their fees. The Scottish colliers and salters, even now, were little better than slaves themselves, bound for life to the owner of the land on which they lived and worked – although they at least earned wages and had certain privileges in exchange for their perpetual serfdom and dismal labours underground. Nevertheless, their action – and that of the lawyers – had been most creditable, something Maclaurin could not now think of his own.

Yet he had had no choice, as an advocate. Men of law developed hard shells that enabled them to behave professionally, argue against their own instincts – fight to ruin a man's livelihood or reputation then go home to cuddle their bairns at night. Maclaurin was no better or worse than Boswell or Cullen or any of the others.

Johnson had addressed him as 'a man of principle'. But was he? He was for liberty but had pleaded – or would have – on behalf of a slave's master. He had argued for Christians to be able to choose their own pastors, but Maclaurin, a Presbyterian in so many other ways, did not really believe in God. When he thought of David Hume, his equanimity in considering death, he envied him. He envied him because he himself thought the same way, but somehow his intellect could not quite stretch to the utter freedom from fear that Hume enjoyed. Once or twice he had tried out his thoughts about this on Boswell and Crosbie: 'Surely we have no reason to expect a future state. It is a beautiful fancy, but what *right* has man to it?' Neither of his friends had been capable of discussing the matter coherently: Bozzy because, lowping back and forth between clap-ridden whores and the arms of religion, he was too anxious about his own state of sin; and Crosbie because he was too drunk.

The hackney was approaching the gates of Dreghorn. It was still dry and warm, and a large moon lightened the evening. Maclaurin decided to risk a few hundred yards in his own grounds. His coat would deliver him from evil. He rapped on the roof. 'I'll walk frae here.' He got out, paid the driver, and saw the carriage turn and head back towards the city. He stood still, breathed in – but not too deep – the fresh, silent air. An owl hooted.

He began to walk towards the house. He thought of Esther sleeping; his four living children, soon to be joined by another. Would it survive? God willing, some would say. Maclaurin held that phrase to be pure cant. It angered him that a supposedly benevolent God could have *willingly* taken three innocent bairns from them. What possible purpose, let alone benevolence, could there be in that?

He stopped again. Dreghorn at that moment was the loveliest place on earth. The owl drifted overhead, a ghostly white splash on the sky. What more could there be than this?

What right, he wondered again, with no friend there to be either appalled or made indifferent through intoxication, what right had man to expect a future state?

Ballindean, August 1773

James Wedderburn woke to the sound of his bedroom door opening. A few seconds later came the drawing of curtains. Light poured into the room. A servant was fussing about with hot water and a basin.

'Good morning, sir. Would ye like assistance tae dress?'

James stretched under the sheets. The bed was extremely comfortable. His head was mildly sore.

'What time is it?'

'It's no lang efter seiven.'

'Good God.'

'Sir John sent me tae wake ye. He is hoping ye'll accompany him roond the loch.'

James sat up. He had not yet got used to hearing his brother referred to as 'Sir John'. He did not even know if the title was officially sanctioned.

The servant, middle-aged and staid-looking, stood expectantly beside the basin.

'Are there no young maids to come and help me with that?'

The man looked mildly shocked. 'Oh, no, sir. That wouldna be richt.'

'Sir John wouldn't approve of it?'

'No, sir. Nor would Lady Margaret.'

'No, I don't suppose she would. Well, what about Sir John's neger?' James waited for a response. The man blanked him. 'Joseph Knight? I thought perhaps he might come this morning and show me his skills at shaving.'

The servant shifted uneasily. James carried on.

'I've not seen him since I came. Sir John has not sold him, has he? Or is he dead?'

'No, sir. But he's no weel.'

'What's the matter with him?'

'I'm no sure, sir. He's been in his bed twa days.'

'I'll look at him later. I'm a doctor.'

'I ken, sir. But – wi respect – ye'll no be able tae help him.'

'What do you mean?'

The man tapped the side of his head. 'It's in here, in my opinion. That's no easy cured. Especially no in a neger.'

'I've cured negers of most things,' James said. He had known within an hour of his arrival that something was amiss with Joseph: that he was nowhere to be seen, that his name was not referred to, that John seemed nervous whenever Jamaica was discussed – all these things pointed to some difficulty. Partly out of courtesy to Margaret, partly out of curiosity to see if or when John did mention him, James had bitten back his questions. But that had been yesterday. He sent the servant away, got up, washed and shaved his face, threw on some clothes and went downstairs.

Back in Scotland for the first time in twenty-seven years, James Wedderburn was adjusting rapidly. He had reached Edinburgh two days before from London, a quicker and more comfortable journey than the one he had made in the opposite direction as a fifteen-year-old. This time he had had overnight stops in good English inns rather than byres. He had spent a day in Edinburgh to see the astonishing changes taking place there, then pressed on to be reunited with his surviving sisters in Dundee, and with his brother John in Perthshire. Yesterday there had been a family gathering here at Ballindean, a great dinner and an evening of stories and recollections. And James had met, for the first time, his brother's wife, Margaret Ogilvy.

In three and a half years of marriage she had already provided John with a son and two daughters, the second girl just a month previously. Margaret was twenty-five, dark, tall – over five foot ten inches – carried herself with a slow, dignified grace, and spoke quietly yet with great firmness, so that James saw his brother acting upon her mildest requests as if they were the orders of a queen. More astonishingly, he found himself doing the same. This amused and mildly excited him. He wondered if he would behave like this with all elegant, rich, white women.

Perhaps both her voice and her history had prompted the odd notion he had had over dinner – that she was a kind of reincarnation of Mary, Queen of Scots. Her speech was tinged with the slightest French accent, the result of her having been born in France and of spending her early years there. Her mother had been so vociferously Jacobite that after Culloden she had been imprisoned in Edinburgh Castle. Several months had passed before she had escaped by impersonating an old servant-woman, and had got across the sea to Boulogne to join her husband in exile. He was Lord David Ogilvy, under whom John Wedderburn had served, and he too, after hiding in the Angus hills for months, had slipped aboard a ship for France. Lord Ogilvy's wife was now dead, he was still in exile, and he had not seen his daughter, who had been sent to live with her grandfather in the family seat at Cortachy Castle, for years.

At Cortachy, within a year of John Wedderburn's return from Jamaica, he and Margaret had been married. It had been a great sadness to the bride and groom, Margaret told James, that not one of their parents had been present for the occasion: John's own mother, who had lived to see him come home to Dundee, had died a few months before the wedding. 'And of course,' Margaret added, 'we would have wished for you to be there. And your brothers, too. But since you could not return to see your mother in her last days, we could hardly expect you to come back just for a wedding.'

Despite the softness of Margaret's voice, James had not missed the implied criticism. Of all their mother's sons, only John had been at her deathbed. She had never seen James again after 1746. Her declining health had been a major factor in John's decision to return to Scotland when he did. He and his sisters had written to James and Peter, warning them that she had not long to live, but neither had come home. It was still a sensitive matter, and James felt that all the implied guilt now lay on his head since Peter, just six months ago, had succumbed to yellow fever, leaving himself and John their generation's only male survivors.

After dinner, James had brought the subject up over cigars in the library. He stood in front of the painting of the three of them – John, Peter and himself – and thought how unreal Jamaica looked to him already.

'Margaret seems to hold it against me that I did not see Mama before she died. Why is that?'

'She feels strongly about such things. Think of the history of her own family.'

'And you? How do you feel?'

'It was your choice.'

'Come now, John. If Peter and I had not stayed on the plantations *you* would not have been able to come home when you did. *You* were here. All our sisters were with her. How many of us did she need?'

'That is unworthy of you,' John said.

'Then it was unworthy of us to go away in the first place. I'm sorry, John, but I cannot abide that kind of sentimentality. What is the *use* of it?'

'Family obligations are not about what is useful.'

'They should be. You and I have been of immense use to the family by being in Jamaica this last quarter-century. We rescued it from poverty and obscurity. But we did not do it through sentiment.'

No more had been said on the subject, but James felt that he had won a point. Now, when he got downstairs, he found his brother waiting for him in the hallway.

'What have you got me up at this hour for?'

'It's a lovely morning,' John said. There was no trace of the disagreement in his tone or expression. 'You'll see the house at its best. Then we'll have some breakfast.'

They walked in silence across the lawn and round the path which circled the loch. A light mist was gradually lifting from the surface of the water. There was hardly a breath of wind. On the far side they stopped to look at Ballindean.

'Well, what do you think?'

'I think you have done well, John. Very well. I must find a place like this for myself.'

'Does it remind you of anywhere?'

'Should it?'

'Not the house itself. Not the loch either. I mean the general position, the surrounding features. Do you not see a resemblance?'

James shrugged. 'Not really.'

'If the house were at the top of the braes instead of in their lee, and if Dundee's harbour were loading barrels of rum, and if the carse were planted in cane . . . ?'

'You mean Dundee is Savanna, and this is Glen Isla?'

'There's something in it, don't you think?'

'Well, you're stretching the point, but I see what you mean. Is that why you bought it?'

'No, not at all. It only occurred to me later.'

James nodded, reassessing his view of the place. Ducks clattered across the water. The vegetation was heavy with dew. He looked down at his boots, which were drenched. 'This is a very different wetness, though,' he said. 'I'd forgotten it, the freshness of it. But it will get into your bones in winter.'

'I never forgot it,' said John. 'Never. I always wanted this climate again.'

'So did Sandy. There may come a time when you will complain about it.'

'You mean, as Sandy would have? Well, let's hope that is many years away. What do you think of Margaret?'

'You've done well there, too. She'll give you plenty more healthy bairns. And I imagine she runs the household pretty efficiently.'

'Do you find her attractive?'

'She's very fine-looking. A credit to you.'

'I feel somehow we were fated to be together – because of our families' involvement in the Forty-five.'

'She was not even born then. You don't really believe in that kind of thing?'

John shook his head. 'I don't know. You mind you met Aeneas MacRoy yesterday?'

'Your comrade from Culloden? The man that's going to tutor your many sons and daughters? He's a dour one, John. A bit too akin to a kirk-session clerk for my liking.'

'There's more to Aeneas than you think. Anyway, remember I told you how he had saved the colours after the battle, how he had kept them all those years? When he came here and gave them to me, it seemed so . . . significant. And when I gave them to Margaret it seemed to close a circle. The colours of her father's regiment, and I handed them to her – I who had served under him, I whose own father had died in the cause, and who was now her husband. That felt like fate.'

James held up a finger. 'But that was *after* you were married.'

John smiled. 'Yes, well, I can see you are not persuaded. Come on, let's find some breakfast.'

It was still not much after eight, and only the servants were about. The brothers took their porridge and a couple of drams in the dining room, then retired to the library. The latest *Edinburgh Advertiser* was there, which James scanned while John wrote some business letters. When he had finished, he asked, renewing their earlier conversation, 'If you want a place like this for yourself, where do you intend to look?'

'I thought we could be neighbours.' James saw the slightly startled look on his brother's face, and grinned widely. 'It's all right, I'm jesting. I'll look nearer to Edinburgh, probably. Perthshire is very fine, it's where our blood springs from and so forth, but I think I'll trade being close to you for being a little closer to society.'

'We're hardly on the edge of civilisation here.'

'You're not far from it, and I've done my time in that location.'

'James, Scotland is a changed country, a settled country. The Highland line does not exist any more. If you buy near Edinburgh you'll pay for the privilege.'

'I can afford it.'

'And you'll be looking for a wife too?'

'Of course. Did I not always say I would? A Fife laird's plump daughter – or better, a Glasgow tobacco trader's. There'd be more money in that.'

James looked carefully to see his brother's reaction. He had always known that his cavalierism made John uncomfortable. Now, safely married and a father, would he feel less threatened by it?

'You'll be ready to start a family, then?' John said. 'I mean a real one.'

'You mean a white one. Of course, and the sooner the better. I'll be forty-three next week. I'll wager you I'm wed before I'm forty-four. That's why I intend to spend the next few weeks in Edinburgh – to see what the availability of young ladies is.'

'Yet you've not brought any of your *other* family with you, to benefit from whatever union you make. I suppose they'd be inconvenient when you open negotiations with these young ladies' fathers.'

'John, sarcasm does not become you. Anyway, you should know me well enough by now. You cannot embarrass me on that count. The father-in-law I get will be perfectly acquainted with the world, and will know that his daughter's husband, if he had not been a-whoring in Jamaica, would only have been a-whoring closer to home. As for my other *family*, as you so quaintly put it, I owe them nothing. *They* owe *me* – there's not a black bastard on that island with my blood in it that is yet a slave. And that brings me to another point – why have I not seen a sign of Joseph since I arrived? And why have you not even breathed his name? I know he is here. What's wrong?'

John got up from behind his table and went over to the window. 'I've been waiting for you to ask. I didn't care to bore you with it yesterday, and Margaret finds the whole affair quite distressing. The truth is, we have been having some considerable trouble with Joseph.'

'Trouble?'

'He has turned recalcitrant. I begin to regret ever having brought him here.'

'What has happened? I hear he is lying sick in his bed.'

'Pretending to be sick. I'm not sure where to start. How much did I write about him in my letters these last two, three years? Did I tell you he was baptised?'

'Yes, I recall that. I mind thinking it was probably inevitable once he was in Scotland. But, as you know, I was ever with George Kinloch on that subject – against Christianising them. How is *he*, by the way?'

'George? He is well, and well established at Kinloch. He is a Justice of the Peace now.'

'George keeping the peace? My God, how we are all come home! Well anyway, tell me about Joseph.'

'To begin with, he behaved very well. We became friends, I suppose you could say, on the voyage home. I felt that he was

194

very uneasy – he'd only once been on a ship before, when he was brought from Africa – so I took it upon myself to treat him with perhaps less formality than I should have. In a way I became more mentor than master. Don't look like that – land rules cannot last two months at sea. We talked on a variety of subjects, and I taught him draughts and backgammon, and sometimes read to him – the Bible, and some easy poetry.

'You'll probably remember, he was a silent, unsmiling, reserved kind of boy most of the time at Glen Isla. I wanted to bring him out of himself, and we had so much time together on the voyage that I believe I was making real progress. He became enthusiastic about learning to read and write for himself. This, I thought, was admirable – it would be good for him to have a *little* culture. We made a start, but then we hit bad weather and that spoiled my plans. He got very sick, was scarce able to lift his head, let alone a pen. In fact, the way he is at the moment, in his bed, is not unlike how he was then. He never groaned or said anything, he just lay in a kind of stupor. It's the same now.'

'Only now it is a pretence.'

'A pretence or a plan, yes, I think so. You know how they get it in their heads that they can outwit you by wearing you down. Well, by the time we made land there was much else to do and I said we would see about getting him lessons once things were more settled. I'll say this, he did not girn for months, but carried himself just as a servant should. His blank face was perfect – gave him a kind of dignity, even if he was not aware of it himself. We were much admired – me for having him, and him for being mine. And of course the women wanted to eat him alive. That was a source of the trouble, though not at first.'

'He was always a good-looking neger.'

'Too good,' John said. He came away from the window, and went over to the bookshelves. He looked for a particular volume, a slim one, took it down and laid it on the table. 'This is instructive,' he said, patting the book. 'I'll come to it by and by. Anyway, the purchase of this property and my marriage were soon the only matters that concerned me – forby making sure of our business affairs, of course, but they, as you know, were running pretty smoothly. The wedding went off at Cortachy, and Joseph played his part adequately –'

'What did you have him do?'

'Nothing very much. He was our page. Really he was there for decoration, and I must say he looked very fine. Then when we got possession here he seemed to settle into his tasks readily enough – looking after my clothes, shaving me, attending me to this place and that, helping with things like unpacking the books in here – but within a few weeks he was deaving me about his lessons, and about getting religious instruction. He said I had promised him, which of course I had not. He was beginning to aggravate me – it was ridiculous, but I kept feeling that I had to find him things to do. And then, like the answer to a prayer, Aeneas MacRoy came on the scene.'

James laughed. 'It must have been an awesome prayer that that fellow was the answer to.'

'Believe me, his timing was perfect. And he has proved loyal ever since. He had a school in Dundee but was closing it down. I got him to meet Joseph, and left them to themselves for half an hour. Then I asked Aeneas if Joseph would do, and he said he would, so we arranged that once a week he would come out to teach him his letters, and sometimes Joseph would go into town and sit in his school, so long as it existed. And then I told Joseph what we had agreed.'

John looked agitated. He picked up the slim volume he had selected, and holding it in one hand began to slap its spine into the palm of the other.

'Would you believe, I thought he was going to object. It was in his face that he did not like Aeneas MacRoy, that he did not want to be taught by him. Well, I thought, I will not have that nonsense. "Joseph," I said, "Maister MacRoy will teach you to read and write, or nobody will." He saw that I was very angry, and he bowed his head and said he was grateful. But I should have realised that he was not. That he was using me. I should have put a stop to it then and there.'

'You should never have started it,' James said. 'Once you have opened that door to them there is no locking them out.'

'Well, it was too late. He was already receiving instruction from the minister at Inchture. And for a while, indeed, he behaved himself. He made progress at his lessons, and he seemed less sullen. But then someone came between him and Aeneas.'

'Let me guess. A woman.'

'A woman, aye. Ann Thomson. She was a housemaid here. She took a fancy to Joseph, and Aeneas took a fancy to her. And she encouraged him, I've no doubt – played him off against Knight, and enjoyed being the prize of two rivals. Not that I knew any of this at the time, you understand.'

'Well, you would be occupied with your own romance. You were just married, after all.'

The book flew from John's hand and skidded across the floor. James bent to retrieve it, glanced at the title page, and handed it back, giving an amused look which his brother did not return.

'James, I could take offence at that. The two instances have absolutely nothing in common. Ann Thomson was no better than a harlot.'

'No better or no worse? What did she do?'

'What all harlots do. She lured an upright man into making himself foolish, then fell pregnant by a knave. She broke Aeneas's heart.'

'Does he have one?'

'Why do you not take me seriously?' John's voice was almost a shout.

'I am sorry.' James held up an appeasing hand. 'Really, I am very sorry. I just find it hard to believe that you are in such a state about a neger and a whore.'

'They were in my house,' John hissed. 'She toyed with the feelings of an old, a trusted comrade, and all the time she was fornicating with Joseph. *He*, meanwhile, was becoming a Christian. Ann Thomson had his child not three months after he was baptised.'

'Does the child live?'

'No, it died at once. That should have been the end of the matter. I allowed the mother to lie in childbed here, and paid for the physician and the funeral, but once it was all over I dismissed her. She was clearly a bad influence on Joseph, and Margaret said that the housekeeper found her to be of a disruptive and rebellious nature. Had she stayed, half the maids would have expected me to pay for them to have bastards. She went back to Dundee, where she came from.'

'But obviously that wasn't – the end of the matter?'

John paced round the room. He had put the book down again, and was now punching the palm of one hand with the fist of the other. 'She had her claws well into Joseph. Even thus parted, they somehow contrived to keep up their liaisons. Aeneas came to see me, most anguished, and said he could not be in the same room as Joseph any more, so the lessons would have to end. I agreed with him – I thought it was a fitting punishment for the way Joseph had behaved, although, as it turned out, he had already learned enough to cause more trouble. But then I was left with what to do with him again. This is something I never thought of before. At Glen Isla he would have been sent to the fields. But it is not so simple here. When you have only one slave, you cannot dispose of him as you could in Jamaica.'

James nodded thoughtfully. 'I see what you mean. And he knew that too, which is why he grew so recalcitrant?'

'Yes, I think so. When the lessons stopped he pestered me to let him improve his skills at dressing hair, and I sent him to a barber in Dundee. He must have met with Ann Thomson there, and she worked her charms on him again. The outcome was, they ran off to Edinburgh and were married. Or at least, they say they were married, by some secessionist.'

'Perhaps they love each other,' James said dryly.

John snorted, a sound somewhere between derision and rage. 'Call it love if you wish. I would not grace their relations with that word. Have you read this?' He picked up the book again, opened it at a marked page, passed it over. 'It is Edward Long's commentary on the Somerset case at Westminster last year.'

'Deplorable decision. As you can imagine, it was much discussed in Savanna. But you are not worried about its implications for Joseph, surely?'

'No. This is Scotland, not England, and if the Union did nothing else it at least preserved us our own laws. But have you read this?'

'No, I've not. Long is very thorough, I hear. I'm keen to read his book on Jamaica when it's finished. What about it?'

'Read that passage there. I might have written it myself.'

James glanced over the page, then read aloud: ' "The lower class of women in England are remarkably fond of blacks, for reasons too brutal to mention; they would connect themselves with horses and asses, if the laws permitted them." Ah, that old favourite. "By these ladies they generally have a numerous brood. Thus, in the course of a few generations more, the English blood will become so contaminated with this mixture, and from the chances, the ups and downs of life, this alloy may spread so extensively, as even to reach the middle, and then the higher orders of the people, till the whole nation resembles the Portuguese and Moriscos in complexion of skin and baseness of mind." Well, John, I presume you find Mr Long's argument persuasive?'

'You do not?'

'I find it exaggerated. It would require a very large number of Joseph Knights to have the effect he suggests. On the other hand, he is of course absolutely right. Why even risk it? Common white women *are* fascinated by negers, because they have heard they are all hung like stallions, and negers lust after genteel white women because of their refinement. Both are grounds for not bringing the blacks over here, which I have always been against – I would not have brought Joseph Knight, had he been mine.'

John took the book back somewhat abruptly, put it back on the shelf, and began pacing again.

'If it puts your mind at ease,' James added, 'I won't be continuing here the habits I had in Jamaica. That was another time and place.'

'Well, we always differed on that particular subject,' John said, 'so we'll not pursue it. And we'll judge Mr Long by his *History* next year. The point is, Joseph came home and announced he was married, and within a very short while he used his newly acquired skills to read all about the Somerset case in this.' He picked up the *Edinburgh Advertiser* and flung it back down again. 'I have no doubt that the Thomson woman pushed him on down the road he has now taken. She was bitter against me and Margaret although we were as fair to her as we could be. But she was not alone in encouraging him.'

'Who else?'

'Others. I do not know.'

'And what road *has* he taken?'

'First he got it into his head that Lord Mansfield had set him free. Then, when I disabused him of that notion, by patiently explaining the details of the case, and that England is not Scotland, and when I had also made it clear that his best interests lay in behaving himself with a master who treated him well and imposed no arduous service on him – after all that, he demanded that I take back his wife – his *supposed* wife – who is pregnant again – and set them up in a cottage on the estate!' John came to a halt, heaving like a bull, and waited for a response.

'Well, there's a spirit in him,' James said. 'I'll say that. I hope you gave him a good whipping to break it.'

'I have never raised my hand against him.'

'You'd not have this trouble if you had.'

'Well, I did not. I told him his request was impertinent and out of the question, that if he really had married her it was without my consent and so he must bear the consequences, and that if he did not quickly learn to control himself I would ship him back to Jamaica.'

'And he said . . .'

'He said in that case he would have to leave my service.'

'He cannot.'

'Of course he cannot.'

'He is an impudent rascal. There is only one thing for it and that is to have him flogged.'

'It is not so simple as that, James. We are in Scotland now.'

'Well, what difference? He is yours to do with as you wish. You would beat such tricks out of a dog, and you would certainly do the same with a neger at Glen Isla. What about . . . what was his name? Charlie. You thrashed him to an inch of his life. Why so timid now you have come home?'

'Because, even if we were not in Scotland, flogging would not work. Did it work with Charlie? He still ran off. He still killed himself. That's why I wanted to try another way with Joseph.'

'Clearly that hasn't worked either. And if you do not deal with him he will run off too.'

'That is what I anticipate.'

'Well, deal with him. Or let me deal with him.'

'No.'

'I'll have him out of his bed and pleading for mercy in ten minutes.'

'No. I'll not have that here.'

'Then he'll run. Maybe he'll run for the hills as they do in Jamaica. Maybe he'll become a sooty Rob Roy.'

'James, you exasperate me. There is a serious principle at stake here – the principle of property, of ownership.'

'I know there is. That's what I'm saying. A slave is a slave. To pretend otherwise is to delude everybody, including yourself and him.'

'Well, we'll see who is the more deluded. I've thought this through. He won't go to the hills. He will go to the Thomson woman in Dundee. I will have been deprived of my property. I will *not* have treated him ill. I *will* have provided him with far more than he could reasonably have expected. He will be in the wrong, and I the one who has been wronged. The law will – must – be on my side. That is why I don't want to beat him. I don't want to give the law any reason to think of him as the injured party.'

James shrugged. 'Well, it's not how I would do it but perhaps you're right. Do everything by the book, John, but for God's sake make sure he does not slip your grasp, or you will have every servant with a petty grudge following his example.'

'No. He is different. Other servants can give notice to leave and I cannot stop them. But I can stop Joseph. That is why I have got Aeneas MacRoy to watch his movements – something Aeneas is more than willing to do. Joseph is forbidden to go to Dundee, forbidden, in fact, to leave Ballindean unless with me. If Aeneas gets a hint that he is about to go – if he sees him folding away his clothes or begging some extra food from the kitchen – he is to tell me at once. I'll know the minute he passes the gates, or before he is halfway to town at any rate.'

'You'll stop him? By force?'

'If necessary. But not by the force of *my* hand. As you said, I'll do it by the book, with a warrant. Our good friend Mr Kinloch is a Justice. So is Mr James Smyth of Balhary – he also has interests in the plantations. So is Sir John Ogilvy of Inverarity – a cousin of Margaret's. I can depend on all of these gentlemen to have either my family's welfare or their own at heart, should it come to it. I foresee no difficulties over securing a signed warrant for Joseph Knight's apprehension.'

James was relieved to see a look of determination in his brother's eyes. 'That's more like it,' he said. 'That's the Wedderburn in you. Perhaps I've been over hasty, John – not been home long enough. I forget how great the law is in Scotland. The law *of* Scotland. You have the law on your side. You cannot fail to keep him.'

Dundee, 16 November 1773

Ann Thomson's sister Peggy was away home, and Ann was alone with her daughter at last. She felt the silence cover her like the shawl that was across her shoulders. She was sitting in one of two old chairs drawn up opposite each other at the ingle. Outside the one-roomed cottage – nothing; nobody going by the gable end on the muddy road, no voices filtering through from the neighbouring buildings. Inside – just the steady clicking of the fire. The spinning-wheels were pushed away for the night. Her mother had gone to the box-bed set in the recess at the far end of the room, closing the doors against draughts. Even the bairn was quiet, giving out none of the tiny murmurs and squeaks that sometimes punctuated her sleep; so quiet, in fact, that it made Ann nervous. She had brought the crib in beside her, close to the fire where she knew never to leave it unattended in case of spitting coals. It was good when the bairn slept so well, but at least when she cried she demonstrated that she was without question, alive. Ann had lost one child already, and could not bear the thought of losing this one.

The cottage was in the Hilltown – a poor part of Dundee north and east of the High Street – a seemingly indiscriminate scattering of narrow, one- and two-roomed houses among a confusion of gardens and kailyards. All but a very few of the roofs were thatched with straw or laid with turf divots, and the stone lums poked through the thatch like ancient markers in a kirkyard. On a windless night such as this, the reek of peat and coal which they puffed out hung in the air like a shroud.

In the cottage lived in by Ann, her mother and her child, tiny thick-glassed windows admitted a minimum of light during the brief winter days, and at night gave out only the faintest flickering indications of life within. The floor was of trodden clay, damp and cold at this time of year. The hearth, built of stone flags, was where their waking life was centred. When the fire faded, Ann would bank it up with dross, then creep into the box-bed with her mother, taking the bairn as well. On the two nights Joseph had been here, Ann and he had made up another rough bed in front of the fire, of plaids and blankets and all the clothes they could fling on top, and had wrapped themselves together against the cold.

But Joseph was not here tonight. They had taken him away yesterday, back to Ballindean. He had gone quietly enough, and Ann herself was calm now, although her calmness surprised her. Yesterday she had been a raging harridan, fighting to keep Joseph when the town constable, Sandy Pullar, came with the warrant. In the Hilltown, officers of the law did not stand on ceremony. Sandy Pullar had been squeezing his enormous bulk past the door even as his knuckles rapped on it. The space behind him had been filled by another two men.

'Noo, lass,' Pullar said, 'let's no hae ony bather. I'm here for your man. It's his name wrote here clear as ye can see, and if there's anither runawa Negro in Scotland cried Joseph Knight I'd like tae see ye produce him.'

She leapt from her spinning-wheel at the other end of the room and planted herself in front of Pullar, hands on hips, her head no higher than the middle of his chest. 'And I'd like tae see ye produce the piece o paper that says ye can tak him awa,' she said. 'Shame on ye, Sandy, tae sinder a man frae his wife and bairn! Shame on ye when he's done naething wrang. All he wants is tae be let alane. What has he done tae ye, that ye come tae tak him awa like this?'

'I am jist daein my duty,' said Pullar, but she could see he did not like it, and would have preferred a case of robbery or assault, where the miscreants he came for tried to fight their way out and he could set his men on them. But here there was no hint of a battle to come: only Ann's mother, hardly pausing at the wheel, as if, half blind and hard of hearing as she was, she did not understand the gravity of what was happening; and Joseph standing behind her with the weak light of the window at his back, cradling the bairn in his arms, saying to Ann he would go with them, there was no sense in bones being broken since he would have to go willing or unwilling. Ann saw Pullar fumbling in his tunic for the document, and she waited till it was in his

204

hand and then snatched it from him, while still barring the way to him and his two brutes.

'Noo, lass –' Pullar said again, but she cut him off with a scream.

'Dinna you *noo lass* me, Sandy Pullar. Ye've kent me since we were bairns. Ye'll jist need tae bide whaur ye are till I read this oot – this *warrant*, as it cries itsel. Hae ye read it yoursel? Dae ye ken the filth ye've been cairryin in yer pooch? Weel, I'm a guid reader, Sandy, sae I'll make it plain tae ye. "Sir John Wedderburn of Ballindean" – a fine title for a man that sends ithers tae dae his dirty work – "claims that Joseph Knight, whom he has hitherto entertained in the same manner as he does his other servants" – aye, that'll be the anes he pays – "and means to continue to do so" – *ha!* – "and humbly presumes that the law will not disappoint him of his service during life, and the said Joseph Knight having within these two days past packed up his clothes and threatened to absent himself from his service, although the petitioner never gave him manumission or promised to release him from his slavery, the petitioner prays that the Justices of Peace of Perthshire grant warrant to apprehend the person of the said Joseph Knight and bring him before them for examination upon the facts as set forth" – God save us, whit facts, Sandy? There's nae facts here, it's aw clash and claivers. It's a pack o lees.'

Sandy moved to the right to get past her. She blocked his way.

'My man has as muckle right as ony man tae leave his maister's service,' she said. 'Mair right, since he was forced intae it.'

'Annie . . .' Pullar and Joseph both said it simultaneously. She ignored them both.

'Whit kind o country is this that ye can come and tak a man back intae bondage, awa frae his family, even awa frae Scotland if *Sir John Wedderburn* wants tae send him back tae Jamaica?'

'That's no for me tae say, lass,' Sandy said, stepping to the left. She blocked him again, turned to the signatures at the foot of the warrant.

'Weel, I'll tell ye,' she said. 'It's a country whaur big glaikit chiels like you dae whit they're tellt by the justices, and the justices that sign warrants are nane but *Sir John Wedderburn*'s

205

cronies and fellow slave-drivers. Justices! Their notion o justice is jist whitever will keep them fat and rich on the sweat and blood o ithers. Here, ye can tak back your trash.'

She thrust the warrant at the constable and stood daring him to shift her. But then she became aware that Sandy was no longer looking at her, and she turned, and Joseph had come up beside them and was holding the bairn to her saying she must be strong, he would have to go, she knew what they had to do, they had discussed it often and she would see him again soon enough. And he kissed the bairn and put her into Ann's arms and then he kissed Ann on both cheeks and once on her mouth and turned to Pullar and his men and stepped between them and out of the door. And all the fight went from her and she clutched the bairn to her and followed them out, tears streaming down her face, and she shouted down the road at him, 'Come back, Joseph Knight!' And the neighbours at their doors were hissing at the procession, and though most of them hissed at Sandy Pullar, some, she knew, hissed at Joseph Knight, and Joseph turned and raised his hand, without a smile, and called, 'Be strong, Annie,' and then he was walking again between the constables, and turned the end of the street and was out of sight. And when she went back into the house, her mother's wheel was clacking away as ever, and without looking up she said, 'Annie, I'm wae for ye and Joseph, and nae man should be treated in that way, but ye mairrit on a black man and ye maun thole the consequences. Sit ye back doun, and we'll spin a way for tae get him back.' And Ann, her face still wet and her tongue unable to speak, put the bairn in the crib, and took her place at her own wheel.

The room was dark except by the fire. Ann had had candles lit earlier, but after her sister Peggy had left she had put them out, and now the fire's red glow was enough for her thoughts. Peggy had been there until half an hour ago. It was she who had said, when the first bairn died, that it was better, if they were to go, that they went sooner and not later. 'That way ye dinna hae time tae grow ower fond o them.' She had said this as one who should know, having lost three of her own, but Ann believed it was not the bereaved mother who spoke but something outside, beyond grief: the need to keep despair at bay. For how could you grow more fond of a bairn than you were when it first slid out of you, mewling and peching and bloody and hungry for life? How could you love it more than the first time you took it to your breast and it sucked the milk from you? Impossible – and yet you did. The love became something solid and immovable, it grew with the tiny life, and so Peggy was right also, in a way. Yet there was not a day went by, not an hour when she held her new bairn, that Ann did not mourn the dead one, that was born and died at Ballindean.

Except for that other one, the new bairn was bonnier than any Ann had ever seen: a wee white lassie with a flat nose and full lips and an astonishing shock of curly black hair. They had called her Sarah, but Ann seldom named her; thought of her as a small unknowable being still to grow into herself, still to be sure of an identity. She had noticed at once how, even when they had agreed on the name, Joseph had shied away from using it, and now she had caught that habit. A name, she understood, was something most people took for granted; but for Joseph a name, the very act of naming, carried a strange and ponderous weight.

Peggy was away back to the man that had given her the three sick bairns, the man that would not come into this house because of the 'blackie'. Peggy's man Chae was a big glaik from Forfar, often half drunk and always wholly daft. He harboured the suspicion that the blackie was 'unco, no chancy', and he did not have the manners or sense to keep it to himself. 'Auld Clootie!' Ann had spat at him, a while back. 'The Deil! How no jist come oot and say it if that's whit ye think? Dae ye want tae see his cloven feet? Awa an hide ahint a dyke if ye're feart frae him. But dinna come here when he's awa –' she had paused significantly '– for he kens when ye hae been and he can pit a curse on ye whether he's here or no.' Chae had not been near them since.

Ann's mother was strong-minded but physically wearing out. For years, since before her husband's early death, she had been at the flax-spinning, and now, though her eyesight was failing, she spun with a thrawn determination, as if her life depended on it. But she spun not for herself but for Annie and her bairn. All day, the two women sat at their wheels with piles of flax beside them, spinning it into yarn, and every week the yarn merchant's agent came with more flax, and took their spindles away to market. The agent, a Fife man called Thomas Ritchie, weighed the flax he brought and the yarn he took away, and made sure, as he did with all his spinners, that his master was getting back what he gave out, allowing for a certain amount of necessary wastage. He entered the figures in a ledger, and each week he handed over what the women were due for their labours. It was never very much.

The yarn merchant was also the landlord, and he deducted the rent of the cottage from what he paid them. Ritchie could also give them credit to buy cheese, coals, oatmeal and so forth from certain traders, and this debt diminished at a painfully slow rate and was always topped up before it was cleared. The tick system was what enabled them to eat and stay warm, but it also bound them to Ritchie and his master, especially at a time, as now, when linen prices were depressed.

Ritchie was not an unkind man, and he had known Mrs Thomson for thirty years, but, as he reminded them when the quality of her yarn was not as it should be, but uneven and knotty, his master was not much interested in charity. In her best days, ten or twenty years ago, Mrs Thomson had earned as much as four shillings a week, but the effects of old age and the fall in prices meant that they now struggled to bring in that amount between them. Ann's mother had been spinning all her life, and would die at the wheel if not in her bed, and sometimes it seemed to Ann that she herself would be spinning into eternity.

Peggy came by two or three times a week. The sisters had had a good laugh at the spell Joseph cast over Chae. 'He's a fool,' said Peggy of her husband. 'It maks it easy tae rule him but there's nae muckle company tae be had frae a man like thon.' Peggy was not afraid of Joseph and it was clear that on these visits to Ann she was happy to get away from Chae and girn about him. This night, she had claimed to come out of sisterly concern in their time of trial. But whatever she said, it was never long before she turned the conversation round to her own woes: Chae's drinking, his stupidity, the long hours they both laboured, she at the spinning, Chae at his handloom weaving coarse linen from her yarn. She complained about their lack of money, though with no family they were better off than many, or would have been if Chae had not poured most of his earnings down his thrapple. And though Peggy always brought something when she came – a poke of tea, a lump of cheese, a pint of gin – she brought only what she could get a good portion of back again before she left. Never a blanket or a bonnet for the bairn, and never siller.

Ann tried not to resent her sister's resentment. It was hard for her, to see the bairn healthy and growing when she had none of her own. But her situation was common – even among the gentry as many bairns died as lived. Tonight, with the trouble over Joseph, Ann had felt doubly oppressed by Peggy's constant moaning. The silence of the night was a blessed relief. How peaceful it was to be alone with the bairn, leaning into the warmth of the fire, and thinking of Joseph nine miles away at Ballindean.

Oh, she could be fierce when she chose, the women of Dundee were famous for it, she could rant and roar with the best of them. But the thing that had fuelled her rage most, the need to protect her family, was also perhaps what now brought her calm. She could hear Joseph's voice, against the hiss of the coals in the fire: 'Be strong, Annie.' It was not what she had wanted to hear. She loved him. She had wanted to hear his love, but she knew how hard it was for Joseph to give his feelings up to her. Still, she trusted him. She always had. But sometimes she wondered, did he trust her?

He had told her many times what he would do when this time came. He had worked it out long before he took off from Ballindean. He would act the way the Wedderburns expected him to act, but when he did run, he would run not to hide, but to be found. More than a year ago he had read in the paper about Somerset, the slave in England, and how the judge there had said he could not be forced to go back to Virginia against his will. Somerset therefore had become free, and the onlooking blacks of London packed into the public gallery had celebrated that freedom with cheers and handshakes all round, and later had held a great dinner at which they had drunk the health of Lord Mansfield. But Joseph had read the reports carefully and repeatedly and had seen that it was only the master's right to take Somerset out of the country that had been overthrown, and that if the master had not been going back to America himself the case would not have arisen.

Ann had said, 'Whit use is it if Wedderburn canna send ye awa but he can keep ye frae me?' So Joseph had read again, and he had talked to some of the servants about the case, and from them he had heard of something that had occurred, right there in Perthshire, only a year or so earlier. A slave woman had run away from her master, and when the master had sought to have her apprehended, the sheriff depute of the county had thrown out the petition. Joseph had latched on to this information like a terrier. This was judgment of a different order. The Sheriff Depute of Perthshire was a man called John Swinton, and it was around him that Joseph had built his hopes.

Since then they had learned enough about the machinery of the law to know what would happen next. Joseph would be brought before the justices and be given a chance to state his case against the petition of his master. The justices, being the friends and accomplices of Wedderburn, would find against him. But – and this Ann had discovered by careful inquiry in Dundee – they would have to make a statement of their decision, and they would have to supply a copy of it to Joseph. With that in his possession, he could then make his own petition against what they had 'decerned'. And the man to whom he could appeal was the sheriff depute of the county, John Swinton.

But all that was in the future. How long Joseph must remain at Ballindean, how long before the sheriff heard their petition, these were questions to which she had no answer. She had the name of a lawyer in Perth, a Mr Andrew Davidson, who could draw up the document for them, but she had no means of paying him. Joseph had sixpence a week in 'pocket money' from Wedderburn, and had been saving what he could of it for months, but this amounted to no more than a pound or two. The work done by Ann and her mother was barely enough to cover their weekly needs, and most of what they earned came in the form of tick. She had to hope that the lawyer would see the rightness of their cause, and work for a nominal fee, or for promise of future payment. If he did not, she did not see how they could reach to the ear of John Swinton.

She wondered again why she was so calm. It was not in her

nature to be passive, to accept fate. Even when she had got the place at Ballindean, through a series of interviews that led her from Mr Ritchie, who had put in a word for her, to a dressmaker cousin of Mr Ritchie's master, and from her to Lady Wedderburn's housekeeper ('Can ye spin, lass? The mistress is maist particular, and I agree wi her, that the maids here shall spin when the rest o the day's darg is done.') – even then she had not reckoned, as other young women in her position might have, that she had *arrived*, that she only had to do what she was told and life would be a more than tolerable burden ever after. A burden was a burden and she didn't believe a body should ever grow to like it, though it might have to be borne. And then she had first got sight of Joseph, and she had known why she had come to the big house out on the Perth road: she had come for him.

The other maids, those that weren't feared of him at least, also tipped their eyes at him and she knew she had to stay ahead of them. There was talk of wild neger lust and the prodigious attributes of African men, but none of that fitted with what she saw. She saw a quiet, deep, thoughtful man, not coarse at all; handsome, clean, soft-voiced and smooth, but with power in the way his body moved; a man whose first line of defence was solemnity, who did not readily open himself to anyone; whose self-reliance seemed a sign of both strength and vulnerability.

Maybe she was also attracted just because he was so different from some of the other menservants, who were crude and leering around the maids when they got a chance, always trying for a fondle or a kiss, whereas Joseph stood off and was cool almost to the point of rudeness, making out that he was not interested in their favours. But surely, she thought, any healthy man would be interested in bonnie Annie Thomson – unless, as somebody whispered once, he was his master's *very* personal servant.

Half the lassies didn't understand that insinuation. Ann understood but didn't believe it – not of Joseph, not of John Wedderburn. The whisper was there, she was sure, only because there was a mystery in Joseph, in his blackness, in his history, in his unique standing in the house, which made him both less and more than the other servants, both closer to and more utterly removed from his master. Ann saw all these things in him, but she also saw something else that made her want to touch him: she saw an aching loneliness.

The story was that he had been plucked from ignorance and savagery by Sir John, had been hand-picked to be raised from field bondage to a position of trust and safety. But Ann, never having benefited from charity, had an ingrained suspicion of such tales. She did not believe that many people, least of all the rich, did things out of the goodness of their hearts. If Joseph had been plucked from anything, it was not from ignorance but from his home, not from savagery but from his family. She understood this because the gentry used the same kind of terms to describe people like her.

The fire was dying away. She should not waste any more coals, but she reached for a couple more and – quietly, in case her mother was still awake – laid them on to coax a little more heat into the room. The bairn would wake soon anyway, hungry; she'd be as well sitting up a while longer, to feed her, and then the pair of them would slip into the box-bed.

She thought again of Joseph, how she had played her own game for him. While the others fluttered and flirted around him, or were offended by his aloofness, she made herself be serious and quietly friendly. She found ways of getting him to help her with this or that task, asked his opinion and acted on it, did him small acts of kindness without seeming to expect thanks. Gradually she began to win his confidence. Once, as she was walking to Inchture on an errand for the housekeeper, Joseph appeared on the road behind her, caught up and escorted her there and back. They said very little then, but she recognised the statement that his silent company represented.

After that, when they could not be away from the house, they tried to find secluded corners of it where they could talk. There was little time for servants to be at leisure – certainly none was allowed for in the pages of Lady Wedderburn's household book – but they would sit together at night for a few minutes, before bed, and he would tell her things about Jamaica; things about Sir John and his brothers, and the terrible cruelties he had seen, and the kind, harsh, feeble, strong, miserable, humorous, brave, bitter people that the slaves were. They were people just like all of them there at Ballindean, he said, good and bad in unequal, changeable portions, leading lives that the white people in the great houses never even knew about. That, too, was like Ballindean, like anywhere – there were the great and rich and there was the rest of the world and a gulf like the ocean lay between the two.

Joseph told her about that also, the ocean he had crossed two times in his life, once when he was brought to Scotland and the other, earlier time when he was taken from Africa in the slave ship. She had heard of slave ships but nothing prepared her for what he described. She listened, appalled, and her hand went out to his and held it while he spoke, and at the end of that long speech it happened, the thing she had longed for, he reached across and kissed her, and she felt a surge of something – love, perhaps, happiness, even, but now she thought it was mainly triumph. She, Annie Thomson, had reached Joseph Knight. But that was only part of it. There was fear in there too. She felt that she was doing something both right and wrong, both good and dangerous: she knew that to act in any way that set herself in conflict with the rich and powerful could destroy her, and that she was about to condemn herself to years, perhaps a lifetime, of trouble. For she knew that her intention to make Joseph hers would mean having to take him away from the Wedderburns.

And there was another obstacle: MacRoy, the dominie from Dundee, who came to give Joseph lessons and who seemed, for a man as unlikely as the one she had opened the door to that first New Year's Day, to have a remarkable skill at keeping in with Sir John. Aeneas MacRoy tilted his bullet head at her and all but pawed the ground in his demonstrations of affection, and she recognised his power, and that she should not fall foul of him. She did not encourage him but she did not discourage him either, and that was how he fell into his delusions, that she might be his, and that was how the three of them were all through the summer of '72, jostling and testing and swarming with desires and jealousies.

That was the summer, too, that Joseph read of Somerset, the English slave, in the newspaper, and began to fix his mind on becoming a Scottish Somerset. And then one day it became clear that the time for prevarication was over, for Ann fell pregnant and Joseph went to John Wedderburn and told him the bairn was his, and he wished to marry Ann. All the faces in the house shifted as if a wind had blown across them. John Wedderburn looked outraged and Lady Margaret, also pregnant, looked pale, and Aeneas MacRoy's face seemed to go darker than Joseph's, thunder dark. Ann thought he might roar out of the house and never come back. She hoped that would happen but it did not – the reverse happened, MacRoy spoke at length to Sir John and soon was winding down his school and had a room to himself at Ballindean and Lady Margaret began to bring forth the bairns of her own that would, in a few years, populate a schoolroom presided over by the dour Maister MacRoy. Meanwhile Ann grew bigger and John Wedderburn, since it was his slave that had put her into that condition, decided that he was under an obligation not to cast her out, at least not till she had had the child. But he could not and did not sanction a marriage to make good what could not be undone, and this he made clear to both her and to Joseph. They wondered about this, since Joseph was now made into a Christian, and she, being a Scotswoman from birth, was already one – they wondered what it was that made John Wedderburn set himself against their becoming man and wife. Now, though, looking back from the fireside, Ann could see quite clearly that John Wedderburn understood what she was about. She saw that he understood the feud that existed between them, that they were engaged in a struggle over the possession of his slave.

And then the bairn came, and it was half Joseph and half her, and she thought that the Wedderburns would have to let them marry, for the bairn was such complete evidence of their union, but it died within a day. John Wedderburn extended his sense of obligation to providing a coffin and a funeral for their bairn, thus neatly disposing of the evidence, and then – and she detected the hand of Lady Margaret here – she herself was disposed of, given the wages due to her to the end of the year and sent on the back of a carrier's cart home to her mother in Dundee.

In this the Wedderburns showed how little they estimated poor folk like her, if they thought that by dismissing her they had heard the last of her. For Joseph had by then become a reader and a writer, and she too had those skills, so there was

214

an exchange of notes between them, and then a meeting in the woods at the back of Ballindean, followed, as winter set in, by more in Dundee, where Joseph had managed to persuade his master to send him for training with a barber. She saw now the interpretation that the Wedderburns were bound to place on these liaisons, which at first went undetected in spite of the suspicions of Aeneas MacRoy – how inevitably they confirmed Sir John and his lady in their view that Ann Thomson was a person of no breeding, indecent passions and habitual deceit. What other kind of woman could so take advantage of Joseph as to persuade him to go with her to Edinburgh, where in March they were joined in matrimonial union by a seceder clergyman of Leith? What else could this be but a pretext on her part, a scheme for making herself comfortable for life?

And the proof of that, for the Wedderburns, came in what happened next. Back came Joseph to Ballindean, without apology for his absence, now claiming that he had a wife to support who should be brought back into their service, or at least that Joseph should get a cottage on the estate where they might live as one as God had joined them together. And John Wedderburn was affronted by the hypocrisy and treachery of his slave, and refused to countenance the idea.

Joseph, Ann thought, might just have had a chance of success had John Wedderburn alone had the decision. But behind Wedderburn stood his wife, with whom he discussed all matters that were not strictly about the plantations or other business. The Lady Margaret would have settled it. Ann detested her. She detested her because she was only two or three years older than herself yet behaved as if she had been born to be mistress of a house like Ballindean. Which, of course, she had. She was fine-looking, soft-spoken, beautifully dressed and always correct. Ann's hands were already coarse, the hands of a spinner, a skivvy, a scudge. Her bonnie, unpainted face would soon begin to acquire care lines and her body would start to crumble from hard and ceaseless toil. Ann's own mother was not much over fifty, but she was an old, done woman, worn out by decades of work. At fifty, Lady Margaret would still be carrying herself like a queen. Ann's daughter Sarah would grow up to be haggard before her time, but the Wedderburns' daughters would be roses, they would bloom in the presence of rich suitors and go off to be the mistresses of great houses of their own. It was not right, it was not fair. And she, meanwhile, was not even allowed to keep the man she had chosen.

She spat into the fire. It gave an answering spit, and she spat at it again. She loathed the Wedderburns and everything about them. Behind their every seemingly charitable or upright deed she saw a twisted, hateful motive. Even Joseph seemed to think less badly of them than she. She had had as little time for the idea of her going back, of making herself beholden to them, as they had. She had been willing to go along with Joseph's request, but only because she was sure it would be rejected. She had known with a certain fatal feeling in the depths of her, that was both despair and contentment, that their options were narrowing and narrowing, till only two would be available to them: either that she and Joseph must part as if they had never met, never loved, never made a bairn, never married; or that he must walk away from his slavery. It was only a matter of time because, weeks before their marriage in Leith, she had known she was pregnant again.

And it was that, the bairn, alive and with her now, that made her calm. Rage and madness would not help the bairn to keep her father. The forces ranged against them were too strong for rage, too rational for madness. She *had* to be calm. She *had* to be patient.

Edinburgh, December 1773

Three men, all lawyers, were sitting round one end of a long rough-boarded table in a steaming, crowded, low-roofed room poorly illuminated by a scattering of tallow candles. What small, greasy light these gave out was further diminished by a thick pall of tobacco smoke, and any remaining pockets of fresh air had long been saturated with the smell of roasting flesh and fish, the fumes of wine and beer and the clamour of forty competing conversations. The rest of the table at which this trio sat was occupied by a mixed company of bareheaded tradesmen and bewigged merchants, and several women – street sellers of various wares, from ribbon and lace to herring – who had joined the men for a drink after their day's work.

The tallest of the lawyers, the one who, from his sallow complexion and long nose, looked least likely to be disposed to frolic, was nevertheless at that moment declaiming a poem with some vigour, reading from a newspaper clutched in his right hand while cutting rhetorical flourishes through the atmosphere with his left.

> 'Ye've seen me roond the bickers reel
> Wi hert as hale as tempered steel,
> And face sae awpen, free and blyth,
> Nor thocht that sorrow there could kyth –'

John Maclaurin broke off, half stood, held up his finger as if for silence – a gesture which had not the slightest effect on the drinking party further down the table – and addressed his two companions:

'And here comes the kick, gentlemen –

> But the neist mawment this was lost,
> Like gowan in December's frost.

Noo, is that no sublime? I challenge ye, James, as I challenge mysel, tae write lines like thae. The man is a genius.'

Boswell shook his head, laughing. 'You'll not catch me at anything so Scotch, unless it's satirical. It's not bad, though, I confess. Genius is too strong, but he's clever, I'll give you that.'

'A genius,' repeated Maclaurin, who was being as Scotch as he damn well pleased, partly to rile his friend. He laid down the *Weekly Magazine*. 'I'd like tae see ye better it. And it *is* satire, man! An address tae his *auld breeks*? Whit's that if it's no satire? It jist has the warmth o humanity in it as weel, that's aw, which is why a cauld-hertit fellow like you disna appreciate it.'

'He may be a genius,' said the third man, Allan Maconochie, also an advocate, speaking in a slow, heavy drawl, 'or jist clever, but I hear he's no very weel. No richt in the heid, even.'

They were in Luckie Middlemist's oyster cellar, a cave deep in the dark canyon of the Cowgate, and the poet under discussion was a bumptious young clerk from the Commissary Office called Robert Fergusson. It was the weekend before Christmas, the start of the Daft Days, but the daftness had started early. Spread out on the table were mugs of porter, a jug of gin punch with three glasses, and the shells of three dozen oysters. The collective advocatory breath was like a stiff breeze off Newhaven. The punch, coming on top of the porter and several bottles of Malaga earlier in the evening, had brought a sweat out on Boswell's brow and a manic gleam to his eyes.

'Insane?' said Boswell. 'Oh, I don't like to hear of mad poets. My brother John – the military one – suffers deliriums. Bad enough in a soldier, but worse – fatal – in a poet.'

'Why?' said Maclaurin. Being an occasional poet himself, he felt he should defend his muse. 'I'd hae thocht it would be bad in either case. Worse in a sodger – he micht run amuck wi his sword, or mairch a haill company aff a cliff.'

'But a soldier is naturally a man of discipline,' said Boswell, who had always rather fancied being in uniform. 'He may be ill, but the madness will not master him so readily as it would a poet, whose mind is already naturally wild and . . . inclined to flight.'

'Aye, but the poet'll hurt nane but himsel if he lowps.'

'Weel, onywey,' said Maconochie, 'I dinna ken Fergusson, but he's in the Cape Club, and Runciman the painter tellt me frae being the life and soul o their diversions he has suddenly ceased his appearances awthegither, and sunk intae some kind o depression. That paper ye're readin frae's a month auld, John. He was haein verses in it gey near every issue until that ane, but he hasna had onything else in it since, forby the tither poem there, his "Last Will" – and *that* disna augur weel.'

'That's a satire tae, is it no?' said Maclaurin, hunting for it.

'If it is, there's nae muckle laughs in it. Runciman says the laddie's feart he's been ower dissolute in this life, and will pey for it in the next ane.'

'Haivers,' said Maclaurin, whose chief objection to the idea of a future state was that it was generally represented as being very disagreeable for the majority, which made him prefer to remain where he was. But to Boswell the explanation struck home. Momentarily he seemed to sober up, pushing the glass of punch away from him. Seconds later, catching the eye of one of the women at the far end of the table, he seized it again and drained the contents.

'Steady, James,' said Maclaurin.

'I wish I was,' said Boswell, 'but this gin has knocked me ajee.'

'Scotticism!' Maconochie shouted. 'For aw ye try, man, ye canna get them oot, and when ye're fou ye canna keep them in!'

'It's being surrounded by men like you that does it,' Boswell muttered. 'It's different in London.'

'Oh, London!' Maconochie sneered.

'Dr Johnson says mine is almost the only Scotsman's tongue that does not offend him.'

'That's because ye're willin tae pit it where maist Scotsmen wouldna,' Maconochie said, but fortunately Boswell did not hear, since the words were drowned by a roar from somewhere else in the cellar. Although he and Maconochie had worked on cases together, Boswell blew hot and cold over the man, who was apt to be distinctly unmannered, something James abhorred in others and tried to restrict in himself to private moments and to his journal – as when he threw plates at his wife, for example, or φυκκτ υιτη α στρυμπετ on Castlehill. But Maconochie redeemed himself by asking after Dr Johnson, who had been back in London for a fortnight after the

Highland adventure, and of whom Boswell never could tire of talking.

'He is well, he is well. He wrote me the other day seeking some information on the clans – I daresay he is writing his book even as we speak.'

'Ye'll be writin a book yoursel? Aboot your journey?'

'I kept a journal, as did he, though I think my notes went further than his. But no doubt his observations on the state of society in those parts will make better reading.'

'Whit I want tae ken,' said Maconochie, 'isna aboot the clans or the state o society, it's aboot the state o Lord Monboddo. Ye took Johnson tae see him at Laurencekirk, I hear? Wasna there a terrible falling-oot atween them?'

Maclaurin gave an exasperated sigh – he had heard all this several times already. Boswell, suddenly friendly again towards Maconochie, reasserted himself over the effects of the gin as he recalled the scene.

'There was no falling-out – though it's true there might have been, and I swithered for a while about risking a meeting between them. At Montrose I debated whether we should keep by the coast to Aberdeen, or cut inland by Laurencekirk. I mentioned to Dr Johnson that by the latter we could take a short detour and visit Monboddo at his home – he'd got out of Edinburgh before we did and had been there some days. Dr Johnson said he would make the detour, so I sent my man on ahead with a note. Meanwhile we pressed on to Laurencekirk, and stopped at the inn there for a rest.'

'Did ye no think tae call on Lord Gardenstone, since ye were in his neighbourhood?' said Maconochie.

Boswell did not like to be interrupted. 'No,' he said sharply. 'He was not there, even had we wished to visit.'

'Ye could hae exchanged fraternal greetings wi his pigs,' said Maclaurin.

'Do you want to hear about Monboddo or not?' Boswell cried.

'Aye, aye,' said Maconochie. 'Let the man speak, John. So ye gaed there insteid?'

'Not *instead* – I've told you, we had no intention of seeing Gardenstone. We left the inn and found my man waiting at

220

the road-end with a message that Monboddo invited us to dinner. This was very welcome, because it had started to rain, and the country there is very exposed. A moorland waste, in fact. Monboddo is no better – cold and broken down and grim –'

'We ken,' Maclaurin said.

'The house, I mean – it's well fitted to its surroundings. But his lordship of course revels in it. "Our ancestors lived in such houses," he told us as soon as we got in, "and they were better men than we." Dr Johnson answered, "No, my lord, we are as strong as they, and a good deal wiser." This could have provoked a fight before we had our coats off, but Monboddo did not rise.'

'He'd no hae come up very high if he had,' Maclaurin said. Monboddo was scarcely five feet tall, and pinched and skinny to boot.

'Did he gie ye a dinner o the ancients?' Maconochie asked. Monboddo's reconstructions, at his Edinburgh residence, of 'learned suppers' in the manner of Roman feasts, were legendary.

'No,' said Boswell. 'He is quite different there. Simple farmer's fare, and we ate with the family. Big hacks of ham, and boiled eggs. "Show me any of your French cooks who can make a dish like this," Monboddo said, holding up an egg. Dr Johnson rather enjoyed himself. Afterwards the two sages entered into a debate as to whether a London shopkeeper or a savage had the finest existence.'

'The sparks would fly then,' said Maconochie hopefully.

'No, they were very restrained. I mean, Monboddo of course was for the savage, and Johnson for the shopkeeper, but they did not even raise their voices, let alone come to blows. In fact, Johnson told me later he would happily have argued for the savage, if anyone else had stood up for the shopkeeper. Mr Maconochie, don't look so surprised. I know Lord Monboddo better than you, and he is always a model of courtesy. He even pressed us to stay the night, but we were expected at Aberdeen, so we declined.'

'Weel, I must say, I'm fair disappointed,' said Maconochie. 'It's a gey lang road tae gang and no get even a sclaff or a dunt for your trouble.'

At the other end of the table a dispute broke out, which seemed to centre on one of the females, who having dispersed her favours fairly liberally among her male drinking cronies, was now being aggressively wooed by two of them. It took another of the women to calm things down by distracting one of the rivals. The three lawyers watched from their end for a minute or two, as if they had suddenly found themselves in a theatre. Eventually Maclaurin restarted the conversation.

'Weel, Allan, Johnson and Monboddo wouldna be very weel matched in a fecht. Johnson would only need tae sit on Monboddo and he'd squash the life oot o him. He probably wouldna even notice he'd done it either.'

'But Monboddo would probably tak the opportunity, afore he expired, tae see if Johnson had a tail,' said Maconochie. 'Aye, they're baith unco chiels. But maybe they hae mair in common than they hae differences.'

'That may be true,' Boswell said. 'Strong opinions respect one another. Physically they could not be more distinct, but intellectually perhaps they're not so far apart. They have a black servant each, too, which is curious. Johnson has the excellent Frank Barber, and Monboddo has a man called Gory, who led us back to the high road to Aberdeen, and seemed equally splendid. It was odd to hear him speaking like a Mearns loun – he has picked up the accent from living there.'

'I hae a black servant too,' Maconochie said.

'So ye hae, Allan. I'd forgotten,' Maclaurin said.

'I did not know that,' Boswell said. 'Well, maybe it is not so rare. When Gory turned back –'

'But it reminds me –' Maconochie began.

'When Gory turned back, Dr Johnson asked him if he was baptised. He is – not only baptised, but confirmed. Johnson gave him a shilling.'

'For being a guid guide or for being a guid Christian?' Maclaurin asked.

'It reminds me,' Maconochie said again. 'Ye ken John Swinton? I mean, of course ye ken him, but hae ye seen him of late?'

'Is he in town?' Boswell asked.

'Aye, he's been here this week past. He was telling me aboot an unusual case that's coming afore the sheriff court at Perth. A petition's been presented – Swinton didna hear it himsel, being in Edinburgh – but his substitute did, and John thocht it would be o some interest tae ye, John. And nae dout tae you tae, Jamie.'

Boswell felt the conversation, and maybe the room, slipping away from him. He resented Maconochie's familiarity, but then that was one of the things about Scotland in general, and Edinburgh in particular, that he found offensive: the uncouth, back-clapping social culture, whereby a man of sensibility such as himself had to put up with the rough intimacy of graceless men like Maconochie, the two Dundases (the Lord President and his much younger half-brother Henry, another advocate and the most ambitious of them all) and anyone else with whom one mixed professionally, which was most of the law. And yet, too, James loved drunken nights like this, and dens like Luckie Middlemist's – the charged atmosphere which might explode at any moment, the women drinking with the men, and keeping up with them, the sense of liberty from the constraints of *being good*. There was, of course, more opportunity to be bad in London, which was one reason why he liked to go there whenever he could, but no city relished sin quite like Edinburgh.

Maconochie was still talking, and James pulled himself back from his thoughts, wondering if he would be able to remember them enough to write them down in the morning.

'It's a Negro case. A fellow that wants tae be free o his maister, and the maister says he canna be. He brocht him hame frae Jamaica and the slave has got mairrit on a local lass but the maister winna release him. Ach, that's no the haill o it, it's mair complicated but I canna mind the details, but the thing is the justices upheld the maister, and noo the slave has petitioned against their judgment and Swinton's substitute heard it and served a copy o the petition on Mr Wedderburn.'

'Wedderburn?' said Boswell.

'That's the maister, John Wedderburn. He's some cousin or ither o Alexander Wedderburn.'

'Him that ran awa tae England when he couldna thole the cut and jab o the Session?' Maclaurin asked.

'Aye. There's a wheen o Wedderburns aboot Dundee, they're

aw related. This John's faither was the ane that suffered in London efter Culloden, d'ye mind, and the son gaed oot tae Jamaica and made a fortune, syne cam hame wi his slave, an noo the slave has decided tae seek his ain fortune. Guid luck tae him, I say, and ye ken John Swinton's fierce against slavery, so he's sure tae want it afore himsel in Perth. Weel, ye ken –'

'Haud on, haud on,' said Maclaurin. 'This slave must hae haen some assistance, jist tae get the length o the sheriff substitute.'

'Aye, John Swinton was tellin me, there's a Perth writer cried Andrew Davidson that's taen the case on, and he's no takkin ony siller for it. He's either brave or stupit – he'll no get muckle business oot o this Wedderburn and his county freens efter he's stood up and spak for the slave afore the sheriff.'

Maclaurin looked pensive. 'I wonder whit the slave's like. He'll need tae be a man o some resolve tae hae got as far as he has.'

'I dinna ken onything aboot him. Swinton tellt me his name but I canna mind it. But ye're richt, he canna be blate.'

'This'll gang further than the sheriff court,' Maclaurin said. 'Or it will if neither party gies way. Maybe that's why Swinton thocht we'd be interested. Are ye, Allan?'

'If it gangs further, ye mean? Aye, but that's no in oor hauns. I mean, we can only tak the cases we're offered.'

'That's true, but ye ken fine weel there are ways o makkin a case come tae ye if ye want it. A word tae Swinton, a word tae this Mr Davidson, so he kens tae approach us.'

'Aye, weel . . .'

'We'll keep an eye on it, then,' said Maclaurin. 'How aboot yoursel, James?'

'Well, I think you're maybe both getting ahead of yourselves,' said Boswell. 'Ye dinna ken . . . know . . . half the facts. These things are always mair complicated.' The jug was almost empty of punch, and most of it was in James, and he was finding his tongue and his head becoming dissociated, his English, like sheets of paper caught in a gust of wind, fleeing away from him as fast as his clarity of vision.

224

'Mair complicated than whit?' said Maconochie. 'Whether a man can own anither man? That seems simple enough.'

'*Can* and *should* are two different things, as I'm sure I don't need to tell you,' Boswell said. 'And there's the fact that this Mr Wedderburn has brought the slave here in the first place. He may not have done it out of charity, but the fact is he hasna left him in the cane fields. What else may he not have done for him?'

Maconochie belched. 'Separated him frae his faimly and freens, perhaps, back there in the cane fields? Wha kens?'

'Weel,' said Maclaurin, 'I dinna like tae concede the point, but James is richt. We are maybe gettin cairried awa. We would hae tae see jist whit the history o the relationship is.'

'The principle stands, in ony event,' said Maconochie.

'But principles are no aye whit the law is concerned wi.'

'It should be. If it were my case, I would mak the principle the foundation o my pleading.'

'There's *should* again,' said Boswell. He knew he was going to have to get outside for some fresh air at any moment, but continued gamely. 'The point is, this Wedderburn's *principles*, his haill behaviour, may be entirely honourable. All planters are not scourge-wielding monsters. If they were –'

'As Dr Johnson alleges,' said Maclaurin mischievously. (Johnson, notoriously, at an Oxford dinner had once raised a toast to the next slave insurrection in the West Indies.)

'– if they were, it would make everything very simple. But they're no. A planter is not some grotesque by Hogarth. He is a man like us, a Christian with a wife and hoose and bairns and books.'

'That makes it worse,' said Maconochie.

'No,' said Boswell, 'it makes it personal.'

The argument might have gone on but for a sudden, loud interruption as the street door burst open and a crowd of young men, about a dozen of them, pushed their way inside. They were loud and drunk and moved en masse like some monstrous construction of arms and legs, bulging bellies and flushed, leering faces. Suddenly the company sharing the lawyers' table seemed remarkably sober and civilised, an impression reinforced by the fact that they swiftly drained their glasses and called the waiter over to settle their bill. As they got ready to leave, the many-limbed monster lurched over, baying in triumph, to secure the table, even though it was far too small to accommodate everybody. There were a few minutes of confusion, with one set of people putting on and the other stripping off cloaks and coats, and all squeezing past each other, treading on toes while trying to maintain a fake fellow-drinker jollity. Boswell, whose last speech seemed to have emptied him of words, sat looking dreamily up at this mêlée with a smile on his lips. Maclaurin leant over towards Maconochie and tapped at his own crotch, then indicated a couple of the newly arrived men, who, in removing their coats, had revealed large coloured kerchiefs tucked into their waists and hanging down in front like gaudy imitations of limp phalluses.

'Whit d'ye think that signifies?'

'God kens,' said Maconochie, 'but they aw hae them.'

Their stares did not pass unnoticed. The man nearest to them, a giant with a maliciously friendly glint in his eye, shouted down at them: 'Ye're lookin at my pintle, man. Ye're wunnerin whit we are, eh? I'll tell ye. We are the Knights o the Naipkin. We've aw taen a solemn pledge tae – here, Bob, whit is it we said we're tae dae?'

'We're tae get fou,' Bob shouted, 'and then we're tae get tae a hoose o ill repute.'

'Aye, aye, but whit was thon pledge we aw took? The wordin o it?'

Two or three more of the group started off in a chorus, which was joined by most of the rest as it progressed, culminating in a mighty roar:

'We pledge oorsels as brithers no tae trust tae Lady Luck,
but spreid oor naipkins in oor laps whene'er we eat and sup,
and aye tae lift oor naipkins up tae glory when we fuck!'

'We're a club, ye see,' said the giant, clutching Maconochie's shoulder as if he were crushing a nut. 'We ken there's aw these gentlemen's clubs, the this and the that and the God kens whit club, and the fuckin gentlemen winna let *us* in, so we thocht we'd hae oor ain.'

'I'm sure the gentlemen will be very happy for ye,' Maconochie said.

'Whit's that?'

'I said, ye're newly formed then?' Maconochie was vainly trying to part his clothing from the hand gripping it.

'Aboot three oors syne. That's how we gae by the mark o the naipkin. It was the only thing we could think o that we aw had.'

'I didna!' one of the group objected, thrusting his pelvis at Boswell's face. A grimy piece of torn-off shirt-sleeve dangled between his legs.

'Ye're a disgrace tae the britherhood,' the giant shouted, releasing Maconochie in order to deliver a punch to his companion's chest which sent him sprawling across three other 'Knights o the Naipkin'. Maclaurin nudged Maconochie, and between them they hulstered Boswell from his seat.

'For God's sake, let's get oot o here afore they mak us join or hae the breeks aff us,' muttered Maclaurin. 'Aye, weel, gentlemen,' he called, putting on a tremulous voice, 'guid nicht, we'll mak mair space for ye, ye'll need tae let us auld anes awa tae oor beds.'

'Here's Luckie comin ower,' said Maconochie, as they dragged Boswell away. 'She'll sort the wastrels oot.'

The waiter took their money, making a face at the prospect of dealing with his new customers, and the lawyers escaped on to the Cowgate with Mistress Middlemist's screech ringing in their ears: 'Noo, sirs, settle doun, settle doun. I'll hae order in this hoose or naebody in it, and ye'll be the first oot the door. Ye can pit your neb cloots awa for a stert – I'm no wantin a rammle if a wheen ither daft birkies come in here sportin feathers ahint their lugs or some such nonsense. Noo, whit are ye for?'

'God, it's no safe drinkin oot these days,' Maconochie said.

'That sort o thing should be kept for clubs in private rooms,' Maclaurin said.

'Weel, you would ken,' Maconochie said. 'You wi your clarty keekin poems.'

Maclaurin grimaced. Back in his mid-twenties, he had composed and anonymously published a satirical mock-epic entitled *The Keekeiad*. In it, an over-inquisitive husband, inspecting his wife's private parts by the light of a candle on their wedding night, accidentally set her pubic hair on fire and left her totally bushless. The remedy he proposed was that she borrow from her friends whatever pubes they could spare, and make a wig to cover her baldness. Having elaborately celebrated the glories of feminine thatch, the poem signed off with a plea for the author to be crowned with a wreath of 'bushy trophies', which he could sport while treading the slopes of Parnassus.

Maclaurin now felt a certain shame over this production, and wished not so many of his acquaintances knew that he was the author. *The Keekeiad* was not a poem he had contemplated taking along to the Boswells' dinner party to be critiqued by Dr Johnson. Thinking of that, he recalled that other embarrassment of his past, his legal work for the slave-owning Fife doctor. 'That poem was jist a bit o daft fun,' he said to Maconochie. 'But thae chiels in there could dae ye serious mischief if their humour turned soor.'

Outside, the fresh air hit them all, with different effects. Maconochie realised how drunk he was and grew eager to get home, Maclaurin started frantically to close up against draughts, and Boswell, from being virtually unable to speak let alone stand a few minutes before, revived like a man come back from drowning.

'Oh, I feel better for this,' he said. 'Oh, far better.' He stumbled, stopped himself. 'Though, perhaps, still . . . a wee bit under the weather . . .'

'I'm awa,' said Maconochie. 'I'll be seik if I dinna get hame.'

He took off without another word, going at that rate which even the very drunk can achieve when instinct says that one's own bed is the only place to be, and leaving the relatively sober Maclaurin in charge of Boswell.

'Dinna abandon me, John. Dinna leave me like that . . . Maconochie traitor. I could not bear to be left alone.'

'Weel, at least can we move in the right direction?' Maclaurin said, trying to turn them to the right, towards the Grassmarket. But Boswell seemed to prefer, for the time being, to amble around in a circle.

'Let's walk up and down here for a while, John, just for a while. Or I swear I'll collapse and die in the gutter. It's cold enough.'

In fact it was not especially cold, only a sharp contrast to the blazing heat of the cellar. Nevertheless Maclaurin had pulled his coat as tight as he could, turned the collar up, wrapped his muffler twice round his neck and thrust his hands deep into his pockets. 'Ye dinna ken whit ye ask o me, James,' he said. 'Staunin aboot in the nicht in December, it's plain madness, that's aw. I'll stay a minute, but could we no jist walk back tae your hame? Ye'll feel better up on the High Street.'

'No, no, I'll feel worse. *Hame* is not where I wish to be. I want to wander. Don't leave me, John.' He staggered into his friend, gripped the left arm which Maclaurin held rigidly against his side. 'I'll tell you what, come with me on an adventure. I'll find Duncan Cameron the chairman and he can find us two comfortable places to lie for a while.'

Maclaurin tried to shake him off. 'Cameron will be lang in his bed, if he's ony sense. And bed is where we should be as weel.'

'Exactly,' said Boswell. 'Well, to hell with Cameron then. I'll find them myself. I ken where. There's a fine lass called Mary. She'll have a friend, I'm sure. A friend for my friend John.'

'Now, James, that's enough. I'll no be pairt o ony sic nonsense. I hae a wife, man!'

'Good God, *I* hae a wife!' Boswell almost sobbed. 'And what a wife! A more charming, loving, sensible, devoted being I cannot imagine being blessed with. And forgiving. Let us not forget forgiving.'

'I think ye should. I dinna see Mrs Boswell forgiving the state ye're in.'

'Oh, she will, she will. She always does. Forgive and forget. I bless Mrs Boswell for forgiving and forgetting. Otherwise she surely would not thole me.'

'But does she forget? Maybe she's storing it all up against ye, for future use.' Maclaurin, deciding to risk a chill to get his friend home, had unmoored one arm in order to oxter him up the nearest close to the High Street. They were making some progress now, a little staggered and uncertain, rather as they were making conversation.

'Ah, now that's where you show how little you know her,

229

John. *She* does not store it up. *She* hasn't the patience. *I* store it up. In my journal. And she reads it.'

'Whit? She reads aboot . . . whit ye get up tae?'

'I don't ask her to. Good God! But she will go and find the damn thing and then she reads it. What can I do?'

'Suppose ye locked it up? Or didna keep it at all?'

'No, John! It is history! I *have* to write it. I write it to be read. I just wish she didn't read it so thoroughly.'

'Nonsense. Ye must want her tae. It's your way o confessing tae her.'

'Do you think so? Aye, maybe it is. God, I am a bad man. Am I, John? Am I a bad man?'

'Probably.'

Boswell frowned; this was too mealy-mouthed a word for the time of night. '*Probably*?'

'Ye are nae dout very wicked. Noo –'

'Then I'll go to hell. If I die tonight – John, d'ye realise if I die tonight, in my unregenerate state, I'll be damned.'

'No ye'll no.'

'D'ye think – I'll be damned?'

'Aye. Definitely.'

'Good God! That *is* definite. John, d'ye think I will? D'ye believe in a future state, John?'

'I believe your future state will be tae be very ill in the mornin.'

'No, no, be serious. Where are we going after this?'

'I'm going hame, efter I've directed ye tae yours.'

'No, I mean, after *this*. After this life.'

'My God, ye never lea it alane, dae ye, James? Even at this oor, and in your state, ye're thinkin aboot it.'

'Well, it's very important. It's *the* most important thing for a human being. This life is just a moment, a blink of God's eye. But that – that's eternity!'

'As a human being, I think this life is mair important.'

'Ah, well, we'll see, we'll see. I'm going to ask our friend David what he thinks. Not tonight, but some time. I'm going to ask Davie Hume.'

'We ken whit he thinks.'

'He's of the same opinion as you, but he's cleverer.'

230

'I dinna deny it.'

'But not tonight. It's too late. He'll be in his bed. Or his hoosekeeper's. Oh, John, that reminds me. We were looking for whores. Where are we?'

Astonishingly, they had come up to St Giles' and were just a couple of hundred yards from the Boswells' residence. Maclaurin was staying in town, at Brown Square. He disengaged his arm from that of his friend. 'That's me, James. Your hoose is up there on the richt, mine is aff here tae the left. And I'm awa tae it.'

'John, come on. Where's the fun in going home? Where's the John Maclaurin that penned the keekin poem? Ah! That surprised you! You thought I was beyond hearing back there. Well, you were wrong. Nothing escapes Bozzy.'

'I'm awa, James,' Maclaurin said, stepping off briskly. 'Dinna let your bed escape ye.'

'Ach, away you go then. You've nae appetite for life, John. I'm going to find a lassie.'

Maclaurin watched Boswell lurch up the street, then set off for Brown Square. There were not many folk about: the Cowgate, as ever, was where Edinburgh smouldered latest into the night. Bozzy would get home safe, probably without satisfying his lust, as most respectable harlots would have long since turned in. Maclaurin knew the pattern well. James would barge into the house, find Margaret stalking the parlour or sitting up anxiously in bed for him, would be both touched, mortified and infuriated by this, would shout at her, fall asleep, wake up with a raging sore head to find her not speaking to him, feel miserable all day, swear never to drink again, and in another day or so meet him, John Maclaurin, and recount the whole episode with equal quantities of guilt and delight. And this was the man who worried about the afterlife? Maclaurin laughed out loud as he headed for his own door. Not for the first time, he wondered how Boswell had time to worry about anything.

Dundee, June 1802

Fate was not something Archibald Jamieson chose to believe in. The idea that chance encounters were not chance at all, but the inevitable outcome of some complex cosmic mechanism, did not impress him. Coincidences could usually be explained rationally, and if they could not they remained, in his eyes, just coincidences.

It was not fate, then, but chance, that led to his meeting Mr Andrew Davidson. If he had not been thwarted on his weekly visit to Pirie's Land by the fact that his acquaintance there was refusing even her most regular guests ('for medical reasons – but naething *you* need tae fash aboot, Airchie'), he would not have been stepping along the High Street at three in the afternoon with a spare hour on his hands. Nor, it followed, would he have seen Sir John Wedderburn's lawyer, Mr Duncan, standing at the entrance to the New Inn talking to another man, and apparently preparing to take his leave of him. These events occurred as all life occurred: a minute's delay here or there, and an encounter would not take place, an opportunity would be missed. The great imponderable, Archibald Jamieson would ponder later, was knowing whether these things made any difference in the long term.

Duncan was large and brosie-faced, with a fat neck emerging like a tree trunk from a white cravat above a dark suit. His companion, identically attired, seemed considerably less healthy, having an emaciated look about him and skin the colour of porridge. He looked like another lawyer. He was unfamiliar to Jamieson, who prided himself on knowing by sight every lawyer in Dundee. This was what prompted him to find out who the man was.

'Mr Duncan,' he called, advancing on the pair. 'Guid day tae ye, sir.'

Duncan peered at him, seemed not to know him for a moment, then nodded curtly. 'Mr Jamieson.'

Jamieson planted himself firmly in front of them. 'A fine day, sir,' he said. 'A very hot day, in fact.' Then, turning to the other man, 'A guid day tae be oot and aboot and no tied tae a desk, would ye no say?'

'Aye, quite,' the man said. In fact he looked as if he might expire on the spot, and glanced at Duncan to see if it was absolutely necessary to be introduced. Jamieson beamed expectantly at them both.

'This is Mr Archibald Jamieson,' Duncan said. 'He is employed by us on an occasional basis. Clerical work, matters requiring some discretion . . .'

'I'd hae thocht that included aw legal maitters,' the man muttered, in a tone of complete exhaustion.

'Very well said, sir,' Jamieson said enthusiastically, and gave Duncan an inquiring look.

'This,' Duncan said, 'is Mr Davidson of Perth. He is about to return there by coach, if the coach ever comes. Forgive me, sir,' he said to Davidson, 'I really must be getting back. I have another appointment. I will write you confirming the details of our discussion . . .'

'Mr Davidson?' Jamieson asked. 'Mr Andrew Davidson the solicitor?'

'The same, sir,' Davidson said mournfully. He looked anxiously up the street for the coach, raising his right hand to shield his eyes from the sun. Duncan seized the hand as it came down again and shook it so vigorously that Jamieson feared it might come off.

'You'll be all right waiting here, sir? Really, I must . . .'

'Aye, aye,' Davidson said, 'on ye go, sir. It'll likely no be lang noo.' He took a few steps away from them into the street, as if this would encourage the missing vehicle.

'I'll wait with Mr Davidson,' Archie said to Duncan. 'Ye needna fash yoursel. I'll mak sure he gets a place on the coach.' There was no queue of passengers, so it seemed this would not be a difficult undertaking.

'Would you mind?' Duncan looked relieved. Under his breath he added, 'I don't like to leave him unattended. He looks as if one more clean shirt would see him out.'

'Aye, he's awfie poukit,' Jamieson said. Then, loudly, 'It will be a pleasure, sir.' While the two lawyers exchanged a last few words, Jamieson went into the inn and asked about the non-appearance of the coach. Word had just come, he was told, that it would be half an hour late, as one of the horses had gone lame and was being replaced. When he went back out with this news, Davidson was on his own.

'Ye'll be as weel coming inside and getting a seat,' Jamieson said, after explaining the delay. 'Some coffee, perhaps, micht revive ye?'

'Jist a glass o water, I think,' Davidson said. 'I dout my wame willna tak coffee.'

Jamieson found them two chairs in a corner and ordered the water, and coffee for himself. Davidson sipped at the glass gratefully and slumped in his chair. 'Thank ye, sir, thank ye. I am no a weel man.'

'I ken,' Jamieson said. He watched as the other man produced a blue silk handkerchief and dabbed at his mouth with it. A network of creases spread across Davidson's cheeks; a patch of silvery stubble on his chin and a few strands of grey hair on his bald head only accentuated the pallor of his skin. Jamieson calculated that if Davidson had been, say, in his twenties when he handled the Knight case, he would now be in his mid- to late fifties. He appeared considerably older.

'Ye ken by looking at me, or ye ken by some ither means?' Davidson asked. 'Ootby, ye seemed tae recognise my name. And I feel I should mind yours.'

'I wrote ye back in February,' Jamieson said. 'I heard then frae your clerk that ye werena weel.'

'And whit did ye write concerning?'

'It was in connection wi some business I undertook for a client o Mr Duncan's. Ye'll be weel acquainted wi Mr Duncan?'

'Moderately, sir, moderately. A guid faimly lawyer and an honest man, I think, which is twa things that recommend him tae me at this particular time. I find mysel unable tae continue my practice as I once did. I am wasting away, apparently, or so my physician tells me. Therefore I am taking the opportunity o a slight improvement – believe me, Mr Jamieson, I looked a hundred times worse in the spring – tae redd up my affairs. I hae nae son in the law, ye see, and naebody in Perth wants the business, which, tae be frank, hasna flourished of late. Mr

Duncan, however, is willing tae tak on my Dundee clients – if they are willing tae be taen on by him.'

'There is nae enmity between ye, then?'

'Enmity?' Davidson became slightly more animated. 'Why would there be?'

'The maitter I was inquiring aboot was an auld affair in which ye represented a slave cried Joseph Knight against ane o Mr Duncan's clients. John Wedderburn o Ballindean.'

Davidson gave a thin laugh. 'Ah, noo I mind your letter! Oh, but that wouldna mak Duncan an enemy o *mine*. Or the tither way aboot. In ony event, it was *auld* Mr Duncan that was in charge in thae days. The present Mr Duncan was still in college. Lord, Mr Jamieson, ye should ken yoursel, if lawyers took the dorts wi each ither on behalf o aw their clients they would gey soon find themsels unable tae practise at aw!'

'But it was, was it no, a bitterly fought case?'

'There was bitterness in it, aye, but no amang the lawyers. Whit was it ye wanted tae ken aboot it?'

'Ye mind it, then?'

'Oh, aye, it was a famous case. I certainly gained a small reputation by it. An unusual case. But is the coach no due?'

'Dinna fash,' Jamieson said. 'I am watchin through the windae, and I'll no let it gang withoot ye.'

'Muckle obleeged,' Davidson said. 'I think if ye werena here I would fall fast asleep.'

'Whit kind o man was Joseph Knight?' Jamieson asked.

Davidson pressed the tips of his fingers together and closed his eyes. Jamieson thought he was indeed dozing off, but it appeared he was collecting his thoughts. When he opened his eyes again a brightness had come into them that had been absent before.

'He was extraordinary,' Davidson said. 'Forby the fact that he was black, which made him – weel, rare, at ony rate. But there was mair tae him than that. If there hadna been – if he had jist been a puir ignorant Negro wi a grievance – I dout I wouldna ever hae taen him on.'

'Extraordinary? How?'

'Weel, in the first place, Mr Jamieson, ye must think back thirty year. The American war hadna happened. The French Revolution hadna happened. Scotland was a douce, quiet kind o place in thae days. Or at least, Perthshire was. Ideas aboot liberty werena exactly rife amang the lower orders, let alane amang slaves. The fact that Mr Knight had the courage and the cleverness – and the thrawnness – tae bring his cause afore the sheriff at all – that was extraordinary.

'He was a guid-looking chiel tae – clean and weel dressed – and maist o whit little he said was sense. He'd had instruction frae a minister oot by Ballindean, and been baptised, and though I dinna think it gaed ower deep wi him he had the carriage o a God-fearing man. These things mak a difference, as ye weel ken, when a solicitor is deciding whether there's a case tae be made. Maybe they shouldna, but they dae. Weel, Mr Knight had thocht through his situation and he saw the things that micht coont for him and the things that micht coont against him, but he believed the natural justice o his cause ootweighed the latter. And forby aw that, he believed the sheriff – Lord Swinton as he later was – would hear his case sympathetically, and that was a necessary and practical consideration. John Swinton was a plodding, dour, tedious kind o man, but he was a fine lawyer and a humane judge. And I, too, considered these things and came tae the same conclusion as Knight did – that his case could be won. But it wasna Knight that first came tae me. It was his wife. Noo whit was her name?'

'Ann. Ann Thomson.'

'That's richt. A bonnie, bonnie lass, but ye could tell she was hard beneath the surface and that was anither factor on their side, for they were likely tae be in for a lang haul. She had got my name frae somebody, and she came aw the way tae Perth and speired at me tae help them.'

Davidson put his handkerchief to his mouth again, but this time he coughed painfully into it. He took more water.

'I was something o a radical in my youth, Mr Jamieson. I hae changed my views since. I dinna haud wi awthing that has happened in France, and I whiles think the radicals today dae mair hairm nor guid wi their wild rantings. But slavery is a thing I never could abide, and when that lassie came tae me wi her tale I decided I would help them though they would never hae the siller tae pay me for my trouble.'

For a man who had seemed at death's door fifteen minutes

236

earlier, Davidson had revived to a remarkable extent. Now he twisted in his chair. 'I hear horses. That's no the coach awready, is it?'

'Na, na, ye may bide a while yet,' Jamieson said. Davidson looked relieved. Briefly, his eyes closed again.

'So ye never took ony money frae them,' Jamieson prompted. 'Even when ye won the appeal at the sheriff court?'

'Win or lose, they couldna hae payed me. Oh, they were puir, puir folk. And efter we won at Perth, and Wedderburn took it tae the Session at Edinburgh, they got puirer. Knight left Ballindean, or was pit oot, and they bade here in Dundee, but it was hard for him tae find regular work. He had nae skills, ye see – he could cut hair, but the barbers o Dundee werena keen tae let him practise.'

'Because o his colour?'

'In pairt, perhaps. But mair because he was Wedderburn's slave. Folk kent aboot the case, and mony o them were feart o upsettin the Wedderburns. So it was a hard time for Joseph and his bonnie wife.

'Weel, I tellt Mr Knight tae haud on, that ane o the very best advocates in Edinburgh was going tae represent him. That was John Maclaurin, Lord Dreghorn as he became, I'd had word tae approach him and he'd taen the case like a saumon snappin a fly. If the Knights could jist keep body and soul thegither for a few months we would see an end tae it. But the case dragged on for years – four years, five years, Mr Jamieson – and I think if they hadna had some assistance frae different quarters they would hae stervit tae death afore there was an ootcome.'

'Who helped them?'

'Oh, there was a number o different folk. A minister raised siller for them frae his congregation, I mind that. But them I mind maist were the anes that could least afford it. The colliers.'

'They were as guid as slaves themsels in thae days, were they no?'

'Aye, but the first Act for their emancipation was passed richt in the middle o the case, jist when the Knights were at their maist desperate. Some o the colliers in Fife had read aboot Joseph Knight, and they raised a subscription for him. By that time I hadna sae muckle tae dae wi the case, it was John

Maclaurin and the Edinburgh advocates that were handling it. But I mind I was very moved when I heard that thae puir craiturs had sent siller tae their fellow-slave. Some folk dinna hae a guid word for the colliers, but I aye thocht that was a noble act.'

Jamieson's coffee was long finished. Davidson drained the last of his water. 'I canna tell ye,' he said, 'hoo little I hae thocht on aw this in recent years. And I canna tell ye hoo glad I am tae think on it noo. When ye're as ill as I am, it does ye guid tae mind that ye did something useful in your life.'

'Hoo ill are ye?' Jamieson asked.

Davidson gave his thin laugh again and held up his forefinger and thumb as if they held a pinch of salt. 'I am this close tae death, Mr Jamieson – or this far, ye can tak your choice. I am riddled wi the cancer, and will be lucky tae survive till August. I suspect I'll be *un*lucky if I survive ony langer. I used tae be as weel fleshed as yoursel, would ye believe? Noo I feel seik at the mere sicht o food.'

'I am very sorry tae hear it,' Jamieson said.

'Aye,' Davidson said, smiling, 'and forby that, ye would much prefer I talked tae ye aboot Mr Knight, eh? Whit's your interest in him?'

'I am lookin for him,' Jamieson said.

'Ye mean, John Wedderburn is lookin for him?'

'No. He was, but no ony langer.'

'Wha's payin ye noo, then?'

'Naebody. It's for mysel.'

'For nae siller? Why, Mr Jamieson, if ye dinna mind me speirin?'

Jamieson shook his head. 'Tae be honest, until I had this conversation wi you, I didna realise I was still lookin for him. As for whit my reasons are – I'm no certain.'

'Loose ends, perhaps,' Davidson said. 'I ken that habit – I like tae hae them tied up mysel. Weel, I'm sorry, but I canna help ye. The last time I saw him was in the Parliament Hoose in Edinburgh, on the day the case was heard at the Court o Session. I never kent whaur he and his wife gaed efter that. And I never heard frae them again.'

He turned again at the sound of hooves and wheels on the cobbles. 'Ah, surely that is the coach at last?'

It was. They stood together and began to walk to the door. Jamieson felt something slipping away from him. Here was a man who had known Knight, worked for him, apparently respected him – a dying man for whom Knight still represented something good, something 'useful'. By chance Jamieson had met this man, but he was unlikely ever to see him again. There should be some kind of resolution but there was none. Jamieson still felt a distance between himself and Knight, a distance that was more than simply all the years that had passed.

'Tell me, Mr Davidson,' he asked, as they left the inn and approached the coach, 'did ye *like* Joseph Knight?'

Davidson stopped. 'That's an interesting question. Wait.' He went over to the coachman and asked how long he had before the coach left. Some parcels and boxes were being handed up on to the roof. 'We'll be five minutes yet, sir,' Jamieson heard the coachman say. Davidson came back.

'Like him? I never had cause tae *dis*like him. But like him? I canna say. I didna ken him weel enough. He didna seem tae let folk ower close tae him. For me, it wasna aboot whether I liked him or no. It was aboot the rightness o his cause. And I never had ony douts aboot that.'

They shook hands, and Davidson went to take his place in the coach. Another couple of passengers had appeared from the inn. Davidson came back again. It was as if he, too, realised that this might be his last opportunity to speak to anyone about Knight. 'He wasna *warm*, ye see. At least I never found him sae. If ye dae come across him, ye'll ken whit I mean. I wish I could tell ye whaur he is, but I canna. But I would be obliged if ye would remember me tae him, if ye ever find him.'

He hauled himself into the coach, and as he went Jamieson saw how the bones of his shoulders poked back through his coat.

'Then ye think he's alive?' Jamieson asked, when Davidson had settled himself.

Davidson laughed again. 'Oh aye,' he said. 'In my state o health, I apply the same rules tae awbody else as tae mysel.

Unless I ken for certain that a man is deid, I assume that he's alive. I'm an optimist, ye see, Mr Jamieson. I hae aye been an optimist. It's the only way tae live.'

Edinburgh, 30 August 1776

It was Friday, a fine summer's afternoon, and, the Session having risen a fortnight before, the lawyers of Edinburgh once again had a little time on their hands. John Maclaurin, Andrew Crosbie and James Boswell had met for a glass of wine in one of the High Street taverns, but all, for various reasons, were unenthused by the prospect of a solid night's drinking: Maclaurin, because on the last two or three such occasions he had got caught up in games of whist and lost a lot of money; Crosbie, because he had an extremely fine claret breathing in his New Town house and did not want to wreck his palate before he returned to it; and Boswell because he was suffering from one of his fits of depression and guilt, and knew that if he got drunk he would, in an effort to dispel the depression, double the guilt by finding himself a prostitute. In addition, all three of them were subdued by the recent death of that emblem of enlightened Edinburgh society, their friend Mr David Hume.

So when, after only one bottle, Maclaurin suggested a walk in the King's Park instead, possibly even a stroll to the top of Arthur's Seat, the others readily agreed, and six o'clock found them setting out from Holyrood across the rough grassland of the park, passing little groups of other walkers, playing children, and a line of elegant-looking white cattle being escorted home round the base of Salisbury Crags by a herd with a couple of dogs. So fine were these cattle that Crosbie paused to admire them and speak to the herd. This gave Boswell the chance to unburden himself to Maclaurin. The last time they had seen each other had been two days before, at Dreghorn, where Maclaurin had had a party out to play bowls. Margaret Boswell had been unwell, so James had gone alone and as a result had got very drunk.

'I have been so dejected since Wednesday,' he said. 'What with Hume, and Margaret's illness, and . . . other things.'

'How is Margaret?'

'A little better. She feared she was consumptive but it is not serious, thank God. But it's not that that vexes me . . . John, I have been a wicked man again. After the bowls.'

'You mean,' said Maclaurin, mockingly wide-eyed, 'when ye left us the ither nicht, ye didna gang straucht hame tae Mrs Boswell? Weel, I'm astonished at ye, James.'

'I don't know what got into me. Anxiety, fear for Margaret's health . . .'

'A guid three bottles o wine.'

'Well, whatever, I wandered about town until I saw a fresh-looking girl –'

'*Fresh-looking!*' Maclaurin said derisively.

'– and lay with her up by the Castle. And then of course I was struck with remorse, and went home and confessed everything.'

'Whit? Ye tellt Margaret that nicht? Wi her seik, and you fou and your breeks hardly done up? James, I dinna ken why I'm freens wi ye. Ye're a monster.'

'I don't know what got into me,' Boswell repeated. 'I cannot help it. My depravity has been exercising me most cruelly in my journal.'

'Dae ye ever think whit would happen if somebody ither than your wife got haud o your precious journal? A disgruntled servant for example? Think o the shame!'

'Oh, I do, I do! Just the other day in the street, a wretched creature caught my eye and tried to lure me off on an . . . adventure. I resisted, and she caught me by the arm and actually begged me by name, "*Mr Boswell!*" Fortunately I was not in company.'

'Wi some men, their reputation precedes them,' Maclaurin said, 'but yours slinks aboot in the shadows waitin tae molest ye.'

'And now, to cap it all,' Boswell said, 'I think I may have caught something. I'll have to get Cameron to find out who this lass is and if she's clean.'

Maclaurin stopped to let Crosbie catch up.

'Not a word now,' Boswell said.

'I wish ye didna feel ye had tae tell me whit ye canna tell him,' said Maclaurin. 'I dinna wish tae hear it, and it seems tae dae ye nae guid tae tell me. Ye'll be awa wi anither strumpet next week, I dinna dout.'

'Oh, do not nag me, my wife does enough of that!' Boswell said, suddenly pettish. As Crosbie reached them, he set off at a pace, leaving the other two behind.

'Whit's up wi him?' Crosbie asked.

'Och, dinna fash, it's jist James. He'll be as sunny as the day in five minutes.'

Nothing, though, would fully shake Boswell out of his mood this evening, although he could not bear to be left out of the conversation and so rejoined them by slowing to a dawdle. They talked of Hume.

'Puir Davie,' Maclaurin said. 'That was a lang, sair struggle he had.'

'Well, scarcely a struggle,' Boswell said. 'More like a mild dispute. I never saw a man face illness with such equanimity. He did not even seem much to resent it, though it must have given him terrible pain.'

'It was very shocking,' said Crosbie, 'tae pass him in the street and see the pounds drap frae him even faster than he pit them on when he was weel.'

'Oh aye, he was a grey, gash fellow at the end,' said Maclaurin. 'And yet it's true, he generally managed a smile if he was receiving visitors. If he couldna manage the smile, his servant didna let ye in.'

'I went to see him buried yesterday on the Calton Hill,' said Boswell. 'There was quite a procession of carriages. I watched from behind the graveyard wall. I didn't feel it was quite right of me to be there.'

'I dout the kirkmen stayed away for the same reason,' Maclaurin remarked. 'Even his moderate minister freens wouldna want tae be seen paying their last respects tae an atheist.'

'Weel,' Crosbie said, 'he would hae preferred it that way. He wouldna hae wanted tae be herried oot o the world by ministers at the hinner end.'

'I saw him just a month past,' said Boswell. 'I missed church and went to see Hume instead – a compound error. You know, I could not get him to shift his views one bit. He was quite calm about being annihilated, even faced with the certainty of death perhaps only days away.'

'Or the uncertainty o it,' Crosbie said. 'Surely that's the point.

He didna believe in an afterlife because ye couldna prove it, so it was a waste o time fashin aboot it.'

'But that's what I find so . . . so shocking. What if he was wrong? I mean, as I'm sure he was. What if you were to die thinking you would pass into oblivion, and then you did not? How would you face God then?'

'Presumably ye would jist hae tae apologise,' Maclaurin said. 'And God would either say, "Weel, Mr Hume, ye were mistaken, and noo ye'll burn in hellfire for your mistake," which wouldna be very Christian, or he'd say, "Weel, Davie, ye were quite aff on the wrang track there but ye're a cosy kind o chiel in spite o your delusions so come awa in and we'll hae a crack aboot it. Your auld freens are here tae – weel, maist o them onywey."'

Crosbie laughed, but Boswell did not like the flippancy of Maclaurin's tone. 'You're as bad as Hume. I did ask him, would it not be agreeable to see your friends again, and he said it would be but he thought it highly unlikely and anyway if he did not exist he would not miss them. Really, he was quite immovable, but perfectly pleasant all the while. We parted on very good terms, for which I am grateful.'

'If ye had been a minister trying tae save his soul frae himsel, he micht no hae been sae nice,' Crosbie said.

'Oh, ministers!' cried Boswell. 'They make me ashamed to be a Scotsman. The fanatics are intolerable, and even the moderates are less moderate than they seem. Mr Blair at St Giles', for heaven's sake, has taken to praying against the Americans, and with a ferocity that is ridiculous in such a mild man. Asking God to defeat your enemies in bloody conflict does not seem very Christian to me.'

'It *isna* very Christian,' Maclaurin said. 'Or if it is, and it's no wrang to ask God tae smite the Americans, it must also be acceptable tae ask him tae smite your opposite coonsel in court, or your ill-mainnered neighbour. But that's religion for ye.'

'No, no,' said Boswell, 'it's not religion's fault. It's the narrowness of men.'

'Ye canna hae it baith weys. Mr Blair isna a narrow man. He's a literary man, a philosopher, a man o taste. He's rid himsel o barbarities like Scotch words, James, so he must be braid-minded, eh? And he was a freen o Hume's tae. Yet he's a Christian that rails against the Americans – jist like your Dr Johnson – when aw they hae done is assert their independence and write it doun in a fine document, *if* ye want my opinion.'

'On that subject – I think we ken – where aw oor sympathies lie,' Crosbie said. He was beginning to pech as they climbed past St Anthony's Chapel.

'I disagree with Johnson on this, as you know,' said Boswell, 'but at least he is consistent. An Anglican, a loyalist, a man who *believes* in authority – whereas our ministers only believe in it when they possess it.'

'Aye,' said Maclaurin, 'a Presbyterian in opposition tae government is a noble beast. A touch fanatical, it may be, but noble. But a Presbyterian licking the Government's fud is a miserable craitur.'

This image did at least draw a laugh from Boswell. 'There should be a cartoon done of that,' he said.

'Whether ye're in favour o it or no,' Crosbie said, 'it seems obvious tae me that the war canna be won by this country. No in the lang term. It grieves me that the folk in London winna see that and get peace noo, afore thoosands mair men are killt on baith sides. If it drags on intae next year, and beyond, the Americans will finish free and independent, jist as they should be, but there'll be aw this bluid skailt in the meantime and bad bluid atween the nations for a generation. Ye canna win a war across such an ocean, no against men in their ain country. Ye may think ye've won, then up it'll flare again, and again and again until ye accept it and come hame.'

'The King canna see that,' said Maclaurin. 'He *refuses* tae see it. And his ministers either winna tell him, or they refuse tae see it as weel.'

'Dundas is the worst,' Boswell said. 'He'll not budge an inch. He always was thrawn, but he's politic enough in law, so why does he dig in his heels so against America?'

'Because he is ambitious,' Crosbie said, 'and as lang as the King says "nae concessions", so will Harry.'

'Maybe he genuinely believes it,' Maclaurin said. 'That it would be wrang tae gie in tae the colonists – an abrogation o responsibility, o authority.'

'Submit or starvate!' Boswell shouted, momentarily gleeful.

Henry Dundas, in a speech in the Commons the previous year, after his elevation to the post of Lord Advocate, had had the House in uproar when he had said that the New Englanders could choose not only between rebellion and 'starvation', they could choose a third way, to submit. The English MPs, who already loved to mock his thick accent and frequent Scotticisms, had hooted at this new invention, and now went about calling him 'Starvation' Dundas. Boswell, never fond of the Dundases in any case, still found this entertaining. The others disagreed with Dundas's views, but they respected his refusal, or his inability, to give up being Scottish, and as for the new word neither of them thought it a particularly awful coinage.

'Dinna be tiresome, James,' said Crosbie. 'Harry's no aw bad. For a Lord Advocate he's quite liberal in some areas o the law. He's got a wise auld heid on him.'

'He's two years younger than I am!' Boswell cried. 'How do you get to be Lord Advocate at thirty-three? He may be clever but he's damned lucky as well. It must help to have a half-brother as Lord President.'

'Ye'd better no start hurling *thae* stanes aboot,' Crosbie said. 'You wi a faither on the Bench, and on dining terms wi twa-three ither o their lordships. It's aye been like that here: faithers and sons and uncles and brithers, Dundases and Fergusons and Dalrymples and Lockharts and Erskines. Good God, man, oor law's as thrang wi relations as a Persian palace!'

'We're a small country,' Maclaurin said. 'It's inevitable.'

By now they were approaching the summit of Arthur's Seat. The last short haul was steep and all talk ceased till they had perched themselves on the rocks, warm from the heat of the sun, which was still well clear of the western horizon. Below them the city was spread out in the softening light. As ever, a few other people were also on the hill top, pointing out particular buildings and streets to one another or just admiring the view in silence. The three lawyers caught their breath. Crosbie, the heaviest of the three, was sweating, Boswell's pulse was racing, and even Maclaurin felt obliged to loosen his cravat.

They saw as a whole what they more often saw as a confusion of layers and fragments – the old city on its rock, the various construction sites on the north side of the new bridge, the houses going up all along Princes Street and behind. It was borne in upon them how huge the changes were that had already taken place, and how, in time, all the fields and gardens as far even as the village of Broughton might become paved over and built on. That seemed incredible, yet looking to the southside, at George Square and Newington, it was possible to see how rapidly such expansion could take place.

'By the way,' Crosbie said to Maclaurin after a while, 'I hear Harry Dundas is interested in your Negro case.'

'Interested?' said Boswell.

'Aye. The case John and Maconochie hae taen on frae Perth. Am I richt, John? Harry wants tae be involved?'

'He *is* involved,' Maclaurin said. 'I've yet tae speak tae him aboot it in detail, but Mr Davidson – our client's solicitor, James – had the notion of approaching Harry tae strengthen oor hand, and I thocht it would dae nae hairm. He agreed tae commit his services the other nicht when we were at dinner at Purves's.'

'What can he offer that you and Maconochie don't already bring to the case?' Boswell asked.

'The fact that he is Lord Advocate,' said Maclaurin. 'His eloquence – dinna smirk, man. His general antipathy tae slavery.'

'Much he has done about it,' Boswell said.

'He moves wi the times,' said Crosbie. 'He kens it canna jist be gotten rid o in a week. But that disna mean he mislikes it ony less. It's the same wi the colliers and salters here at hame.'

The previous year, an Act had been passed emancipating these workers from their peculiar bonds of servitude, guided through Parliament by Dundas's predecessor as Lord Advocate. Dundas had not been involved, but had approved of the measure. Until then, Scottish colliers and salters had been bound for life to their masters, the mine and saltworks owners. It had been something of an embarrassment among enlightened men, that such bondage should survive in a society as advanced as Scotland had become. And yet, as Crosbie, Maclaurin and Boswell all knew, the driving motivation in the movement for change had not been the liberation of the oppressed labourer. Instead an argument had raged between conservative and modernising masters. The former resented any outside interference in the way they exploited their coal reserves. The latter were keen to open up mining to a much larger workforce, subject both wages and prices to competition and make far bigger profits. Only by destroying the old labour system, which was in effect a closed shop, could this be achieved.

There were some colliers and salters who, miserable though their lot was, were as fierce against gaining their liberty as some of their masters were determined to impose it on them. With life bondage came back-breaking labour, danger, disease and an early death, but also certain benefits: higher wages than those of other workers such as farm labourers; free or cheap housing; security of a sort. There were other colliers and salters who bitterly resented their serfdom, the fact that not only they but their wives, sons and daughters were bound into the system for life. Among both owners and workers there had been much argument, anger and confusion over the way forward. As a result the 1775 Act was so beset with age qualifications, exclusions and time lags that it had not made a clean break with the past. Dundas, the feeling was, wanted a further Act to make the emancipation complete.

'You would think,' said Boswell, 'with his great enthusiasm for the war, and all his other ploys, he had enough on his plate without interfering in this Negro case. Who's acting for Wedderburn?'

'Young Ferguson, Pitfour's son, Robert Cullen, and Ilay Campbell,' Crosbie said.

'That's a team of the first rank. Your Negro will be up against it.'

'Our client has a name,' said Maclaurin testily. 'It is Joseph Knight. He's no a zoological specimen.'

'Ye're richt, of course,' said Crosbie. 'Still, it is aboot his race, is it no? If he wasna a Negro he wouldna be a slave.'

'Quite,' Boswell said. 'That is why people speak of the "Negro case". It is not just about one man. It's about the institution, our trade, our empire, our prosperity. Ignore all that and of course there is no good reason why Mr Knight should not be free. But you cannot ignore it, and there is the difficulty.'

'So ye would sacrifice Knight and the rest o his race for oor trade?' Maclaurin asked.

'I see no other option.'

'Be grateful ye were not born an African, then.'

'Believe me, I am.'

'If ye're richt, James,' said Maclaurin, 'that ye canna isolate Mr Knight frae the bigger picture, then ye lead us back tae the very point Dr Johnson made that nicht at your hoose. We must get back tae first principles. If we canna omit the haill question o slavery in oor colonies – the immorality, the illegality, the barbarity o slavery – if we canna leave aw that oot, then we must keep it aw in. As, indeed, Allan Maconochie and I decided some while back. Oor memorials, therefore, are an entire *history* o slavery, frae the ancients tae modern times. Even Monboddo ought tae approve oor classical references.'

'I could ask Dr Johnson to contribute, if you wish,' said Boswell, suddenly enlivened. 'You know his views. His opinion would, I am sure, lend a good deal more *gravitas* to your arguments than anything Dundas may come up with.'

'Aye, weel, that would be fine,' said Maclaurin. 'Every little helps.'

'I'm sure it would be more than a *little*.'

'And we'll welcome it if and when it comes, James. But oor memorials were delivered months ago, so it would be guid only for the day in court, and I dinna ken when that's tae be. It's Wedderburn's side that's haudin the process up. I've complained tae the President aboot it, but they jist winna submit their papers. Meanwhile Joseph Knight is half destitute in Dundee, scrapin a livin at God kens whit. It's as weel we're no chairgin him fees or the puir man would likely hae gien himsel back tae his maister by noo. And he's a wife and bairn and the wife's mither tae fash aboot tae.'

'Maybe Wedderburn's draggin his heels deliberately, tae break him,' Crosbie suggested.

'No, I think it's Cullen that's at fault. I believe the miners' and salters' Act has sent him away tae think again. Whitever else it has or hasna done, it has certainly destroyed the idea that perpetual servitude is something we should accept jist because it's Scottish! Did I tell ye, by the way, that the colliers in Fife raised some money for Mr Knight? They sent a representative tae meet him the last time he was in Edinburgh. They see him as a fellow-sufferer.'

'They're certainly about the same colour,' Boswell said.

'Aye,' Crosbie said, 'but the colliers start aff as white as you and me.'

They sat in silence for a while, until Boswell said, indicating the scene below them with a sweep of his arm – the castle, the city, the broad gleaming firth, the green fields and woods extending westward, the Pentlands, the coast of Fife – 'Am I hopelessly prejudiced, or is there another view in the world to better this one?'

The others added their murmurs of appreciation. The previous discussion suddenly seemed out of place, as if that shining expanse could contain nothing disagreeable. But the argument continued in Maclaurin's head as they lay there, and later as they made their way off the hill nose to tail like the cattle they had seen earlier. That night it revisited him in the form of a dream.

He saw himself in a strange building, a cross between a Persian palace and a luxurious Scottish tavern hung with crimson drapes, with tables groaning under vast amounts of food and drink. Fat, cheerful lawyers and merchants reclined on plump cushions, helping themselves to whatever they fancied. Maclaurin was in the midst of an argument, not with Bozzy or Crosbie or even Cullen but with a roaring oaf who had a dishcloot hanging from his waistband, some ignoramus drunk on wine and patriotism. The oaf was deaving him with the kind of sentiments many Scots found hard to resist: 'Aye, sir, we've aye been hot for liberty. We focht for it against the English wi Wallace and Bruce, and we'll fecht for it against the French. It's in oor banes, it's in oor banes. Of course we'll fecht for the freedom o the Negroes, sir. We're Scotsmen. It's in oor banes.'

But Maclaurin, in his dream-world tavern, did not scuttle for safety but roared back into the oaf's face, 'Ye've drunk yoursel hauf blin, man! Ye see the past but ye dinna see the present. It's Scots that run the plantations, and if ye dinna believe me read Mr Long's book on Jamaica.' (Mr Long, seated in a corner, a yellowish, sneering man with a black beard, raised a glass to him on hearing his work cited.) 'The place is rife wi us. Look at the names, ye blin beggar, and tell me I'm a liar.' He whipped the cloot from its place and began to thrash the drunkard about the face with it, a blow for every name: 'Wedderburns!' *Skelp!* 'Wallaces!'

Skelp! 'Aye, Wallaces!' *Skelp!* 'Kerrs!' *Skelp!* 'Campbells!' *Skelp!* 'MacLeans!' *Skelp!* 'Gordons! Gillespies! Grants!' *Skelp! Skelp! Skelp!* 'Robertsons! Rosses! Ritchies! – Jamaica reads like an Edinburgh kirkyaird! And the plantations are a map o Scotland – Glasgow!' *Skelp!* 'Haddo!' *Skelp!* 'Fort William! Braco! New Galloway! Newmiln! Strathbogie! Drummond!' *Skelp! Skelp! Skelp!* The oaf was now a cowering, wincing jelly before Maclaurin's righteous anger. Mr Long was clapping, slowly and sarcastically. The other men in the place continued to stuff themselves. 'The truth is, we're swimmin up tae oor mooths in the bluid o Africans, but when we tak some in the sugar has sae sweetened the taste that it disna scunner us.' He flung the cloot and the last dregs of the man's glass in his face. 'If ye're a true Scotsman, sir, ye wouldna be proud. Ye would be ashamed!'

He woke with a start, and saw Esther, who was pregnant again, sitting in a chair by the bedroom window. He sat up. 'Are ye no weel?'

'No, John, I'm fine. Jist a wee bittie uncomfortable. I came through tae speak tae ye but ye were asleep. And then ye started thrashin aboot like a horse wi a colic, and I thocht I should stay in case ye were ill. I thocht ye said ye wouldna drink much tonight.'

'I didna. Dinna catch a chill there, my dear.'

She had the window open a few inches. 'It is swelterin, John. I'll no catch a chill. Go back tae sleep.'

He lay back down, pulled up the covers, drifted off again. He knew now that the drunken oaf was not real, and yet was. Courteous Cullen, who in addition to mimicry had made something of a speciality of the study of dreams, would have a field day with his. He had of course no intention of telling him about it. He understood that in his dream he was, in some way, apologising for the failings of the past. But to whom?

Dundee and Ballindean, October 1802

Something had been nagging at the back of Archibald Jamieson's mind for weeks, and it was not the familiar girns of the new Mrs Jamieson. In fact, the new Mrs Jamieson had been remarkably quiet since the end of summer: her complaints about the boys had dwindled to sighs, her rare appearances at the dinner table were peaceful. Some days she did not get out of bed at all. This, at first mildly pleasing to Archibald, had become increasingly disturbing, causing him to wonder, guiltily, if her health was in a worse state than he had supposed. But the doctor had been unable to diagnose anything specific, and Janet Jamieson had absolutely refused to be bled 'jist for the sake o fillin a bowlie'. In this, Archibald had a certain amount of sympathy with her. Last week, however, her obduracy had given the doctor the opportunity to shrug and say that he could not help her if she did not trust him. Mrs Jamieson had replied that indeed she did not trust him, as she knew of several people whose moderate illnesses had developed, following the attendance of their physicians, into full-blown crises rapidly succeeded by death, and that she could not help but feel that these events were connected. The doctor had stalked out in a rage. After he was gone, Archibald Jamieson had sat on the end of his wife's bed and asked whether she wished another doctor to be called. 'They are aw the same, Archie,' she had told him placidly. 'I think I prefer tae decline withoot their assistance.'

The item ticking away in Jamieson's thoughts was one he had not discussed with Janet. This in itself was nothing unusual. As far as he could tell, she had neither curiosity nor care about his work. She did not in fact seem much interested in anything that went on beyond the walls of the house: he had learnt not to bother her with news of the town, the world and their ongoings. But he had not mentioned this particular subject partly because he believed she *would* be interested in it and, because it involved a young woman, that she would draw a number of hasty and ill-judged conclusions.

He was worried about Miss Susan Wedderburn. There had been no contact between them since June, when he had decided that she was both naïve and manipulative, intelligent but also rather silly. Yet she kept interrupting his thoughts. He doubted that Aeneas MacRoy would have betrayed her to her father, but strangely the idea that this might have happened made him tingle with excitement. Sometimes he found himself imagining just that scenario, and the confrontations he, Archibald Jamieson, her protector, would have to have – first with MacRoy, then, in that Ballindean library, with Wedderburn. Working out in his head why he should feel like this was easy: he was connected to her by Alexander Wedderburn's journal.

He still had it, and would bring it out once in a while not to read but to inhale the scent of its linen wrap. He should return it, enable her to put it back where she had found it (assuming it had not been missed). A discreet replacement, a restoration of the former order of things. He needed to persuade her to do this so that he could get her out of his head.

Jamieson had been in his line of work long enough to know how easily, and how often, apparently settled middle-aged men could get into awkward scrapes by letting their imaginations or their instincts run away with them when a second party of the young and female kind entered into proceedings. So, he could stand outside himself and wag a warning finger. He would not be so foolish as to embarrass or compromise either of them. Yet he longed to see her. Why? Surely he was not in love. Ridiculous thought! – the worm of desire that periodically uncurled in him was satisfied in Pirie's Land. With Susan, he told himself, his intentions were strictly honourable: he wanted to make sure that she did nothing irredeemably foolish. And he wanted to tell her what Davidson had said about Joseph Knight.

The journal was the object around which he built his plans. Wrapped in its protective cloth, it nestled against his chest as, one slack October morning, one sunny day with a light westerly blowing leaves in his face, he rode off along the Perth road on the same hired horse as before.

He reached the village of Inchture about eleven, turned the

horse in at a dwelling, slightly larger than the others, that served as a very simple inn, and strolled around the scattering of cottages. The place seemed run down for the principal staging post between Dundee and Perth. This state of disrepair was largely because Lord Kinnaird, who owned it, had plans to knock it all down and construct a model village on the site. Such 'improvement' was something of a fashion among landowners.

Jamieson did not suppose that the inhabitants had any say in how, or whether, their homes were to be improved. From a casual inspection, though, they could not get much worse. The remnant of an old castle, the manse, the kirk and the schoolhouse were the only buildings of any real substance. He stopped to admire the manse, a fine if ramshackle pile covered in ivy and standing behind the graveyard wall. He noticed a rodden tree, barrier to witches, growing at the gate, its autumn foliage flame-orange and lit with smouldering clusters of red berries. He wondered if God was offended by this extra layer of protection against evil, or if He even cared.

Joseph Knight, Davidson had said, had been made a Christian by some local minister. Was it here he had come for instruction? Jamieson was tempted to chap the door and ask to see the current incumbent, a Mr Davie, but there was no point. Davie, a middle-aged bachelor, had only been there a couple of years. The previous minister had died in 1799, but it would probably have been *his* predecessor, or even the one before that, who would have had any dealings with Knight. And even if Davie did know anything, why would he tell it to a strange man who came unannounced to ask questions? More likely he would go straight to Ballindean, where it would not take Wedderburn, or MacRoy, long to work out who the stranger was.

Jamieson walked back to the 'inn', passing through a small group of brown-faced, barefoot children loitering by the road in anticipation of the Dundee coach. He had considered coming out on the coach and catching the afternoon one back, but the times were not reliable, and he did not know how long he might need. He cast a few sharp glances at the older boys and, observing what looks were returned, went inside.

He found himself in what was really the enlarged front room of a cottage. He settled himself near the unlit fire, the only customer, and the woman of the house brought him a tankard of ale. Jamieson waited.

Before he was halfway through the tankard a scrawny, black-eyed lad of ten or eleven sidled in to stand a few feet away. Jamieson was pleased with himself. It was the one he wanted, the eager hireling, the one who understood. He could have put a bet on it.

'There's a penny here for ye,' he said, tapping the coin on the table, 'if ye are tae be trusted? Are ye?'

'Aye.'

'D'ye belang this hoose?'

'Na.'

'Whit's your name?'

'Neil Murray.'

'Come closer, Neil Murray.' The boy approached till they were almost touching. Jamieson dropped his voice. There was no sign of the woman, but he was not taking any chances.

'D'ye ken the big hoose, lad?'

'Aye.'

'How d'ye ken which ane I mean? Drimmie or Ballindean?'

'I ken them baith, so ye can mean either.'

'Ye dinna stand much on ceremony, eh, Neil? Never mind. Ballindean is closer, is it no?'

'Aye. A mile awa, nae mair. Drimmie's twa.'

'Wha bides at Drimmie?'

'The muckle laird's folk. The Kinnairds.'

'Weel, ye seem wise enough. Let's see how fast ye are. Can ye rin tae Ballindean and back?' Neil Murray nodded. 'Dae ye ken the folk there? The great folk, I mean?'

'Aye, Sir John and that.'

'D'ye ken the dochters, the Miss Wedderburns?'

'Aye. Five o them.'

'But can ye tell them apairt?'

'The auld ane's Margaret. The wee ane's Anne. The bonnie ane's Louisa.'

'It's nane o them I mean. I want ye tae tak a message tae Miss Susan. D'ye ken her?'

'She's the dark-haired ane o the ither twa.'

'Guid lad.'

255

Jamieson reached inside his coat, felt for the folded, sealed note behind the journal, pulled it out. It had nothing written on the outside.

'Ye've tae find a wey tae gie this tae her. Tae naebody else, mind. No tae a sister nor a servant nor onybody. Only tae her.'

'Whit if she's no there?'

'Bring it back. How will ye find her?'

'My cousin's a hoosemaid. She'll ken.'

'Dinna gie it tae your cousin. Dinna show it tae her. Tell her there's a penny for her as weel if she speirs nae questions but gets ye tae Susan Wedderburn. Gie Miss Wedderburn this paper when she's alane and wait till she opens it. Then tell her a man at Inchture sent ye.'

Most idiot bairns would have wanted to know what name to give. Neil Murray was quite a find: he only asked, 'Whit'll she say?'

'Naething, I hope, but that she's coming here. But if she canna, she may gie ye a message back. Speak tae naebody else and there's twa pennies in it, ane for you and ane for your cousin.'

'How lang will ye wait?'

'I'm in nae hurry.'

'There's mair nor twa pennies' work in this.'

Jamieson scowled, really in order to hide his delight. He saw the quick mind working behind Neil Murray's dark eyes. Already the boy was thinking of how not to involve his cousin, how to get both coins for himself. This was highly commendable. 'Dae it weel, and there will be,' said Jamieson, and Neil, apparently satisfied with this half-promise, slipped out of the door.

The coach bound for Perth arrived and a couple of passengers got out to stretch their legs. Jamieson watched through the window as the Inchture bairns gathered round as if they had never seen a coach or strangers before in their lives. He ordered a slice of mutton pie to soak up his ale. The coach departed again. Jamieson ate, settled up, then wandered back outside.

The children paid him no attention. The broad dusty street was splashed with sunlight dripping through some fine old oak trees. Dead leaves lay in drifts against a dyke on one side of the road. Doubtless the trees themselves would not survive the rebuilding of the village. It was something of a surprise that they had stood even till now, since there seemed to be a mania – at least the would-be gypsy in Jamieson thought it so – for cutting down the biggest and best trees in the land.

Nearly an hour had passed since Neil had left. Jamieson's sense of anticipation overcame his patience. He returned to the inn, reclaimed his horse, and rode slowly in the direction of Ballindean. He passed a few poor but clean-looking cottages. A man working in one of the gardens exchanged the time of day. The open gates of Ballindean appeared on the right. Jamieson remembered the long curving avenue that led up to the house. The boy came trotting out of the thick woods and through the gates.

'Aye, Neil?'

'She's coming. On her ain horse,' Neil said. He did not seem in the least excited by his news.

'Jist hersel?'

'Aye.'

'Wait here for her. Tell her no tae gang tae Inchture. This way.' He pointed ahead, a track leading into the hills behind Ballindean. 'Ye understand?'

'That's anither penny.'

Jamieson laughed. He saw that Neil had him in his power now. He had probably spent the last hour calculating what the man from Dundee's secret manoeuvres might be worth. Jamieson flicked him two coins, one after the other in a spinning arc, then a third, and a huge smile appeared on the boy's face. A captain of commerce in the making. Jamieson kicked his horse into a trot as Neil hunkered down by one of the stone gateposts to complete his errand.

After a few hundred yards the track turned to the west and seemed to be heading towards another collection of cottages. This was the old Perth road, now superseded by the turnpike. On his right a broken-down dyke separated the track from woods which formed part of the policies of Ballindean. It suddenly occurred to Jamieson that he was riding very close to danger – not physical danger, but risk of his rather clumsily arranged liaison with Susan being discovered. No great calamity for him, but it could be for her.

That word 'liaison' rather surprised him. It popped into his head and sent a small thrill through him, one he immediately mocked. Then he thought – and this was part of the rising tide of excitement in him – that there might really be some threat to his safety. What if Susan Wedderburn, outraged at his forwardness, was setting a trap, coming to meet him while her brother and Aeneas MacRoy were outflanking him armed with horsewhips and cudgels? But no, if she was coming it was in response to two words and four letters on a single sheet of paper, which her own previous actions would have prevented her from disclosing to anyone else: 'I HAVE JK. AJ.' He was intrigued to discover how she had interpreted this; if she would be angry when she found he had played her own trick back on her.

He dismounted, guided the horse through a gap in the dyke, and waited among the trees.

Presently he heard hooves approaching at a smart trot. One horse, and Susan Wedderburn on it. As she drew level he whistled. She turned her head, saw him, lifted her hand in acknowledgment and pointing forward continued on her way. He emerged from the trees and saw that she had left the track where it turned to the west, and had taken a very narrow and overgrown path due north that he would otherwise have missed. He mounted up and followed.

After a short steep climb, the vegetation thinned again and the path opened out on to a hillside scattered with birch scrub. Here, resting her horse by a large boulder, Susan Wedderburn was waiting.

'I am much obliged tae ye, miss,' Jamieson said, coming up to her. 'I didna ken if this would be possible. I was concerned for ye.'

'I am pleased to see you,' she said. 'And I thank you for your concern.'

He was immediately struck by the sombre tone of her voice. She seemed more formal than before; gracefulness banishing gaucheness almost entirely. It was as if she had left childhood quite behind her in the intervening months.

'This winna cause ye trouble?'

'No. Neil Murray is very discreet.'

'Ye ken him?'

'I ken most of the Inchture bairns. Anyway, there is more than enough occupying the hearts and minds of Ballindean at present for anyone to notice whether *I* choose to go out riding or not.'

Again, he sensed a change: a note of pride; bitterness even?

'I misled ye, perhaps,' he said, 'wi the note.'

'Not at all. I understood it perfectly. I had no illusions that you had hidden Mr Knight behind a tree for me.'

Their horses were standing patiently alongside each other, head to tail. He took out the package from his breast, realised too late that he had smelt its scent for the last time, and handed it towards her. She made no effort to take it, seemed in fact to shy away from it. But he kept it there, and at last she took it.

'Was it missed?' he asked.

'If it was, nobody has remarked on it.'

She looked at it in her hand, but did not unwrap it.

'I thought it was exciting when I found it. Now I can hardly bear to touch it. I find it repulsive.'

'Your uncle?'

'The whole of it.'

For the third time, Jamieson heard the melancholy in her voice.

'Miss, has something happened?'

'What do you mean?'

'Ye seem different. Unhappy.'

'No. I am happy. Life is gathering pace, that's all. There are to be changes here.'

Jamieson thought of his own fantasies – the gypsy ones. What would the tinklarian life be but a slowing down of life, an attempt to put a brake on change? That was perhaps what he longed for. He did not say anything.

'Papa is not at all well,' Susan said. 'He has had a stroke. We fear he will not last the winter. Yet even he is anxious to hurry things along.'

'What things?'

'My sister is to be married.'

'I am happy for her.'

'Pff! *I* can say that. I am her sister. You don't even know which one I mean.'

'I hardly know *you*. Which of your sisters is tae be married?'

'All of them in time, doubtless.' Again, that bitter note. 'But

Louisa will be first, and now we all expect Margaret to fly the nest in the spring.'

'Louisa? But she's younger than you.'

'Sixteen. But that's old enough, whereas Margaret would probably be thought a little *too* old. For what we are best at, that is. Families.'

'This is aw very sudden, is it no?'

'Well, Margaret has been a dark horse. She spends whole weeks in Edinburgh with various friends, and there she has been *seen* with Mr Philip Dundas – one of *the* Dundases, Henry Dundas's young brother in fact. A lady can't be seen often with a Dundas before either something *happens* or she ceases to be seen with him. So I predict an announcement. But as for Louisa, yes, I suppose it is quite sudden.' She broke off. 'Listen.'

Jamieson looked around, half expecting to see men creeping through the scrub. But Susan's head was turned skyward. There was the ragged cry of geese, and shortly afterwards a V of them passed overhead.

'I love that sound. It's as if they are saying, how clever we are, to have found our way here again.'

Jamieson nodded, but he had never thought much about geese. Susan carried on.

'After you and I last met, Mr Jamieson, that day in Dundee, we all went to the shows in the Meadows. And we found a spaewife. Margaret wasn't there, but the rest of us had our fortunes read, and swore not to reveal what we had been told till some months had passed. Well, last week, Louisa and I rode over to our friends the Threiplands at Fingask for the morning – a day just like this – and we were about to come home when they asked us to stay on to meet General Sir John Hope, who was expected. You know who he is, don't you?'

'Aye, he focht the French wi Abercromby in Egypt – a tremendous hero, they say.'

'Exactly. And also one of the Hopes of Hopetoun, which one day he may inherit. So we did stay, and were introduced. For a soldier he is very gentlemanly, but also much older than I imagined – he is certainly nearer forty than thirty, *and* a widower. The next day – where are we now? – last Friday, the very same

260

Sir John Hope rode up to Ballindean, requested to see Papa, and asked for his daughter's hand in marriage!'

'That *is* heroic!'

'Yes, especially since, when Papa inquired which daughter, Sir John was unable to say. He did not know her name. We'd been introduced to him as the Misses Wedderburn.'

Jamieson detected now, in the way Susan's narrative had re-animated her, a certain heroism of her own. If, as it seemed, the story was to have a happy ending, it also looked as if it would have an ugly sister.

'Papa told us about it later – he is so proud that he is to have Sir John as his son-in-law. The first we knew of it was when they entered the schoolroom – Louisa and Anne and I were all there, with Maister MacRoy – and Sir John inclined his head towards Aeneas and Annie and me, then positively bowed to Louisa. And Papa said to her, "My dear, I have something very important to discuss with this gentleman, and then with you," and they went back out again.'

'Ye'd hae haen an idea whit was afoot?'

'Oh, Aeneas couldn't keep us in the room! We had to get out to talk about it. Then Louisa was summoned and we had to wait for an age before she came back and told us, half laughing, half crying, that she was to be married. And she said she'd fallen in love with Sir John Hope the moment she saw him at Fingask, which I'm sure ... well, I expect it was true. And she said that what the spaewife had told her was that she would marry John Hope, which she had thought till that moment was a figure, a riddle of some kind, like John the Commonweal or John Barleycorn. I expect that was true, too, but Annie spoiled it a little by insisting that the wife had said *she* was to marry John Hope. She was quite upset, because either Louisa was telling a lie or she was, or the spaewife was a cheat for telling the same prophecy twice. And the rest of us I'm sure would have settled for blaming the wife except that then Louisa *would* stand *her* ground and say Annie was just jealous. It was a shame, but we've agreed to say no more about it. I think Annie's upset because she'll be losing Louisa, who is closest to her.'

'Very likely. What, may I ask, was predicted for you?'

'Oh, a number of things. But I didn't put much faith in any of it at the time and I certainly don't now.'

All this time she had been holding the wrapped journal in her hand. Now she held it out to him. 'Will you take this back?'

'I canna.'

'My father has not missed it. He does not know where half the things he looks for are any more. It is a horrible book. When he is dead I do not wish anyone else to find it and read it.'

'Whit dae ye want me tae dae wi it?'

'Destroy it.'

'I canna, miss.'

'It's a commission. I gave it into your hands, now I ask you to destroy it. Are you wanting a fee?'

There was a new note in her voice now. Back in June she might have tried coquettishness to get him to do what she wanted. That was gone, and in its place was something he did not like as much: an attempt at imperiousness.

'Miss Wedderburn, I would gladly dae whitever ye asked that was reasonable, but I canna dae this. It isna mine or yours tae destroy.'

'I had no idea reasonableness or morality entered into your work. Perhaps *you* would like to return it to my father instead?'

'Ye should never hae sent it tae me if ye felt like this.'

'I did *not* feel like this when I sent it to you. Then it was about Mr Knight. Now it is . . . Now it is not.'

'It's aboot your faither.'

The haughty look she had been maintaining crumbled a little. 'Yes, and my uncles – my whole family being so . . . involved in slavery. I am ashamed, for them and for myself. That is why I ask you to take the book away and destroy it.'

'But you – they – still hae slaves. The plantations still exist. I tellt ye that afore. It's slavery that keeps ye in Ballindean. Destroying that wee book winna change that.'

'It is the detail in it. The fine, vile detail. It is as if they are murderers.' Her hands were restless: the one holding the journal jerked up and down rapidly, the other picked at the horse's mane. Her lower lip was trembling. 'They *are* murderers. I do not recognise them.'

Jamieson reached his big coarse hand over her small gloved

262

one and the journal; stilled the movement. It was an instinctive act, insanely forward, but he was relieved to find that it had nothing in it but concern and pity and . . . fatherliness.

'He is your faither,' he said. 'Whitever else he has been, he is your faither.'

She shook her head, fighting back her distress.

'If I burn this book,' he said, 'I burn a pairt o him. A pairt o you. It isna my business tae dae that. Pit it back where ye found it, miss, or keep it tae yoursel till ye ken better. But ye canna undo whit's in it. If it maks ye hate slavery, fine and guid.'

'But it makes me hate my father!'

'No,' he said, 'this isna hate I'm seeing.'

Somewhere to the east a gun was fired. The echo of the shot carried like a rasping cough over the hill.

'My brother, probably,' she said. 'I should not stay much longer.' He lifted his hand, and she gazed at the wrapped book. She had a little satchel slung across her shoulder, and now she unfastened it and put the journal inside. 'You're right,' she said. 'I cannot expect you to do what I ask. I will do it myself.'

He shook his head. 'Think hard first. Ye can only make that decision once. Ye can defer it as often as ye like.'

'I feel it is time to stop deferring,' she said. 'I could defer all my life and not achieve anything.'

'It's true,' he said. 'But when ye act, ye can tak back yer haun but no the action.'

'That is to be human,' she said. 'To act is to be alive. I don't feel I am truly alive. I cannot act. A woman cannot act as you can, as my father has.'

'Then ye are withoot responsibility, and it is men that should envy you.'

'Do not mock me, Mr Jamieson. We are without *choice*. There is nothing to be envied in that.'

He thought at once of the new Mrs Jamieson, lying in bed, refusing the doctor, and a shock of guilt jolted through him. Suddenly he hoped she would still be awake when he got home. He felt he would like to sit and talk with her for a while. Not about this, but about her, Janet Jamieson.

'Ye'll no hae had much thought of Joseph Knight these last few weeks, then?' he asked Susan Wedderburn.

'Not much. He was here, now he's gone. I think – something tells me – he is dead. And you?'

'I've been thinking a guid deal aboot him. Aboot all of ye oot here – you, your faither, Aeneas MacRoy. And Joseph. I think he's alive.'

'Why?'

'The same reason you gied: something tells me.'

'So you'll keep looking for him?'

'Ah, miss, I'm no a man o leisure. I hae tae work, and Joseph isna work ony mair. But I'm due in Edinburgh soon – I'm gaun tae seek oot some o the papers frae the case. I'll think aboot him some mair. In a way, that's looking for him. Like reading thon bookie. I thocht it was nae help, but somehow it is. That's anither reason I'm sure ye shouldna destroy it.'

'That's what I thought,' she said. 'When I read what was in it I really wanted you to find him. If he and Papa could have been brought together, could have been reconciled in some way . . .'

'That isna gaun tae happen, miss. It never was.'

'Yes, now I see that. That's why I would rather the journal was destroyed. You see, it's not just that I believe Mr Knight is dead. I feel . . .'

'Aye, miss?'

'I feel it would be better for everybody if he were.'

There was another shot, closer this time, and a rattle of wings among branches.

'I must go,' Susan said quickly. 'No – you should go first. It will surprise nobody if I am found riding up here.'

'Aye, ye're richt.'

He made as if to leave; hesitated. Words began to come from him that he did not expect to hear himself say. 'Miss Wedderburn, I am your servant, as ye ken. I hope ye will consider me your friend as weel. If ye should ever lack a friend.'

She smiled warmly. 'I appreciate that.'

He smiled back, but still he was reluctant to leave. What madness was this? He did not, could not, want anything from her. She was younger than his own daughters. Yet her younger sister was to marry a man who might be his brother. Something seemed very wrong, and yet it was all entirely normal. He could not figure it out.

Susan Wedderburn made up his mind for him by reaching out and shaking his hand. Before he could contemplate kissing the back of hers, it had been withdrawn, and she had turned her horse and trotted away up the hill. '*Au revoir*, Monsieur Jamieson!' He waved briefly, then made his way back to the old road.

The reliable old hired horse knew its way home, which was just as well, for Jamieson took in nothing of the nine-mile ride. He was too deep in thought. It was not until he was on the outskirts of Dundee, with the long clouds turning deep and bloody behind him in the afternoon sky, not until he had turned over every phrase, every look in their conversation, that he understood the weight and true meaning of Susan's words: there was, indeed, nothing to be envied about being without choice.

He thought also about the fact that he had not told her of his meeting with Andrew Davidson. The dying, possibly by now the dead Mr Davidson, who assumed that everybody was alive unless he had proof to the contrary. Jamieson had not forgotten to tell her about him: he had chosen not to. Davidson wanted him to find Knight, wanted Knight to be alive. Susan Wedderburn thought it would be better if he were dead. Better for everybody, she had said, but what she surely meant was better for her and her family. Even as he had been offering her his friendship, Jamieson had been struck by her Wedderburn conceit, the cool arrogance of wealth. Would it be better for Joseph Knight if Joseph Knight were dead?

He kicked the horse hard and the poor beast broke into a half-hearted canter for twenty yards, then slowed down again. Archibald Jamieson apologised aloud for making it the recipient of feelings he should have been directing at himself: irritation that he still had not bothered to find out its name; disgust at his own hypocrisy; anger that it should take a seventeen-year-old lassie to remind him, in three or four sentences, of all the petty and gross injustices of life.

Ballindean, 28 November 1802

It was, once again, the anniversary of his father's death. Sir John Wedderburn forgot what he had had for breakfast these days, but he did not forget this or the other significant dates of his calendar. He was where he almost always was when he was not at table or in his bed – in his library. The fire was built up, throwing out heat across the room. Most days someone would check periodically to make sure there were enough logs, that he was warm enough. Every afternoon one of his daughters would come and read to him, which they seemed to find reassuring, especially when it sent him off, as it invariably did, into a doze. But the mornings were still his, and this morning in particular: he had asked not to be disturbed till noon, promising that he would not let the fire die out.

He no longer went outside now that winter had come. He looked through the window at the naked trees and the wet brown leaves decaying on the grass, he saw small birds valiantly darting about in the wind, and he was happy to be indoors. Everything ached: his back, his legs, his fingers, his neck. The stroke had made his left side partially paralysed, so that he could hardly raise his arm; his fingers were clumsy lumps and his leg dragged his foot like a stone in a sack. The doctor could prescribe any number of ointments, embrocations, decoctions, pills and powders, he could urge therapeutic exercises of a most tedious kind, but he could, he admitted, offer only temporary relief. 'A hard and eventful life is catching up with you at last, Sir John,' he said, smiling gravely. And although Sir John had never trusted doctors much, having been one, of sorts, himself, the man was probably right: that was what it felt like to him – life's trials and tribulations wearing him down at the end, getting ready to crumble him into dust.

He wondered if this day would come again, if this might be the last anniversary of the execution of which he would be conscious. How strange to contemplate not being conscious – of anything. But he did not think it would be like that. There *was* a heaven, and he trusted he would get there. There *was* a God, and he would see Him. But sooner rather than later, of *that* there was little doubt. And he would, presumably, see his other, earthly father again: Blackness and Ballindean would embrace, and Blackness would perhaps say, 'I misjudged you, John, I was wrong. You did very well in the end.'

For nearly sixty years he had kept this day apart. On it, he did no work, and kept no company except that of his immediate family. And for what? To remember someone who was less than a shadow. He looked at the painting of his father. That was how he saw him now. The man, the physical man, was quite gone. He still heard his words on Drummossie Moor, he still saw a figure mounted on a horse going away from him, but the voice was his own voice, the face was the face of the painting, the memory was a likeness of the painting. That was what time did to memory: it washed it away and left only a representation of it in its place.

Yet that was not quite correct. For time erased the nearer memories first, or at least the trivial, daily ones that allowed a man to function with something like dignity. Sir John knew that the whole household treated him now more like a lost child than as the head of the family. Then they wondered why he grew irritable. What they did not know, what they did not understand, was that, however feeble they thought his mind, there were things in it stronger than time itself: memories that could not be wiped out. And these came before him, as he sat by the fire, as vivid and hot as the flames themselves.

Aeneas MacRoy. Was he still in the house? Yes, Sir John believed he was, in spite of what had happened, in spite of the fact that he did not come near his master any more, crept away into the darker, furthest corners of the house. When had it happened? After the stroke anyway. Yes, he minded the rage he had felt that could not be acted upon, that had got stuck in his dead side and in his numb mouth. But what had happened was between the two of them, and always would be, and because of that, and that alone, Aeneas MacRoy remained beneath his roof. Sir John would not humiliate the family by casting him out and having to explain why. He would not humiliate his daughters and his wife. Above all, especially in his already diminished state, he would not further humiliate himself.

If the man would only go of his own accord – but he would not. He had got in years ago, trading on some notion of loyalty and he was in it now like a bat in the bauks. One traitor out and another inside. What had he ever done to deserve them?

It must only have been a few days ago, yet it seemed like years. Dreamlike. One of his first mornings back in the library, after a week in bed. He had insisted on getting up, had dragged his leg down to this room, gazed out of the window, sat in front of the fire. Even when exhausted he had fought them trying to get him back to bed: 'I am quite comfortable. Will you not leave me be? Another ten minutes, and then I'll go. Where's Aeneas?'

So they had sent in Aeneas, or Aeneas had come of his own accord, to sit and wipe his master's slaivers no doubt, the faithful old comrade in arms. And Sir John had waved at the chair opposite – 'Sit down, Aeneas, for God's sake!' – but MacRoy had stood hovering, towering over him although he was a shrunken wee man, until it became evident, even to Sir John in his wreckage, that the dominie had something to say.

'Well, what is it?' He heard the slur in his own voice, hated it.

Aeneas MacRoy coughed, began in measured, clipped tones. 'I have not yet congratulated you, Sir John, on your daughter's engagement to Sir John Hope. Your illness has prevented . . . It would gratify me to do so now.'

'Speak Scotch, for God's sake, man. You approve of the match?'

'It wouldna be for me no tae approve. It's a guid match.'

'You're pleased, then?' A half-chuckle fought its way out of his throat. The idea of the schoolmaster being pleased at anything . . .

'I am pleased for Miss Louisa, aye. Disappointed for mysel, of course. She has been a fair student.'

'She has no need for more learning now. But you've taught her well, Aeneas. You've taught them all well.'

'And Miss Margaret is tae be wed tae. Ye'll soon hae nae dochters left in the hoose.'

'I'll get some peace then.' A forced attempt at mirth. 'Anyway, there's Anne and Susan and Maria yet.'

268

'It was Susan I wished tae speak aboot.'

There was a note in MacRoy's voice, of doom or regret or something grave at any rate. Sir John made an effort to sit up.

'If she has not been diligent or something, see Lady Alicia about it. I am not to be fashed with that kind of thing, you see.'

'She has aye been diligent. I couldna find faut wi her in that respect. In ony respect. She's the cleverest o them aw.'

'Then what is it?'

His vision was affected by the stroke too. MacRoy seemed a little hazy, as if he had retreated a little. Then he loomed forward again. In fact he was going like a pendulum.

'She is intelligent and handsome and decorous and a credit tae yoursel and Lady Wedderburn,' MacRoy said in a rush. 'If she has a failing, it is an inclination tae feel ower passionate on maitters that she kens little aboot, but this isna sae muckle a failing as a mark o a noble inheritance and a virtuous character. In short she is a young lady that ony man would be prood tae cry his wife.'

Sir John had never heard so many words issue from Aeneas's mouth in so short a time. He focused harder on the swaying face.

'I humbly ask ye, Sir John, tae acknowledge my lang service tae ye and your faimly, tae set that agin ony douts, ony hesitation ye may hae anent my humble beginnings, and tae grant permission that I micht speir at your dochter Susan tae be my wedded wife.'

Another laugh began to erupt from the Wedderburn throat. With severe difficulty he suppressed it. '*What*?'

'She has found a place in my hert, sir, and I implore ye as her faither and as a fellow man no tae keep me in agony, no tae –'

'You want to marry *my* daughter?'

'Aye, Sir John.'

'My daughter *Susan*?'

'Aye, Sir John.'

Sir John discovered that words were, literally, failing him. His brain could not construct, could not transmit to his mouth, the sentences he needed. He tried to summon the strength to launch himself out of his chair and attack MacRoy, but succeeded only in slipping nearer to the floor. The next thing, MacRoy was over him, trying to lever him back up. Sir John vainly head-butted him in the chest, but the dominie did not seem to notice.

'Get off – you – I –'

'Ye wouldna be expectin this, I ken –'

'I – nnngh – this – joke –'

'I was never mair serious.'

'– nnngh – never –'

'Aye, never.'

'I mean – *never*. Can't – unnh – believe it. You – damned schoolmaster –'

'I ken, but –'

'– left you – nnngh – charge of my lassies – now this . . . Out!'

'Sir John –'

'*Out!*'

'I dinna mean tae offend ye.'

'Get out! Could not – offend – more. Sight of you – offends me.'

'Sir John –'

'I will – unnh – cry murder.'

'I only –'

'*Help!*'

The shout surprised them both, it was so loud. Sir John saw the word ballooning up from his lungs and out of his mouth, like a cartoon. He liked the look of it; tried again.

'*Help! HELP!*'

And then Aeneas MacRoy joined in: '*Help!*' He was still holding him in place on the chair. Suddenly there were people everywhere, pushing Sir John and clutching at him and trying to give him brandy, when all he wanted was to throttle MacRoy. But MacRoy was lost in the crowd, and Sir John's body gave in to the pressures and he felt it collapse in on his mind, so that it was his mind that they carried to the bedroom, like an egg slopping in a glass.

'Where is he?' he asked at one point. 'Where's the dominie?'

'He has left us to manage things,' somebody said. 'Thank heaven he was there with you, but you must not fret about him now. You'll see him in the morning.'

He recognised the voice. 'Who's there?' he shouted, like a sentinel.

'It is only me. Your wife.'

'Margaret?'

'You have quite overdone it, my dear. This is your wife Alicia.'

He remembered that blunder. After that they had had him beaten. He had asked again for the dominie but they had said he could see nobody else that day. And his mind had lain there and seen that the thing that had happened had not happened, that Aeneas had never made his outrageous request, that he had gone away with his question and would never bring it back, would tear it up and eat it, chew it thirty-two times, destroy all possibility of ever having asked it. Yet it was there, in Sir John's head. He *had* asked it. Unbelievable. Very like a dream, yes indeed.

He had not seen MacRoy since. Perhaps he really had gone. But no, somebody would have said. One of his daughters, coming to read to him, would have said. He wondered who would come today. He would like Susan. No – he would not like any of them. Today was the day of his father's death.

There had been one time – one only – when this day had been different. He had been caught out by circumstances. It was in the middle of the Joseph Knight business – one year or other of the interminable years that the case dragged on. The precise year was unimportant except that it must have been after the death of his first wife, dear Margaret. Yes, that was it, late on in the case. He had been obliged to go to Edinburgh to meet with his counsel, what was his name, Cullen. Cullen was under pressure from Knight's people. They had complained about his slowness in lodging memorials with the reporting judge, and the court had fined him, and Cullen had asked Sir John to come in to straighten out some of the circumstances. It was easier to do it face to face than by correspondence, he wrote, an argument which Sir John had put down to laziness. But when he acquiesced and journeyed to the capital and met with Cullen, he realised at once that something more was afoot.

Cullen had got them a private room in one of the smarter taverns, and they ordered some dinner: venison soup followed by roast grouse. There, as they ate, he began quietly to express his doubts about the wisdom of proceeding with the case. The recent legislation emancipating the miners and salters was given as one reason: it made their arguments much less secure. The mood of the Bench was another. Cullen had assessed the opinions of each of the fifteen Lords of Session, and he reckoned, at best, that they might expect the sympathies of five. At this Sir John almost exploded. 'I *have* their sympathies, sir! Five? That is pitiful accountancy. The Lord President wrote me when my wife died. Lord Elliock wrote me. Lord Pitfour wrote me. I am obliged to all of them. Will they show more *sympathy* to a Negro than to me a Scotsman?'

'With respect, Sir John,' Cullen said, 'you have named but three, and Lord Pitfour is ailing. I do not doubt the sympathies of the entire Session for your grievous loss. That is not what I meant. I meant their leanings for or against the cause of slavery.'

'But that is not their business. Their business is to determine a matter of property. Knight is part of my property. There is no doubt of it.'

'It is disputed. Otherwise we would not be before the Session. And, as we have discussed before, the other side will make certain the case is heard in the broadest context. That is why we cannot rely in our arguments on property rights alone. That is why we are stressing your generosity toward Knight, your kindliness to him, the fact that you have educated, clothed and fed him and made him a Christian, that you have never mistreated him. And it is also why I have built up the historical case *for* slavery, to show that it has always existed wherever there have been societies and nations, that it is – that it can be shown to be – natural to them.'

'Do I detect, Mr Cullen, that you do not fully subscribe to the points you are making?'

'That is neither here nor there, sir. I am an advocate and I make the case for my client with all the force of argument I can muster.'

'You cannot do it with passion, if you do not passionately believe it.'

'The Session is not interested in passion, only in law.'

'Then,' said Sir John, 'their *sympathies* are irrelevant also. For they should put aside such feelings and look at the cold, hard facts, and those will tell them that I am right, and Joseph Knight and his abettors are wrong.'

'The Act liberating the miners changes the facts. It suggests that the only reason for keeping Joseph a slave is the accident of his race.'

'What about economy? The security of our colonies? The prosperity of the nation? What about these?'

'These are general issues, which we will duly address. But there are arguments, equally strong perhaps, on both sides.'

'Perhaps I should find myself new counsel, sir. One who will fight my cause with more vigour.'

'That is your choice, sir, but I would not advise it. Their lordships will not countenance further delays. They would dismiss the case. We are stuck with each other, I believe.'

'And you think I should surrender?'

'I think you should consider withdrawing.'

'I will not. This must be resolved one way or the other.'

'Very well.'

The rest of the meeting had been conducted coolly, with Cullen making notes as they talked, and trying to look as though he were still confident of winning. Sir John Wedderburn gave him what information he needed. He had seen Cullen's papers and they were impressive, but what use were pages of dry words if the men who were to make the decision were already inclining towards Knight? Cullen began to summarise their position, and as he droned on Sir John tried to add up the judges himself, for and against. He knew three quite well. Four others he had spoken with at one time or another. None of them, of course, was in any way a radical. He believed a further two – Monboddo and Gardenstone – would vote for property and thus for him. That made nine. He thought Auchinleck and old Kames were likely to be against him. This did not take any account of those judges he did not know, and yet he had a majority without them, even if one of the nine went the other way. Furthermore, his other counsel, working with Cullen, was James Ferguson, the son of Lord Pitfour. That must count for something, surely – Pitfour's fellow judges would not want to see him embarrassed. Cullen was being too negative.

Then again, there might be other alliances and enmities in the court. The Dundases, for example . . . But here he stopped himself. He was doing what Cullen and his cronies did – weighing up ifs and buts and notwithstandings, calculating personal politics. This would get him nowhere.

There was another way to test the ground, though, and that was to seek out Knight's counsel and see what they thought they were up to. It was this which determined Sir John to stay on in Edinburgh an extra day. He knew John Maclaurin – by sight, at least – because he had seen him perform at the preliminary hearing before Lord Kennet, the reporting judge, some months before. A tall, angular, dreary-faced fellow, who looked like he would snap like a twig. Sir John decided to test this out. The suave Cullen no doubt 'would not advise it', so Wedderburn was careful to avoid a public scene. He went to see Maclaurin at his town house in Brown Square, early the following day.

It was a bitter morning. The wind was so cold it felt almost solid. He was peevish at the temperature and at the fact that he had not got back to Perthshire the previous evening: somehow both seemed to be Maclaurin's fault. He quite forgot the date. A servant took his card and made him wait in the lobby. After a few minutes Maclaurin appeared, all in black except for his white cravat, wearing fingerless gloves and with a species of wool bonnet crammed on his head.

'If this is a social call, sir, ye are of course welcome. But there is law between us. I needna say that if it were a criminal case I wouldna even hae admitted ye.'

'I am not here for pleasure,' Sir John said. 'It is, however, a private visit.'

'Weel, come in here, please.'

Maclaurin showed him into a small study off the lobby. There was a good fire in the grate, a set of shelves lined with books, a large table covered in papers. Condensation streamed down the panes of the two windows. On a smaller, round table set between these sat a tray on which were a crumb-strewn plate, a used cup and saucer and a coffee pot: beneath the tray was a copy of the *Edinburgh Advertiser*. There were three upright hard chairs around this table and Maclaurin indicated to Wedderburn to take one.

'I prefer to stand, thank you.'

Maclaurin shrugged. 'Then ye should state your business.' He was between Wedderburn and the fire, and made no effort to move aside.

'Mr Maclaurin, I'll not beat about the bush. You are acting for Joseph Knight, and no doubt your motives are honourable. But it is well known that you, and his other counsel, are not being paid for your work. This can only mean that you are treating this case not as a matter of law – not *just* as law – but as some moral crusade. Well, that is your right. But I wish you to understand how mistaken your position is.'

'*Mr* Wedderburn,' said the advocate, 'aw this can be debated in court. How I treat the case is my ain business. That is my profession.'

'And my profession is practicality, sir. Joseph has got into bad company and listened to some bad advice – not, I assume, from yourself – and as a result he has got some wrong ideas in his head. I tried to reason with him but he would not listen, and now, obviously, we do not communicate. But with me he had everything – more than most Scotsmen could expect to have, let alone a Negro. He has damned himself to poverty and misery in Dundee, and his so-called freedom, if he acquires it, will probably be the death of him.'

'I take it frae "bad company" ye refer tae his wife. As for poverty, frae you he had sixpence a week, if I mind richt. That's no much o a cut above poverty.'

'Pocket money. In addition he had clothing, a room, warmth, food, comfort, education. His duties were not arduous.'

'He prefers tae be free. He has told me so withoot ony prompting frae third parties. He understands the principle o liberty.'

'He does not. He never had a principle or a notion in his head but someone else put it there. He is a child in this – all his people are. *I* am the man of principle. My principles are both liberty *and* property. To liberate the Negroes would be a disaster for them and for our nation. I want the best for both. I am a reasonable man, Mr Maclaurin. I am not a barbarian.'

'We can explore that in court, sir.' Maclaurin's voice rose up a tone. 'I amna willing tae discuss it further here.'

'I brought that fellow *away* from slavery. His whole life has been a journey out of darkness into light. Do you not think he is better off here in Scotland, in my service, than playing with bones in a mud hut in Guinea? Even this, now – I have brought him to it: this choice that he must make. I do not want him to go back into the darkness.'

'Your concern is touching. The point is, nane o this has been o his choosing, no even whit ye cry his *choice*. He never chose tae be in your service in the first place.'

'Why are you doing this, Mr Maclaurin? What possible obligation can a man like you have to a Negro? This is about property, the right of honest gentlemen of your own race to own and dispose of their property without interference. If you aim too many blows of your axe at that tree, well . . . we all know where that is likely to end.'

'Where, Mr Wedderburn? In revolution? So are ye for or against the slave-owning colonists noo in rebellion? Ye would ken aboot it, haein been oot in a rebellion yoursel.'

'Ah, now I begin to see where you come from. This is a matter of honour, is it? A runaway Negro is less offensive to you than a Jacobite who stands and fights?'

'This is ridiculous,' Maclaurin said.

'A young lad of sixteen follows his father in a noble and dangerous cause, as what father would not hope and expect his son to do, and thirty years later a man who was scarcely out of petticoats at the time finds ground to oppose that cause again.'

Maclaurin moved to the door, opened it. 'This interview is over. It should never have taken place. Good morning, Mr Wedderburn.'

But Sir John was now unstoppable. 'Your father scuttled around organising the defences of Edinburgh, which opened its gates as soon as the white cockade approached its walls, and now you take up paper weaponry on behalf of a deceitful African. I had thought better of you than that, sir.'

'I dout ye've never gien me muckle thocht at aw, Mr Wedderburn, so I amna distressed. But keep my faither's name clear o this, if ye will. He was a better man than ye'll ever be, and he stood in a better cause tae. He stood against tyranny, however gallant it seemed and however bonnie it looked wi its cockades and plaids. It was on accoont o tyranny, sir, that the Pretender's grandfaither lost his throne. But it seems tyranny is alive and weel, and needs tae be cowpit again. Noo, please leave my hoose.'

Sir John stalked past him. 'We will settle this before the Fifteen,' he said. Seconds later he was back out on the street, filling his lungs with icy air. Furious, he marched towards the High Street. He would collect his belongings and go straight to the ferry. At that moment he would happily have seen all Scots law and all Edinburgh lawyers swallowed up by England. They were a self-satisfied club and they owed their first allegiance to that club. Maclaurin was a prig and Cullen was duplicitous. He felt almost like forgetting the whole business.

But he could not. He could not then, and he could not now, a quarter-century later. Sir John felt his pulse beating hard, as if the rage of that day – further fuelled in the coach to Queensferry by the shock of remembering what day it was – had never dispersed, as if there was still a quantity of it running about in his veins. The rage of all his days, of his impotence. Knight was like Culloden – a knot in time that he could not untie but could not leave alone. Why must he always be looking back, and not forward?

Because there was no future. He was seventy-three and winter was upon him. He felt the absence of a future with horrible, chilling intensity. And yet there might yet be one. For, from somewhere, he had gathered into his mind the news that the French had captured Toussaint L'Ouverture and shipped him over to Europe, and that Bonaparte had him in a prison high up in the mountains where he could cause no more trouble. With Toussaint out of the way, there was a chance of the French armies regaining control of San Domingo, though God knows what there was left to control after years of bloodshed and destruction. If that happened, the revolutionary threat to Jamaica would recede, and Glen Isla and Bluecastle would continue to prosper, to shore up the Wedderburn fortunes.

Meanwhile, here at home his daughters were queuing up to be married in the New Year. An expensive business, but better married than be old maids, so long as they did not marry schoolmasters! One to a soldier, scion of a noble family, the

277

other to a Dundas. By God, the Wedderburns had come home with a vengeance! How they had come home! They were joining with the greatest families in the land. Even *that* family! He had done what he had set out to do.

Yet the weddings would be quiet affairs, here at Ballindean. Sir John did not want too much fuss, or too many guests. In particular, when Margaret wed Philip Dundas he did not want Uncle *Harry* turning up.

On the Wedderburn side, as far as uncles went, there would be only James. A shame, that. Uncle James was popular with the girls, a handsome charmer, but still it would have been good if they had known Peter, or Sandy. Sandy would have been in his sixties now. Good God. He'd be quite rotted away out there.

A future then, of sorts. But not for him. He was fading away. His daughters would outlast him. His second wife would outlast him. His father's portrait would outlast him. James would outlast him. Sandy's picture of Peter and James and himself in Jamaica would outlast him. They all would. All except Sandy, who was not in the picture, and Joseph Knight, who had been, but was no longer.

He remembered the journal. He had always meant to destroy it. James had told him to. Had they not burnt it together? He recalled doing so. Or did he? He struggled over to the mahogany writing-table. It had always been in there, in one of the drawers on the left. He clawed at the handles and pulled the drawers open one by one, feeling with his good right hand for the familiar calf covers. He clawed and clawed and clawed. Yes, there it was. He pulled it out. But he had burnt it before, he was certain, almost certain . . . He had burnt *something*. Well, he must burn it again.

He dropped it on to the table and adopted an awkward leaning posture, holding one corner in place with the weight of his left hand while his right roughly opened the book for one last look. He was trying to decipher the scrawled lines on the final page, when the wag-at-the-wa began to whirr as it prepared to strike twelve. This induced an odd sense of urgency in him, as if somebody was coming, as if all the years in Jamaica, long since ticked away, were contained in Sandy's journal and he must consign them to the flames before the twelfth chime, before whoever was coming could prevent him. And so he did not read it. He let it fall shut and, lifting it in his right hand, shuffled back to the fire, and cast it from him with a sudden jerk, as if a large spider had suddenly scuttled out of it. But the action was less a throw than a drop. The book fell short, a foot from the fire. Now he would have to bend to retrieve it. He would have to think his legs through the motions.

Before he could manage this there was a rustling sound, a figure beside him was swooping down on the book, and a familiar voice was saying, 'What are you doing, Papa? Please sit down. There is something we need to discuss.'

Dundee, 15 January 1803 / Edinburgh, 15 January 1778

Archibald Jamieson sat at his wife's bedside on a Saturday evening, holding her pale hand, and feeling the great empty wound in his chest which, when he spoke, made his voice hoarse and breathless. Janet was propped up against four pillows, smiling bravely at him. It was the smile that had opened Archie's wound. It kept doing it, whether he was in her presence or out of it, when he woke in the still heart of the night and when his mind drifted at unexpected moments of the day: she smiled, he saw it or thought of it, and was torn apart again. It never ceased to surprise him how much it hurt.

The new Mrs Jamieson had, in the space of just a few months, become the auld Mrs Jamieson, the cancerous, the faded, the dying Mrs Jamieson. And yet not once since she became ill had she complained about anything. She had simply, day by day, got weaker, thinner, paler, and her face had become more drawn with pain. The doctor – a younger, more sympathetic doctor than the last – came regularly to check on her condition: not to make her well, for he admitted frankly that he could not do that, but to ease her illness. He gave her a variety of drugs to help her sleep and to dull the pain, and he showed Archibald Jamieson how to administer them: laudanum draughts, essence of guaiacum, Dover's Powder. There were days which she passed in a kind of trance, breathing short breaths but at least not in agony. There were other days when the pain seemed to mock the drugs, and she made Jamieson and Betty and everybody else stay out of the room so that they could not see her distress. And then there were evenings like this one, when it was as if the pain had got bored with tormenting her and had gone to sulk for a while, and she was left, exhausted but pleased to see him, and smiling.

Sometimes he read to her, sometimes they talked about trivial matters, and sometimes they said nothing. Once, a week or two ago, she had said it was like a courtship, and he had laughed and agreed that it was, and then apologised because their real courtship had not taken half as long or involved nearly as many conversations, or silences. Janet had shaken her head. 'It's aw richt, Archie. We're makkin up for it noo.'

Tonight, she had an unusual request. 'Tell me something aboot your work, Archie. Whit work hae ye had lately?' And he was astonished, because she had never asked such a question before. But as he had spent the last few weeks taking on as much writing and copying as possible, to pay for the doctor and keep a good fire in her room and also to keep himself in Dundee so that he could be home every night, there was nothing of any great interest to tell her about his work. There was something, though, work-*related*. He had it with him, as he thought it might entertain her. More than that, he *wanted* to tell her about it.

'A letter has come,' he said. He had it on the floor by his chair-leg, and picked it up and showed it to her.

'Guidsakes, that *is* a letter,' Janet said. 'It looks mair like a book withoot boards.'

Archie was again struck with guilt. How could he have failed to appreciate her sense of humour? But then, perhaps she had never shown it when she was well. Certainly he had no memory of it.

'Weel, are ye gaun tae read it tae me?'

'Aye, I thocht I would. It's frae a man in Paisley. I wrote him nearly a year past. I had gien up ony expectation o hearin frae him. In fact, he'd gane oot o my mind completely.'

'Whit is it aboot?'

'It's a lang, lang story, Janet. I would need tae tell ye so much afore I read ye the letter.'

'Weel,' she said, 'I'm bidin whaur I am for the present, if you are.'

'It's odd it should hae arrived this day,' he said. 'Today is exactly twenty-five year since it happened.'

'Since whit happened?'

'A court case, my dear. It was a gey important case in its day, though I think maist folk hae clean forgot it since. It concerned a Negro slave that had left his maister, and whether he could be

281

kept a slave here in Scotland. The maister was John Wedderburn oot at Inchture.'

'The case o Joseph Knight, ye mean?' Janet said.

Archie almost dropped the letter. 'Ye've heard o it?'

'Och, Archie, I mind them aw speakin aboot it. I was only a lassie, but it was in the weekly papers, and I aye mind the name because my faither made a pun aboot his coat being as black as Knight. It was the Dundee connection that gart them speak aboot it, I dout – what wi the Wedderburns, and then of course the Negro was bidin in the toun at the time. But he gaed awa soon efter.'

'I suppose,' Archie asked cautiously, 'ye dinna mind whaur he gaed tae?'

'How would I mind that? I was only aboot fourteen, nae mair. But I'm no sure if onybody kent. What hae *you* tae dae wi aw that, onywey? That's a lifetime awa.'

'I had a commission,' he said, 'aboot a year ago, tae find him. Frae the maister, Wedderburn.'

'Whit for did he want tae find him?'

'I dinna ken.'

'But ye werena successful?'

'Na. It made me tak an interest in the case though. When I was in Edinburgh last summer, I had ane o the advocates I ken look up some o the details in their library. And this day is twenty-five years since the case was decided. Would ye . . . I would be happy tae tell ye aboot it. As I see it in my heid, that is. But it micht tak a while.'

'Archie,' she said, 'we hae aw nicht.'

How did he see it? He knew that he would have to take Janet into the Parliament House, where the courts sat. She had never been to Edinburgh, and, until he was there in the summer, Parliament House was a place he himself had never been inside.

From previous visits to the capital he was familiar enough with the immediate surroundings, the jostling throng of Parliament Close. This was a square enclosed by St Giles' Kirk on the north side, by the Parliament House and Goldsmiths' Hall on the west, by the merchants' Exchange on the south and by tall tenements on the east. On a stone plinth in the middle was a lead statue of

King Charles II on his horse, the latter disrespectfully pointing its rump at the Great Door of the Parliament, over which statues of Mercy and Justice stood sentinel. The Parliament building was austere and forbidding. Its ashlar walls were broken by the door and a number of ornamented windows, and topped by a broken parapet and several turrets. All along the side of St Giles' was a row of two-storey shops, which continued, at ground level only, for the length of the east side below the tenements. There were goldsmiths, clockmakers, printers, booksellers, engravers, vintners, tobacconists and coffee houses, and the Close was a constantly shifting mass of people going about their business. When the Session was sitting, only at the Cross on the High Street was there more activity.

Archie led Janet through the Great Door and into a large square room, the walls of which were lined with yet more stalls or 'krames' selling books, cutlery, hats, toys and jewellery, and a coffee house owned by the famous kidnap victim 'Indian Peter' Williamson. They went on through a partition into the huge hammerbeam-roofed hall, where in a previous age the Parliament had sat, and here a new world was presented to them. It was a vast, draughty expanse, its walls decorated only with a few dark oil paintings of pale kings and stern nobility. Down one side, set back in plain, raised niches, were chairs where the Lords Ordinary – individual judges dispatched from their inner den to converse with the outside world – sat and heard pleadings, like so many oracles perched in birdcages. The hall was filled with advocates in wigs and black gowns, and other men with them, the solicitors or agents of their clients, arguing or agreeing, protesting or instructing, and all the time walking the length of the hall, turning and retracing their steps without a pause. Most mornings, the vast roof echoed with these dozens of conversations, while those advocates who were actually addressing the judges in their alcoves strove more vociferously to make themselves heard above the din.

This was the Outer House of the Court of Session, where preliminary hearings took place, or where, in cases not requiring the attentions of the entire Bench, an individual judge might dispense justice as the Session's representative. But for matters of greater complexity or moment, the 'haill Fifteen', the full quorum of the Session, met to deliberate and vote. They did this in the Inner House, a room off to the left at the far end of the hall, a sanctum into which few women, least of all a casual tourist such as Janet Jamieson, ever ventured.

It was a square room divided by the Bar, the line separating the advocates from the Lords of Session – or more properly, the Senators of the College of Justice – themselves. On the advocates' side there was little space and less dignity. All kinds of persons, including those whose cases were to be heard but also others – lawyers, would-be lawyers, know-alls and busybodies – who were not directly involved but curious to watch the proceedings, crowded into the room, or into the gallery suspended over it. This gallery extended quite far out, and was barely six and a half feet above the floor, so that the crush of bodies had a lid as well as walls to contain it. Here, on this half-lit January morning, preparing their speeches amidst the general babble for what would be the first case of the day, were the counsel for Joseph Knight and the counsel for John Wedderburn.

On the judges' side of the Bar, the atmosphere was more sedate. There was a high, semi-circular bench, of dark unpolished wood, with seats for the Fifteen. In the well of this hemisphere was a table for the clerks of court. Behind the Bench was an enormous fireplace: a miserable pile of wheezing sticks and coal in the grate sneaked an inadequate heat up the backs of their lordships' seats. In wooden frames, one on either side of the fire, picked out in gold thread on a black velvet background, were the Lord's Prayer and the Ten Commandments. They looked as though they had been made, and positioned, a long, long time ago. The whole room was layered with dust and grime, and littered with the marks and detritus of many hearings – ink-stains, idle scratchings in the wood, scraps of paper, stray hairs from venerable wigs, lost buttons, crumbs dropped from hastily consumed snacks, the dried-out extractions of a thousand nose-pickings. It was like a cobwebbed cave into which a light had been unexpectedly shone, and the Lords of Session, entering through a side door from another room where they had put on their dark-blue robes lined with crimson, seemed like a family of disgruntled, winter-coated bears awakened by the intrusion.

In they came, preceded by a court officer carrying a large

silver mace: the Senators of the College of Justice, the Fifteen (although in fact they were only fourteen, Lord Alva being indisposed). The whole court rose to receive them. First, the Lord President, coarse old Robert Dundas of Arniston, half-brother of Harry Dundas but, being twenty-eight years his senior, more like an uncle to him. He deposited himself in the centre of the Bench, right in front of the smoky fire. Then there was Lord Kames, a man born in the seventeenth century and, at eighty-two, the oldest member of the Session: irreverent in speech, sharp of tongue – 'bitch' was his favourite epithet, applied without discrimination to man, woman, beast and inanimate object – sharp of thought, tall, long-nosed and disdainful of youth. Ten years his junior was James Boswell's father, Lord Auchinleck, gouty, terse, Calvinistic but humane. There was Lord Justice-Clerk Barskimming, an Ayrshire neighbour of Auchinleck's, an astute listener, scrupulous in the letter of the law; Lord Kennet, quiet and unassuming, who had been the judge charged with summarising and reporting the case to his colleagues; Lord Hailes, English-sounding bibliophile and man of taste; Lord Gardenstone, the genial pig-fancier, whose conversation was noted both for its liveliness and for its quavering, stammering delivery, a pleasant, ugly man with a nose empurpled by excessive drink and enlarged by the inhalation of vast quantities of snuff; amiable Lord Elliock, with a grin so fixed on his face it was as if he had forgotten it was ever there; Lord Braxfield, a bullish, florid man with a flicker of humour in his eyes and a fiercely Scots tongue in his mouth, with which he could crack a joke in the first half of a sentence and send a man to Botany Bay in the second; Lord Covington, as old as the century, raised to the Bench three years before at the grand old age of seventy-five when everybody had thought he would die as he lived, an extremely wealthy advocate; and Lords Ankerville, Stonefield and Westhall, of whom it could be said that they made up the numbers. (Lord Westhall had only in the last few months been elevated to the Bench, replacing the recently deceased Lord Pitfour.) Finally, five feet tall and bustling like a maid, Lord Monboddo entered, darted round the end of the Bench and took a seat alongside the clerks at their great table. He habitually sat in this place: it was rumoured that this was because he liked to keep a distance from the other judges, some of whom he disliked; but the truth was he was growing deaf and did not like to miss anything.

At the Bar, the two sets of counsel were several feet apart, but there was little sense of antagonism between them: Messrs John Maclaurin and Allan Maconochie on the one hand, and Messrs Robert Cullen, James Ferguson and Ilay Campbell on the other. They were well acquainted, if not all close friends, and on entering the court room had greeted one other amicably enough before separating to make their last-minute preparations. And now, a little late, and bowing an apology to his half-brother the Lord President, came Henry Dundas to join Knight's team. As Lord Advocate, Dundas was entitled to sit within the Bar, in the well of the court. He had joined this cause in an unofficial, private capacity but he still took up his official seat.

As soon as he had done so, the macer called the case: 'Joseph Knight, a Negro of Africa, Pursuer, against John Wedderburn of Ballindean, Esquire, late Planter in Jamaica, Defender.'

'But, Archie,' Mrs Jamieson asked, 'where *is* Joseph Knight aw this time?'

'That,' Archie said, 'is a very guid question.'

There were two men among that mill of lawyers who seemed not wholly part of the proceedings, but without whom the lawyers would have been redundant. They seemed somehow removed from what was going on around them. They were seated at opposite ends of a long bench situated under the gallery on the advocates' side of the Bar. Their counsel could sit with them to confer, then step forward to plead before their lordships. One of these men was an African, the only black man in the courtroom. He was wearing a plain, somewhat frayed suit of grey clothes. His feet, in cracked but polished boots, were planted firmly on the floor, slightly apart, but he rested his hands on his thighs almost delicately. He looked anxious and careworn, and though he did not move his head his eyes were constantly shifting, taking in everything before him. When the judges entered, he came to his feet swiftly, and remained standing until nearly everyone else had sat down again. This looked like the act of a man habituated to deference, but it might equally have been the behaviour of one who felt out of place but recognised that he was the focus of attention.

The other man seemed more relaxed. His face betrayed no emotion whatsoever. He was also plainly dressed, but his clothes were clearly of a better quality than those of Joseph Knight. John Wedderburn's gaze wandered around the court, lingered on the Lord's Prayer, took in some of the other features. Once he turned to look behind him, raising a hand to acknowledge the presence of a slightly younger, better-looking version of himself standing under the balcony: his brother James. Then he faced the front again. When their lordships had taken their seats, he resumed his as if they had all sat down to dinner together. He even nodded politely to the Lord President and Lord Elliock, who responded in the same manner.

The macer who had called the case looked up and paused, as if to allow anyone who had inadvertently come to court on the wrong day the opportunity to leave. Then he bowed to the President.

Lord Arniston checked his papers, cleared his throat. 'Twa points, afore we stert. First, as this cause originated in Mr Knight's petition tae the Sheriff of Perthshire against the findings of the justices of Perthshire, and his suit is against Mr Wedderburn no jist in respect o asserting his right tae liberty, but also in respect o seeking back-wages as a free man, he is designated pursuer, and Mr Wedderburn defender. I mak this point tae the court in order tae clarify the situation, as in ither respects it micht be thocht that Mr Wedderburn has been in pursuit o Mr Knight.'

There was a thin ripple of laughter around the room.

'Secondly, this case has been ongoing for several years, and mony pages of memorials and informations hae been submitted tae the court. The informations hae been printed and dispersed amang us, and hae received oor due consideration. It is therefore unnecessary for coonsel tae repeat the exquisite detail nor tae quote chapter and verse o every reference gien in these documents, which I may say are o the highest quality and reflect weel on the diligence o baith sides. I would therefore urge coonsel for the pursuer and for the defender tae be as brief as the importance o these maitters allows.' He reached down below the Bench and produced a large sand-glass, which he set beside him. 'I do not say I shall call a halt to any speech which exceeds the play of this instrument, but gentlemen, please, dinna mak me turn it up ower mony times.'

Again, the advocates, and above them the members of the public in the gallery, showed their appreciation of the Lord President's methods with some polite laughter. Arniston's dislike of long-winded pleadings was well known, and in the eighteen years of his presidency he had been a stickler for completing business and preventing a backlog of cases building up. The sand-glass was the symbol of his determination.

Arniston turned to the men gathered alongside Joseph Knight. 'Mr Maclaurin?'

Maclaurin gave a quick smile to Knight, rose, approached the Bar, and launched straight in. 'My lords, this is a cause o the utmaist significance and I crave therefore your patient attention. The pairties concerned in it are, in effect, representatives o twa different races, and we submit that the ootcome o this case will affect no jist these individual men, but the future relations between thae races. This isna simply a maitter o property, whitever the defender may claim, but gangs deep intae the foundations o law and morality. It is for these reasons that I prefixed tae the information the motto *Quamvis ille niger quamvis tu candidus esses*, the import o which I dinna need tae explain tae your lordships, but which for the benefit o them no acquent wi Latin I translate, "As black as he is, so should you be white" – meaning, of course, fair, impartial, candid.'

'Very guid, Mr Maclaurin, very apposite,' Arniston said. 'But hardly necessary tae tell us oor business.'

The nasal voice of Lord Kames issued from further along the Bench. 'Perhaps ye should also tell them that dinna ken that it's frae Virgil, or they'll be awa hame thinkin ye made it up yoursel.'

'Thank you, my lord,' Maclaurin replied, looking suitably humble. He pressed on: 'I should say as weel that the present contest between Great Britain and her colonies in America has also raised in the public eye the haill question o the institution o slavery. Therefore, the decision o a supreme court such as this may hae some tendency either tae retard or accelerate its fall. This is why the arguments in oor written pleadings hae been so extensive. It is impossible tae treat of this cause within narrow bounds. But we will endeavour tae tak up nae mair o the court's time than is absolutely necessary, and tae this end I intend tae speak only tae the main points contained in oor informations and syne sit doun tae let my colleagues Mr Maconochie and the Lord Advocate speak on oor behalf.'

Before Maclaurin could continue the Lord President was wagging a finger at him. 'Now, now, Mr Maclaurin, that *is* the Lord Advocate sittin doun there afore ye, but then again it isna. This isna the Crown's cause and he disna hae his public hat on. That is Mr Dundas.'

Maclaurin dipped his head in acknowledgment.

'I jist thocht I'd point that oot,' Arniston said to his half-brother.

Henry Dundas half stood – 'Much obleeged, my lord' – and sat down again.

'My lords,' Maclaurin said, 'the pursuer was cairried aff frae the coast o Guinea by a Captain Knight when a mere child perhaps eleiven or twal years o age, and was sellt tae the defender Mr Wedderburn in Jamaica, wha used him no in the field, but as a servant in his hoose. When Mr Wedderburn quit Jamaica aboot nine year syne, and returned tae this country, he brocht the pursuer wi him. Frae that time on, he gied him an allowance o sixpence a week in pocket money.

'Here in Scotland the pursuer learned tae read and write, and was instructed in the principles o the Christian faith. He was baptised under the name Joseph Knight, though I must remind your lordships that this name, like everything else in his present circumstances, isna his by choice, but as a consequence o his haein been abducted frae his parents and his country at a very early age.'

'Whitiver the bitch micht hae been cried afore, *that* wouldna hae been his choice either,' Lord Kames observed to no one in particular. Maclaurin was well used to this kind of interruption from the Bench. He pressed on.

'In 1773 the pursuer was mairrit on a lassie that had been a maid in Mr Wedderburn's hoose, although she was by then removed tae Dundee. They had a child, and Joseph Knight, finding his sixpence-a-week pocket money quite inadequate tae support his faimly, applied tae Mr Wedderburn for a cottage on the estate, or ordinary wages, so that he could live as normal a life as ony ither free man. These requests were rejected and the pursuer declared his intention o finding work elsewhere.

'It was at this point that Mr Wedderburn applied tae the Justices o the Peace o Perthshire tae prevent his taking aff in this mainner, on the grounds that he had aye treated him kindly and furnished him wi claes, bed, board and pocket money, and that in consequence o haein acquired him legitimately in Jamaica he had the richt tae detain him in perpetuity in his service for life. The justices, all, let it be said, guid freens o Mr Wedderburn's and some wi their ain interests in the plantations, upheld his petition and the pursuer was arrested and returned tae him.'

Cullen, who had been becoming restless, coughed loudly and stood up. 'If there is any substance in that remark about the justices, my lords, we should like to hear it spoke out plain.'

'Mr Maclaurin?' the President asked. 'Whit did ye mean?'

'I meant naething in particular, my lord. I jist thocht I'd point it oot. The relationship, that is.'

Cullen had not sat down. 'That will not do, sir. If you have some reason to think that Sir John –'

'That *will* do, Mr Cullen,' said Arniston. 'Address the Bench if ye please. Mr Maclaurin, I must warn ye. This is a civil case, and naebody is on trial. The Perthshire justices arena on trial for their decision, ony mair than the Sheriff is when ye come tae his decision.'

'I *was* jist coming tae him,' Maclaurin said. 'I apologise.'

'Guid. And Mr Cullen, the case before us is between a *Mr* Knight and a *Mr* Wedderburn, however your client is kent by common usage. Nae offence, of course, ah . . .' Arniston, looking directly at Wedderburn but unable to address him without seeming to contradict himself one way or the other, left the sentence unfinished. He swung back towards Maclaurin. 'Continue, sir.'

'Mr Knight remained in Mr Wedderburn's service a while langer, but his situation was intolerable – his wife and child were in Dundee and he had nae opportunity tae see them, let alane provide for them. So he saved up his sixpences and petitioned the Sheriff o Perthshire, and he, tae his everlasting fame, found that the state o slavery is not recognised by the laws o this kingdom, and that the laws o Jamaica do not extend tae this kingdom. It's true Mr Swinton – I beg pardon, the Sheriff – rejected the pursuer's claim o wages, since, of course, nae wages had been agreed, but equally, and crucially, my lords, he found that perpetual service withoot wages *is* slavery and therefore unlawful in Scotland. Whereupon Mr Wedderburn took the cause tae this court, where it was heard first by Lord Kennet, who then made *avizandum* tae the haill Fifteen, and memorials and informations were prepared and printed, which ye hae before ye, and here we are at last tae see it brocht tae a conclusion. That, my lords, is a summary o how we hae got frae Guinea tae here.'

He paused, and Monboddo, twisting in his chair to speak to Arniston, said, 'As this is likely to get complicated, may we hear now from the defender whether what we have heard is a fair representation of the story thus far?'

The Lord President, glancing along the Bench, received a few nods, and addressed Robert Cullen. 'Ony comments, Mr Cullen?' Then, with a thin, sour smile: 'Ye'll ken aw aboot whit constitutes a fair *representation*.'

Cullen rose again, ignoring the goad. 'My lords, the facts are pretty much as stated. But one can paint facts to give them a – I will not say false – an unnatural gloss, and I should like to correct one or two misleading impressions.'

'Misleading impressions?' Arniston hooted. 'I hae warned ye aboot them afore noo, sir.'

There were a few chuckles. Cullen smiled at the Lord President as upon a wayward child, then continued. 'First, my lords, it is most unjust to place the burden of the whole slave trade, and the institution of slavery itself, upon the shoulders of Mr Wedderburn, who is after all only one man defending his property rights. Whatever one's view of slavery, one cannot blame Mr Wedderburn for its existence, nor load this case with responsibility for its continuance or fall. Secondly, my worthy friend was very careful in the way he described the pursuer's circumstances since he came to Scotland with his master. We heard that he acquired education and religion, and that he

291

lived in a perfectly comfortable manner. I should like to remind the court that these things did not occur by chance. They all stemmed from the generosity and humanity of Mr Wedderburn. Thirdly, the order of events by which the pursuer's personal circumstances altered were not quite as we have heard. He deviated a little from the Christian path in which he had been instructed by getting the girl he later married with child, and it is ever to the credit of his master that he not only allowed this girl to lie in childbed at Ballindean, but paid the doctor's bills and even the expenses of the funeral when the child died. It was only after the girl was better that she was dismissed from the household and returned to Dundee, where she and the pursuer continued their secret liaisons, and in time produced a second child. I make no further comment on the insinuations concerning the justices of Perthshire, except that, given these examples of Mr Wedderburn's humanity and reasonableness, it should I think count for rather than against them that they are friends to him. Thank you, my lords.'

Cullen bowed, turned and repeated the gesture towards Knight's counsel, and sat down. John Maclaurin returned to the Bar.

'Noo, my lords, let us look a little further intae this cause. The defender, Mr Wedderburn, has been at pains in aw his written submissions tae the court, tae emphasise his kindness and generosity tae the pursuer. We will leave aside, for the moment, whether these words can ever be applied tae a relationship founded upon ae man's absolute power ower anither. But we note that he seeks frae the court no jist the richt tae the pursuer's service in perpetuity, but also the richt tae send or cairry him back tae Jamaica if he should choose it. He insists that he has nae *intention* o daein that, but, as he acquired him legitimately there, he must be *entitled* tae return him there. Whit, though, would be the purpose o assertin that richt, were it no tae exercise it? My lords, if Mr Knight behaved in Jamaica as he has done here, that is if he claimed his freedom and acted upon that claim, he would be subjected tae the maist horrific punishments for desertion. Are we tae believe that if he were sent tae that island, it would be for his security and happiness and the guid o his soul?

'Furthermore, the defender's memorial contradicts itsel at various points. He maintains at ane point that he never mistreated Mr Knight but kept him for a personal servant, but at anither that by bringin him tae Scotland he saved him frae hard labour in the sugar fields, "by which", I quote, "he would probably have expired". That single sentence, my lords, tells us mair aboot the plantations than we could ever wish tae ken. Can we dout that though Mr Knight's situation here became intolerable frae his lack o wages and freedom, it would be still mair intolerable were Mr Wedderburn tae hae the richt tae send him tae Jamaica – a country, I remind ye again, whaur he never wished tae be in the first place.

'Noo, as tae the expense o the pursuer's education, it is true that he got some learnin frae a schoolmaister in the defender's employ. But that schoolmaister is employed tae teach Mr Wedderburn's ain children in ony case. As tae ither expenses, I dinna think hauf a guinea paid tae a barber in Dundee tae gie him some notion o dressin hair can be coonted as excessive largesse.'

This scored a round of laughter not only in the public gallery but on the Bench. Joseph Knight smiled briefly. John Wedderburn did not.

'My lords, I winna dwell on the slave trade, as the written arguments already before ye prove ayont aw dout the cruel, immoral and un-Christian nature o that species o commerce. But it is relevant tae oor cause, insofar as Mr Wedderburn maintains that he got Joseph Knight legally and fairly, and that therefore the rights o property he exercised ower him in Jamaica should apply equally here. We must ask, whit proof is there, even if we accept the legitimacy of ae man buyin and sellin anither, that *this* transaction was legal and fair? The defender bocht the pursuer, he tells us, frae a Captain Knight. Where is the bill o sale? How much did he pay? Mair important, whit richt had this Captain Knight tae sell the boy? He either kidnapped or purchased him frae the coast o Guinea, syne transported him across the sea. By whit law either o nature or o nations does this mak oor client a chattle tae be bocht and sellt? That, my lords, is something ye must reject as ootrageous.

'It will be argued, nae dout, that the laws o African nations, as wi ancient nations, permit and justify the practice o slavery. Yet slavery is only ever, *can* only ever be, maintained through violence. Let it be a custom for generations, the present generation that is enslaved willna accept it unless they are forced by violence tae accept it. And if proof is needed that it is a criminal raither than a lawful practice, I need only quote the testimony o my colleague Mr Maconochie's servant, himsel an African and formerly a slave, that was included in oor submissions. He remembers perfectly being taen up when a child at play and pit in a poke, and in it cairried on board ship. The abduction o bairns, my lords, is nae basis for ony legitimate system o society.

'It is true that in Jamaica, accordin tae the laws there, the pursuer was the defender's property. But should the law o Jamaica hae ony effect here in Britain? We say no, baith because it is repugnant tae the first principles o justice and morality, and because, even if it can be excused or justified *there* on grounds o expediency or necessity, nae such grounds can possibly be justified *here*.

'We hae seen in the defender's informations aw species o arguments raised aboot the historical legitimacy o slavery; that in aw ages it has been customary for men and women tae be made slaves through military conquest, as punishment for wrang-daein, or through a contract entered intae by themsels. But Joseph Knight was a mere boy o eleiven when he was taen: he couldna hae been a sodger and therefore couldna hae been, in ony true sense, a prisoner-o-war; nor, being sae young, could he hae committed sae heinous a crime as tae forfeit his freedom in perpetuity; nor was he auld enough tae enter intae a contract tae sell himsel. And again, if it is said that slavery is a way o life in mony pairts o Africa, and that parents aften sell their ain bairns intae slavery, can we say that *this* child must therefore lose his liberty for life? Surely it is the parents that are guilty o a terrible crime against their young, and likewise guilty is the man that buys him. My lords, if Mr Wedderburn has legal right tae the pursuer in Jamaica, he got it through a trade that has nae regard for ony rights whitsoever, and he must lose it whenever he sets foot in a civilised country.

'The fact is, legitimacy disna enter intae it. If it did, how could ony society that was baith legal and moral tolerate a system that cairries a hundred thoosand Africans a year frae their hameland, kills upward o thirty thoosand o these either in the passage or in whit they cry the seasoning, and by overwork, barbarous punishment and neglect kills maist o the rest in a further sixteen years? There is but one thing that maks a slave a slave in the plantations: his colour. A Negro is a slave because he is black. The only legal question then is, tae whom does he belang? For the laws dinna protect him in ony way, no in his person, his liberty or his life. Like the slaves amang the Romans, the Negroes are not considered as *persons* but *things*, though these *things* can hae bairns that also become the property o them that own the parents. I wouldna wish tae cause embarrassment tae the pursuer in this venerable place, but I would ask your lordships tae look upon him, and ask yoursels, is this a man or a thing?

'But there are ither arguments used by the apologisers for slavery which we must also refute. It is said that the cruelties we hear aboot in the colonies are much exaggerated, that it canna be true that slaves are ill-used there, because it is against the interest o the proprietors tae maltreat them. Weel, my lords, ye micht as weel say that a fermer in this country never overcrops his land or overworks his beasts, because it is against his interest. But we ken that the passions o men aften counteract their interest, and that these things occur. In the case o the planters, their passion and their interest are baith the same: it is tae mak as muckle money as they can in as short as possible a time, and that requires them tae work their slaves hard, and feed them ill, because that is the way tae mak the maist o them.' Maclaurin cast a rapid but direct glance at Wedderburn. 'And syne when they are rich they come hame tae enjoy the fruits o their slaves' labours.

'It is further said that the climate in the colonies, and the culture o sugar, tobacco and so forth, renders it absolutely necessary tae employ Negroes, as we puir white people dinna hae constitutions strang enough for the required labours. But this isna true. Slaves are worked where ploos micht mair usefully be employed, and white people, *if taken care of*, are nae mair unfit for such work than Negroes. The fact is, Negroes are *not* taken care of, because it appears tae be cheaper tae work them like beasts, kill them like beasts, and replace them wi mair o the same. But mony sensible thinkers, such as Mr Adam Smith, argue that this is false economy; that the wear and tear o slaves falls entirely on the maister, and that it is exacerbated by the practices o cruel or careless overseers. A free man labours for wages, and maintains himsel in order tae be able tae work. A slave has nae incentive tae work but the scourge, which when it is used injures him and prevents him frae workin, and nae maitter whether he works hard or little his reward is the same – naething.

'My lords, I dinna intend tae rehearse the arguments aboot whether a person coming frae ane country intae anither can expect tae be governed and protected by the laws o the country he left, raither than the laws o the ane he is in. That is aw before ye in the papers. But I will say this: the law o Jamaica never afforded *ony* protection tae Joseph Knight. He wasna born under that law; he never lived there but against his will; he never received ony benefit frae that law. Mr Wedderburn may find it convenient tae respect Jamaican law, and ask us tae respect it; but why should Mr Knight care a docken for it?'

Arniston's fingers were stretching towards the sand-glass. Maclaurin, noticing, began to wind up.

'My lords, my learned friend Mr Dundas will summarise some mair general points, maistly wi regaird tae the law here in Scotland. I will finish noo by askin ye tae consider the intellectual and moral climate in which we find oorsels in this year o 1778. This isna Jamaica, but Scotland. We submit that, leavin aside aw the niceties o written law, whether there or here, there is a natural law frae which stem oor first principles o morality and justice, and that that natural law finds slavery utterly repugnant. The herts o aw men that hivna been corrupted by money or hardened by bad habits must bear witness against it. In this age and this nation some o the finest minds the world has seen hae devoted themsels tae the science and study o man, and examined thae twa principles that seem tae guide us through oor lives: self-interest on the ae hand, and benevolence towards oor fellows on the tither. True happiness and virtue consists in findin a proper balance between the twa. He that acts frae self-love alane, acts as if man were intended for solitude, whereas nature, as oor best philosophers and thinkers hae demonstrated – and some o them are sittin afore me as I speak, my lords – whereas nature meant him for society. When we dae guid tae ithers, we feel pleasure. When we dae evil, we feel pain and guilt and we ken that evil is whit we hae done. I trust that the common law o Scotland will be found tae act and exist for the cause o guid, no evil.

'If your lordships' judgment be pronounced for the pursuer, he and his faimly will rank wi the inhabitants o this fortunate island. We dinna hae the natural advantages that Africa enjoys, and Africa we canna restore tae him, but in ither respects this is a better, happier place tae be than maist o the rest o the world, and for that he may tak comfort, though he must ever regret his haein bein torn, when a child, frae his parents and native land. If judgment shall be pronounced against him, he, and his faimly, must either be reduced tae a state o bondage and misery in this country, or be transported tae whence he last came, and atone *there* for the valiant effort he has made tae assert his liberty *here*. I canna think so badly o my country, and its law, that it would so treat a man. But as I said at the ootset, my lords, this isna jist aboot twa men, but aboot twa races. The supreme court o Scotland has it in its power tae strike a blow for the liberty and dignity no jist o Joseph Knight, but for aw his countrymen.'

Maclaurin stood for a few seconds, gangling and awkward yet strangely impressive, staring at the Bench as if daring them to disgrace their country. This, he knew, was a crucial moment. He observed the appreciation in one or two of the old faces – Boswell's father's, Kames's – and the cold hard stares of others, such as Covington's. Then he bowed and turned back to where Dundas, Maconochie and Knight were seated. There was a general murmur throughout the court, as people took the opportunity of the hiatus to cough, blow their noses, take snuff, pass a word or two to a neighbour. But the Lord President did not allow this to go on long. 'We hae a great deal tae get through today,' he said, 'forby this important maitter. Mr Cullen, would ye care tae continue?'

Kames said loudly, 'There are haill battalions o them drawn up on each side. Hoo mony o the bitches are intendin tae speak?'

The President did not seem to think this a ludicrous intervention, and scowled at the titters it generated. 'It's true, gentlemen, we shall be here aw day if each o ye taks as lang as Mr Maclaurin. Is it necessary that ye should aw speak?'

Knight's counsel conferred. Maclaurin stood up. 'Mr Maconochie respectfully relinquishes his place, my lords, but will pass the main points o his argument tae Mr Dundas, if that is acceptable.'

Wedderburn's counsel also had a quick consultation. Cullen said: 'We could insist that we should match the pursuer's counsel exactly, my lords – that is, that two of us should speak. However, if we are permitted to have the last word, and if we may have a five-minute adjournment before we plead, we will forfeit that equality of numbers.'

Arniston cast an eye along the Bench; met with no objections. 'Very well, gentlemen. If awbody is content wi that arrangement – Mr Dundas,' he said to his half-brother, 'would ye care tae finish for the pursuer, so that we may then hear what the tither side has tae say?'

Dundas started from his seat like a prizefighter. Thick-set and bluff in stature, he leaned forward, shoulders hunched, as he faced the Bench, his dark eyes constantly searching for signs of reaction among the judges. When he spoke it was with a quiet passion that carried a tone of immense authority – almost as if he were the Lord President addressing the court, and Arniston only an impostor in borrowed robes. Whether this authority had grown in the three years Dundas had been Lord Advocate, or whether it was a manifestation of the ambition which had propelled him into public office in the first place, was an open question. Most would have said the latter, that Harry Dundas had been born to perform on stages such as this.

'My lords, I hae little tae add tae whit Mr Maclaurin has already so eloquently expressed. Like him, I begin wi a general point, and then move tae particulars. A perfect equality amang men is impossible, and all schemes for establishing it are visionary. There must – there always will be – a disparity. One man will hae servants, anither will be a servant, and there is neither hairm nor disgrace in either situation. But there are natural rights, such as my learned friend has already described, which every man, o whitever race, ought tae enjoy.

'The defender has argued in his informations that Negroes are inferior tae white people in point o capacity, and that it is therefore natural and justifiable for the whites tae enslave them in America and the West Indies. Weel, first we may ask, is it true that Negroes are inferior? The answer is, there is neither proof nor presumption that the fact stands so. The Negro slaves in oor colonies are made and kept miserable by their condition and by the laws that govern them. It is hardly surprising that they *appear* inferior. In spite o this, as we ken, there are examples of insurrections when these *inferior* beings hae risen up against their subjection. In Jamaica the Maroons fought for and won their freedom by force of arms, and are today a proud and independent people. It may be that, as the late Mr Hume has said, nae Negro has excelled in ony art or science, but how few labourers in Scotland have? Multitudes o white men hae lived and died unkent and unlamented. Every kirkyaird is packed wi the banes o men whase talents, if poverty hadna repressed them, would hae been recognised. If this is true o puir white men in Scotland and England and all across Europe, how much mair true must it be o the Negroes? Is there reason tae dout that multitudes o black men, men o talent and capacity and even genius, are at this moment consuming their strength in raising sugar and tobacco, indigo and rice, for West Indian and American planters – that noble and virtuous Africans are forced tae work for nae recompense other than tae be spared the lash, in order tae enrich men far less honourable, civilised and deserving than they? This surely canna be a right situation.

'But let us suppose for a moment that it were true, that Negroes *were* far inferior tae whites. Would that inferiority be a reason why they should be treated wi injustice and inhumanity? Surely it would be the Christian duty o white men tae care for and protect their lesser brethren. Or else there can be nae moral obligation on onybody tae behave in a civilised mainner. Why then should a puir strang man no be entitled tae rob a weak rich man? The tane has whit the tither wants, and the tither has the power tae tak it. This is nae different frae the idea that Negroes are inferior and therefore should be slaves, or that slavery is justifiable because it is necessary for the commerce o this nation.'

Lord Monboddo, lounging at the clerks' table, had periodically been making faces or noises of exasperation during both Maclaurin's and Dundas's speeches. At this point he could contain himself no longer.

'This is absurd,' he said. 'I have heard Hume quoted as if his opinion has any authority, and I have heard Smith quoted although it would seem from his book on trade that he never read any of the writers of ancient times. Whether slavery is good for commerce or good for Negroes is immaterial. The point is, slavery is *only* found in civil societies, not among barbarians, who either kill or adopt their prisoners. Prove it is against the *jus gentium*, the law of nations, not against the law of nature, for it has nothing to do with man in a natural state.'

'My lord,' Arniston said quickly as Monboddo drew breath, 'we may all offer oor opinions later. Please let Mr Dundas continue.'

'And remember too,' Monboddo breenged on, 'that the highest civilisations the world has ever seen, of Greece and Rome, countenanced slavery.'

'My lord –' Arniston tried again, but Dundas was quicker, and louder.

'My lords,' Dundas said, 'I am aboot tae address this very point – the law of nations – or at least, the law of *this* nation. And by that I mean the Scottish nation. It is certain that neither oor law or custom presently gie the least countenance tae ony species of slavery. I do not propose tae waste the court's time discussing whether it ever took place amang us. It is all one whether it did or it didna. If we once had it when we were barbarous, and it has died oot amang us, this surely is not an age for relapsing intae such an abuse. If we never had slavery, even when we were barbarous, we certainly will not adopt it noo that we are a civilised and an enlightened nation. That may or may not satisfy Lord Monboddo, but it is whit *we* believe.

'Mention has been made in the informations of the servitude of the colliers, which until recently existed here. Noo this, my lords, though it was inconsistent wi the state of oor nation as I hae jist described it, was by nae means a state of slavery, however much some thocht it so. Oor colliers and salters were protected in their person and property by the law o the land: they were not mere chattels or things. It is true that a man who wrocht at a coal work a year and a day was bound tae continue at it for life; and that his children, if they once entered that work after puberty, were also obliged tae work there for life. And it is true that, through the circumstances o their particular labours, the colliers and salters hae been considered awmaist as a race

300

apairt frae the rest o oor people. But in nae ither respect were the colliers the personal slaves o the coalmaister. They received wages, aften mair than the average, and hooses and ither things as pairt o the contract between themsels and the maister. There is *nae* contract between a maister and a slave. By comparison wi the Negroes in the plantations, the colliers' servitude was mild indeed. Yet even in the last few years an Act o Parliament has abolished it in principle, and the last remnants o that system are falling away, and in a generation will be quite gone.

'Again, my lords, I will not rehearse the many legal opinions aboot the freedoms o this country, and o oor sister kingdom England, tae which we are noo joined, except tae say that there is nae ither country in the world where the principle o liberty is mair widely kent and accepted in baith law and practice. Insteid, I will come tae the recent case o James Somerset, determined in London by the King's Bench six years syne. Noo the defender maintains that in this instance the decision went against the maister on whit we micht call a speciality, a technicality if I may be allowed such a term. That is tae say, when the slave absented himsel frae the maister's service, the maister had him seized and pit on board a ship wi the intention o cairryin him back tae the colonies tae be sold; and the King's Bench decided that the maister could not so act, as he broke the laws o England whaur he then was, since it is unlawful tae seize a man by force tae be sold abroad. Therefore, the slave James Somerset must go free. But had the maister merely taken Somerset wi him, under the warrant o a judge issued against the slave for desertion, withoot expressing his intention tae *sell* him, then nae offence would hae been committed. That is how the defender sees the Somerset case.

'My lords, we say this is a gey selective interpretation of Lord Mansfield's ruling. Can it really be supposed that the Lord Chief Justice of England would deliberately choose tae deliver an enigmatical opinion wrapped up, on purpose, in darkness and ambiguity?'

'I'd hae thocht it quite likely,' said another voice from the Bench. This time it was Braxfield, speaking loudly to his neighbour, Lord Gardenstone. It was widely rumoured that Lord Mansfield had blocked Braxfield's appointment as a judge the

301

first time round, but had expressed effusive delight at such an addition to the Scottish Bench when he could not prevent it a year later.

Henry Dundas, smiling, continued. 'We say, my lords, that the judgment was a general not a specific ane, and that it said that a Negro, brocht intae this country, canna be cairried back tae the plantations against his will for *ony* purpose. Certainly, frae the uproar that arose amang the slave traders, planters and their agents, and frae the numerous papers and pamphlets they hae written against the judgment, it would seem that *they* understood it in this way. And the maister, Mr Stewart, also understood it in this way, and that he had lost on the general point, otherwise he would certainly hae applied tae a judge for a warrant tae recommit the Negro, but he didna.

'It is undeniable, frae the accumulated doctrines and authorities that we hae presented in oor informations, which I will not burden ye wi again here, that, as in France, Germany, England, and ither countries of Europe, every man existing in these countries that isna a criminal is free, whether he be a native or a foreigner, and whether he was aince a slave in anither country. Therefore nae ither man may tak him awa against his will. This idea is founded in the principles of natural justice, and it must apply equally in Scotland. The clear consequence is, then, that every Negro, as soon as he sets foot in Scotland, must become a free man.'

All this time, Dundas's voice, controlled but with an edgy violence to it, had been rising in volume. Now he paused, turned so that he was in profile to the gallery, and put down his notes. Even had the Lord President wished to intervene, Dundas for the next few minutes was unstoppable.

'Again, my lords, I dinna wish tae deave ye wi mair examples than are awready afore ye of the harsh treatment and punishments meted oot tae the Negroes in Jamaica, but let me remind ye that Mr Knight could hardly expect justice and consolation frae that colony's laws should he once again set foot there, especially as he would be considered a slave that had deserted his maister. By contrast, does not a Negro frae that place, once here, deserve the full protection of the humane and equitable law of Scotland? Similarly, even if the judgment of the English courts should rest on a narrow ground and not, as we maintain, on the wider principle – even if the common law of England should say that the condition of perpetual service is tae be upheld, though the original transaction that began it is manifestly unjust – it is hoped that the authority of neither it nor the law of Jamaica will ever be countenanced in Scotland. In ancient times, the free and warlike spirit of the Scots beat back the infection of slavery: Tacitus records the noble sentiments of the Caledonians; Sir William Wallace and Robert the Bruce are not forgotten; and in modern times the equality, the justice and humanity of oor religion and oor laws, hae preserved tae us the right of freedom. Whaurever slavery has existed in Christendom, religion, reason and law hae hunted it frae its sordid abodes. France, England, Germany, Denmark and Holland surround us: in aw these countries the oppressed Negro finds his freedom. Is Scotland alane tae chain him up? We are ridding oorsels of the last vestiges of whit micht be *considered* serfdom in oor society, by Act of Parliament. At the same time, are we tae assert that whit isna guid enough for a white man is simply bad luck for a black man? There is nae logic in that, my lords. There is nae logic in oor attempting tae justify the oppression of the Africans.

'The defender has laboured tae conjure up gigantic spectres of future evils frae a judgment in favour of the pursuer. It is claimed that the haill African fleet micht be driven by storms tae Scotland, and a hundred thoosand Negroes, the number shipped annually tae the plantations, would at once become free men; that Scotland, as soon as word got oot of this judgment, would become the general receptacle of fugitive Negroes, wha would arrive in multitudes; and that the pure Scottish blood would be contaminated wi a tinge of African dye. My lords, such suppositions dinna deserve a serious answer. We can hardly arrange Scottish law in order tae protect the institution of slavery throughout the rest of the globe. But I will say this, if some in this court are fashed by this prospect: the maist effectual means tae preserve Scotland frae a breed of Africans is tae render it the interest of their tyrants tae keep them at a distance frae it.

'My lords, I am done. Whit I hae said is but a summation of, and an addition tae, the detailed arguments laid before ye in writing. The pursuer's case has been made, and he, and we his coonsel, noo rest, wi tranquillity, his future fate on the justice and humanity of this court.'

This sudden conclusion, reached before the President had even thought of reaching for his sand-glass, was delivered in a hushed tone, the quiet after the storm. The performance was greeted with stamping of feet and a few cheers – but these were cut off after only a few seconds by Arniston repeatedly pounding the Bench with the wooden base of the sand-glass and sweeping the court with a furious, imperious stare. 'We are *not*,' he roared into the silence, 'we are *not* in a bear-pit. I will clear the court if that occurs again. Mr Cullen, ye hae five minutes.'

Arniston heaved himself upright and made for the side door. A court officer arrived only just in time to open it for him. The other judges filed out, with the exception of Monboddo, who presumably wanted neither the company of his fellow-judges nor a share of the claret that would be waiting for them. With the Session gone, a general clamour broke out among the crowd.

Cullen, Ferguson, Campbell and John Wedderburn huddled together, deciding which parts of their argument could be removed or abridged and which parts were essential. Across the room Knight's counsel were also in deep consultation. Maconochie seemed to be emphasising some point of urgency to Dundas, speaking very directly into his face, while Maclaurin listened intently. The atmosphere under the gallery was thick and oppressive. Knight himself was for a moment forgotten. Suddenly he turned and started towards the door. A route through the crowd opened before him, and a few hands clapped his shoulders as he went, but he made no response, did not seem even to feel them on him.

Before the crush closed behind him, another man had also decided to leave the room for some fresh air, and pushed himself along in the black man's wake.

Despite Arniston's desire to keep proceedings moving, it was apparently harder to get the Session back into the chamber than it had been to lead them out. Nearly fifteen minutes elapsed before they reappeared, wiping their mouths as they did. The President however saw no reason to blame himself. 'Ah weel, Mr Cullen, if ye hadna asked for an adjournment ye could aw hae spoken jist as ye meant tae in the first place. But that canna be helped. Ye may stert noo, onywey.'

Cullen got up and glided to the centre of the court. He knew that Maclaurin and Dundas between them had captured the moral ground. He was not interested in that, since he could not win it back from them. To win this case, he could be concerned only with the law.

But then something else occurred to him, something which was clearly occurring to several of the judges, and to a nervous-looking John Maclaurin, at the same time.

'My lord, I will start. I cannot help observing, however, that an important item has gone missing in the brief period since we last met. Not for the first time, the pursuer appears to have absented himself.'

There was a general gasp from the gallery, where most of the people could not see who was or was not present beneath them.

'I do not know whether we should read anything from this unexpected development,' Cullen said, '– if indeed it *is* unexpected. The defender –' turning to smile at John Wedderburn '– does not look very surprised.' By now there was laughter in the public space and even along the Bench. 'This kind of behaviour is quite characteristic, perhaps.'

Maclaurin jumped to his feet. 'My lords, Mr Cullen's jokes are cheaply made. Mr Knight was feeling unwell. He went out for air. Mr Maconochie –' Maconochie set off as if to fetch their client, but at that moment the door at the rear of the room opened and Knight burst through. He seemed very wound up, furious or frightened, or perhaps both.

'Tak your place, sir,' Arniston said. 'We dinna like tae be kept waiting here.' Knight made no sign of apology. He scowled up at the Bench as he reached his seat. Some of the judges recoiled, as if animated by fears they had not known they possessed. Knight would not return Maclaurin's anxious inquiring glances.

Cullen received a nod from the President. He knew that he had been presented with a gift by the opposition, and set about making the most of it.

'My lords, we have heard much, so very much about the

immorality, the injustices of slavery, the alleged cruelties of Jamaica, and so forth, that we are in danger of forgetting the facts. My lord, you spoke very true when you said this is not a bear-pit. Nor, as Mr Dundas himself pointed out, is it a place where we may legislate for the world. We are here for one purpose only, and that is to decide whether Mr Wedderburn, the defender, has the right to the perpetual service of the pursuer. All the bombast and rhetoric of the other side must be discounted, and the plain facts looked at.

'In a country where the blessings of liberty are so completely enjoyed as they are in Britain, it is natural for a good man when he hears the very name of slavery to take the opposite side of the question at once, without examination, and to make judgment solely on the basis of his natural prejudices. It does not occur to him to address the issue according to the law of the land as it stands, nor to leave it to the legislative power to correct that law if it should require any amendment.

'But here we are in a court of law, and this court is surely aware of and superior to such prejudices. We have no reason to be afraid of our cause, though we will not be surprised if the popular clamour should rather be against us.

'We find it almost unfair to hear the word "slavery" quoted against us, since there is no need – or ought to be no need – to enter into a discussion of that question in the present cause. All that Mr Wedderburn claims is a right to the service of the pursuer, to which he cannot doubt but that he is well entitled.

'The pursuer's counsel have thought proper all along to plead their cause exceedingly high, insisting that Mr Wedderburn had no title to the property of the pursuer as a slave even in the West Indies, because of the doubtful manner, as they say, by which he was acquired. They demand evidence of ownership. If by this they mean to insist on a written contract in the Whidah or Anamaboe or indeed some other African language that we know not the name of, the defender acknowledges that he has none. It is the custom to transact these matters only verbally, and as *he* purchased the pursuer in a fair sale, it is not necessary, nor indeed possible, to go farther back. Nothing can be more ridiculous than to suppose that for every Negro in the West Indies his master should have a proof of the particular manner in which he had been purchased on the coast of Guinea. What is very clear is the fact that by all the custom and law of Jamaica the pursuer *was* the legal property of the defender.

'Furthermore, as our written submissions show beyond any doubt, that custom and law is founded upon the laws of Britain, by Acts of Parliament and by royal decrees, as well as by hundreds of years of practice. Nowhere do these statutes advise the planters of the Indies that in consequence of returning to the land where these very laws were made, they should be deprived of their right, and be forfeited of their property – under the same authority by which they were enabled to acquire that property in the first place.

'If Mr Wedderburn's title to the pursuer is invalid, then the entire system of slavery, the entire industry and commerce of the plantations, the entire wealth and prosperity and trade of this nation, is also invalid. This is a palpable nonsense. Do the honourable gentlemen opposite drink coffee? Do they drink rum? Do they take tea with their wives? Do they wear cotton? Is the cotton dyed with indigo? Do they eat rice puddings and sprinkle them with sugar? Do they smoke tobacco? All these activities, these pleasures and necessities of our lives, are invalid, my lords, upon their argument. I repeat, to claim that this court should be passing judgment upon slavery when we should be deciding upon the property rights of Mr Wedderburn is a wilful pretence.

'Like my learned and emphatic friend Mr Dundas, I do not wish to *deave* your lordships with arguments you have already read at length. Nonetheless, I must repeat what was said earlier: Joseph Knight is so far from being a *slave*, as that term is generally understood, that one must wonder what oppression it is from which he seeks to free himself. Mr Wedderburn trained him, at considerable expense, to be his own personal servant. He has ever treated him with tenderness and indulgence. No hardship was ever imposed on him. In place of being left in Jamaica, to toil at cultivating sugar cane under a burning West Indian sun, he was brought to Scotland to live the life of a gentleman's servant; was clothed, fed, housed, taught to read and write, and instructed in the principles of the Christian religion. My lords, we have heard of poor forgotten genius Scottish labourers rotting away in kirkyards. Many a Scottish labourer must dream of such a life as the pursuer has enjoyed! The colliers and salters, of whom it was said that their lives were easier than those of the Negro slaves, could scarcely even dream it, it is so far removed from their reality – but I will return to them later.

'And so you might think that mere gratitude alone might have secured, upon the pursuer's part, inviolable fidelity and attachment to such a master. His behaviour, sadly, does not advertise any of the decency and kindness that clearly reside in Mr Wedderburn. Every good deed done to the pursuer is repaid with an ill one. His master has never mistreated him: he therefore forms a scheme for deserting his service. He is made a Christian: he proceeds to seduce, or allow himself to be seduced by, a housemaid, a girl of low morals –'

A voice, quite low but very firm, cut across Cullen's. 'Steady noo, Maister Knight. I warned ye o this.' It was Maclaurin's voice. He had a restraining hand on Knight's arm, and at the same time as he was holding Knight in his seat, he was using him to lever himself upright. 'My lords, this is unwarranted. The pursuer's spouse's character has nae place in this cause and the defender's coonsel should withdraw that ootrageous remark.'

'Restrict your remarks tae the cause, Mr Cullen,' said Arniston wearily. 'Mr Knight, I willna tell ye again. Tak your seat, and stay in it.'

'I withdraw the remark,' said Cullen coolly, knowing that it was said anyway and would lodge in the dry roof-space of the less liberal judges' minds; as would Knight's apparent contempt for the legal process. 'To continue, then. He is taught to read: he picks up a newspaper, reads of the case of his countryman Somerset, and at once decides that he has no further obligation to his master. He proves himself, in other words, at every turn undeserving of that *freedom* to which he presumes to aspire. Freedom, my lords, does not come, if I may put it this way, unfettered. It comes with duties, and obligations, and responsibilities. These Mr Wedderburn has exhibited in all his dealings with his servant. How is he repaid? With desertion.

'Yet the pursuer expects the court to blame Mr Wedderburn for his own shortcomings. More than that, he expects the court to blame Mr Wedderburn for the occasional abuses that are committed in bringing the Negroes from their native country, or in their treatment in the West Indies. Yet, as is demonstrably clear, Mr Wedderburn has never abused the pursuer, whom he purchased in good faith and according to usual practice from Captain Knight. While the law of Britain remains in its present state, authorising and protecting the slave trade and the planters' property rights in their slaves, courts of law can never be at liberty to dispense with that law from any supposed considerations of its inhumanity or inexpediency.

'My lords, I will not enter again into the arguments about whether slavery runs contrary to the principles of natural law or the law of nations. All historical evidence shows, as has already been mentioned from the Bench, that it is a practice which has prevailed in every nation that ever existed, from Greece and Rome to the present, and it prevails today over the greater part of the world. We have heard of France and Holland and Britain being havens of liberty: slavery exists in the colonies of each of these nations, and is protected by their laws. In Africa, from whence the slaves are brought, slavery is so much a part of society that parents sell their own children. Did the rapacious Europeans descend upon the west coast of Africa and invent slavery? No, it was and is practised by the Africans themselves, as a consequence of conquest, as a form of punishment for crime, and as a form of commerce. Furthermore, it is accompanied in Africa by the most shocking and barbarous cruelties. Being taken from such miserable and savage conditions to the New World, where they are well fed and clothed, and able to live in safety and peace and be useful labourers, can only be seen as an improvement in the circumstances of the plantation slaves. They are well suited to the climate there, which is, though often fatal to whites, temperate in comparison to that which they left, and they are well fitted for the employment to which they are put. We understand, my lords, it became a common saying in the Indies that "unless a Negro happened to be hanged, he never died" – a saying which could scarcely have become widespread were there any truth in the vast numbers of mortalities claimed by the pursuer's counsel. How much more, then, is it true of the pursuer, that by being brought to Scotland his circumstances have been still further improved, and that, until he deserted his master, he was ever on an upward journey towards civilisation, comfort and happiness.

'Let it also be said that Scottish patriotism provides no haven for those who would do away with all bondage. Scotland has in no way distanced herself from the institution of slavery. Fully one-third of the planters of Jamaica are Scotsmen. They own a quarter of the land there. In Virginia and the Carolinas, Scots, both Highlanders and Lowlanders, are so thick on the ground that some of the Negroes there speak the Gaelic, and others the Scotch tongue. Go to Glasgow and see the great buildings and the busy commerce of that city, founded on tobacco and sugar. One might almost say that Glasgow is *made* of tobacco. Even before this age, though, when the Scots aspired to their own empire, it was with the utmost reluctance, at the time of the Union, that they – I should say *we* – surrendered the rights of the African Company, and ever since it has been with the utmost enthusiasm that we have engaged in the ventures opened up to us by the Union, including those that could not prosper without slavery.

'Ever since then, too, Negroes have been brought by their masters from the colonies to Scotland, but no question with respect to their becoming free arose until very recent times. I think we should not indulge in the cant and false patriotism of pretending that we are a nation who so love natural justice that we would welcome thousands of black men among us when they steal across the Atlantic seeking liberty on our shores. My lords, I think our attitudes have not yet been sufficiently tested on that score, but if thousands do come among us – well, we shall then be put to the test. I say this to the court: they may come among us, and we may not like it. What song will Scottish patriots sing then, my lords?

'With regard to the colliers and salters, it is very clear that the pursuer's counsel would not have drawn attention to this group had there not been the recent law relaxing their state of servitude. But what does this have to do with the matter in hand? The fact that a law has had to be passed to alter their status merely strengthens *our* argument – that it is not this court's task to legislate, but only to interpret the law. Parliament alone can change laws, and, as we have shown, slavery exists by and in accordance with the laws of this country. In any case, despite the new legislation, servitude *does* still exist among the colliers and salters, and will do so unless or until a further law is made to do away with it all together. We respectfully dispute, in addition, the notion that to be bound to work at the dangerous physical toil of a collier throughout life is a milder form of servitude than that of being a gentleman's personal servant. In short, we feel that the law freeing the colliers is doubly supportive of our cause.

'It has been claimed that a Negro, by being baptised into the Christian faith, must thereby win his liberty, and although the pursuer does not much insist on this – which perhaps indicates how little was his sincerity in adopting our religion – still it is worth touching on. If this claim be true, what message does it send to the planters? It suggests that a good master such as Mr Wedderburn, who encouraged and enabled his servant to become a Christian, would have served his own interests better by keeping him in a state of savage ignorance – in other words, it suggests that Mr Wedderburn should act as an un-Christian to those in his employment and under his protection.

'I am almost finished, my lords. I do not intend to detain you by engaging in a discussion about the supposed cruel manner in which it is alleged the Negroes are reduced to slavery in Africa and brought from thence to the West Indies, nor in a refutation of the greatly exaggerated accounts of the ill-treatment of the Negroes in the plantations. None of this is of any pertinence to the present question, but in any case, as I have repeatedly said, none of it can be laid at the door of the defender, who has always conducted himself with kindness, honesty and generosity.

'I need now touch only on two issues, which are closely related. The first is the precedent of the case of James Somerset, decided in England. Without going back into this in detail, it is not true to say that that decision was made on a general point. On the contrary, the honourable Lord Chief Justice expressly said, that he "confined his opinion to the only question before him", and that the intent of the master to *sell* his slave when abroad once more, was crucial. The second issue is this: a consequence of Mr Wedderburn's right of property in the pursuer should and must be that he ought to be allowed to carry him back to Jamaica, or send him there, if he should choose it. We emphasise that in fact he has no intention of doing so, just as he has no intention of selling or disposing of him or in any way mistreating him. But the right of property cannot be limited by locality. Mr Wedderburn undoubtedly owned the pursuer in Jamaica; we maintain that he owns him in Scotland; and that therefore he may carry him back to Jamaica if he pleases.

'My lords, that is all. After all that has been said today, and all that has been written and read by your lordships in these last three years, we are confident that the facts of this case are clear, and clearly in favour of the defender. We conclude that it cannot be agreeable to the principles of justice, to divest the master or owner of a Negro, of his right of property, by the mere accidental circumstance of his bringing that Negro into the island of Great Britain.'

There was something fatally conclusive in the way Cullen delivered all his points. There was no sense of passion, and every appeal that went beyond the letter of the law to the feelings of the Bench seemed dry-measured, precise, a reminder that the letter of the law was all they really had to be concerned with. He bowed and turned back to Wedderburn, who neither smiled nor made any movement. His eyes were fixed on the Lord President.

'Thank you, gentlemen,' Arniston said. 'This is a significant cause, as we aw ken. In a minute I will ask for the opinions of their lordships, and their votes. But I may say, for mysel, I find Mr Cullen's last remark is the maist important. The pursuer was the slave or bonded servant of Mr Wedderburn in the West Indies – naebody disputes that. The question is, whether this service be considered as ended by his coming intae this country. I see nae reason why this should be so. If the maister abides by the laws o this country – disna hurt or hairm the servant in ways that are unacceptable here – why should he no continue tae hae his service for life? If the maister submits tae this consequence of *oor* law, then it seems tae me the slave or servant must submit tae the consequence of Jamaican law. Mr Cullen is richt: the law as it exists is aw that should concern us. But that is only *my* opinion. The court, my lords, is anxious tae hear whether ye agree wi me or no.'

*   *   *

Archibald Jamieson had not, of course, been reproducing every syllable of these learned speeches to his wife as she lay silently in the fading light. Not having been present, he could not have known everything that had taken place in that crowded courtroom. Nevertheless, he had been speaking for a long time, explaining the complexities of the arguments and the clashes of the personalities, and, it must be said, letting his imagination fill in gaps with details of which he was none too certain or indeed entirely ignorant. Now, somewhat abashed at having gone on at such length, he said to Janet, 'Ye must be tired. I've been deavin ye like a minister in a pulpit. Ye should try tae sleep.'

'I am wide awake, I assure ye. Ye paint a guid picture.'

'I wasna there of course. It's jist hoo I hae biggit it in my mind frae the papers I hae read.'

'I wonder if Knight's wife was there. Whit would she hae made o it?'

'I would think she must hae been there. Up in the gallery, nae dout. She'd no hae liked Cullen.'

'I dinna like Cullen, frae whit ye've said. A bluidless kind o chiel.'

'*Lord* Cullen noo, of course. Weel, my dear, it's past eleiven. I should let ye be.'

'The morn's Sunday. Ye'll no hae work – ye can tell me the rest o whit happened at the court then. I ken the ootcome onywey. But ye hinna read me the letter yet.'

Archie picked it up from the counterpane where it had lain all this time. 'It's gey lang, Janet. I'm feart aw this must be boring ye.'

'How could it be boring? Whit could be mair interesting than a man seeking his liberty, *gaining* his liberty?'

'A man gaining his life?' Archie suggested tentatively.

'But a life withoot freedom, whit is that? It's like a life withoot health – a shadow o being alive. Imagine hoo wrang it is, the life o the Negroes in the colonies.'

'I imagine it is not intolerable, or they wouldna tolerate it.'

'Dinna be souple, Archie, it disna become ye. Look at me – d'ye think I tolerate this? I dinna hae a choice in it. Imagine the life of Joseph Knight if he had been sent back tae Jamaica.'

'It seems that was never the intention.'

'Aye, and dae ye believe in fairies? They micht no hae killt him, but it would hae been the cane fields for him until that wore him awa. Would that be tolerable? There is mair tae life than jist living.'

Archie bowed his head. 'I hinna aften seen it like that, I fear.'

'Oh, Archie, there is much ye hinna seen. But there are quiet millions o us everywhere that see whit's richt and whit's wrang.'

He did not answer, nodded thoughtfully, traced the diamond pattern of the counterpane with a finger.

'I am sorry,' Janet said into the silence, 'that I hae been a disappointment tae ye.'

This was so unexpected, and yet so much what he had been thinking of saying himself, *about* himself, that he could not bear to look at her. He mumbled a reply, 'No, no, Janet . . .'

'Aye, it's true. But ye can mairry again – a man is never ower auld – perhaps hae mair bairns, the anes I couldna gie ye . . .'

'Please, this is ower sair.'

She went on as if she had not heard him. 'But if ye dae, listen tae whit I hae tae say. Your present children are fine young people – even the laddies, I ken, in spite o their noise – but they are grown awready. If ye hae ony mair, dinna raise them up for the world as it is. Raise them for the world as it micht be. A better world. Then it micht come aboot.' She stopped, sniffed. 'Noo, read me thon letter, and efter that I promise I'll try tae sleep.'

Archibald Jamieson blew his nose and wiped his eyes, astonished to find that he appeared to be married to a saint. After a minute, he began to read the letter to her. The handwriting was neat and regular, but the candles were flickering and he had to concentrate or lose his place. When he glanced up at the end of each page, he saw that Janet was staring into the shadows as if there were no shadows there. After three pages, she settled back against the pillows and closed her eyes, but he could tell from the slightest occasional press of her fingers on his wrist that she was still listening. It was not until he was more than halfway through the letter that the fingers relaxed and she seemed to fall asleep, and by then he

314

was afraid to stop in case the silence should wake her again. And so he continued to the end, his quiet voice threading the words of Mr Peter Burnet into whatever dreams she might be having.

From Mr Peter Burnet of Paisley

8th January, 1803

Mr Archibald Jamieson, St Clement's Lane, Dundee

Sir,

It is more than nine months since your letter addressed to me was sent, and near as long since it was put in my hand. You may have wondered if the want of a reply was owing to my not having received it – be assured that the direction *Black Peter, Weaver, Paisley* found me without the least trouble. I am a kenspeckle person in this town, and have been for many years. No, sir, there was no answer because, for long, I felt an unease about giving you one, since you did not specify a reason for your wishing information concerning the gentleman in question, other than it relating to his famous legal cause, and I have in the past been made painfully aware that a man of colour, howsoever respectable he be, may not always welcome the attendance of a *lawyer's agent* such as you state yourself to be. I mean this not as an offence to you, sir, whom I have never met, but as a lesson hard learned by myself. But, on consideration, I am of the opinion that there's no harm in telling you what I know of Mr Joseph Knight, since what you particularly wish to know, namely his whereabouts, I cannot tell you.

I will add that my good friend Mr Robert Tannahill, also of Paisley, has agreed with me on this matter, and offered to write this reply. This is not owing to a lack of letters on my part, but this will be a lengthy epistle, and Mr Tannahill, being a poet and writer of songs, has a speedier and neater hand than I, as well as being better acquaint with the finer points of the English language.

In relating to you the circumstances of my brief acquaintance with Mr Knight, it is first necessary that I mention some of the particulars of my own life, because our experiences both in Scotland and in the Americas have been so very different. I was born a free man, but in a land far from that of my race: he was born an African in Africa, but violently seized from his home and carried thence to be a slave. From an early age I have counted many white people, male and female, among my friends: he received from white people only enslavement, oppression and disdain until he reached these shores, whither, unlike me, he was brought against his will; and even when he found comfort in the arms of his wife, this itself brought fresh anger and despisal upon his head; whereas I have been twice married in Scotland, and neither I, nor my first dear wife, nor my second, have suffered more than slight grazes from the darts of narrow prejudice. When Mr Knight and I met, therefore, it was a meeting of two men who were alike and yet utterly unlike. We saw and recognised one another, but we were not at all the same.

Know then, sir, that I, Peter Burnet, was born about thirty-eight years since on the estate of Thomas Todd in Virginia. My grandfather, a gardener, had been brought there from Africa and on account of his loyal and faithful service he and my grandmother were made free by their master, and all their children, including my father, likewise were released from the yoke of slavery. This manifest blessing did not blind me to the travails of my fellow Africans, but it did impart in me from an early age a notion that is far less true in reality than it ought to be – namely, that loyalty, dignity and courage will ever be rewarded.

At the onset of the American war, it became plain even to me, a mere boy, that my freedom might not be assured in a country that in some parts held no obligations to these principles. I therefore enlisted as a cabin boy on a British privateer. At this time I was about eleven years of age. I was not long in discovering that my notions of fair play were sometimes as lacking among the British as among the

Americans, as not once but twice I was nearly tricked by the very officers I served into being kidnapped and sold as a slave to the planters of Jamaica. In each case I narrowly avoided this cruel fate only through the timeous warnings of my friends in New York, where I then was. In that town, having discovered that the ocean life was fraught with worse dangers for a black boy than mere storms and piracy, I made my home, being employed by a Mr Torrance, who kept a store, and whose father was a merchant in the Saltmarket, Glasgow.

Here commenced my association with the Scottish people, which I will ever count among the chief pleasures of my life. Mr Torrance was a good and kindly master, who treated me with gentleness and honesty, and never took advantage of me. He was, however, sadly addicted to drink, to the detriment of his health, and I was often left in charge of the business when he, owing to his love of the bottle, was either unable to rise from his bed or unable to get to it. After some years, when I was about sixteen, Mr Torrance's condition declined so much that he could no longer manage the store, and he desired to return to Glasgow to live out his days in his native land. He asked me to attend him as his servant, which request I joyfully accepted, as I had a great desire to see more of the world. At length we set sail and after stopping at Cork, safely reached Glasgow, whereupon my master retired to his bed and could scarcely be prevailed upon ever again to leave it. But he was not unaware of his responsibilities toward me, and set me on the road to Kilmarnock, where he knew of someone who would employ me.

I will not further trouble you with details of events which, though of singular interest to me, are doubtless of little to you, except insofar as they relate to Mr Knight. Suffice it to say that through Mr George Tannahill of Kilmarnock I came to Paisley, where he thought I would get on better, the weaving then being in a prosperous condition. Mr James Tannahill, a silk weaver of distinction, took me in and I became an apprentice. From this time dates my intimacy with the Tannahills, who from the first extended to me the hand of friendship as if I had been a son to them, and

318

a brother to Robert who is writing this. I will not say it was as if they did not see my blackness, for I was certainly a curiosity, but in a little while it was no more remarked upon than if I had a set of large ears or red hair. I have never been ashamed of my black face, and have, when occasionally subjected to the derision of ignorant people, made a point of saying that I would not exchange it for their stupidity in any event.

Not long after the occasion which I am about to relate, I was falsely accused and imprisoned for a debt I did not owe, and I believe my skin did not help me to prove my innocence. Or rather, the way my skin was *viewed* did not help. But I refused to pay on a principle, and the Tannahills gave me every support and comfort at this time, until, completely vindicated, I was released. You may understand now, sir, why I am wary of affairs involving men such as yourself.

In about the year 1789, fourteen years ago, I had left the weaving during a period of slackness in that trade, and removed to Edinburgh in search of work. I was servant for a time to the Clerks of Eldin in Midlothian, who kept a town house, and of whom the now famed advocate Mr John Clerk was the son. Sometimes I went with the young Mr Clerk to the court at Parliament Close. He had one shortened leg from a childhood illness – so much contracted that it swung in the air when he stood upright, and caused him to pitch like a ship at sea when he walked. To ease his progress he would have me accompany him, carrying documents, books and such. On one occasion, I remember well, a lady remarked within our hearing as we passed, 'There goes Mr Clerk, the lame lawyer.' Quick as a flash, he turned around and said, 'Ma'am, I may be a lame man, but I am no lame lawyer!'

When not needed by him, I might spend an hour on the High Street, enjoying the crowds, the colourful stalls and shops, the constant fair, as it seemed, of conversation and bartering, the fine-dressed ladies and gallant soldiery, the many folk all going about their various businesses. Paisley is a thriving town, but it is as nothing to the commotion of Edinburgh.

One day, standing near the entrance to the courts, I saw strolling up the street towards me another black man. Though we were by no means the only two black men then in the capital, we were sufficiently rare to catch each other's eye, and as he advanced he held my glance, as if searching in my face for recognition. He was wearing plain and not altogether new clothes, and therefore was a contrast to myself, for I have ever been proud to turn out in style, and on this day I was quite the macaroni in a brown brass-buttoned coat and a black velvet vest picked out in gold thread in the Paisley pattern. But whatever advantage I had over him in dress, he made up for with his proud, even fierce demeanour.

As we met, the first words he addressed to me were: 'What are *you* looking at, man?' I remember this distinctly, because he was staring at me at least as hard as I was staring at him, and I felt that he was in some way demanding the answer from himself.

I said I was looking at him, since he and I had one thing in common, if it was the only thing, and I put out my hand to him. He hesitated for a second, as if he would march on past me, but then he gave a very brief smile – more a stretching of the mouth, in fact, than a smile – and shook my hand. He was a fine, slender man, with a good crop of hair which was just beginning to whiten at the edges. I guessed him to be no more than thirty-eight or forty – about what I am now – which seemed a great age to one who was then only in his early twenties. He had not an inch of wasted flesh on him, and though he did not look excessively muscular, yet there was a strength in his way of standing, and in the grip of his hand, that a much greater man might have envied. I noticed also a peculiar graininess in the palm of his hand, which I could not identify.

I told him my name, and said that if he would give me his I would buy him a drink in the nearest tavern (indicating it). He said he would prefer to go to one a hundred yards further away, since it was the scene of a great triumph of his and as he was not often in Edinburgh he was minded to recall to himself the day of that triumph. I agreed, and asked again for his name. 'They call me Joseph Knight,' he said. And without another word he strode towards the law courts, and I went after him about half a step behind.

I knew at once who he was, and of what triumph he spoke. It had taken place some eleven years before, and there had been a great stir about it in the west. Although I was not then residing in Scotland it was scarcely possible that the cause of Joseph Knight should not have reached my ears within a few months of my arrival. I heard of it both from my friends the Tannahills, who regarded it as greatly creditable to the Scottish law, and from other black men in Glasgow and thereabouts whom I chanced to meet from time to time. Its effect, of course, did not apply to me as I had always been free, but the name Joseph Knight was spoken of with reverence, as belonging to one who had liberated not just himself but all African people in Scotland. (Mr Tannahill, however, tells me he has heard of at least one poor African who continued in servitude until his death about five years since in a distant part of the country, not, it is true, maltreated, but certainly unable to leave the old house in which he was an unpaid servant, because he would have been like the madman let out from the bedlam after fifty years, who starved from not knowing how to be sane.) And so I hurried along beside Mr Knight, eager to hear what he might have to say.

We turned into the Parliament Close, and my companion, without a faltering step, marched up to and through the Great Door into the old Parliament building itself. I had been in and out of this place once or twice myself, but never lingered much, preferring the light of the street to the gloom within. Here, as you will know, there used to exist – I do not know if they still do – a number of shops and booths, and a place where men of business and law would sit absorbing coffee and the day's newspapers. This establishment went by the name of INDIAN PETER'S COFFEE HOUSE, but it was a house only in name, since it was really little more than a series of compartments propped up

321

against a wall, the internal dividers made of the thinnest of materials, including, if I mind right, some of brown paper. Mr Knight drew up a seat at a vacant table in one of the 'rooms' so formed.

'I like this place,' he said. 'Indian Peter is a man after my own heart.'

This was the proprietor, Peter Williamson, who also went by the name 'Peter Williamson from the Other World', a reference to his having been among the savage Indians in his youth. He was kidnapped when a boy in Aberdeen and sold into slavery to America, and was then captured by the Indians, who treated him most cruel. But he made his escape, and came to Edinburgh, where he became a celebrated figure, and set up the penny post.

'He was sold by his own kind,' said Mr Knight, 'then fell among those who cared little whether he lived or died, so he had a notion what *my* feelings were. When I came here with those who helped me, he took my hand and treated me with great civility. There was an argument used in the court that I should be happy with my lot, which they said was a comfortable one, but Mr Williamson would have none of that. "If you are bound with silken cord you are as wretched as he who is bound with hemp," he told me, and he was right.'

I will not attempt to represent the sound of Mr Knight's voice. I myself, though born a British subject in America, have acquired a fair smattering of Scotch words and noises over the years, so that my speech is an odd enough mix. But Mr Knight's was a veritable patchwork. There was, if I may express it in this way, a rich Jamaican ground, overlaid with Scotch sounds and occasional Scotch words, probably pronounced in the tones of Dundee or Perth; and I daresay the stitching itself may have been done with an African needle. Listening to him was like listening to a ship's company all speaking at once, yet in a kind of harmony. I must, though, leave the resulting effect to your imagination, and reproduce only the general run of his words.

Mr Williamson was not in his shop that day. A waiter approached and asked what we required.

'Coffee,' said Mr Knight, 'and rum to chase it with.'

'The same for me,' I said, and the man took away our order.

I was aware that our entry had caused something of a stir. Two black fellows together in such a place was an uncommon sight, and not a few glances and whispers flew around, so that I half expected my companion to roar out at somebody, 'What are *you* looking at, man?' He did not, indeed he hardly seemed to notice the attention we were getting, but sat flaring his nostrils and breathing in deep, noisy breaths, while I amused myself with the conjecture that we might be thought an advance party of Jacobins come to overthrow King Harry Dundas (the French Revolution was then in its earliest stages), and that the City Guard would shortly burst in and haul us away to the tolbooth. But we were left undisturbed, and in a while the waiter returned with what we had requested.

'Well now,' said Knight, inhaling strenuously. 'Did you ever smell the like of that? Coffee, rum and sugar all in the one breath. The smell of riches, the smell of blood!'

I could see, of course, what he drove at, but he spoke so loud that I really feared his talk of blood might bring the Guard upon us, so, making a jest of it, I implored him to lower his voice lest we be taken for conspirators against Mr Dundas.

He smiled at me – and this time it was a real, shining smile. 'You are nervous, man,' he said. 'You'll not find me plotting against that gentleman. What he does in the Government is his own concern, but I owe him for his part in my triumph – just in through that door there – so he need have no fear of designs from me.'

'Henry Dundas spoke for you?' I asked.

'He and others,' he said. 'Lord Dreghorn was the leading counsel.' (This was Mr John Maclaurin, who had just in that year been appointed to the Bench.)

'You were well represented, then,' I remarked.

'So was the other side, according to what the papers wrote of it.' This was said with a certain bitterness, which was confirmed by what followed. 'They were more impressed

323

with the quality of the arguments than with the result, I think. Than with my triumph.'

'Well,' I said, 'that may be, but what I have heard is that the Scottish people were proud and pleased that you won.'

'It wore off pretty quick, then,' he said. 'They forgot me in a month.'

'No,' I said, 'they were still talking about it when I first came to Paisley, and that was two years after.'

'Ah, weavers,' he said. 'Aye, they would remember. Weavers and spinners and black folk like us, it would mean something to all them. But the high and mighty, they soon found other things to talk about. Whether apes might be a kind of man, for example. But I think they did not much entertain the idea of an ape who might be a *white* man.'

I did not follow this, and asked him what he meant. It turned out he was speaking of one of the judges in his case, Lord Monboddo. 'A small monkey himself,' he said. 'He voted against me.'

He had a precise memory – much more precise than mine now, I confess – of exactly which of the Fifteen had been for him, and which against. Those against were four in number. One was the President, Lord Arniston, who said that the coming of master and slave to this country did not alter the fact of that relationship. Another was Monboddo, who said there was nothing in this country's statutes to stop the master taking his slave back to Jamaica, where he had been a slave by law, contract or no contract. And what vexed Mr Knight most, this judge seemed to base his vote for slavery on the fact that the Romans had it – I am recording these things as best I can remember them, and from a few notes I made later that day, which I still have for I thought Mr Knight worthy of notes. 'When Monboddo said that,' he told me, 'I saw why he was such a shrunken, shrivelled wee man. It was because he was fifteen hundred years old.'

On the other side, Lords Gardenstone and Braxfield – nearly all these judges were still alive at the time I met

Knight, though they are all dead now – said that whatever had obtained in Jamaica, it was quite beyond the master's power to carry Mr Knight back there from this, a free country. And old Lord Kames said it was not the court's job to enforce the laws of Jamaica, but to enforce *right*, not *wrong*. It was, however, Lord Auchinleck of whom Mr Knight spoke most warmly. He gave his opinion in less than half a minute, apparently, and it was this: 'Is a man to be a slave because he is black? No. He is our brother; and he is a man, in a land of liberty with his wife and child. Let him remain there.' Mr Knight raised his glass of rum, tossed it off with a toast to Lord Auchinleck, and signalled to the waiter for another. Naturally, I could not do other than join him.

'Well, anyway,' I said, 'a law court is for arguing points of law, however disagreeable. I suppose you must have been happy that a majority of the judges upheld your cause.'

He looked at me coldly. 'I was happy to be found a free man,' he said. Then his voice suddenly rose. 'I was not happy that it took fourteen old men four years to decide it – fourteen old men in a country I never wished to be in, when the best of my youth was over.'

A few nearby heads were raised again, and I begged him to calm himself.

'I am calm,' he said. 'I have learned since that day what it is to be free. It is not to be free at all. I am well used to it now, so I am quite calm about it.'

'Not free?' I said, astonished. 'What do you mean? We are free, both of us. This is where we *can* be free.'

'You said yourself you were *born* free,' he replied. 'I was made a slave before I knew what freedom was, and when they gave me my freedom they left me stuck here. I could not go back to Jamaica. I could not go back to Africa. I could not go *home*. They had left me no such place.'

'But you have a family? Are they not your home?'

'That is not the same. John Wedderburn, he came home. When I think of the grievous wrong he did me and all those other people on his plantations, it makes me angry even now that he, who was a rebel against his country, should be welcomed back. Even the Government call him Sir John these days, though they took the title away from his father. But as for me, once they had used me as a symbol of their justice, they did not care about me as a man.'

I said, 'Perhaps that is what freedom is. People do not care, they don't see you any more, because you *are* free.'

'How could they not see me?' he said. 'Look at me. They still don't care about all those others, the ones making them rich. They do not see *them*. They had to take notice of me when I stood out among them. But once that was over, well, you are right, I became invisible.'

'Like all the other free men and women of Scotland,' I said.

'No,' was his reply. 'Invisibility is not freedom if you are black. I'll tell you what it is to be black and invisible in this country: it is the proof that they choose not to see us. They want us growing sugar for them in Jamaica, but they do not want us here.'

I was much saddened by all this bile. I felt it demeaned him. I felt that his freedom had festered like a wound, had not healed him.

'No, Mr Knight,' I said, 'I cannot agree. When I came to Scotland, I came because I had met good Scots people in America, and I came knowing I would be safe here from kidnap, from enslavement, which was ever a threat to me there. But I was a free man. Now all men here are safe, whatever their colour or condition – because of *you*. They set you free, Mr Knight, and that ought to make this place special to you.'

He only sneered, and said, 'Am I supposed to feel grateful for the honour and the riches they have heaped on me?'

'No, but feel grateful for the bounty of God,' I said. 'I don't believe I am invisible to them, as you say, but if I were, what of it? When I was in Paisley I was a weaver, like other weavers. When I go back there, I will be a weaver again. I will be among friends. If times are good or hard, I will prosper or suffer as a weaver, the same as the rest – not as a black man. They are good people. This is a good country for people like us.'

'I grant you,' he said, 'there are some good people here, some who helped me then and some who are friends to me now; but there are good and bad people everywhere. Every country has its share of evil men, and Scotland is no different. Scotland has been good to you, you say. Let me tell you what Scotland has been to me. It has been the source of my tormentors and the wellspring of my torment.'

I could not persuade him out of this mood, and I wondered why he chose to sit in this place, to savour his old triumph, since it seemed to bring him no happiness. We spoke a little more, and had more rum, for which he offered to pay but then found that he had not enough money. I was just able to pay the reckoning, though it put an end to our stay at Mr Williamson's, and we went back out on to the street. I asked him if he still lived in Dundee, and he said, 'We've not been there some years.' I took it from this that he lived nearer to Edinburgh, with his wife and family, but the truth is he never gave a hint of why he was there that day, nor where he was living, and that was fourteen years ago.

We parted then, with another shake of the hand, and I felt again that odd harsh texture of his palm. Then he continued walking up the High Street, almost as if he and I had never stepped aside for an hour to have our talk. I thought of what he had said, that we were invisible, and it gave me the fanciful notion that I had not met with him at all, that he was an illusion. I was much disturbed by this, and went up the Castlehill and stood on the ramparts looking over the city, turning over in my mind all that he had said.

I felt that, had I known I was going to meet Mr Knight before I did, I would have been filled with a great expectation of meeting a contented, proud, grateful and courageous man. Well, I do not doubt that the pride and courage were there, but gratitude and contentment were not. I felt a disappointment that this was the case.

I was so moved by this that I lingered at the Castle well into the afternoon, and it made me late for rejoining Mr Clerk. He was not angry, however, when I explained what had happened. He said, 'Well, Peter, perhaps he needed to be thrawn to achieve what he did. You are naturally a cheerful and optimistic fellow and so think others are always downcast. Mr Knight may be happier than you think. There's many of us Scots are happiest when we are at our most miserable. Perhaps he has simply become a native.'

It was a joke, of course, but I cannot help but think that there may have been a truth in it. Mr Clerk often made such pithy and interesting observations.

I find, sir, having given all the information I can recall anent Mr Joseph Knight, and as my friend Mr Tannahill has for some while now been obliged to rest his pen and stretch his fingers between sentences, it is time to end this very long letter. I fear I have not helped you in your quest, but I am, for myself, pleased to discover that it has enabled me to unburden my mind of many thoughts and impressions which had long lain dormant there, and which I had seldom considered in recent years. Mr Tannahill declares that the story is most interesting, and reminds me that Mr Robert Burns, the late poet, in whose memory he intends to establish a club here in Paisley, penned a touching song in which a slave laments being torn from the sweet shore of Senegal and sent to Virginia. I, a native of Virginia, came to Scotland of my own will, and Mr Knight, against his, from Africa by way of the plantations of the Indies. Mr Tannahill reminds me also that Burns was about to leave Scotland for those plantations when his muse burst upon the Edinburgh scene, assuring him of literary fame. One wonders how such a man could possibly have acted as the oppressor's lieutenant: Mr Tannahill is of the opinion that either he would have been on the first boat home, or he would have begun a rebellion among the Negroes. He wrote the lament, apparently, in Dundee, at which place I trust this will find you. Such are the many strands which connect us all together.

I could never say I was a friend of Mr Knight, but we were acquainted, however briefly, and should you ever meet with him, I would be obliged to you for reminding him of that acquaintance, and of the deep conversation he once had with his fellow man, and fellow African,

Peter Burnet.

IV

Knight

FOR BLACK RIVER AND SAVANNA LA MAR, JAMAICA, *to call at Madeira.*
The Coppered Ship AJAX, *Alexander Maclaurin Master, is now ready to*
take goods on board, and will sail in November. For freight or passage
apply to BEGBIE & MILNE.

N.B. Tradesmen, Husbandmen, &c, will meet with good encouragement to
go by the above ship. Leith, Sept 24, 1802

CALEDONIAN MERCURY, 9 OCTOBER 1802

JAMAICA JULY 24

The French have abandoned the island of St Domingo to the blacks, who
now reign victoriously there, and hold out a dreadful example to this
colony. And, accordingly, a few days ago, a conspiracy was discovered
in a miraculous manner among the negroes of this island. A slave having
displeased his master, was sent to the house of correction. His companions
knowing he was in the secret of their plot, and fearing he might confess,
sent him some victuals which were poisoned. The unsuspecting negro ate of
the victuals, when finding the poison beginning to operate, and knowing
whence it came, enraged at the treachery of his companions, he confessed
the plot which they had laid to set fire to Kingston, and massacre every
white inhabitant.

If they had succeeded in this, their intention seems to have been the
extermination of all the whites in the island. Some of them have already
paid the forfeiture of their lives, and we are now quiet, but still under
apprehensions.

The inhabitants of this island have reason to curse the day they ever
received the fugitive French blacks from St Domingo, for they have
poisoned the minds of our blacks with their revolutionary principles. These
things, combined with the war, have depreciated the value of negro and
landed property.

CALEDONIAN MERCURY, 1 SEPTEMBER 1803

Dundee, 24 June 1803

'Noo, Mr Jamieson, ye're a bit afore yoursel there, I'm thinkin.'

Betty gently but firmly removed her employer's hand from her waist, where he had placed it almost unconsciously, as if it were something he did every morning when she set down the coffee pot. Archibald Jamieson rather sheepishly apologised.

'Whit are ye sorry for?' she demanded. 'If ye didna want tae touch me, ye shouldna hae done it.'

'It was a liberty,' he said.

'Aye, it was, but dae ye wish ye hadna taen it?'

'No, but –'

'Weel, dinna say ye're sorry if ye're no.' A line had been crossed, or a barrier removed. Betty pulled up one of the other chairs and plumped herself down on it; looked him in the eye.

'It's early days yet, Mr Jamieson,' she said. 'The puir mistress is scarce oot the hoose. No that she would be surprised – or even fashed, I would say. But there's nae rush.'

'I should be ashamed o mysel,' he said, 'but I'm no.'

'And whit for should ye be?' she said. 'Ye're a man, wi a man's lusts. Dae ye think I hinna noticed? But I'm nae fool, Mr Jamieson, and I'll no be taen for ane. I'll look efter the laddies till they're awa, and yoursel, and syne we'll see whit comes o it. There's a few things we would need tae settle, though.'

She lifted the pot, and poured out his coffee. He stared at her as if she were performing a magic trick.

'Whit things?'

'Ye would need tae gie up your freen in Pirie's Land afore I would coontenance onything.'

He grew wider-eyed still. Had she been spying on him? Good God, had Janet known too, and never said a word? He felt himself flush. Betty might say there was no rush, but to him things seemed to be moving very fast indeed.

'It is done already,' he muttered.

'Aye, we'll see,' she said.

'No, truly.'

'Weel, there's ither things I winna coontenance at aw,' Betty said. 'Nae bairns, for a start.'

'Nae bairns?'

'Aye. Ye're a guid faither but ye're no needin mair. I've stayed oot o childbed ten year and I'm no gettin intae it noo, no for ony man. That is a tribulation I amna willin tae thole, and I ken hoo tae avoid it. Nae wedlock either. I ken whit happens then: awthing that's mine becomes yours, and naething that's yours becomes mine unless ye're deid. That's no richt, it's no equitable. As we are, we ken whaur we stand ilk wi ither. So, plenty o time tae see whit it is we're baith wantin, if we're wantin it at aw.'

She got up, clapped him lightly on the shoulder and left the room. Archibald Jamieson stared at the steaming cup of coffee, which eventually he lifted and sipped tentatively. He was not sure what he had started, but it appeared, whatever it was, that Betty had taken the matter clean out of his hands.

Janet had died three months before – surely, he thought, trying to justify himself, a more decent interval than Betty's 'scarce oot the hoose'. She had clung on longer than anyone expected, till she was little more than a reed. Only in the last week had she been unable to speak, unable to do anything in fact. Horribly, those last few months had been the happiest of their marriage.

Still, as Betty had said when she went to wash and lay Janet out, 'naebody ever raised a smile by girnin at life'. Jamieson had been hard at work since, the elder boy had finished school and found a clerical post with a shipping merchant, the younger had a summer job at the harbour where his brother could keep half an eye on him. And Archie had been tolerably happy, in spite of his loss. They had put the new, late Mrs Jamieson in the ground at the Howff and, ever since, he had felt that he was living in the warm afterglow of their many conversations and the evenings he had sat reading to her. His mind, and then his hand, had turned to Betty only in the last few days.

Other things had kept him occupied. Ten days ago Sir John Wedderburn of Ballindean died after a long decline. Today he too was to be buried in the Howff graveyard, and Jamieson intended to go along and watch the proceedings. He had no real expectations, but he did wonder if by any chance a black man might turn up at the grave. To do what, though? Weep beside it or piss into it – Archie slurped his coffee, laughing – one or the other.

There was that slight possibility, because Archie now believed that Joseph Knight was not far away, that he might very well have heard of the death of his former master. The whole business seemed to require a *coup de grâce* of some description, the 'melting blow' as the slaughtermen called it, and only Knight could deliver it. But then, maybe he already had, twenty-five years earlier.

The previous week, Archie Jamieson had indeed paid a visit to his friend in Pirie's Land, after a long absence. She had not been best pleased to see him – he had become most irregular since his wife took ill, she had told him insensitively. 'I didna come tae be scauldit,' he had retorted. 'I came tae say I wouldna be back.' This was a lie, but one that became a truth as soon as he uttered it. They parted without a transaction taking place.

To make up for it, and to nurse his injured pride, he took himself down to Nannie's stinking pit, and drank half a pint of whisky. He had not been in there since his session with Aeneas MacRoy. The place was as dark and foul as ever. He took a seat in a corner and began to work his way through the whisky, still wondering if Janet could have known about Pirie's Land.

A few surly-looking men were also in Nannie's shop, crowded around the makeshift gantry, and Jamieson thought he recognised one of them. This always bothered him, for a half-remembered face coming out of the past could mean trouble, especially in a place like Nannie's. Eventually he placed the man, and relaxed. It was an old weaver from the Hilltown, an informer who was usually too drunk to realise he was informing. Archie had not seen him for two or three years, and had no intention of renewing the acquaintance, but the man caught his eye and, recognising him as someone who used to buy him drink, slid over to his table.

'Aye, Chae,' Jamieson said.

'Aye, sir,' said Chae. 'You ken me, and I feel . . . I feel I should ken you. Would ye spare us some o your whisky?'

'No,' said Jamieson, 'I wouldna. No unless ye can tell me something I want tae hear.'

Chae looked hard at him, seemed to place him. 'Ah, noo I hae ye. Whit is it ye want tae hear?'

'I dinna ken.'

'Weel, hoo can I tell it ye then?'

Jamieson shook his head – the man was destroyed with drink. 'I'm no wantin tae ken onything,' he said. 'Lea me alane, Chae.'

But Chae had now got it into his head that there must be some nugget of information that would earn him a drink. 'Noo whit micht it be?' he said half into himself, as though he had been set a riddle. Then, after a minute: 'Eh, I ken. The spinners at Lochee are restless.'

'They're aye restless.'

Chae gave him an absurd *significant* look. 'There's a boat o strange men pit in at the Ferry wi foreign accents. They're wantin tae buy whisky and ither things. They micht be Frenchies.'

'They are Welsh.'

'Ach, weel. Oh, I ken, I ken. Sir John Wedderburn's deid.'

'That was in the paper yesterday.'

Chae looked dejected. Then, brightening, he tried again. 'I'll tell ye something I ken *wasna* in the paper yesterday.'

Jamieson laughed. 'How, Chae? Ye canna read.'

'I used to ken auld Wedderburn's neger.'

Jamieson coughed, trying not to show any interest. 'Is that richt, Chae? Weel, ye'll no hae been the only ane.'

'Ah, but I kent him better. He was mairrit on my guidsister.'

All this time Chae had been hotching, half leaning on the table, torn between sitting down, in the vague hope of being offered a drink, and returning to his cronies at the counter, who were probably dispatching his share of whatever was being drunk there. Jamieson pointed at the bench next to himself – 'Sit doun, Chae' – and called Nannie over. 'Anither half-pint o cask, and anither gless,' he ordered, and she shuffled off to fetch them. The other men's interest was aroused by the fact that Chae had found a new, or old, acquaintance, and one of them broke away to investigate. Jamieson warned him off with a murderous look. When Nannie returned he gave her a further instruction. 'Keep that pack ower there, Nannie. The first ane that comes within reach o me, I'll break his fuckin heid.'

He was pleased with the way it came out – it made him sound much harder than he really was. Aeneas MacRoy would have been proud of him.

Chae's hand strayed towards the jug and glass. 'Aye, on ye go,' Jamieson said. 'Tell me aboot the neger.'

'A wicked man, a wicked man,' Chae said, gulping back whisky. 'He bedded my wife's sister and gied her black bairns.'

'Why was he wicked?'

'Weel, he was black.'

'That made him wicked?'

'He didna like me. He was a cauld, thrawn craitur.'

'When did ye last see him?'

'Oh . . .' Chae stopped himself, looked cunning, suddenly aware that his answer might stop the flow of whisky. 'A while syne.'

'Years?'

Chae seized the jug and filled his glass to the brim. He drank greedily. 'Aye. Efter the trial.'

'Naebody was on trial, Chae. It was a civil case.'

Chae gave a rasping laugh. 'Oh, was it? I think it wasna very civil. Wedderburn was on trial for slave-driving and the neger was on trial for . . . for being a neger.'

Jamieson shrugged. There was no arguing with that. 'So ye've no seen Joseph Knight for twenty-five year?'

'Oh, no as lang as that. They bade here a while, but he never likit work.'

'If he was kin o yours, that's nae surprise.'

This was too subtle for Chae, who was more interested in getting to the bottom of the jug before Jamieson stopped him.

'Whaur did they gae, then?'

'I dinna ken, and I dinna care. Tae the deil, I would say. They were baith a bad lot, the neger and Annie. They never likit me.'

'Och, weel, Chae,' Jamieson said, and took back the jug. 'Ye're tellin me naething.'

'Dinna ask me then. Ask the auld mither.'

'Whit auld mither?'

337

'Kate Thomson. Annie's mither. My wife's mither. My wife's deid but Kate bides in the Hilltoun yet. She'll ken whaur they gaed.'

Chae earned himself the rest of the jug with this bit of information, once he had told Jamieson where to find the old woman. 'But dinna tell her I sent ye,' he warned. 'She disna like me either. And dinna lea it ower lang – she's an auld, auld bitch.'

The cottage Kate Thomson had once shared with her daughter and grandchild was now in a state perilously near to collapse. Old Mrs Thomson, who by now was in her eighties, had been joined by another woman, perhaps twenty years her junior, and between them they just managed to live without starving or freezing. But it was a life so close to the edge of human existence that to Jamieson they did not seem quite human when he entered the cottage. Both were covered in so many layers of clothing that it was as if they were composed entirely of rags, and only their faces, and their fingers projecting like twigs from a hedge, proved that this was not the case. Even though it was midsummer, the place smelt damp and was as dark as November. Kate Thomson, still working the treadle of her spinning-wheel, would not stop until Jamieson offered her some coins to buy her a respite.

'There's naething in spinnin ony mair,' she said. 'The mills are takkin it awa frae the likes o us. But whit else can I dae? Sixty year I hae been spinnin. I hae seen Tam Ritchie in his grave and a wheen ither folk that should hae lived ayont me. I'm hauf deif and three-pairts blin, but I dinna need my een for this work ony mair. I could dae it in my sleep. In fact I *dae* dae it in my sleep. Whiles I dinna ken if I am wakin or dreamin. If I stop noo, I'll dee.'

A few months ago death might have seemed to Archibald Jamieson like the better option, but now he found her resilience impressive. She and the other woman, who never uttered a syllable the whole time he was there, were surrounded by piles of flax, and the floor was covered in wasted scraps of the stuff.

'I am lookin for somebody,' Jamieson said cautiously. 'I thocht ye would ken whaur they micht be?'

'I dinna ken onybody ony mair,' Kate Thomson said. 'They're aw deid.'

'No,' Jamieson said. 'I dinna think so. I'm lookin for your dochter, Annie. And for her man, Joseph.'

Kate became still. She peered hard at Jamieson. Eventually she said, 'Wha are ye that ye want tae ken aboot them. Let them be. They had trouble enough in their time.'

'Dae ye ever see them?'

'Na,' she said. 'No for mony a year.'

'But they still live?'

She was silent again, thinking. Just as he was about to repeat the question, she spoke. 'I heard John Wedderburn is deid.'

'Aye, he is,' Jamieson said.

'If he'd died years syne, they micht hae lived better,' she said. 'Are ye frae him?'

It was on the tip of Jamieson's tongue to say no, when he thought that this would only lead her to ask what his business was with them. 'I am tae cairry the news o his death tae them,' he said ambiguously.

'Oh.' Again, she paused to think. 'Will it be worth onything tae them?'

'I canna say,' he said.

At first she would not be drawn on where they might be. But the longer he sat the more she seemed to trust him, or perhaps it was the addition of a few more pennies into her hand. 'When ye hae been a prisoner for years,' she said, 'and ye come oot intae sunlicht, it blins ye. Ye canna thole it. And naebody understands. Joseph tried, aye he tried, but it was nae use. He had tae tak cover again. Whaur would ye gang, sir? Eh? If ye wantit back oot the sunlicht and tae be amang folk that understood? He wasna the first black man that cam oot the dark. Ye're a clever chiel, I can tell. Work it oot. Whaur would ye gang?'

'That is whit I need tae ken,' he said.

'Wemyss,' she said. 'I dinna ken jist whaur it is but it's somewhaur in Fife. Look there for Joseph Knight.'

Coming out into the street, Jamieson had found himself dazzled by the day, and his head rotten with the effects of Nannie's whisky. Kate Thomson's words had rattled around in there too. The remark about Joseph not being the first had puzzled him, and so had the name Wemyss. It had reminded him of something in all the information he had accumulated on the case over the previous eighteen months. At last he had hit on what she must mean. A case that John Maclaurin had been involved in, many years earlier. A slave called Davie Spens, the parish of Wemyss. And he had thought of something else: something Peter Burnet had written about the texture of Knight's hands.

Today was Friday. Tomorrow, he was going on a journey across the Tay, and into Fife.

First, though, there was the Wedderburn funeral. They were putting Sir John at the foot of the elaborate tomb he had erected to his wife Margaret, the first Lady Wedderburn. The interment was a family affair. Nevertheless, such a local grandee could not be buried without attracting public interest. Numerous indwellers of Dundee gathered to watch the cortège enter the city, and, at a respectful distance, they also stood in the Howff itself. Among them was Archibald Jamieson.

It was a fine, bright day. The firth was skinkling, and the town lay like a contented dog in the heat. The Wedderburns arrived in a procession of carriages made mournful with crape. The horses drawing the hearse were decked with black plumes. Jamieson was surprised to see the female Wedderburns in attendance. He tried to work out the various sons and daughters and cousins: David, the eldest son and new laird of Ballindean; Margaret and Jean, his sisters; then the half-brothers (two of them – a third was in Jamaica) and half-sisters, Maria, Susan, Louisa and Anne. There was a silver-haired man of about seventy, handsome and proud-looking, whom Jamieson took to be Uncle James from Inveresk; and a couple of young men who were probably his sons. Lady Alicia was there in her black dress and veil, and behind her the stooped, weary figure of Aeneas MacRoy. There were others too, perhaps husbands and wives of some of these, so that the party gathered round the grave numbered more than twenty. A clergyman was in attendance, but the ceremony was kept brief – there would have been a full service at Ballindean. Although the Penal Acts against Episcopalianism had been repealed some ten years previously, following the death of Charles Edward Stewart, the popular mood was still not entirely conducive to public displays of any faith other than that of the Kirk.

Afterwards, the family party broke up into smaller groups. Some of them stood quietly at the grave, others moved away, talking a little, wandering among the gravestones. The beautiful weather seemed to make them all reluctant to get back in the carriages. Most of the onlookers drifted. Jamieson walked over to the small, simple stone that marked the grave of both the first Mrs Jamieson and the second. He stood there, head uncovered, his presence legitimised by that stone, and waited. He had spotted Susan Wedderburn walking by herself in that direction, along one of the paths that criss-crossed the Howff. She was almost upon him before she saw him.

'My sympathies,' he said, bowing his bare head to her.

Her bonnet had a little veil but he could see through it that her eyes were red.

'Do you mean that?' she asked.

'I dae.'

'Then I am grateful to you for coming.'

Her presumption nettled him. 'I would hae been here onywey,' he said.

She looked at the stone in front of them. The dates of the second Mrs Jamieson, beloved wife of Archibald, were freshly cut below those of the first.

'Oh,' Susan said, 'I see. You have suffered a loss too. A very recent loss.'

'Aye, weel. How are ye?'

'I am tired,' she said. She turned to see if anyone was watching them. 'It was not, of course, unexpected, but so much has happened of late. I am desperately tired.'

'I ken,' he said. 'But it will get better.'

'I am sorry for you,' she said, indicating the stone.

'Dinna be, miss. I am perfectly fine.'

They stood together looking at the grave. It occurred to Jamieson that seen from a distance they could be father and daughter.

'I didna think you or your sisters would be here,' he said. 'It isna usual.'

'We insisted,' she said. 'Along with Mama, so they could not refuse us.'

'Whit did ye dae, in the end, wi thon book?' he asked after a while.

'In the end?' she said. 'In the end I did what I said I would do. I burnt it.' He sighed. Before he could make a comment she went on, 'But I also did what you advised. I put it back where I had found it.'

'Then ye changed your mind again?'

'No,' she said, 'not really. Papa and I destroyed it together.'

'I dinna understand.'

'I found him with it a few weeks after I put it back. He was very ill by then. He had been about to throw it on the fire but he did not have the strength. I made him sit down and we talked about it. I told him I had read it.'

'He must hae been furious.'

'No, he was beyond fury by then. At first I thought he was going to weep. I had never seen him weep. But he did not. He asked me to forgive him.'

'For whit? For whit he did tae Joseph Knight?'

She frowned. 'No, no. He had no remorse for Joseph Knight. He was sorry that he had not told me about my poor uncle Sandy.'

'Poor Uncle Sandy whase journal sae disgusted ye?'

'He said I must not feel disgust for Sandy. It was not Sandy's fault that he was weak and sick. Jamaica was a cruel and hard place. They were bairns out there, my father said, all of them, and they behaved in their own different ways, and some survived and some did not. My father said if he had not fixed his mind on coming home he would have been like Sandy. "I saw myself in him," he said, "and him in me. If I had weakened, none of us would be here now." His speech was not very clear but that was what he was telling me.'

'That he felt guilty about their lives in Jamaica?'

'No.' She sounded surprised, as if he had completely misunderstood. 'That he had made the best of a bad situation, and come through it.'

'And ye believed him? Ye accepted whit he said?'

'Yes,' she said, 'I did. And I do. He was my father. I felt that I had no right to judge him. We took the journal between us and consigned it to the flames.'

'Ye've changed your tune, miss. There was a time no lang syne ye believed in goodness.'

'If you remember, you told me that that was because I did not know the world. Perhaps I know it better now. Or have you become *less* wise?' He was aware of a growing coolness between them, even though they remained just two feet apart. There seemed to be resentment on both sides.

'Then ye dinna think Joseph Knight is sae heroic ony mair?' He heard the jibe in his voice, was surprised at its force. She heard it too.

'He cannot be heroic. He is dead. Do you know why my father employed you to search for him?'

'Tell me.'

'To make certain. He did not expect you to find Mr Knight. He wanted to be sure that he had outlasted him.'

'So that he could think that he had beaten him efter aw?'

'To *know* that he had beaten him.'

She spoke in such a flat tone that Jamieson could not tell whether she was reporting what her father had actually told her or simply voicing her own opinion. He turned to catch her eye, but was distracted by a movement beyond her. 'We are observed,' he said.

Susan turned too. Aeneas MacRoy, standing alone among the graves, was staring at them, and though he was some way off his face was dark with anger. Susan stared back impassively, then turned away from him. Archie saw MacRoy walk stiffly over towards the white-haired old man, who was talking to one of Susan's sisters.

'Would you really have been here anyway?' Susan asked. 'Or were you expecting . . . *him*?'

'I come here maist days,' Jamieson said. 'But aye, I did wonder if he micht appear.'

'He is dead,' she said again. 'I am sure of it.'

Jamieson stopped himself from replying. He could see that whether he thought Knight was alive or not did not matter to her. Her father was dead and therefore so must Knight be. He saw that Joseph had only ever lived, in her mind, because of her father.

'What is happening now?' she asked, seeing him look past her again. Aeneas MacRoy, pointing in their direction, had said something to the older man, who had turned his gaze towards them. MacRoy said something else and set off, but had taken only

343

a few paces when he was called back. Slowly, the white-haired man began to stroll towards them, alone.

'I am tae be investigated, I think,' Jamieson said.

'How novel for you,' Susan said. She glanced behind her. 'My uncle James.'

'You are merely paying your respects, as am I,' Jamieson said.

'Quite. Do you not think he is very distinguished looking?'

'He looks better than he did in that picture in the library.'

She raised her eyebrows, as if to indicate that his remark was in poor taste. 'I discovered the truth about that, too,' she said. 'It was not my father who had Joseph Knight taken out of the painting. It was Uncle Sandy. He took an aversion to Joseph near the end, and removed him. Papa said it was the best thing he ever did to that painting. He said he would certainly not have kept it there if Knight had still been in it.'

'The mystery is solved, then,' Jamieson said. He felt a thousand miles from her now. He was tempted just to walk away, but he was standing in front of Mary and Janet's grave and he did not wish to move. 'Here is your uncle now.'

She did not take the hint and go. 'I may go to live with him,' she said. 'At Inveresk. My brother David won't want two spinster sisters haunting Ballindean for ever.'

She sounded very definite about that number. 'Two?' he asked.

'Maria and I. Louisa married Sir John Hope in February – I told you that was to happen. And Margaret married Philip Dundas just a month past. But the strangest thing is, Anne is to be married soon also. She is to marry Sir John Hope too, just as the spaewife said she would.'

He frowned. 'How can that be?'

'*Another* Sir John Hope – of Pinkie. He is a neighbour of our uncle's. So it seems neither of my sisters was telling a lie.'

Now that she was talking of these other family matters, she seemed more animated. Safe matters, Jamieson thought: she has settled for safety. Had it been a game for her all along?

James Wedderburn, unsmiling, approached them, his cane tapping dryly on the stones of the path. 'Susan, we shall be leaving in a moment. Who is this person?'

Archie inclined his head slightly, feeling distinctly hypocritical. 'Archibald Jamieson, sir. My sympathies tae your faimly.'

'Mr Jamieson has recently lost his wife,' Susan said, as if they had just met. 'We were exchanging condolences.'

Wedderburn glanced at the headstone, seemed satisfied. 'Very well. But you must take your leave of him now, my dear. Give me your arm back to the carriage.'

'One moment, Uncle.' He nodded, glanced curiously at Jamieson, then stepped away a few yards. Whatever MacRoy had said, Jamieson must have seemed to pose no great danger to his niece.

Susan put out her gloved hand and Archie took it in farewell. 'Goodbye,' she said. 'We shall not meet again.' Then, almost in a whisper, but very precisely, as though she needed his answer also to be precise, the truth, she added, 'Did you love her?'

Archibald Jamieson had come a long way in the last few months. He could not dissemble in front of Janet, dead though she was. 'Aye,' he said. 'I did. I didna think I did, but I loved her greatly.'

'I loved my father,' she said. 'That is all that matters, isn't it?'

He felt as though she had somehow made him an accomplice in something he did not agree with. Before he could object, she had let go his hand and was walking to her uncle. She put her arm through his. Together they set off towards the waiting carriages.

'Goodbye,' Archie said, but Susan Wedderburn was already too far away to hear.

Wemyss, 26 June 1803

He woke and lay for a minute, panicking and alone, until the sounds inside and outside his head sorted themselves, and he knew he was not alone after all. Outside: Ann, breathing regularly beside him; a brief skelter of a mouse in the wall; Andrew, his son, coughing in the other room. Inside: animal screeches; sailors talking in strange tongues; some men arguing; another weeping. When he identified this last sound he bit his lip, put fingers to his face, found it wet. Again. Always, again. This was how it was with him.

It must have been two, three o'clock. A wee laddie had said to him yesterday, 'Man, ye're black as the howe o the nicht.' He had laughed and said, 'Ah, but whaur does the coal stop and me stert?' And now here he was, in the howe o the nicht, and it was as black as himself coming home from the pit. It made no difference whether he had his eyes shut or open. Pit-mirk, and silent as a kirkyard.

He thought ahead to the day that would soon come. Again. Always. Years and years of howking away at the rock. As if somehow it would reveal something buried, hidden by other years, thousands and thousands of them. Down there where there was no light, the coal sometimes gleamed with a brightness that could be paradise breaking through clouds.

Paradise. Lots of the people in Jamaica, they believed when they died they would be going back to Africa. They said they wouldn't mind dying. They looked forward to it, they'd welcome it. A good end to their bad story; going home again.

His story was different. He had no idea where he would be going when he died. That was another thing that had been taken from him – the end. Just as the beginning had been taken.

Just lately he had been getting glimpses of a beginning. Away back, another place. Dream sightings that woke him in the night, sudden flashes in the middle of the day; in the depths of the

346

coal-dark day. There were huts with gardens, and low clay walls that separated them; fields where a boy stood scaring off birds; a hot dry wind huffing over grassland; a green river sliding through great trees thick with the screams of . . . birds, monkeys? He didn't know, didn't remember. For this was the beginning of a story that had never happened, that had come to a sudden and complete stop.

There was a woman who he understood must have been his mother. But he could not see her face, and that blindness coiled a deep pain in his belly, left him breathless with regret. His father was not there at all. He had often thought that his father must have gone the same road before him, the road that he himself was taken on. Because why else could he not remember the least thing about him?

But he would never know. His father was an empty space.

Africa. These glimpses, these dreams, sometimes woke him less gently than tonight. They could cause him to moan and thrash and shake with grief. He would come to with Ann leaning over him, trying to calm him. Africa was repossessing him after more than forty years. But he had no distinct sense of what Africa was like. For years he had had to lean on the memories of others, people taken when they were older than he had been. Now, away from them, he had only dreams.

This was what he thought: that place – home, whatever he'd have called it – could not have been too far from the coast. Far enough that he had never seen the sea until he saw it, but not so far that he, a young boy, could not be made to walk there. How many hours' or days' travel? He did not know. He had no recollection of making that journey – whether it started with him in a sack, whether he tried to run away, whether he was chained to others, whether he was beaten or starved or threatened with murder. The thing he did remember was the sea, and the ship like a great bony bird out on the water, the feathers of its many wings wrapped tight on the bones. Hot golden sand, and a boat that carried him out to the ship. But even this . . . he was not sure. Maybe he was not remembering at all. Maybe he *thought* he recalled these things because of all he had since heard and read.

Ann said he did not remember because he chose not to. It was

347

blanked out of himself because what had happened to a boy of ten or eleven was too appalling for the mind to hold. She was maybe right, except that it was never a question of choosing, and except that others had not forgotten. Memory was not about choice. That was the time when choice was taken from him, from all of them, seemingly for ever.

And it was the time when life split for a while, between pictures and sounds. In his head, thinking back there, the pictures were disjoined from the sounds. He saw people speak but he did not hear what they said. White men. It was noise; noise that he had to make sense of by watching, guessing, by the interpreting and making of gestures. Many of the Africans were from different parts, different communities and peoples, and he could only understand a little of what they said. Most of them did not say much. It was the white men, whether they shouted or said nothing, who were in charge. When he imagined them now, he could hear the things they must have said.

One night recently he had had a very bad dream and Ann had been there to comfort him when he woke; then he could not sleep again. He had sat up in bed, calmed by the lie of her head on his shoulder, her hair greying but still fine, and the tiny kiss she had given to his collarbone before she drifted off. He felt that kiss there like a butterfly at rest. But even that, and her presence, had set him wondering: he loved her, he could not imagine having found his way to where he was without her, but would he have loved a black woman more? Or differently? This was a puzzle, something he thought about all the time. It made him feel guilty, and the guilt enraged him. That *he* should be made to feel guilty . . .

'I love you,' she had said, another night when the tears came. She said it often. 'Ye ken that. I'll never betray ye. I'll never dae ye hairm. But ye've tae be strang for me tae, Joseph.'

'I am strang for ye,' he had said. He had heard his voice in his chest, the words that had once been new and were now old and familiar, that he had made his, that he spoke in his own distinctive way. 'Hae I no been strang for ye thirty year? Jist in the nicht though, like noo, I dinna aye need tae be strang, div I?'

'No, lad, no,' she had said. 'Greet awa. Greet aw ye want. Ye're safe noo.'

'It's no jist me. It's aw the ithers.'

'I ken,' she had said, holding him tight.

She was strong too; he could not fault her; sometimes he wished he could. Sometimes he wished she would burst out at him, 'Dae ye think it's been easy for me? Dae ye think I hinna suffered?' *Because ye're a neger. And I stood by ye in spite o it.* If she had flung that in his face just once, he might have got an answer to his puzzle. But she never had. Not ever.

A picture. The ship had moved further along the coast, and had lain at anchor in one place for weeks, along with two more ships, while more and more people were held in a stockade at the mouth of a river. White men rowed back and forth between the stockade and the ships, bringing boatloads of prisoners out to them. Two men in each longboat sat with guns trained on their passengers.

The black men were shackled together, and put below deck. He saw himself, a boy alone, and he saw the men going down through the hatch in awkward stumbling couples, then brought up again during the day, still in chains, and made to jump and stretch their limbs. The sun beat down relentlessly on the bright reflective sea and the blistering wooden ship. The women were kept apart from the men, both below and above deck, and were not shackled in the daytime, and any children went with the women. But there were few women and fewer children, and for a long time no other boys of his age. He was small for his years: had he been any bigger, or had there been more boys to cause trouble as a group, he would have been put with the men.

Overwhelmingly this was a world of adult males, of shouts, curses, blows, the surface brutality of the white men, the submerged threat of retaliation of the black men. The whole ship trembled with anger.

The sailors let the boy – in the picture it was him and yet not him – move around fairly freely in the daytime, so long as he did not go near the edge of the ship. Once he did this and looked over at the sea below and a sailor yelled at him, thinking that he was about to go overboard. This had happened before – pairs of men with such weight of misery on them that they would let the chains sink them to the bottom of the sea, rather than live in them. The boy did not want to die, nor did he want to live on the ship. But he could not swim. The water was too far down, the shore too far away, and his home too far from the shore. Only the ship was where he could be.

There was a white man who was old enough to be one of his grandfathers – two more people he did not remember. This white sailor was tall, thin, red-eyed, his mouth half hidden by a straggle of grey, coarse beard. He always carried a short, solid, leather-sheathed cosh, attached by a strap to his right wrist. He was indifferent to the boy, seemed hardly to notice him. His mind was on other things as he and a younger crewman approached the section of the deck where the two dozen women huddled, separated from the men by a wooden barrier. The older sailor had something in his left hand which he offered to one of the women, a young one, beckoning her over. She watched cautiously, drew a little closer, and so did the watching boy. One of the other women said something and the one the sailor wanted stopped, lowered herself and looked away.

The sailor spoke. What did he say? What had he, would he have said? Forty years on, Joseph heard the fleetching, coaxing voice. He imagined the words. 'You come wi me, my darlin. It'll be better for ye on the trip ye're gaun, I swear.' She did not move, stared down at the wooden planks on which she was squatting. His words to her were a jumble of sounds. His left hand opened and was full of colours, shining things. She crept a little closer, within reach, and the sailor smiled, leant over and let the colours fall into her lap while, quite gently, he cupped the hand under her breast. She started away and his other hand, dangling the cosh, came over and seized her shoulder. 'Come, nae need tae be like that noo. You be nice wi me and I'll be nice wi you. You needna fear naething frae me.'

He slipped his hand from her breast to under her arm, and pulled her to her feet. As he did so, the watching boy sensed a movement among the men, a shift in the atmosphere, and glanced over there. The sailor felt it too and turned quickly, still gripping the girl tight. One of the African men, across the wooden barrier, had half risen from the deck – as far as his chains would allow him. There was a low murmur of protest from those around him, but the boy could not tell whether it was caused by the action of the sailor or that of their companion.

The sailor let the girl go and took half a dozen paces across to the barrier. He stretched across till his face was an inch from the face of the half-standing man. 'Dinna you flash your een at me, my son. Ye're at sea noo, this is sailors' country. My country. Ye better learn that. It's the only way life's gaun tae be worth the livin for ye, frae noo on. Ye dinna ken whit I'm sayin, div ye? But ye will, freen, ye will.' He flipped the cosh into his hand and smashed it into the black face, sending the man crashing to the deck. 'Aw white men's your maisters noo. Aw richt, my son?'

Then he turned back to the women, among whom a soft crying had begun in the wake of the blow. He seized the girl, much more roughly than before, and pulled her out from among them.

That was the start, Joseph saw. That was where the taking, the smashing, the raping, the torturing, the killing started. It started there and it would go on for years, until every single person on the ship was dead. It had gone on for centuries so why would it ever stop?

'Pick one for yourself,' the sailor said to his young companion. 'They'll dae your biddin fair enough and it's a lang haul ower the Atlantic so you may as weel get the benefit.' He saw that the other sailor was watching the prone body of the man he had struck. 'Dinna fash aboot that. That's a lesson for you as much as for him. That's whit they're like, your African. They're a kind o horse, or some ither animal ye can train up a bit. Your male neger's a docile, daicent beast when he's broke in, but ye must never forget the wildness lurkin at the back o him. When his ee lichts up like that, he's like a horse aboot tae buck or kick. That's when ye hae tae act, and act fast. It's you or him at that point, mak nae mistake aboot it. There's planters in the Indies let their negers get above themsels, they try tae treat them the same as us, and it disna work, it disna work at aw, and it makes problems for awbody – them, their neighbours *and* the negers. Teach them hoo tae see richt frae wrang and they'll choose wrang every time. There's a badness in them and ye canna get it oot, no wi books nor baptisin nor fine claes nor naething. Ye can tak them thoosands o miles across the ocean but ye canna get Africa oot o them, ye jist canna. It's in them and if ye try tae get it oot like as no ye'll get a blade in the back for your trouble.'

Joseph shifted his weight, trying to ease a slight pain in his shoulder without waking Ann. He had run that scene in his head so often that he heard the sailor like a bell now. Maybe over the years his dreams had put words in the sailor's mouth. Maybe, but he knew they were not far wrong. This was how it had been: the start of very bad times; the start of a war. And now, in this bed in a tiny cottage on another, colder coast, he felt the truth held in the sailor's evil words: Africa was in him, had always been in him.

This was a bed. No rough timber board, no bodies rank with sweat and shit fettered together in the darkness in the stinking belly of a slave ship. This was a bed. They were lying in a bed, their bed. He had slept with Ann, night after night now, for how long? Near on thirty years. And he would never get used to it, the sheer joy of the bed he shared with his wife.

This was a bed and he was Joseph Knight. He had not been Joseph then. He had been someone else. There was a time when he had hated that name, but he had made it his and no one was going to take it away now. But neither would they take away his other, older name. It was the one thing he had left from that other beginning, the one thing that was his and his alone. And he had never uttered it. Not since he was on the ship. Not since Captain Knight favoured him with his own name. He had known – a ten-year-old but he had known – that he must keep it from everyone. They could not take it if they did not know it. Not even Ann knew it.

She used to ask him, 'Whit was your name? Whit is your real name? Ye must hae an African name.' At last she wore him down, and he admitted it, he had. But it was his, and he would not give it to her. 'Dae ye no trust me?' she said. But it was not about her. It was about himself. He had to keep his name whole, away from others, away, especially, from white people. Even her. She thought hard about that for a day or two. It must have hurt her, because it surely hurt him to keep it from her. But it was necessary. Eventually she saw that. She never asked again.

He thought of a conversation he had once had, a long time ago now. A man had told him: 'People don't see you any more, because you are free.' He hadn't believed it then, and he didn't believe it now. Freedom was the very opposite, it was being seen and recognised and acknowledged and still let alone. Being named and taken as a whole. He didn't believe that this country he had ended up in was ready to dispense that kind of freedom. Not yet anyway.

Prejudice could have one eye closed, or it could be blind. Justice was sometimes depicted as blind. He wanted a country, a world, which saw with both eyes open.

That man he had met. He had forgotten his name but he had heard it again recently. Peter Burnet. Another black man. They had gone for a drink in the court house. Burnet had had on a fine velvet waistcoat and he had paid for what they drank. Joseph had told Burnet what they were – invisible – and he had been right about that too. He never saw an African face these days, not here. Even the Africa that was in his own son, Andrew, was diluted by the blood of his mother. His daughter Sarah was married and had given him a grandson who, apart from his tightly curled hair, seemed not to bear a trace of him. In another generation or two his blood would be swirling unseen and unrecognised through the veins of men and women who had never set foot furth of Scotland.

But although there were no other African faces around him he was not alone. He was surrounded by the faces of men who had also once been slaves, near as damn it. They were all around him, and when they went down to the shore and into the earth together there was a joining of their souls that was like no other feeling.

Where he had met with Burnet, that was the scene of what he used to call his triumph. The old men peering down at him and Wedderburn. Wedderburn's counsel goading him, and Maclaurin – Lord Dreghorn, dead now – holding him back. 'Steady noo, Maister Knight.' It was that 'Maister' that had saved him. Maclaurin had always treated him with respect, right from when they first met. Sometimes he would call him Maister, sometimes sir, sometimes Joseph, but there had always been politeness and respect in the address. It was the way one man ought to speak to another, when they were equals.

He remembered sitting in that room, waiting for the judges to come in. And looking across at Wedderburn. There was, briefly, a crush of finely dressed white bodies that obscured his view.

A strong smell of snuff was in the air, and wig powder, and somebody's shirt or maybe their entire linen and person could have done with a thorough wash. But Joseph hardly noticed – it was the moment that was important. An ending; maybe also a beginning. And as he thought that, it became important to see Wedderburn again, before the judges entered and the moment changed. He leaned forward and with his right arm carefully but firmly pushed aside one particularly large silk-wrapped belly, clearing a line of vision.

And there he was: Sir John Wedderburn of Ballindean. Wedderburn was staring at the ceiling, and Joseph expected to be enraged at the sight of him, proud and cold and unyielding, but it was not like that. When he saw the weary lines on Wedderburn's face, he was utterly amazed to discover in himself a feeling he never expected to have. He felt sorry for him.

Why? Because Wedderburn had lost his wife? Because he looked exhausted? No. Then why should he feel sorry for him? It flashed across his mind then: because Wedderburn had failed. Wedderburn had been planning ever since he got off the boat in Kingston: planning and scheming and preparing and building and becoming hugely rich and trying always to make everything secure. But nothing was secure. Life was a step, a second away from disaster. And he felt sorry for Wedderburn because he understood this, and Wedderburn did not.

But that feeling lasted for only a moment. For just then the court rose, and they were enemies again, one trying to beat the other.

It was a cold day but it grew hot in that courtroom. The place was thick with people, their combined breath and body heat and body smells rising to the beams under the gallery and filling up the whole room. And as Maclaurin and Dundas stepped clear to make their speeches, Joseph began to be revisited with memories of the slave ship – those same memories that he still had: the packed, chained filth and nakedness of the people; the rancid smell; the slittery mess of shit and piss and puke running back and forth with every shift of the vessel; the groans of men and the crying of women; the groans of the ship, the sounds of people dying. What terrible waste was that? – people taken for slaves who would never even reach the

354

plantations, who would be thrown overboard, waste literally, when they expired. He tried to block those sounds out and concentrate on the speeches, the fine white words being uttered on his behalf, but they would not disappear. Maclaurin finished. Dundas began. Monboddo interrupted. Then there was a pause, while Wedderburn's lawyers consulted among themselves. His own lawyers formed a huddle, discussing how they had done. Maconochie was complaining that Dundas had omitted some important point. Joseph was outwith their circle. For a minute, even Maclaurin had forgotten him.

And even Maclaurin, good and well-meaning though he was, could be insensitive. His Latin motto, designed to impress the court, hurt. His invitation to the old men to look on his client and see if he were a man or a thing, that hurt. The heat, the close air, the backs turned against him – Joseph had to get out.

He went right through the great hall, past the bookstalls and the coffee shop, out into the Parliament Close. Ann would have come down from the gallery, perhaps, would be back in there looking for him, but just now he didn't want anybody, not even her.

Outside it was wonderfully, sharply cold. There was an empty spot in a corner formed by one of the buttresses of St Giles'. He stood there, eyes closed, breathing in the fresh air, regaining control. He realised how tired he was. Tired of everything.

'Hello, Joseph.'

For a second he thought John Wedderburn had followed him out. He jumped forward, wide awake again. It was not John Wedderburn. It was his brother.

'Hot, isn't it?' James Wedderburn said, smiling. He was blocking him, so that Joseph would have to push him out of the way to leave. Joseph did not wish to touch him. 'I mean, in there,' Wedderburn said. 'Not out here. Brrr! But in there – almost as hot as Jamaica at this time of year. But it's always hot there. You've not forgotten that, have you?'

'Lea me alane.'

'You're getting a right Scotch accent, Joseph. You'd almost pass for a native.'

'I dinna wish tae speak wi ye.'

'But I wish to speak to you. And if I were you, I'd listen. For your own good.'

Joseph made as if to get past him but Wedderburn stopped him with a hand to his chest, pushed him back against the wall. And now he began to speak very hard and very fast, and there was not a trace of a smile on the handsome face any more.

'You're not thinking of going back in there, surely? That would be very foolish. Because you know what's going to happen, don't you? You're going to lose. All the fine words of Maclaurin and his cronies won't save you. They're done, finished. All that's left is the law. And that's what they do in there – law. That's all that matters. You haven't a chance. But just to make sure, we've taken a gentle line with their lordships. We don't want to alarm them. Even if they say you are not to be a slave here, we've asked them to accept that you were a slave *there*, as a point of principle. Of course my brother, your master, has said that he has no intention of sending you back to Jamaica, but he'd like to establish that he has the right to do so. They can't throw over Jamaican law any more than Jamaica can throw over Scots law.

'So my advice to you, Joseph, is to do what you're good at. Start running. Start now. Don't go back in that room. There's a ship leaving Greenock in less than a week, bound for Savanna-la-Mar. You're going to be on it if we catch you. And we will catch you. We've got your place booked already with the agents. I'd happily see you safe on board and bound for your old friends at Glen Isla. But as it happens, somebody else has volunteered to escort you.'

Now he stood aside. Across the close, standing below the statue of King Charles and staring over at them, was Aeneas MacRoy.

'I'm going back inside now, Joseph,' Wedderburn said, 'to hear the arguments against you. It's up to you whether you come in, or set off running. Maister MacRoy will keep an eye on you either way. Goodbye, Joseph.'

If it had been John Wedderburn, he might have struck him. He might have elbowed him out of the way and gone back to the court. But James Wedderburn was different. There was a fire in him. He held you with the intensity of his look. He did not pretend.

For a moment Joseph thought he was going to run. For more than a moment. He began to walk towards the High Street. At the corner of the kirk he stopped and turned. MacRoy was behind him, at a safe distance. Joseph took another twenty paces.

Then he stopped. This was exactly what the Wedderburns wanted. They wanted him to act like a slave, they expected it. Whereas Maclaurin expected him to act like a human being.

Joseph turned round. He broke into a run. As he passed MacRoy, heading towards the Great Door, he dropped his shoulder and caught him a glancing blow, sending him staggering to one side. Joseph was furious: with himself, with MacRoy, with the Wedderburns. Mostly, though, he was furious at the thought of the Court of Session deciding his fate without him. Which was why, when the judges looked askance at his reappearance, he had stared back at them without flinching, refusing to be cowed.

He did not see either MacRoy or James Wedderburn afterwards, when it was all over. He never knew if John Wedderburn had countenanced what they had done, and he did not want to discuss it with Maclaurin. Along with Dundas and Maconochie and Annie, and Mr Davidson down from Perth and a number of other well-wishers, Maclaurin insisted on celebrating the victory at Indian Peter's, and raising a glass to him and to freedom. And Boswell was there too, Auchinleck's son, fretting at the edge of the circle, and complaining to Maclaurin because in their pleadings none of them appeared to have used Dr Johnson's argument, that Boswell had gone to considerable trouble to take down when last in London. And Maclaurin said, calmly enough, 'Och, Jamie, we used some o it, I'm sure. Onywey, oor arguments had enough weight without bringin in the English, did ye no think?' Everybody laughed except Bozzy, who thought that was a remark that did little honour to Samuel Johnson, who had been much taken with Maclaurin, did he not remember? At this Maclaurin grew quite short with his friend, and said, 'Whit would ye hae had us say, James? Should we hae gien their lordships Johnson's Oxford toast: "Here's tae the next insurrection in the West Indies"? Dae ye think that would hae clinched it?' Everybody else roared, and then Maconochie, seeing the other side coming out past them, raised that toast anyway, very loud: 'Here's tae the next insurrection in the West Indies!' And of course several of them, Joseph and Annie the loudest, repeated it, and they all, with the exception of Henry Dundas, who looked embarrassed, drank.

John Wedderburn was subjected to this as he and his counsel went past, and he could not ignore it. He refused to acknowledge Joseph, refused even to look at him. Instead, he turned on Henry Dundas, who was nearest to him. 'You are a rank hypocrite, sir. You attacked me, who never mistreated that Negro, and you attacked slavery, yet I do not see you move against it elsewhere, where it matters. Why are you not calling for abolition in the House of Commons? You accuse *me* of expediency, yet it seems you are one man here and quite another in London.'

Dundas tried to brush it off – 'Mr Wedderburn, we had aw thae arguments jist noo in court' – but Wedderburn would not move on. Cullen's gentle attempts to persuade him only further infuriated him.

'Mr Cullen, I am done with you, sir, apart from your fee.' Cullen held up his hands, glanced at Dundas and shrugged, then walked off. Wedderburn stayed. 'Well, Mr Dundas, are you to present a bill in the House to wind up the rest of my property?'

Dundas shook his head. 'Mr Wedderburn, I am not blind to the situation in the West Indies. I am not unaware of the wealth that comes frae them, or the advantages they bring tae this country. But that is a different maitter frae whit we hae resolved this morning. I am a practical kind of man.'

'As I said, you are a hypocrite.'

Wedderburn stormed out. Those were the last words Joseph ever heard from him.

All this was pouring through his mind as he lay in the half-light. Although the dreams of Africa came often to him, he seldom thought of Wedderburn these days, but he was thinking of him now because he had heard that he was dead.

Yesterday, Saturday, he and Andrew had come out of the pit as usual with the other men. Their bodies were aching and soaked from hours of toil; soaked, too, from the water they had laboured in up to their knees after the steam-driven pump broke down. The mine shafts were down by the shore: one of them, the main one, went down a hundred and eighty feet, out under the sea. This was the shaft Joseph, his son and another sixty or seventy men had been working twelve hours a day since the early spring.

Men had been howking coal out of the earth at Wemyss for hundreds of years; first scratching at it on the surface, then sinking bell pits and working them till the seam was exhausted or the pit flooded, then constructing deeper, more productive but more dangerous pits, with wooden walkways, ladders and stairs. Every year thousands of tons of coal were shipped from the little harbour across the Forth to Falkirk, to Germany and to England. There was enough coal down there, it was said, to fuel the Carron ironworks at Falkirk for a thousand years. At night the colliers could look far out into the firth and see the warning light flickering on the Isle of May. It was fuelled by coal they had howked. Night after night it burned, an emblem of their endless labour.

The women and bairns, who bore the coal up a wooden staircase that spiralled round the shaft, had finished a few minutes earlier and were already on their way home. The colliers, black and bent and exhausted, loaded with their picks and shovels and ropes, blinking at the bright, cloudless sky, must have looked like creatures emerging from another world, but nobody ever remarked on this because there was never anybody there who was not from that world.

They trudged up the hill in silence, towards the rows of cottages. At a certain point on the rough track, they became aware that there *was* someone unusual observing them: a fattish man none of them knew, sitting on the verge while his horse grazed the long grass in the sheuch. Some of the men were suspicious of the stranger. They glowered at him or turned their heads away and would not catch his eye. Others stared, resentful of a man who had the leisure to sit in sunshine while they had been crawling in darkness. One or two nodded and the man nodded back. He was watching them all very carefully. When Joseph and his son passed by it seemed as though he lifted his head a little more, even raised his hand slightly. No more than that, but Joseph saw it, and when he glanced back the man was still watching him.

At the cottage door a wee laddie, one of his neighbours' boys, said, 'Man, ye're black as the howe o the nicht.' He laughed and said, 'Ah, but whaur does the coal stop and me stert?' The laddie said, 'Dinna ken. But there's a man been speirin efter a black man like you.' Exhausted though he was, Joseph became alert. 'Whit man?' he asked. 'A man wi a horse,' the boy said. 'But I didna tell him ocht.'

Joseph Knight and Andrew went into the house and Andrew collapsed into a chair. Annie was dozing in another, catching a little rest before she made the evening meal. Joseph went to the water-butt at the back door. He dipped the tin in and splashed water over his face and neck. By the time he came back, Ann and the lad were asleep.

Joseph set off down the track again. When he came to the spot where the man had been he was still there, eating an apple while his horse grazed. Joseph stopped a few feet from him. They stared at each other. The man smiled and got to his feet. He threw the apple core to land by the horse's mouth and held out his hand. 'Mr Knight?' he said.

Joseph did not acknowledge this. He did not take the hand. He did not like the fact that the stranger knew who he was.

'My name is Archibald Jamieson,' the man said. 'I hae come frae Dundee.' He paused, as if to see what effect this would have. 'Ye needna fear. I dinna come tae cause ye trouble. I come wi news.'

'I'm no feart,' Joseph said. 'Whit news?' But he knew there were only two kinds of news that might come from Dundee: news about Annie's mother, or news from his own past.

Jamieson let his hand drop. Joseph thought he looked tired. This was not surprising – the man would have ridden nearly forty miles. He would be saddle-sore. Nevertheless, it was hard to believe that he could be more tired than Joseph felt.

'I hae been lookin for ye for weeks,' Jamieson said. 'Months, in fact. Since a year past January.'

'Why would ye dae that?' Joseph asked.

'At first, I was employed tae search for ye by John Wedderburn of Ballindean.'

Joseph did not move. His heart began to pound but he did not allow the blank expression on his face to change.

Jamieson went on. 'But that's no why I'm here noo. I'm here tae tell ye that Wedderburn is deid.'

Joseph felt a jolt inside him, but still he said nothing. He was

360

not willing to concede anything until he knew what all this was about.

'He died twa weeks syne. He was buried yesterday. I was there. I thocht ye should ken.'

'Why would I need tae ken onything aboot John Wedderburn?' Joseph said cautiously.

'Because o whit he did tae ye. It's finished, ower.'

'Whit is?'

'Whit happened atween ye. The court case.'

'That's been ower a lang time.'

'Ah,' Jamieson said, 'then ye admit ye are Joseph Knight?'

Joseph looked at the ground, then at the sky, then back at Jamieson. 'Hoo did ye find me?' he asked at last.

'A number o coincidences,' Jamieson said. 'But in the end it was Kate Thomson – Ann's mither – that tellt me whaur tae look.'

Joseph nodded. 'How is she?'

'Frail. But still workin awa. She canna stop.'

'Whit did Wedderburn want wi me efter aw this time?'

'Tae ken whit had happened tae ye. If ye still lived or no. I couldna find ye and that seemed tae satisfy him. But it didna satisfy me.'

'How no?'

'Because ye interested me. I ken hoo ye were brocht tae Jamaica, and frae there tae here. I ken aboot the Wedderburns, the fower brithers. They are aw deid noo, aw save James, the doctor ane. I ken aboot your case – Knight versus Wedderburn. But I didna ken you, and I wanted tae meet ye.'

'And whit is it ye want?'

Jamieson said, 'Naething. I want naething frae ye. I jist wanted tae see ye – and tae hear ye.'

This made Joseph think of the way he sounded. Although he had the words of the people around him he sounded some of them differently. The colliers did not care or comment any more. What did how he looked or spoke mean to this total stranger? He said, 'I dinna believe ye. There's aye something. Whitiver it is, ye hae wasted your journey.'

Jamieson held out his hands, palms upward. 'I swear there is naething.'

Joseph said, 'Then ye hae whit ye cam for. There's your horse.' He began to walk up the brae.

'Wait,' Jamieson said. 'I hae a message for ye. Twa messages.'

Joseph turned back.

'The ane is frae anither black man like yoursel. A Mr Peter Burnet, a weaver by trade. Ye had a drink wi him some years syne at the Parliament Close in Edinburgh.'

Joseph said nothing. He remembered Burnet and the conversation they had had. He remembered being annoyed.

'Mr Burnet wrote a letter tae me,' Jamieson was saying. 'He spoke very highly of ye. He said if I should ever find ye, tae remind ye o your meetin.'

'Ye didna come aw this way tae tell me that,' Joseph said.

'The ither message,' Jamieson continued, 'is frae a Perthshire gentleman that ye kent.' He seemed to be stalling. Joseph felt himself growing angry. He knew no Perthshire gentlemen forby those that had had him arrested.

'Mr Andrew Davidson, the lawyer.'

Joseph was astonished at the instant calming effect this name had on him. It seemed also to transform Jamieson in his eyes, as if a password had been uttered, a code that proved his good intent. 'Mr Davidson,' Joseph said. 'Ye hae seen him?'

'I confess,' Jamieson said, 'it was a year syne. When I met him he wasna weel. I dinna ken if he is alive yet.'

'Mr Davidson,' Joseph said, '*was* a gentleman. He never misdouted me or my cause. Never.'

'That's whit he tellt me,' Jamieson said. 'And he asked, if I ever did find ye, tae be remembered tae ye.'

Joseph recalled a large, serious man with intense eyes and a rapid understanding. A kind man. 'He is remembered,' he said. 'I named my son Andrew efter him.'

'That was your son I saw ye wi earlier?' Jamieson asked.

'Aye.'

'A fine-looking lad. The work will be hard on him, though.'

'He is paid for it,' Joseph said. 'He labours wi me but no because o me. When he is a man, he will labour for himsel. If he disna he'll sterve, but it will be his choice.'

'Ye had a dochter, if I mind richt.'

'I hae. She bides in anither village.'

'Is your wife still wi ye?'

'Of course.'

'I'm sorry, I meant, does she still live?'

'Whit is it tae you?'

'I am a faimly man, Mr Knight. I hae sons and dochters and grandbairns, but my wife is deid.'

Something in the way Jamieson said this made Joseph less wary of the questions. Jamieson could keep neither the pride nor the pain out of his voice. Joseph relaxed a little more. 'Aye,' he said, 'she still lives.'

He felt the evening sun on his face, a soft breeze coming off the sea. He was no longer so suspicious of Jamieson, but he did not want to be having this conversation. He wanted to go home and eat, to sit outside with Ann and Andrew until the light went. He would tell them about this visitor, this man not of the past but bearing news of the past. Thinking of that, he was surprised to discover that Jamieson was right: that what he had thought was over years before had not been.

'Mr Jamieson,' Joseph said, 'if ye should see Mr Davidson again, I hope ye would say that Joseph Knight wishes him weel. But I hope also that ye winna say whaur ye found him. I hae made mysel a new life here and I dinna want the auld ane disturbin it – no even Mr Davidson.'

'Ye needna fash,' Jamieson said, as he had a few minutes earlier. 'Naebody will ken but mysel.'

Joseph went to the horse and clapped its neck, picked up the loose reins and passed them to Jamieson. He said, 'If ye're tae get back tae Dundee the nicht ye'll need tae set oot noo.'

'There's nae rush,' Jamieson said. 'It's settled weather and it hardly gets dark these nichts. On this beast I could sleep aw the way hame. But I micht turn in at Cupar. I'll see.'

Leading the docile animal, they set off back to the rows of collier cottages. The track rose past these and on through thick woods till it rejoined the coast route from Kirkcaldy. At the first of the cottages Joseph stopped. 'There's your road,' he said.

'Aye,' Jamieson said. He hesitated for a moment. 'I said there was naething I wanted frae ye, and there isna. But there is something I would like tae ken. Was it worth it?'

'Was whit worth it?' Joseph asked.

'Weel, ye gained your freedom but, forgie me, I'm lookin at ye and it disna seem that ye gained that muckle. Was it worth it?'

'If ye had been a slave ye would never hae asked that question,' Joseph said. 'Dae ye no see why I am here? Because the folk here *ken*.'

'Aye, that's whit I thocht,' Jamieson said. 'I see that.'

Joseph spat on the ground. 'No ye dinna. If ye saw it ye wouldna hae asked it. And noo I'll ask ye the same question. Was it worth your while tae seek me oot?'

Jamieson said, 'Mr Knight, I dinna expect ye tae understand this or tae believe it, but jist speakin wi ye these few minutes – ye hae gien me something in spite o yoursel.'

'I hae gien ye naething.'

'Ye hae shown me whit a free man looks like.'

Joseph spat again. But Jamieson seemed to mean it, whatever it might mean. He held Joseph's disdainful stare and stared back.

'Weel, and are ye disappointed?' Joseph said.

'No,' Jamieson said. 'Ye are exactly as Mr Davidson described ye.'

Whit did Wedderburn want wi me efter aw this time? Joseph's own question, not one of Jamieson's, was the one that had lingered. Jamieson certainly hadn't had a satisfactory answer to it, either from Wedderburn or from thinking it through for himself. Wedderburn, even if he had really known what he wanted, had not told Jamieson, and now he was dead. The only person who could provide an answer was the one they had both sought: himself, Joseph Knight.

It wasn't, Joseph believed, about the court case, or about slavery, or about revenge or recompense. These things were part of it, but it was about something much bigger. It was about life. Wedderburn had seen the life spirit in Joseph and it had consumed him with envy. It had stripped him to the bone. Only Joseph had ever seen him so exposed. That had given Joseph a strange power over him.

Another ship: the one in which they had crossed the Atlantic, from Jamaica to Scotland. Sailors' country. Out there on the ocean, rules of behaviour – codes of ownership and obedience – reshaped themselves. Joseph, who had been terrified of going aboard, remembered this as they lost sight of land.

The cabin they shared was cramped, though luxurious compared with the conditions of the slave ship in which Joseph had made his only other sea journey. On opposite sides of the six-foot-wide space were wooden beds which in the daytime served as benches. A hinged table swung down from a third wall between the beds, filling half of the cabin. The table could be put away at night, but the midshipman who showed them the workings of various lockers, fitted under the beds and overhead, suggested that it was best left down, as it provided useful additional purchase in the event of rough weather, when they might be in danger of being thrown to the floor. There were various ropes attached to the beds for strapping oneself in, but these were apt to chaff in prolonged storms. 'Let us hope,' Wedderburn said to the midshipman, 'that we are not called upon for anything too heroic, eh Joseph?' But Joseph said nothing, for he was already feeling ill.

'Well, sir,' the midshipman said, 'you know what they say – no man can ever be a hero to his valet. And if that be true on land, it be ten times more true at sea.'

'Because you see me naked, Joseph, and you may also see me sick and helpless. That is the gentleman's meaning – is it not, sir?'

'It is, sir. But maybe I'm speaking out of turn. The saying might not hold good for a neger.'

'Well, we shall see. Joseph and I are pretty close acquainted, but I expect we'll be closer in the coming weeks.'

For the first few days of the voyage the weather was fine, the skies clear, the sun strong and the westerly winds steady. Wedderburn and Joseph spent as much time as possible on deck, stretching their limbs, watching the sailors at their tasks – anything that kept them out of the stuffy, dark cabin where the ship's rolling motion seemed magnified. Wedderburn read from various books while Joseph shielded him from the sun with a large parasol. There were one or two other passengers on board, but none with whom Wedderburn wished to keep company. Most of the ship was given over to its cargo of rum and sugar.

In the evenings Wedderburn taught Joseph games – whist, rummy, draughts and backgammon. His motivation, Joseph guessed, was more about providing himself with a playing opponent than about educating his slave. But the games were levellers. They obliged them to be equals for as long as they played. Joseph was quick to learn, which clearly pleased Wedderburn. He even seemed to take pleasure in being beaten by him.

From reading the cards it was a natural progression to learning the alphabet. Wedderburn would read aloud from the Bible, then take a verse and write the words out on a sheet of paper, with space underneath for Joseph to copy them. It was a crude method of teaching, but it worked. When Wedderburn grew bored of it, Joseph took the Bible and copied passages directly. Then he asked Wedderburn to read out what he had written. In this way, reading and writing began to open themselves to him.

But after two weeks at sea, the first of a series of storms changed everything.

Even in fine weather the ship rolled and pitched unexpectedly. Joseph had fought to keep seasickness at bay, but the smell of caulk and salt-laden wood, the constant sawing of ropes and creaking of timbers, and the lurching motion, all reminded him too much of that other voyage. His stomach remained queasy at best. When the weather turned, and they were forced to keep below decks for days at a time, and every wave found a new way to angle and spin the ship, what had been a constant nagging nausea became violent and uncontrollable pain.

His bed became a prison. He could neither get up from it nor bear to be in it. He alternately boiled and froze. His head pounded. Sweat poured from him. He vomited till there was nothing left to come up but bile. The tepid drinking water did nothing to ease his thirst, and refused to sit in his stomach. His body was dehydrated and saltless. The cabin stank of his illness. He fully expected to be moved to another part of the ship, so as not to inconvenience his master. But there was nowhere else that he could go. Master and slave were bound together in the tiny cabin until either Joseph died or the storm abated.

He drifted in and out of consciousness. Sleep was fitful and filled with bad dreams, but it was a mercy compared with lying awake. He began to wish he would die. Never before had he experienced that wish, but the seasickness was overwhelming. It demanded relief. There was none, only a swirling hole of pain down which he seemed to be endlessly falling.

And then, after what seemed like weeks, Joseph began to piece together what had been happening to him. He had been sick, over and over and without any ability to direct what forced itself through his mouth. He had soiled himself. He had soaked his sheet with sweat. And each time he had done these things, someone had cleaned him. Someone had wiped his brow, sponged down his body. Someone had gently raised his head and helped him to drink. Someone had lifted his body from one bed to the other, and then, when he had wrecked the second, lifted him again to the first and laid him on a dry sheet. Someone had sat holding his hand, speaking to him, soothing words in a soothing voice. A familiar voice.

It was not always calm, though. He remembered it growing frantic at times when Wedderburn thought he was asleep. Through the darkness, close by his head, came the pleading: 'Don't die on me, Joseph. Do not die on me. Please God, do not die on me. Please God, do not let him die. Almighty God and Jesus Christ, do not take Joseph from me. Let him live. Do not die on me. Not you too. Please, Joseph, do not die.' On and on, for hours, until Joseph really did sleep, and, waking, found Wedderburn still at his side.

Joseph felt something stir in his heart. That this other man should tend him, should so devote himself to his needs, was remarkable. Out there in the Atlantic, master and slave were reduced to this simple humanity: one man caring for another. Wedderburn the master did not chastise, did not curse, did not neglect: as if he were his father, the father Joseph did not remember, he cared for him. Lying unable to speak, Joseph saw that Wedderburn was desperate to love and be loved; but he was denied those things because of the way he was. And Joseph was touched, since it was the same for him: he had been torn from love, and he did not know how to give or receive it. For a moment there on the ship, they were two sides of the same coin.

Once, there seemed to be a space somewhere in the storm. The ship rocked rather than shook, and the waves slapped rather than crashed against the timbers. Joseph was strangely aware of his own serenity. It was as if he were clinging like a bat to the low cabin roof, looking down at his body. He was beyond exhaustion, beyond despair. And there was another man in the room, the ship's surgeon, talking to John Wedderburn. 'It is the calm before death, Mr Wedderburn,' the surgeon was saying. 'I have seen it often, and not just in negers. The body is defeated, and the mind gives up the will to live. When the sea fever has taken someone the way it has this fellow, it's common enough.'

'I agree he is very sick,' Wedderburn said. 'That is why I sent for you. But I do not wish him to die. I am taking him home to Scotland.'

There was a silence. Joseph felt the surgeon's hands moving across his body, checking his pulse, pushing back his eyelids.

'He cannot die,' Wedderburn said. 'I will not allow it.'

'With respect, sir, there's very little you can do to prevent it.'

'I am a medical man, too, sir,' Wedderburn said. 'I have looked after him thus far. If you can do nothing for him, I will continue to do what I can.'

'He'll be dead in two days,' the surgeon said. 'I'm sorry to say it, for he looks a well-built lad, but I've seen it too many times.'

Alone again with Joseph, John Wedderburn got down on his knees, squeezed in between the table and the bed. Up above, bat-like, Joseph watched.

'Joseph, can you hear me? No, don't speak. Turn your head a little if you can hear me. Look at me.'

The neck of Joseph's body felt as though it were bound in iron. With immense effort, his head turned to look at John Wedderburn. Joseph was shocked to see that Wedderburn was crying.

'Joseph, I beg you, do not die on me. This is no place for you to die. There is nothing between us and God out here. If you die, I will die. He will not take you and let me live. He is watching us both on this cursed piece of wood. He is watching me with you. Joseph, if you die He will blame me. He will say it was my fault. Do not die, Joseph Knight.' He took Joseph's left hand in his two, brought it to his mouth, kissed it. Joseph was too weak to resist. But he felt the kiss.

And afterwards, when the tempest died away and he began to recover, he did not forget it. He remembered it and he understood it. He remembered it even as John Wedderburn distanced himself again, leaving him alone to sleep while he got out on deck for fresh air, rebuilding the boundaries between them as the ship approached landfall. He remembered the kiss when he looked in Wedderburn's eyes and saw the weakness masquerading as strength, the fear behind the confidence. He remembered the kindness Wedderburn had shown all through the terrible time of bad weather and sickness, and he despised it.

He had come so close to rewarding that kindness. If Wedderburn had not kissed him, he might even have done so. But the kiss was a mark not of kindness but of guilt. And it flooded in upon Joseph that it did not matter whether Wedderburn was a good master or a bad master. It did not matter whether he was a good slave or a bad slave. Even though Wedderburn had helped him to read and write, had nursed him and perhaps even saved his life, these things did not heal the injury he continued to inflict. In claiming to own Joseph, he destroyed the possibility of goodness between them. Wedderburn's kindness was conditional. Joseph, sick as he was, saw that, and made up his mind always to reject it.

And he knew now, lying in bed next to Ann, why John Wedderburn had tried to find him. Jamieson was right in saying that Wedderburn had wanted to know if he was dead or alive. But the reason: he had *needed* Joseph to be alive. When Jamieson had failed to find him, Wedderburn had called off the search. It was better that way. It was better not to *know* that Joseph was dead. That way he might yet be alive, and John Wedderburn could get to his God, or wherever he was going, before Joseph did. He *needed* Joseph to survive him; to survive the great wrong he had done him.

Life had been a trial to Wedderburn, a burden. How could that be? – that a man that had been a slave came to cherish every rotten moment of being alive, but a rich man with all he could want in the world looked at life as if it were going to jump up and bite him at any minute, as if it were something best kept at a safe distance? How could that be?

Because for a man like Wedderburn life was like a neger. If you once loosed your grip on it, it would rise up and overthrow you.

His mind was racing now. He would not sleep again before daybreak. The Sabbath was over and the new week's labour was about to begin. Sometimes he did have pangs of guilt about having brought Ann here, about Andrew growing up to such a life. But they were here now. There was no going back. And they were alive.

He thought of James Wedderburn, his threat to send him back to his 'old friends' at Glen Isla. Nearly all those people now, they must be dead. He remembered the kindness he had had from Newman. How Newman used to tell him about Charlie, whom he had once been, and the great days of Tacky's War, before Joseph was ever in Jamaica. Newman would let him trace with his fingers the scars of the terrible flogging he took for being out in the rebellion, and he would talk about his days on the run. They were the best days he had in Jamaica, he said, even though he was half-starved and faced death every day for months. But you were always hungry as a slave, and death was the overseer of all the plantations, so what was there to lose? Newman schooled Joseph. There were many ways of being free, he said, and none of them was easy. But they were all better than being a slave, so when you saw your chance, you had to take it. All your life before that happened, all your life was just waiting, and all your life after was thinking about it happening again. And *they* knew that too. If you looked in their eyes you would see it there. The fear. It was guilt in another form. They should never be allowed to rest easy in their beds at night.

That was before the other Wedderburn, the sick one, drove Mary from the house and Newman mad by killing her. The fear was in that Wedderburn, all right. It was in all of them except James. And he was the one that still lived, so Jamieson had said. But even James Wedderburn had found slavery clinging to his back and that it could not easily be shaken off. The black son, Robert, that he had had by Rosanna, had come to Edinburgh to haunt him in the year of Joseph's triumph. Joseph had never met Robert but he had heard about him. A regular nuisance to his father's family, and probably still was. Good luck to him, Joseph thought.

Robert's grandmother was Talkee Amy, that came to Glen Isla once to cure the sickness in Alexander Wedderburn. She cured the sickness but not the weakness. While she was there she told Joseph stories about Anansi. Anansi was the spider, always outwitting the other animals, always getting himself out of trouble. He'd forgotten the detail of the stories but he remembered her telling them. 'Anansi always win out in the end,' she said, 'because him clever and him patient. Him prepared to wait long, long time.'

Joseph thought of the toast they had raised at Indian Peter's that day. He thought of Newman, and Tacky, and Apongo, and the Maroons. He thought of Toussaint L'Ouverture, whom the French had killed this year with cold and hunger because they could not defeat him in war. These men were heroes. The Scots had their heroes too: Wallace and Bruce and now the young chevalier, Charles Edward Stewart, the one John Wedderburn had fought for. But they were not Joseph's heroes. They were nothing to do with him. And like all the others, they were dead.

He would go to the coal tomorrow, and Ann would walk with him and the lad too. They would go their separate ways, he and Andrew climbing down the shaft and then crawling deep into the earth while Ann and the other women bore the great creels loaded with coal to the surface. And the men and women he worked with would call him Joe and laugh and girn as always and treat him as one of themselves. It was a sair, sair life but it was true, he was one of them, a collier. Colliers. The only people who had never held out against him. They knew that life was only ever a second away from disaster, from death. They saw him black, they knew him black, and it didn't make them hate him or love him, they just accepted him. And he understood why this was.

Slavery. It had set them together against their country, against the world. He remembered the time in Edinburgh, in a room in a tavern with John Maclaurin. Maclaurin said, 'Joseph, there is a man here that wishes tae meet ye.' A tiny, wizened man in threadbare working clothes had stood up and given him his hand. When Joseph grasped it he felt it rough and cracked and hard, and when he looked at it he saw it black, deep-grained with coal stour. That stour was never going to come out. The man said he was from the colliers at Wemyss in Fife, they had heard of his trouble and they had made a subscription for him. He said he was sorry for the smallness of the sum, but he hoped it might help. Joseph nearly wept at that. The collier said, 'We aw ken, man, dinna be feart, we aw ken.'

It was true. They were all free now, he and the other colliers, but there was something in them, a deep buried part, that would be slave till the day they died.

Joseph would not welcome death. The men he got on with best, they would not welcome it, hard and grinding and rotten though their lives were. They lived with death every day so they knew its face was ugly and cruel, just as he did. Maybe it was *because* of that, because of all he had been through, that it made him mad to think of not being alive, of not being on the earth to breathe any more.

Sometimes on a Saturday night his friends would queue outside the cottage and he would draw out his old scissors and razor and trim their hair, make them nice for their wives. He would not take money for it. Some of the men had wee square-rigged yawls that they raced on the sea and caught fish from, and they would give him some fish in return. They offered to take him out fishing but they could never entice Joseph to join them on the great grey waters. Others would buy him a drink, or leave a few rabbits poached from the laird's parks. *That* was life, that was heroism: friendship, and trust, and once in a while a little stolen delight.

No, Joseph would not welcome death. Whether it came underground, or here in the bed, or some other way he could not imagine. Whether it took him to Africa, or to Jesus, or just into a hole in the earth. He would not hold out his hand to it. He was alive and he did not want to die. It might not be much, life, but he wanted it all the same, all he could get of it, so death would have to wait. He had beaten Wedderburn and he'd beat death as long as he was able. He was alive and here and now. He was alive.